Karl has a unique story.

From being the most awarded advertising creative in Australasia, to professional wrestling heavyweight champion of New Zealand, to completing a Masters in Creative Writing, to writing the first three books in his thriller series, The Truth Files.

Karl is 'the body-slamming adman-turned-author.'

Also by Karl William Fleet:

Novels
The Truth Files series:
01: Corporate Truth
02: Criminal Truth
03: Fractured Truth

Coming soon
Emily and the Missing Mansion, a young adult fantasy novel.

Short Films
Signs
Jet Black
Consequences
Finders Keepers

Also by Karl William Fleet:

Novels
The Truth Files series:
01: Corporate Truth
02: Criminal Truth
03: Fractured Truth

Coming soon
Emily and the Missing Mansion, a young adult fantasy novel.

Short Films
Signs
Jet Black
Consequences
Finders Keepers

The right of Karl William Fleet to be identified as the Author of
the work in terms of section 96 of the Copyright Act 1994 is hereby asserted.
Published by Chaos360, New Zealand
123 Western Springs, Auckland, New Zealand

ISBN 978-0-473-43925-5 (soft cover) (A-format)
ISBN 978-0-473-43926-2 (kindle/mobi) (B-format)

For Andrew.
My brother of a thousand years.

CRIMINAL TRUTH

BY
KARL WILLIAM FLEET

Chaos 360

COVER DESIGN: COTTONWOOD STUDIO

MARK BENOIT WAS STILL DRUNK—not uncommon for his Saturday mornings. He had no desire to be awake as he faded in and out of a conscious state. His toxic slumber seemed like a far more attractive option than the inevitable heavy hangover.

A distant, muffled beeping reminded him of a popular Taylor Swift remix. The repetitive sound echoed around his skull like broken stilettos on a cold concrete floor. He imagined for a second that he might have passed out in one of the dingy clubs he frequented at the end of a drunken night out, hidden in a dark little corner all by himself.

He tilted his head upward and discovered his tongue welded to the roof of his mouth, his throat a Sahara. He worked his jaw up and down to encourage saliva. Half-heartedly he tried to open his eyes; full-heartedly they remained closed.

The beeping got louder as fragments of the previous night filtered back into his murky memory. Mark worked for a broker on Wall Street; he made money, just not the big money. Still, he liked to suit up and talk the talk as if he were a big fish, but in reality, he was just lucky to be in the water. Yet his lack of funds didn't limit his fun.

Mark had a tried-and-true method of impressing party girls. He knew they were more impressed by certain branded bottles of champagne than the actual champagne. After a few drinks, their taste buds weren't that refined. One night, while removing the wet label of a bottle he regretted buying with his rent money, Mark realized that once it was "naked," it could be any bottle. If he stuck another label on it, an even more expensive label, one downloaded from the internet onto the right paper, would half-drunk girls notice?

The beeping that threatened to wake him got closer and grew louder, so Mark rolled to one side, squeezed his eyes tighter, and gritted his teeth. He summoned all his willpower to descend back into the darkness of sleep. It worked; the annoying sound faded from his consciousness.

Mark's method of switching bottle labels worked like magic the first time he'd tried it, so it became a regular late-Friday-night thing. He'd wait until the timing was right, go to the bar and order three of the cheapest bottles of champagne, a bucket of ice, a bottle of water, and a double shot of house whiskey on the rocks. He'd then pour the water into the bucket and leave the bottles to soak at his feet, taking his time sipping his whiskey.

The cold water made it easy for him to remove the labels from the cheap champagne bottles—which he would do while pretending to tighten his shoelaces. The "naked" bottles were then dried with a napkin, and the five-hundred-dollar sticky labels perfectly attached. Mark had it down to a fine art, and like a magician, nobody would see him do the switch.

Back at the table, he'd bang the bucket down and pop open a bottle. "Who wants to get fucked up?" he'd yell to a raucous applause.

He'd pulled this stunt twice last night to impress his latest dream girl, Elizabeth. She was playing hard to get, so he tried to get her more drunk. It had worked with plenty of other girls. But maybe he drank too much himself because the night turned into a blur. He lost Elizabeth at some stage; he recalled cold air hitting his face as he left the club in search of her. He had a vague memory of vomiting against an alley wall, spinning lights, and then nothing. Until now.

A terrible odor entered Mark's nostrils and forced his eyes open. He hoped he hadn't shit the bed. But he wasn't in bed, he was surrounded by darkness, and the air smelled sickeningly rancid. The beeping was even louder now, and it was right by his head. He could barely move, and strangely shaped objects dug into him.

Suddenly, his dark, suffocating world shook. Mark yelled as he realized that the beeping belonged to a garbage truck lifting the dumpster he was in. He reached for the opening to pull himself out, but he slipped on the moving trash and fell further into the vile garbage. The higher the bin went, the steeper the angle became, and the harder it was for him to find his balance.

The dumpster shook violently, and Mark tumbled out with the rest of the trash into the compactor below. His screams for help were in vain, as no one could hear him above the sound of the truck's engine and hydraulics. The only person who knew to help him was the dark-suited man responsible for Mark's current predicament. The man had found Mark passed out hours earlier, gently picked him up, and put him inside the dumpster, knowing the garbage truck would pass by to empty it early in the morning.

The compressor hissed into a second gear, and with a low, metallic screech, the walls slowly began closing in on Mark. He kicked and clawed at his surroundings, trying to get leverage to escape the shrinking tomb. As the surrounding trash compacted tighter and tighter, he shoved his back hard against one wall of trash and slammed his feet on the opposite wall to halt its movement. He let out a high-pitched scream as the closing walls blew out his kneecaps, tearing skin and snapping bone. His skull cracked and contorted beyond recognition as metal crushed every part of him.

The dark-suited man watched as the truck returned the empty dumpster to its original position with a thunderous clank and continued on its way. Happy with his morning's work, he stepped out of the dark alley into the first rays of the morning sun.

JUSTIN TRUTH STOOD and stretched his muscular legs. He spent way too many hours sitting behind his desk. For the last ten months, he had been the CEO of American icon Soda-Cola. With its vast empire of products, there wasn't one country in the world that didn't sell Soda-Cola products, and he controlled all of it.

He walked over to the large windows that overlooked Manhattan. Justin checked himself out in the reflective glass and flexed his biceps. He was more interested in looking at himself than at the panoramic view. He liked how his tailored shirt wound tightly around his toned upper body, and how his vest emphasized his powerful, broad shoulders. He stroked his perfectly groomed stubble-beard and ran his hand through his wavy, dusty-blond hair.

For the last three months, Justin had been modeling himself after Ryan Gosling: from the suits, to the physique, to the Botox injections that gave him Gosling's famous "bedroom eyes." His charcoal three-piece Gucci suit was of the same cut as the one Gosling wore to the *Gangster Squad* movie premiere. To complete the look, Justin wore a bright orange, handmade, Italian silk tie with a matching pocket square and his initials stylishly embroidered into them.

After taking over from Carlton, the former CEO, Justin had sliced through the hierarchy of Soda-Cola, firing anyone who he didn't believe was on his side, a time the survivors now infamously referred to as "Tornado Tuesday" during their watercooler chats. A few threatened legal action, but Justin had obtained some form of dirt on everyone. He used the smallest of reasons—visiting inappropriate websites during work hours, arriving late, or even taking stationery home—as grounds for dismissal.

When Justin first joined Soda-Cola, Carlton was a healthy sixty-four-year-old silver fox. But to edge him more quickly into retirement, Justin slowly and regularly poisoned his daily glass of Scotch until Carlton was too sick to work. Once he was out of the way, Justin let the former CEO return to his former healthy self. He would stay healthy as long as he limited his time to board meetings and left the running of Soda-Cola to Justin.

Steve Barker had been Justin's rival for the CEO position until his reputation was ruined. Justin still smiled at how easy it had been to set up Steve so everyone thought it was he who'd raped Montana Cruz, destroying the man mentally and financially. Steve ultimately avoided jail time, but that was the least of his problems; Justin heard that Steve had taken up heroin, killing himself one injection at a time.

Montana, who'd been so desperate to bring Justin down and have him fired from Soda-Cola, was now his broken plaything. He'd made her apply for a job at Soda-Cola's fiercest competitor, Phizz. How quickly they had snatched her up, thinking she would bring all of her Soda-Cola knowledge with her. They were wrong. She still worked for Justin and kept him up-to-date about everything Phizz was doing and planning. He'd give her tasks to perform to help keep Soda-Cola one step ahead.

Justin's office phone beeped.

"Debbie," Justin said, hitting the speaker button. Debbie was his personal assistant. Nothing happened in the building without her knowing about it. After proving her loyalty to him again and again, Justin promoted her to office manager, which gave her a little power and a few people to manage. Debbie's main job was to take care of Justin's calendar, and she protected it with a venomous zeal.

"Hello, Mr. Truth," Debbie chirped. "Just a reminder that you have drinks with Mr. Rip Gordon tonight. And on Saturday afternoon, I've booked the Soda-Cola chopper to take you to Bell Island to visit that awful Ross Smith. God, after what that man did to your poor mother! How can you even look at him?"

"It actually helps me focus on the good things in life. He wanted to hurt me, but all he did was hurt himself. My visits show him how strong he has made me."

"You have such strength, Mr. Truth," Debbie fawned. "I've set up the Number Two boardroom for your management meeting—they're all there waiting for you."

"Great, tell them I'll be there soon." Justin ended the call.

Detective Ross Smith was serving a life sentence for the murder of Justin's mother—a murder Justin had committed himself. He'd thought about having Ross killed; it would be easy enough to have some gang member stab a dirty cop without anyone batting an eyelid. But he liked the irony of Ross being in the exact place he'd tried so hard to put Justin into. He found his monthly visits therapeutic, as he could rub it in Ross's face that he was in prison while Justin was free to do as he pleased.

Justin checked his much-loved reflection one more time, running through a few favorite poses and looks. He grinned, happy with himself. It was time to feed his Young Lions, throw them some raw meat and watch them fight over it.

EIGHT MINUTES LATER Justin's The Number Two boardroom was surrounded entirely by glass walls that frosted over during meetings, obscuring the interior from passersby. It was white, bright, and featured wireless equipment that could be controlled remotely. A plateglass table ran down the middle of the room, surrounded by rippled, white leather office chairs. Justin had designed it himself.

When he took over as CEO, he also restructured the management team, whom he named "Young Lions." He split the accounts amongst them to create fierce competition. In meetings, Justin cranked up the testosterone; he wanted warriors fighting for him, men who would do whatever it took to impress him.

All conversations stopped as Justin entered the room with gusto.

"My Lions!" Justin roared.

The entire room roared back at him. The energy was primal, almost savage.

"When I took over, I knew it would be a fight to revive this dying dinosaur. As a company, we were slipping, growing old, and fast becoming irrelevant. Today, because of me, Soda-Cola is transformed. This company is now a flesh-eating monster of magnificent proportions." The group applauded enthusiastically.

"And as each of you know, I have big plans—new products, smarter marketing, and tighter, more focused advertising to take Soda-Cola to new heights of global domination. We have heard the weak-minded idiots say it's too hard, that we expect too much, that we should roll over and embrace mediocrity. But those fuckers are weak, pathetic, and quitters They are the cancer eating away at this great country of ours!"

The group roared again, banging on the table with their fists. Justin glared at his warriors, his eyes encouraging them to be louder. When he wanted them to listen, he prowled the room slowly, and the group went silent.

"Caleb," Justin said. "Caleb-Motherfucking-King. Please stand up."

Caleb looked at everyone and stood boldly.

"Caleb is crushing it on NiceTea, fighting to make it the number one iced tea in the market. It's the best tasting iced tea in the world, goddammit!" Again, the Lions banged their fists on the table just as Justin had trained them to do each time he made a point.

"Our competition, Tea-Sip"—the Lions responded with well-trained boos and more fist-banging—"got the drop on us and secured a tight sponsorship deal for the college football championship game. They shut us out. Those assholes at Phizz thought they were so damn clever, right? So, what did Caleb do? Did he say, 'Good one! We'll get you next year.' No he didn't, because he's a Young Fucking Lion! He hired ten of the sexiest bitches that ever walked this earth. He had them wear the tiniest-of-tiny denim shorts and the tightest-of-tight white T-shirts, with NiceTea emblazoned on them, big and in your face, just like their enhanced cleavages. They set themselves up outside the main beverage stand and each time a teenager emerged with a Tea-Sip, they gave him an option. They could keep their disgusting pitiful choice of a drink and sit in the stands like the losers they are. Or if they poured that shit into the gutter, where it belongs, we'd give them a bottle of water to pour over our sexy-as-hell NiceTea girls' tight white T-shirts.

"Did they pour it out? Goddamn right they did. Each guy who did then had their picture taken, and that shit got Instagrammed, hashtagged, and Facebooked. Splashed all over social media! Tea-Sip paid for sponsorship, but we owned that event. That's what it means to get business done!"

The Lions got louder and more boisterous. Caleb raised his arms like Rocky Balboa as the men close to him slapped him on the back.

"Now, what did we learn from this?" Justin scanned the room. "If the competition tries to out-think us, we out-fuck them.

"Michael. Please stand up." Michael got up from his chair, his eyes darting around the room. "Michael, Michael, Michael… Can everyone look at the big screen, please," Justin said, lowering his tone. He pushed a button on his iPhone. The lights dimmed as the screen came to life and played a ninety-second commercial for Diet Soda-Cola. Everyone in the room watched silently.

Once the ad finished, the lights came back on, and Justin turned back to Michael.

"Michael, how did this ad get made?"

"I saw an opportunity to get one over the competition and went for it," Michael stated.

"Tell me more," Justin replied, tapping his iPhone against his chin.

"Um, yeah, so four weeks ago, R and R Advertising came to me with this idea. They discovered this artist who has no arms, right? It was incredible—she dances and paints at the same time. The floor is one giant white canvas, and she spreads glue onto it with her feet while moving around the room to music. You can't tell what she's painting because the glue is white, you know? Toward the end of the dance, she kicks over containers of colored glitter, a giant fan blows the glitter around, it sticks to the glue, and the picture appears like magic. It all ties into the music and dance. R and R pulled it together and presented me with a finished ad to play during the final of *American Idol*. The media company pulled some strings and got us the spot for next to nothing. They got a sixty at first, but I pushed them for a ninety. It was truly inspirational."

Justin prowled the room again. "I don't remember signing it off?"

"I had to move fast to seize the opportunity," Michael answered gingerly. "I tried to show it to you, but you were in meetings, or out of the office. I couldn't see you."

"So, it's my fault?"

"No, you… It's my fault, sir."

"Damn right, it's your fault. What makes me mad is that we had a spot during the final of *American* fucking *Idol*, with millions of eyeballs, and that shit is what went to air. Could anyone read the branding at the end? Was there a range shot? Our end sting? I did not see one person in the ad drinking Diet Soda-Cola, not one person holding an actual bottle. Not one Diet Soda-Cola, the product we are selling."

"I researched it…" Michael mumbled.

"You did what?"

"I researched it, I asked a few girls in the target audience and around the office. Sally on reception said it was the most emotional TV ad she'd ever seen. It talks to the target audience in a way we haven't before—it reached them on a new level. Helping them see the unachievable is achievable."

"So Sally on reception thinks it's great?"

"Yeah…"

Justin used his iPhone. "Hello, Sally… can you join me in the Number Two boardroom please. Yes, now. Right now."

The Lions sat in silence as they waited for Sally. No one dared to say a word.

The doors opened and a slim blonde meekly entered. Each Lion stared at her with lustful grins as she tentatively took a few steps toward Justin.

"Hi, Sally," Justin said gently. "A question. What is your job description?"

"I work… I work at reception," she stammered, shyly dropping her head as her cheeks turned bright red.

"Have you ever been the CEO of this company?"

"Umm, no."

"Thanks Sally, glad you could clear that up." Justin flicked his fingers to tell her to leave. With the poise of a ballet dancer, she turned on her toes and left the room.

"There you go, Michael. Sally confirmed it. She is the receptionist. Now I ask you again: How did this ad, that I never signed off, with fuck-all branding, and featuring a bitch who can't even hold the product, get to air?"

"I thought—"

"Well, you thought wrong," Justin stated. "Nothing, and I mean nothing, ever goes to air without me saying so. Do you see me now?"

"What?" Michael asked.

"Do you fucking see me now?"

"Yes, yes I do."

"Good. You have twenty minutes to gather your shit and get your fired ass the fuck out of my building."

Michael looked around his colleagues' faces for support. Finding none, he exited the room. As soon as the door closed, Justin addressed the remaining Young Lions.

"Now I have an option for you all. I can hire someone to replace that worthless bag of shit, or you can divide his workload among yourselves along with his salary. Make a group decision and email me your collective answer by noon. We are here to get rich, not to get fucked. And that pussy just got fucked!"

THE AIR CONDITIONING INSIDE the Phizz International Building had been malfunctioning for weeks. Montana Cruz could hear technicians slowly working on the air ducts, their tools echoing above her desk.

Bang, bang, clank. Bang, bang, clank.

She sat staring at the wall behind her computer, zoned out. Every now and then she ran her hand through her black hair, catching herself surprised at its new length. It used to be a lot longer—about halfway down her back—but now it stopped short of her shoulders.

Bang, bang, clank.

Montana often stared at the wall and spaced out these days, wishing to be anywhere other than where she was. She felt like Justin had sliced open her skull and used an industrial blender to turn her brain into liquid mince.

Bang, bang, clank.

A shiver ran down her spine. She was glad she had an office to herself so when her body reacted violently to thoughts of Justin, she didn't have to explain why she suddenly banged her fists on her desk in fits of anger or threw up in her wastebasket.

Bang, bang, clank.

Her job at Phizz was basically the same job she'd had at Soda-Cola. A little easier, in fact. She was good at what she did and was shining in her new role, despite her trauma. In fact, she was killing it—so much so that she'd already received a pay rise and an all-expenses paid trip to Rome.

Bang, bang, clank.

There was a courtesy knock at Montana's door as Kenny Longwater walked in. He was the general manager for Phizz and in charge of the marketing team. He had headhunted Montana personally and was eager to make sure she got what she needed. Even after five months, he still dropped by frequently to check up on her. Kenny seemed to always wear a broad smile beneath his large, hawk-like nose, which made his eyes, already naturally close together, look even smaller. The whole look accentuated his curly mop of blond hair.

"Hi, Montana." Kenny smiled. "I have the case studies you asked for. You really do put in the hard yards. I knew you were good, but you're better than good. You're knock-it-out-of-the-park good!"

Montana returned the smile. She knew Kenny didn't have to drop the files off in person. His dark gray suit and white shirt were too big for his small frame. He'd lost a lot of weight recently, due to his increased interest in long-distance cycling.

"When I said I'd come here," Montana said, "it was to make you guys number one, and to do that, I need to know your strengths and weaknesses—what you have tried, what you are planning, and what's been successful. As my mom says, 'Every little crumb makes the cake.'"

"You're amazing, you know that?" Kenny asked genuinely.

"Thank you, Kenny." She smiled again. She didn't find him at all attractive, but if his liking her made life easier, she'd smile as much as he seemed to need her to.

Kenny licked his dry lips. "We all love having you here."

His eyes scanned the front of her blouse. Montana's hand twitched, her throat tightened up, and she could hear her own heart beating like a tribal drum. She closed her eyes to stop the world from spinning. She needed to get him out of her office. She centered herself and opened her eyes to gaze at him. Then, she picked up a gold-plated letter opener and played with it while she seductively stood up, exhibiting her curves.

"I think about you," she whispered, as she placed her hand on Kenny's chest, feeling his heart beat faster beneath her hot palm. She moved her body in close, sliding up against him as she flicked the inside of his ear with the tip of her tongue. He got hard and pushed against her. She moved her hand from his chest to caress his face and hair, her fingers toying with the curls. Slowly her hand tightened its grip on his hair until he let out a little whimper of pain.

"I want you…" she gasped longingly. "I want you… to fucking die!"

She stabbed the letter opener again and again into Kenny's exposed neck. His eyes widened in fear and confusion as blood exploded out of his gaping mouth. Montana released his hair. He fell back against the wall, blood gushing from his neck. His hands desperately tried to stop the torrent of crimson liquid flowing out of him. He slid down the wall and onto the floor into a pool of blood, his beady eyes wide and terrified. Montana stood over his body, his blood dripping off her hands.

"Montana," Kenny said.

She couldn't understand how he could talk with such a gash in his neck.

"Montana? Hello? Earth to Montana…?"

Her eyes opened. She snapped back. Kenny stood in the doorway, very much alive. She gazed at her bloodless hands. Her vivid daydreams about killing were getting stronger. She dropped the letter opener onto her desk and stood, desperately wanting him out of her office. She put a hand on his shoulder, pulled the files from his hands, and leaned in, speaking softly.

"Thanks, Kenny. This will be a massive help. Can't wait to compare the forecasts and write up a course-of-action report on the changing market trends for you." She subtly turned him around and motioned him to leave. "You're the one that's amazing, Kenny."

"Thanks, here whenever you need me," he said hopefully, playing with his wedding ring as he shuffled out.

Montana closed the door and slumped her back against it. Slowly she lowered herself to the floor, clenching her eyes shut to hold back tears as she wrapped her arms around her knees. She had to pull herself together. She was meeting Justin for lunch in under two hours.

She hit her head against the door to the incessant rhythm of the echoing air conditioner.

Bang, bang, clank. Bang, bang, clank.

A SMALL BROWN PAPER BAG bounced up and down on Nick Harvey's knees as he sat in an upscale dental waiting room. He fidgeted a lot, but it had nothing to do with the five cups of coffee he'd consumed. He got bored easily and needed constant stimulation. He stood five-foot-nine and was twenty-eight, but looking at him, anyone would think he was twenty-one. He tried to grow stubble to help age him, but it didn't do much.

Nick played with his tie and smoothed out his white shirt. He wore a slim-fitting suit with a shirt and tie. They were far from designer—he'd purchased his entire attire for under a hundred dollars at Walmart—but they fit his small frame well and he liked how he looked. He never had to think of what to wear, it was always a suit and tie.

"Mr. Harvey," the receptionist called out.

"That's me!" Nick said, raising his hand in the air.

"Dr. Wagner will see you now."

"That's the best news I've heard all morning." Nick sprang to his feet and did a slight tap dance. The receptionist smiled behind her rectangular glasses as she watched him skip down the corridor to the awaiting white room.

"Take a seat," Dr. Wagner said. The dentist was in his fifties, his white hair swept to one side. His face was well tanned, and his extra chin revealed a man who fancied a second helping of dessert. He sat on a small swivel chair at his desk, peering at a computer screen.

Nick leapt onto the dentist's chair, clutching the paper bag in his lap.

"How can I help you?" Dr. Wagner smiled, pushing his chair away from the computer and gliding over to Nick.

"Doc, can I call you 'Doc'? Man, I love this room." Nick looked around the room with an animated expression as if he were in Disneyland. "It's so white and clean. And that smell—so good. I love a clean-smelling room."

Before Dr. Wagner could reply, Nick continued. "Now Doc, I have this problem. How is the best way to say this? I like to piss people off. And sometimes they don't like it and will punch me right in the mouth. Would you believe that? In this day and age?"

"Did you lose a tooth?" Dr. Wagner asked with a half-raised eyebrow.

"Not yet, knock on wood." Nick tapped his knuckles on his head. "But Doc, I guess it's the people I piss off, they kinda deserve it, you know? I don't just walk up to strangers and go, 'Hey you, you suck!' or 'Oi you! Fatty boom sticks! Eat less donuts, porky.' Or 'Hey ugly! Stop scaring small children, it's not Halloween.' It's mainly people I meet in my job. I bet you meet some crazy people in your line of work, too… people with some weird, fucked-up teeth, right?"

"I meet a large selection of people, Mr. Harvey."

"I bet you do. In my job, I deal with all kinds of creeps and weirdos," Nick chirped on. "It's my job to uncover them, expose their dirty little secrets."

"Okay," Dr. Wagner replied quizzically, looking toward the door. Nick picked up on the subtle change in attitude from the good doctor and opened the paper bag. He pulled out a soft toy, a Lopsy Lulu doll with large button eyes and floppy pink hair.

"This is for you, by the way," Nick smirked, throwing it toward the dentist.

"I'm a bit old for this." Dr. Wagner laughed.

"Yeah, you are," Nick laughed back. "I just thought you'd like to have it as the little girl who used to own it no longer needs it. Her name was Emma, cute as a button she was." Nick removed a photo from his paper bag and showed it to Dr. Wagner. It was a picture of Emma on a swing sporting an infectious smile. "You see, she got hit by a car in a small vacation town about eight months ago. The car was speeding, lost control, and hit her as she played in her front yard. The driver didn't stop. He must have seen her, as her body smacked across the windshield." Dr. Wagner moved uneasily in his chair. "The local police looked into it, but found nothing. It was as if a ghost had done it. Do you believe in ghosts?

I get called 'the ghost hunter' because you know what, Doc? I find these ghosts. I sat in that front yard, in the exact spot her body landed. For six hours, I lay there watching the clouds roll overhead, holding this very photo. Waiting for her to trust me enough to tell me what happened. What type of car it was… a sleek black convertible driven by a guy with shiny white hair."

"I don't understand why you're telling me this." Dr. Wagner moved his chair away from Nick.

"I'm sorry. I just thought you might like to know that you killed Emma. I would like to know if I'd killed someone, seems only right. Wouldn't you? Did you know she was dead? Maybe it didn't cross your mind as you sped away. Or maybe you did know and just didn't give a fuck. Yeah, that could be it. You just don't give a fuck."

Dr. Wagner's voice became agitated. "You can leave now. I have no idea what you're talking about!"

"Good one, Doc. You tried really hard to cover your tracks, even booking your car in for a detail. That was one clean car, no scuff marks from Emma's body. Lucky for me they don't clean the ventilation intake at the base of the windshield. That little vent collects everything."

"Get the hell out!" Dr. Wagner grabbed Nick by the collar of his white shirt, dragging him out of the chair and throwing him onto the ground.

"Ease up, Doc." Nick got to his feet and produced a Ziploc bag. "You see this little hair in there? This little hair puts you at the scene, and this little hair will make sure that you're held accountable for what you did. And you know what I said about getting punched a lot? I wouldn't try."

Dr. Wagner swung a wild right at Nick's head. Nick pivoted, easily blocking the punch, and returned his own with interest, striking the sweet spot on the dentist's jaw. He dropped instantly, falling face-first into the spit basin, smashing out his front teeth before crumpling onto the floor.

"Thanks, Doc, that felt good! You can now add 'attempted assault' to your long list of charges. And I'm thinking you have about two minutes to clean yourself up before the cops get here and haul your ass out in front of everyone. No need to rush."

Nick leapt back into the dentist chair and listened for the distant sound of police sirens to drown out the groaning Dr. Wagner.

CHAPTER SIX

JUSTIN WAS LATE. He always was, and Montana knew he did it on purpose. He liked making her wait, yet if she didn't arrive on time, he would make her pay. He'd taunt her in great detail about how hard her parents' life would be if he had them deported back to Mexico.

So Montana sat and watched the bubbles race each other to the top of her crystal flute. Justin always preordered her champagne. "It's a celebration every time we meet," he'd tell her.

Montana didn't see Justin, but she could feel him enter the restaurant. Her skin crawled the instant his hands touched her bare shoulders, and she wished her light blue halter dress had sleeves. Montana drained half the glass of champagne and placed it back down. She wearily greeted Justin with a sour smile as he sat opposite her.

"You look ravishing today. I love what you have done to your hair." Justin leaned across the table and ran his hand through her newly cropped locks. "But you should have asked me first." He traced his fingers gently down her neck.

God, how she loathed him. And now with his hipster-groomed facial hair and god-awful designer silk ties, there was even more to loathe.

Justin leaned back and clicked his fingers to summon a waiter, who was by his side in an instant. "Two grilled porterhouse steaks, steamed vegetables, and a baked potato," he commanded, without taking his eyes off Montana. "And the chicken Caesar salad for my delicious companion."

"Excellent choice. I'll let the chef know at once, Mr. Truth." And with that the waiter disappeared.

"How's work going, sweet lady?"

"Fine, thank you," Montana replied icily.

"Good girl. I hear you're doing well. You've implemented the educational program per my instructions. Was it hard?"

"No, people thought it was a great idea."

"It is a great idea. After all, I came up with it."

"I don't know why you wanted me to action this? It will actually benefit the brand, your competition, the people you want to crush." Montana drained the rest of her glass, a waiter appeared and quickly topped it up.

"Oh, I know, Montana. But don't worry your pretty little head about why. It will make you look amazing. When things start to go wrong, you will be the star in a dark sky, the only port in the storm, a rose among thorns. I'm looking out for you. You are very special to me."

Montana sunk into her seat, wishing the earth would open up and swallow her whole.

"Now sit up straight, brandish those wonderful breasts of yours, and smile," Justin ordered. Montana shifted her position and put on her Justin-friendly fake smile.

The waiter arrived with their lunch. Justin's order was always prepared immediately. The staff knew that the faster he got his meal, the more he would tip. Montana's lunch quickly followed.

"Enjoy your meal." Justin cut into his grilled steak and signaled for Montana to eat hers.

Montana picked up her knife and fork and cut into her chicken tenderloin. The blade was sharp and sliced through the chicken effortlessly. She looked up at Justin as he hungrily stuffed a large portion of steak into his mouth.

"Excuse me," she said. "I need to go to the powder room."

Justin grinned and patted her ass as she passed him. She took in a deep breath. Her heart pounded like tribal drums, her fingers twitched.

Montana spun behind Justin and grabbed his head, pressing the sharp blade against his throat. She yanked it back as hard as she could, ripping open his jugular. Justin's hands grasped at his neck, trying to stem the gush of blood erupting from the incision. Montana dropped the knife, grabbed the back of his head, and smashed it hard onto the table, over and over.

"I had lunch with Carlton yesterday," Justin said, glancing at Montana.

She jolted back to the real world, the tribal drums fading, and hid the knife behind her back before turning to face him. "He asked about you. I told him you were doing well."

"That… that's nice of him," Montana replied, dizzy from her violent daydream. She forced a smile and continued to the ladies' room.

Once inside, she threw up in the sink. Her throat burned from the acid reflux. It was a taste she was getting all too used to these days. She stabbed the knife into the wall with a shaky fist. Her stomach convulsed, and she threw up once more.

Montana returned to the table with reapplied makeup and her mouth freshly rinsed. Having left the knife stuck in the bathroom wall, she picked up the fork and tossed her salad around. Justin continued as if she'd never left.

"Carlton said he reached out to Steve. Have you also reached out to the man who raped and beat you, Montana?"

Montana lowered her fork as flashbacks of the Soda-Cola party tortured her. Much of it was still a blur. Reminding her about Steve and the rape was a game Justin relished playing.

"I haven't spoken to Steve, you know that," Montana spoke in an even tone.

"Good girl. He's not good for you. I think it would be an excellent idea to call Carlton and remind him of the amazing job you hear I'm doing."

"I'll call him tomorrow."

Justin leaned across the table and grabbed her by the wrist. "Yes, you will. And forget all about Steve. He's dead to you, hear me? Dead."

CHAPTER SEVEN

THE RUSTLE OF OLD NEWSPAPERS flying around the room wasn't what woke Steve, nor was it the stench of the urine-soaked mattresses. It wasn't the moaning and groaning of the drug addicts coming off their last hit. It wasn't the obscene yelling of the destitute prostitute in the corner letting two college students fuck her, as rough as they liked, for just fifty dollars each. No, it was the hard kick to his ribs that woke him.

"Motherfucker," a high-pitched voice shrieked. "You is in my bed. This mine!"

Steve's eyes gradually focused on a skinny Texan with a wispy white beard and brown-stained, broken teeth. His filthy denim shirt and rotting jeans hung loosely off his frail body.

"Motherfucker, my bed. Mine. You fucking fuck, my bed, you hear me!"

"Sorry, I didn't know." Steve tried to sit up, his neck protesting against any movement.

"Everyone knows this be Rattlesnake's bed. Me Rattlesnake! Not you."

Steve painfully rose to his feet. His arm still itched from the previous night's misadventure. "It's all yours." Steve gestured with his spotted arm. Rattlesnake flopped onto the mattress, coughing loudly.

Steve stumbled toward the door. The fresh air outside was a welcome relief, and he drew in a deep lungful while the wind tussled with the dregs of a dirty beard he couldn't remember growing. He had fallen a long way from the lofty position he'd held at Soda-Cola. His six-figure income, his beautiful wife and children, his stylish house, respect from his colleagues and the power that came with it were all gone—all because Carlton had hired Justin Truth.

Steve had heard that the rich never went to jail, and now he believed it. Even though Montana didn't press charges, the police followed through and prosecuted him.

The first thing Steve did was enlist a shark lawyer. He instructed him to do whatever it took to clear his name, but each day he'd watch vast sums of money evaporate into what looked like a lost cause. Finally he cut a deal just to avoid jail time.

Part of the settlement was a thousand hours of community service, which was a bit of a joke, really. All he had to do was pay his caseworker to report to the courts each month that he'd completed his allocated hours.

He hired a second lawyer to deal with the divorce, leading to the disappearance of more chunks of money from his bank account. His wife had been far more organized than him, and she'd hit him hard and fast. She'd taken the high ground, and all he could do was try not to drag the kids into the matrimonial meltdown.

Steve stumbled down the alley from the drug den, searching his pockets for money, finding only his hands in them. His stomach growled, and a half-eaten pizza he scavenged from a discarded pizza box helped a little. Collapsing in a doorway for a rest, he held out his hand to passersby for loose change.

He remembered how, after one brutal court session with the divorce lawyers, he'd wandered the streets aimlessly until his legs were too sore to take another step. He sat on a park bench with no idea what to do. He felt he was fucked, and the only thing that made sense was to get more fucked up.

Across the road from where he sat was an Irish pub. He walked in, plonked himself down at the bar, and ordered a Guinness. The bartender told him that once a person had drunk a hundred pints of Guinness, he'd add their own personal glass to the wall behind the bar. Always up for a challenge, Steve told the bartender he'd complete the challenge by the end of the week.

And so he did; with his pint glass firmly mounted on the wall, and a whole load of new friends in tow, "King Steve" was born. Dropping money on the bar made him popular, and with his newfound friends came interesting new experiences. He tried some coke, loved it, and inhaled a king's share. Before he knew it, he threw down pills and whatever else he could get his hands on. One hazy night, he took up an offer to try heroin, and the high was incredible. King Steve felt invincible.

From then on Steve got loaded every night, dropping money and living the king's life. Once the bar closed, his entourage often ended up back at his apartment where King Steve, with a hot girl on his arm, funded the never-ending party. But when his money dried up, so did the hot girls and party friends.

It wasn't long before Steve found himself trying to scrape together enough money just to get himself a score, but none of his so-called friends would hook him up; it was like he'd never existed. He wasn't sure how he'd been able to blow so much money so fast.

Eventually, Steve pawned everything he owned and hit up anyone he knew for cash. Luckily, he'd paid rent eighteen months in advance on his apartment in the trendy suburb of Tribeca. He had a place to sleep, but that was about it.

The sun felt blissful on Steve's gaunt face as he corralled himself back to his apartment. The door was unlocked, and as he stumbled in, he tripped over his own feet and fell flat on his face. His nose bled, and he cried.

CHAPTER EIGHT

A SPLUTTERING SPRAY of hot water splashed over Ross Smith's shaved head. Small rivers snaked their way down his hardened body. His shoulders were wider, his waist slimmer, and his chest broader. A man of fifty-three typically didn't have such a physique, yet it was vital that he did. He ran a hand over his head, feeling the stubble as he spat out water from his mouth.

Justin had set Ross up good, and as soon as his trial started, Ross knew it was a lost cause. They were going to make an example of him; too many stories had popped up in the media about dirty cops planting false evidence. He wasn't surprised when they sentenced him to thirty years in one of the most notoriously violent prisons in America, Bell Island.

Bell Island was originally built as a naval base in Broad Channel, Queens. Its name came from an enormous iron bell in one of its towers. When rung, its *clang* would roll over the ocean and could be heard for miles around. During World War II, Bell Island was turned into a military prison. That was short-lived, and the base went unused until it was bought by a private consortium. They turned it into a maximum security prison and positioned it as a place that would accept prisoners that other prisons turned down. It was frequently referred to as "Hell" Island.

As a convicted dirty cop, Ross knew he'd have a huge target on his back and wouldn't last a week in his old, flabby condition. He'd need to develop some serious muscle and create a strong visual change or else he'd be dead meat.

Pulling as many strings as he could and calling in a few favors, Ross managed to get his hands on some serious anabolic steroids to kick-start his transformation. The first shot had nearly killed him; he felt as if his heart might explode. He altered his diet and spent his time between court hearings working out furiously to build up strength and endurance. If he was going to have to fight for his life on a daily basis, his body had to be ready for it.

The high steroid dosage he was on made him hyperactive; he'd rotate between squats, push-ups, and pull-ups to combat his inability to sit still. He did hundreds and hundreds of reps per day, any chance he could, and use anything he could find as weights to lift—breaking down his muscle and rebuilding it stronger.

The side effects of being on the juice were vicious. He could feel his testicles shrink and his sex drive slowly disappear. He didn't care, having sex in prison was the last thing on his mind. He was on an emotional rollercoaster too. One minute he'd yell abuse at his wall; the next, he'd cry, tears streaming down his face.

Ross lifted his right hand and looked at his knuckles as the water glanced off them. He had broken his hand so many times on the inside that it had virtually no natural movement left. It was more like a club than a hand—a club that was his primary weapon.

His mind bounced back to the bus ride into prison six months ago and the cold eyes of the other prisoners slicing him to ribbons as they muttered *pig, dead cop,* and *prison justice* under their breath. He'd ignored their words, and instead run through scenarios of what might happen if they jumped him. He scanned every seat, every person, and every possible strike and counterstrike he could use.

The bus jolted to a stop, and everyone was ordered off. Ross remembered the cool air on his face as he stepped onto the gravel outside the prison entrance. New inmates always brought a crowd of prisoners to the gates, and a dirty cop coming into their world was big news. The guards did little to control the abuse, threats, and spit slung toward Ross. Every step he took that day in his ankle cuffs had to be focused and with purpose. Ten steps in, one of the other new prisoners leaned in close so Ross could hear him clearly.

"You gonna die in here, pig."

Ross fired his elbow back, smashing the guy square in the mouth, breaking most of his teeth. Before anyone else could move, he'd selected his next three targets, gripping his hands tightly together to use his fists like a human sledgehammer. A roundhouse swing to one man's head knocked him out cold. A low gut-shot and swinging uppercut knocked the second guy clean off his feet. Ross then thrust out his hands and grabbed the third guy around the throat, delivering three thunderous headbutts to his face and crushing his nose into a bloody pulp. Ross dropped him, then turned around to face the crowd.

"You fuckers know who I am! What you don't know is what I am! Want to fuck with me? You gonna be the one who gets fucked! Like a bitch! Come after me and you're dead. Simple. I'm here for life. I don't give a shit about taking a few lives while I'm here. Step up and you're gonna get knocked the fuck back down."

The guards were on him quickly after that. He didn't resist. Taking a few cheap shots from them was small payment for the message he'd delivered. He was confined to solitary for four weeks. Four weeks of squats, push-ups, and pull-ups. Four weeks of getting stronger.

Ross was relieved to be out of the hole. He'd been out three weeks now, his personal best. He lifted up his face and let the warm water rain gently down on him. Showers were one of the few pleasures he got to enjoy these days—when he wasn't in the hole. No doubt that was where he would continue to spend most of his time. He had to protect himself, and the most violent and vicious way was also the fastest way to achieve that. It worked, as most prisoners avoided him now. Even just a slight shoulder bump in the corridors would send Ross into Beast Mode, and he'd instantly fuck up the offender, damning the consequences. He couldn't let anyone get away with even the smallest infraction against him.

Ross looked around the empty communal shower. It was rarely empty. He'd noticed guys leaving as soon as he walked in, but that wasn't unusual, given his fits of violent rage. For him to be here by himself right now only meant one thing—he was right about the shower.

He heard the *click* of the shower room door shut and lock.

"Peekaboo," said a deep, croaky voice.

CHAPTER NINE

ROSS DIDN'T NEED TO LOOK UP to know Ezekiel was strutting in. The West Spiders, one of the top gangs in Bell, was having an internal power struggle, and Ezekiel wanted to be the head of the web. To achieve this, he needed support from his fellow Spiders and respect from the other gang leaders. He'd announced just the day before that he was "gonna take care of the motherfucking dirty cop." And here he was.

Ross remained calm and counted the slow, methodical footsteps coming closer. Ezekiel seemed to be taking his time, toying with him, knowing he couldn't escape.

Ezekiel arrived at Bell Island two weeks ago, and he'd made aggressive moves from the outset. At six feet four, he was a mass of solid muscle, and his hard, black body was covered in primal ink. Like all upper echelon West Spiders, he had an intricate spider web tattooed on the right side of his face. Ezekiel first rose to notoriety on YouTube by filming his own street fights. Tweets and viral shares fueled his vanity, making him feel like a Hollywood star. One night he got sloppy though, let himself get caught on camera hammering his fist into another guy's face until it caved in. It was impossible to avoid a murder conviction after the clip went viral; at least 850,000 people saw it before it was removed.

Ross picked up the plastic bottle of gel he'd brought in and squeezed its contents over his shoulders and torso. The transparent lubricant slid down his body to make him extra slippery. He discarded the container.

"This shower's taken. Come back in ten minutes," Ross said.

"Motherfucking funny fucker, is that what you is?" Ezekiel replied.

"I can tell a joke or two," Ross stated matter-of-factly. "The one about your mom and the donkey is a real crowd-pleaser."

"You is the joke, cracker. Motherfucking dirty fuckin' cop."

"Dirty?" Ross raised his head. "You need to come over and check my nuts. They are squeaky clean, man."

"I'll rip your fucking nuts off, cunt!" Ezekiel roared.

Ross's plan to fire up Ezekiel was working. He'd planned to focus Ezekiel's mindless anger on his words so that Ezekiel wouldn't notice the pools of soapy water all around, or remember that his prison-issued shoes had no grip, or see that Ross had covered his entire body with gel.

Ross smiled at Ezekiel. "Take your best shot, bitch. All I hear is how you faked your fight videos, how you're a reality-TV-wannabe slut. No real banger. Just a dumbass bitch!"

Ezekiel's eyes widened in rage.

"Fuckin' cop cunt!" he roared and charged at Ross. He watched as Ezekiel slipped and struggled to regain his balance, then Ross launched himself off the shower wall and thrust the ball of his foot deep into Ezekiel's solar plexus. It was a hard shot and forced the wind out of his rival's lungs. Gasping for breath, Ezekiel dropped to one knee while Ross drove a backspin-kick to his face. The force of it sent Ezekiel flying backward, cracking his skull as it bounced on the concrete floor.

Ross moved quickly and straddled his downed opponent. He needed to finish this quickly, so he dropped elbow strikes to Ezekiel's face, one after another. To Ross's surprise, the man recovered almost instantly and covered up to deflect his incoming strikes. Ezekiel twisted and popped his hips to push Ross off him. He stood and spat out a mouthful of blood.

"That all you got, old man? You gonna fucking die now."

Ross scrambled to his own feet. He was marginally impressed by how physically strong this man was, but he still had a few tricks up his sleeve.

"Come here, fucker," Ezekiel bellowed, as he methodically stalked his opponent, cutting the distance between them one step at a time. "Where you gonna go, white cunt?" He spat out another mouthful of blood and a dislodged tooth.

"You kiss your mother with that mouth? Because if you did, you would have smelled my cock on her breath."

Ezekiel grounded his back foot, shot in, and grabbed Ross around the waist, slamming him against the shower wall. Holding Ross tight and trapping his arms, Ezekiel began to squeeze. Ross felt the wind getting crushed out of him. As Ross twisted and turned, the gel did its job and he managed to free one hand. He had one chance. Ross used all his strength to ram his thumb into Ezekiel's eye. Ross felt the eyeball detach as his thumb went in deeper. He fell to the ground as Ezekiel released his grip and covered his face, screaming.

Ross leapt to his feet and hurled himself onto the larger man's back, slipped his forearm under his chin, and, in a vice grip, shut off the oxygen supply to Ezekiel's brain. The big man stumbled, swinging wildly until he hit the ground hard. Ross maintained the chokehold until Ezekiel passed out on the shower floor.

Ross dropped his head back and let out a roar intended for the Spiders outside the room. "This all you got? Get this washed-up cunt out of here before I kill him!"

Ross got to his feet and limped back to his shower, head down, hands against the wall as blood and soap floated away down the drain. He didn't look up when Ezekiel's boys entered the room and dragged their unconscious leader out, leaving Ross alone once again.

CHAPTER TEN

AFTER LUNCH WITH JUSTIN, Montana stumbled out of the restaurant. Justin's smell clung to her like a damp wool sweater. She could only think of one way to drown out her revolted senses.

She hailed a cab and told the driver to take her to Mazed. The cabbie raised his eyebrows—clearly he knew of the bar and was surprised that a classy lady would want to go there, especially at this time of day.

Montana pulled out her cell phone and emailed the office that she'd be working from home the rest of the day. Then she activated her OUT OF OFFICE notification, turned off her phone, and put it away.

She'd discovered Mazed after a drunken Phizz marketing event at the Museum of Modern Art. A drugged-up accountant introduced her to the place, just around the corner from the museum. That introduction was the start of too many nights she would rather not remember.

The buildings blurred by as Montana searched her bag for cash. Mazed was cash only—no exceptions. The cab turned right after the museum, then a sharp left into an alley between a secondhand book store and an S&M store.

Montana got out of the cab. The stench of urine and vomit made her gag, but it smelled better than the lingering stench of Justin. Tall buildings surrounding the place blocked the afternoon sunlight. Overflowing trash cans lined derelict walls, rusty fire escapes led to nowhere, and abandoned stairs dropped into dark, dingy holes.

The door to Mazed was down a flight of broken concrete stairs. A faded hexagram with an "M" painted in the center was the only indication that the place was there. Montana could hear hypnotic beats of heavy bass as she pushed open the door. The obese bouncer on an antique stool cocked his head at her before turning his eyes back to his '80s *Hustler* magazine.

Mazed was the sort of place people discovered at times in their lives when they shouldn't. It never closed and had a rolling clientele of drunks, drug addicts, and porn stars. The owner of the joint was Paul Starlight, an infamous porn producer from the '80s and '90s. He was always on-site and enjoyed a cult following.

Montana's eyes adjusted to the murky dark as she stepped through the Mona Lisa-print beaded curtain into the main bar where about twenty people lounged in oblivion.

The bar was called Mazed due to its layout—it was a maze of corridors and dens that all branched off the main lounge. The place had the effect of emptying a person's soul, and soon nothing there seemed shocking; nothing was off-limits. In fact, if you didn't see something depraved, you'd most probably end up feeling deeply disappointed.

Montana perched at the bar that doubled as a fully functional tropical fish tank. The gothic bartender approached her as if he was floating. He didn't ask her anything; he just observed her with an emotionless expression through white contact lenses that gave the impression he didn't have any pupils, only blank eyeballs.

"Island Maze," Montana ordered. The bartender slowly turned his back on her and went about preparing the cocktail. It had the same ingredients as a Long Island Iced Tea, with the addition of a shot of champagne, a shot of absinthe, a spoon of brown sugar, but without ice.

Montana picked up the muddy jar of liquid the bartender placed in front of her, downed it, and slid the empty vessel back toward the goth with a look that said *same again*.

As she handed the empty jar back over to the bartender for her third refill, Montana was oblivious to the large hulk of a figure appearing next to her.

"Fuck me if I'm wrong," he started. "But you want to fuck me." Montana swiveled on her stool to face the tobacco-rich voice. The man sitting next to her was a patched biker. He smelled of smoke, wore aged leather, and was one evolutionary step away from Neanderthal. His hands were heavily tattooed, and his face featured a crisscross of scars that alluded to a pleasurably violent lifestyle. A thick handlebar mustache made his cleft chin even more prominent.

"You want to fuck me?" Montana asked, holding his gaze.

"No. I said you want to fuck me."

"Do I now?" Montana returned to her drink.

"Yeah, because you've never been fucked with a cocaine condom, and I'm in the mood to teach one lucky girl something she'll never forget."

Montana placed her drink in front of the biker.

"I'm going to call you Maggot." Montana smiled and motioned with her eyes that he should drink her Island Maze. Maggot took a drag of his cigarette, dropped it in the jar, and downed the liquid. He stood up, put his arms around Montana's waist, and kissed her neck.

"Come," he ordered.

"I'll show you something first. A trick," Montana said in a husky voice. "See that empty wine glass over there? Bring it to me, and a trick I shall show you."

Montana stumbled slightly as the rhythmic, tribal beating in her ears returned.

Maggot returned with the glass and presented it to her as if he were offering her a sacred sword from the age of knights and dragons.

"Watch very closely because I'm only going to do this once," Montana said before shattering the head of the glass on the bar. No one raised an eyebrow. The sound of smashing glass wasn't uncommon there. She placed it in the center of the bar and looked at Maggot with a sideways smile before putting her hands behind her back. Hovering her head above the broken glass, she let a glob of saliva drop from her mouth onto the top of the broken stem.

"If you wanna fuck me, I've got to know you have good aim. Your turn," she smiled. Maggot wiped his mouth with the back of his hand and placed his hands behind his back. As he opened his mouth, Montana slapped her hands onto the back of his head and drove it down with force, impaling the stem into his left eyeball. Maggot fell backward in reactive shock, knocking over a table while desperately trying to pull the stem from his eye. He dropped to his knees and tried to yank it out, but cried out in pain every time he touched it. Montana stepped in front of him and watched the blood leak from his eye and trickle down his cheek.

She kicked the stem, sending it further into Maggot's head.

Towering over him, the tribal drums got louder, making her vision double. She held her head in her hands to muffle the sound. She looked down again and couldn't see Maggot. He was standing next to her holding the unbroken glass.

"What ya got?" Maggot asked again shaking Montana's shoulder.

"What?" she asked confusedly.

"The trick?" he demanded.

"What are you talking about?" She swayed from side to side.

"You said you wanted to show me a trick and then you just stood there, wasted as fuck, looking at nothing."

"Forget it." She grabbed him by the hand and lead him through the maze of corridors into a single cubicle with a strobing light bulb.

Maggot was a brutish man. His pants were quickly down, Montana's dress was hitched up, and her underwear dispatched.

"Show me, Maggot, show me this cocaine condom you rate so highly," Montana huffed, pushing him away.

Maggot pulled out a large plastic bag of cocaine.

"This is the good shit. Not that shit office cunts suck up their noses pretending they're Pablo fuckin' Escabar. That shit's cut with aspirin. This shit's pure fucking white gold." He sprinkled it over his throbbing hard-on. Then lifted Montana onto the basin, spread her legs and thrust his cock deep into her. Montana felt completely numb, mumbling in a dazed voice, "Fucking kill me… Just fucking kill me. . ."

CHAPTER ELEVEN

THE VALET LEAPT INTO ACTION when he saw Justin pull up in his Audi R8 Spyder. The Buffalo Room was one of the most exclusive gentleman's clubs in New York, and a valet could make a tidy profit in tips by targeting the right person. Justin had been noted as a high tipper.

"Mr. Truth," the valet greeted him. "You look incredible—like you just stepped out of GQ."

"This old thing?" Justin said, brushing some invisible lint off his bespoke Alexander Amosu suit. This evening, Justin had decided on a bright purple Prada tie with a matching silk pocket square. An antique Breguet pocket watch perfected his look.

"I had to tell my girlfriend to stop coming in when you're here," the valet schmoozed. "All she could talk about was you, and how handsome you are."

"She has excellent taste," Justin replied, slipping the valet a generous tip.

Two doormen opened the heavy oak double doors, and Justin strutted in like he owned the place. He took a deep breath. The smell of old money filled his lungs. He felt at home.

He made his way to the billiard room where Rip would be waiting for him. Justin and Rip had gone to Harvard together and become like brothers. A dark secret formed the foundation of their friendship.

Justin spotted Rip in a corner. He stood around six feet tall with short black hair, a square jaw, and bright blue eyes, and he was all suited up like a double-0 agent from a Bond film. He'd retained his posture from his time as an army pilot.

"Lord Justin Justice!" Rip announced as soon as he saw Justin.

"Sir Rip Rippington!" Justin bellowed back with gusto from the other side of the room. They bowed in front of each other and then embraced in a brotherly bear hug. This ceremonious, over-the-top English gesture had started on a trip to the UK they'd once taken together, and they'd continued the ritual ever since.

"Alfred!" Rip yelled at the frail seventy-year-old waiter, whose name wasn't Alfred but who acknowledged him anyway. "Bring us some Scotch. The good stuff, from my father's private stash."

"Yes, sir," the waiter replied dryly, and he ambled off to get the drinks.

"Come and tell me of your adventures in the world of cola and soda, and that orange stuff with bubbles," Rip laughed. They both sat down in luxurious leather chairs, much older than both men's ages added together, and relaxed into easy conversation.

"It's a dirty job rotting people's teeth, but someone has to do it," Justin said.

Rip was employed by his father, which meant he didn't work at all. He loved to hear all about Justin's sexual conquests and high-powered business meetings.

"And how is that French neighbor of yours? The last time we spoke, you said you'd lined up a threesome with that hot Polish friend of hers."

"Well, I have to tell you, 'justice' was served that night." Justin pulled out his iPhone and handed it to Rip. "As you can see, a good time was had by all."

Rip swiped through a few pictures of the two women Justin had shared that night with. One showed them kissing, another showed them playing naked with each other, and the last photo was a close-up of one eating out the other's pussy.

"Fuck me, Justin. How do you do it? They're so hot!"

"I have a magical cock, my good man. It can play the flute like a snake charmer."

They both cracked up laughing.

The waiter returned with the hundred-year-old Scotch in a square-cut crystal decanter and two Baccarat crystal tumblers, placing them on the small mahogany table between the two grand chairs. They ignored him as he poured the drinks neat. Each man then picked up their tumbler and offered their toast.

"Fortune favors the bold, and fucks the whores. The gold is ours, for a thousand scores. If you be a bitch, be bitched out. If you be a man, then man up. For the gentleman will ride hard forever, and like a stallion, fuck forever more. Motherfucker." They ran through their brotherly mantra in unison before taking a sip.

"Lord Justice, have you found time in your calendar to join me at the Baxtor Street soup kitchen. I'm helping all weekend."

"I wish I could. Would a thousand-dollar donation cover me?"

"Would like you to lend a hand? People I served overseas with will be there. Tell me you will think about it."

"I will, *Dad*. Now, sir," Justin asked with sincerity. "Is your father joining us tonight?"

"He told me he was going to try and drop by, depending on how his meeting goes. His company is in negotiations with the military for the contract to service the on-base canteens in the Middle East. Do you know how much they sell your sodas for? Forty-five dollars a case!"

"Not one of mine," Justin smiled.

"I bet you wish it was. Mo' money, bitches."

They laughed again and downed their drinks. Alfred quickly returned to refill them.

"Speak of the devil and he will appear," Rip said, looking toward the door. Justin turned to see Peter Gordon walk in. The man was a beacon of power, with a mind as sharp as a razor and eyes that could cut you in half. He didn't pity fools or enjoy small talk. With him was Gilbert Gruber, his personal assistant, a Yale-educated German. Rip called him his father's tall shadow. Gilbert was a lanky six foot ten, and wherever Peter was, he would be lurking close by.

"Father!" Rip called out.

Peter acknowledged his son with a slight wave and made his way over. Gilbert hung back before leaving the room.

"Glad you could make it," Rip said.

"I told you I would," Peter replied as if he were talking to a pet dog: short, sharp, and bereft of emotion. The family resemblance was strong between father and son—they both had the same piercing blue eyes and strong jaw. Peter's once jet-black hair was now speckled with gray, yet it remained thick and distinguished. He was larger than Rip and stood with his head slightly hunched forward, his tie hanging loosely around his fat neck.

Justin got to his feet. "Mr. Gordon."

"Justin, glad you could make it," Peter exclaimed. "Hope you've been talking some sense into this errant son of mine."

"We haven't gotten to that point yet." Justin grinned.

"Father, you know I'm going to do it. I married the girl you wanted, and I've been keeping my nose clean."

"Not clean enough, Rip."

Peter had been planning Rip's life since he was born, a curriculum vitae fit for a future President of the United States.

"Father!" Rip sounded like a ten-year-old boy who didn't want to eat his vegetables.

"Rip, you have to protect your name and the family. Things go viral in no time these days."

Sipping his aged Scotch, Justin observed the tension between the two. He secretly wished Peter was his father, but while Justin had embraced Rip like a brother, he knew Peter didn't see him as a son. Justin was surprised, then, when Peter turned his attention from Rip to him

"Justin, come for a walk with me."

Justin followed Peter into the cigar room, a smaller, more intimate room down the corridor from the billiard room. Peter selected a fine cigar displayed beneath a glass counter. He rolled it slowly between his fingers, appreciated the aroma, and gestured for the attendant to bring two. In course, they were cut, lit, and the two men enjoyed them in front of a large, roaring fire.

"Sorry to hear about your mother," Peter said brusquely.

"Thank you, sir."

"I'm hearing good things about what you are achieving at Soda-Cola. Some large dividends have been shared. You have shown me you can rise up and get things done. I have two questions for you…"

"Sure," Justin nodded, and took in a puff of the cigar. The expensive smoke tantalized his taste buds and he savored its taste.

"Number one: I'm very close to sealing a deal with the top brass for a service contract in Iraq. I want you to bring your company to the party.

Your competition is in bed with my competition. Word is they are just ahead of us and I need to get this deal over the line. When we win, it will open the door to a few more opportunities that I have my eye on, but I won't get into that right now. I need you to make this deal happen on your side. Show me you can do what needs to be done."

"You can count on me, sir."

"Number two: Here's an opportunity for you. My son is going to be the president of this great country of ours one day—I will make sure of it. The current Republican governor of New York isn't going to run for another term. I have the numbers behind Rip to make him the Republican front-runner. He will be the youngest man ever to be the governor of New York. I'm assembling a team for his campaign train. And when that train leaves, whoever is on board will be taken along for the glorious ride. There is a seat for you, Justin, but to get on the train, you need a ticket."

"And how do I get a ticket?" Justin asked calmly.

"You buy one. It costs ten million dollars." Peter blew a plume of rich cigar smoke into the fire.

CHAPTER TWELVE

NICK STOOD IN THE DOORWAY of a busy downtown Pennsylvania bar. The walls were gimmicked with street signs from all over the country, and hubcaps adorned the front of the bar. Red and white gingham-checked tables lined the room, and in the center was a dance floor that had yet to see any action. People were drinking, talking, and laughing out loud.

He'd spent the day doing routine paperwork at the local police station for Emma's killer, Dr. Wagner. This had taken up far too much of his precious time. He'd delivered them the bad guy along with enough evidence for a five-year-old to convict him, yet, they'd kept him waiting for hours and failed to thank him. And they'd eaten into his personal drinking time.

Nick yanked the entrance door closed behind him. It made a loud bang, interrupting people in mid-conversation, and a majority of them turned to see where the sound had come from. The girls who looked at him for more than five seconds seemed to like what they saw. The girls who turned back to their conversations were in relationships, or not interested, he figured. He counted seven girls who held his gaze long enough for his liking and committed their faces to memory. He then made his way to a small table at the end of the bar.

A waitress approached him.

"Hi, hun, what can I get you?" she said in a cute Oklahoman drawl. She had big brown eyes, a small pixie-like nose, and wore her blonde hair tied back in a slick ponytail. Her tight white T-shirt highlighted her large rack, and her denim skirt accentuated her curvaceous behind. Her smile was professional, warm, and inviting.

"Hi, you." Nick smiled. "What I would like is a Corona and two shot glasses, one with gold tequila, the other left empty. Every twenty minutes, I'd like you to return and top up my shot glass. And once I have company, could you top up both glasses, please?" Nick pulled out the contents of a pocket. He didn't carry a wallet; he just moved items from one pocket to the next when he changed pants. He pulled out a wad of crumpled notes and placed them on her tray. "I know it's going to get busy later, but if you could look after me, the change is your tip."

The waitress smiled, and this time he knew it was genuine. He watched as she counted the money on her way back to the bar. Nick bet five hundred dollars would make this a good night already for her.

Nick scanned the room again, deciding that there were four girls in the bar he could pick up for sure. All he needed to do was throw out the bait and see which one he caught first.

The waitress returned with the Corona, two shot glasses, a bottle of Sauza gold tequila, as well as a shaker of salt and some wedges of lime. "You didn't ask for the extras, hun, but they kinda come together."

"I knew you would." Nick smiled.

"Oh, really," she replied playfully.

"It's a talent, I know things."

"Really?" She placed a hand on her hip, accentuating her hourglass figure.

"It's true. I know you will be friendly to me all night, but you won't go any further."

"You don't know that," she said flirtatiously, leaving the interpretation open-ended.

"But I do. I know you're in a relationship with the bartender, and you two look good together. But his girlfriend of six years and their newborn wouldn't agree. You know it's wrong, but you're infatuated with him and choose to overlook some shaky details. He says he sleeps on the couch, but deep down you know they share a bed. This is your place together, and she never visits. He gets the best of both worlds. Happy home, happy work."

"What? No. . . who told you that?" The waitress crossed her arms and screwed up her face.

"You did. I watched you when you got my drink. The way you two just interacted told me everything I needed to know. The baby was one;

the stain on his shoulder is common for burping toddlers. But you don't look like you've had kids yet. I'm not judging. I don't care. If it makes you happy, I'm all for that. As I told you, I just kinda know things. And here's a game we can play." Nick pointed to four different girls in the bar. "One of these four fine young ladies will be sitting next to me in the next hour enjoying a tequila from that extra shot glass. At the moment, I don't know which one, but if I had to make a bet, the girl in the denim shorts, red shirt, with the cropped blonde hair is the one I'd put the house on."

Nick turned his eyes back to the waitress; her lips were still pursed.

"I know," Nick continued, "that guy over there with the sideburns will generously tip tonight if you slip him a bowl of popcorn with his next drink order. That couple with doe eyes will too if you get some Elvis music on while they eat chicken wings."

She leaned in. "What else do you know?" she asked, her eyes brightening. "What about him, the guy with the loud tie, he's always in and never tips. What can I do to him?"

CHAPTER THIRTEEN

JUSTIN FLOORED IT, leaving a trail of rubber on the road outside the Buffalo Room.

"Ten million? Give him twenty," Rip said, with the arrogance of someone who had never worked a day in his life, when Justin told him about Peter's offer. Justin had amassed a sizable fortune through his portfolio of stocks, bonds, and property, but he didn't have the amount of money that Peter required in cash. Besides, to sell everything would take time, but Peter had given him four weeks to contribute to the election fund, or the ticket would go to someone else. "Someone who could afford it. . ." Peter's words rang harshly in Justin's ears.

Justin sped into the underground parking building of the Luxor Apartments. He'd acquired his parking spot—a premium one—after getting a neighbor kicked out.

His mind raced as he wracked his brains about all the ways he could pull together the required funds. This door would only be open for a short time, and once closed, he feared Peter would never open it again

Just as he reached his own front door, the door to the adjacent apartment opened. Wearing a sheer black lace bra, a matching G-string, and stay-up stockings that accentuated her long, toned legs, Alex emerged. Her elegant, flawlessly manicured fingers played with a glass of deep red wine, rolling it back and forth seductively, knowingly.

"There you are, you naughty boy," she purred in her sweet French accent. "I was feeling a little dirty, I need a bath… You would like to help clean me, no?"

Justin felt the air in his lungs being sucked out, replaced by her perfume. Alex had an amazing catwalk body, which he'd experienced a few times, enjoying every inch.

"Alex, honey, run the bath, and I'll grab my special back scrubber."

"Be quick, Justin. I would very much like some sex too."

Justin raised his eyebrow, blew her a kiss, and disappeared into his apartment. He threw his jacket on the black leather couch, unbuttoned the top of his shirt, and sat down at his desk. Crunching numbers and figuring out how he could get the ten million was his number one priority, and soon he even forgot about Alex and her bath.

Thirty minutes later Justin stood up angrily, rubbing the faint scar on the right side of his head, just below his temple. He moved about the length of his spacious apartment. He couldn't swing it. It was impossible for him to get his hands on that much money. As he'd predicted, the bulk of his funds were tied up in shares and investments, plus he'd heavily leveraged himself to get the apartment building up and running.

Justin was going to have to reach out to Black Wolf and hope he'd come up with a Plan B. Black Wolf successfully brokered underground business arrangements and would know some people. Maybe that was the only way.

Justin typed a cryptic coded email.

To: thebw316@gmail.com
From: justin.truth@thetruthfoundation.com
Subject: Friendly invitation.

Hi BW,
Hope this finds you well. The new job is great. You were right, no rest for the wicked. I used my telescope the other night. Wow, it was like ten million stars were out there just within reach. I would like to show you some time. I know you're busy but you should fit it in.

Your friend, Justin.

Justin stared out of his window toward Central Park, leaned his right forearm on the cool glass, then rested his forehead against it. Black Wolf would know what he was asking for. Now he only had to wait and see what the response was.

Justin's eyes drifted to his masterpiece on the far wall. The grand oil painting was a celebration of every life Justin had taken. It had a gray gradient background featuring multiple red handprints. Justin looked at his hand and stretched his fingers. It was time to add another handprint. Soon, he thought to himself. Soon…

Suddenly Justin remembered Alex, and the thought of her naked body tied to her bed made him grin. She wouldn't be happy that he'd made her wait, but a few lines of coke would sort that out. Justin grabbed a small bag of pure Bolivian from his hidden floor safe and his special $10,000 bill featuring President Woodrow Wilson. When he snorted coke that good, he liked to break out this special note. He was going to get loaded and fuck Alex as if her life depended on it.

CHAPTER FOURTEEN

"WHY YOU WANT ME TO hurt you, Yury?" Misha asked in a heavy Russian accent. "You see, I don't care of past we have. I will hurt you. Break finger. Break leg. Crack skull open like ripe melon. Cut off cock and feed to dog. These are things I do without even thinking."

"Please!" Yury sobbed. Blood and snot oozed from his European-shaped nose and down into his trembling mouth. "I'll tell you everything!"

Yury knew there was a small risk he would be caught. Yet, like so many before him, he thought he'd get away with it.

"I can get it back... all of it," he sniffed.

"You can get back? That is funny. It is gone, Yury. All drugs, all money, gone. You forget business we are in. You work for me, and I work for people. Money goes one way, and along way, people get piece of pie. My piece bigger than your piece, and people above me, their piece of pie is very big. People forget this, Yury, you forget this. I never forget this. Everybody has to earn, everybody has to pay every month. If I not pay, then people will come and give me a visit. It make sure I look after my business."

Misha ran the New York connection of the Bratva, a common name for the Russian Mafia. He had worked hard in his homeland then emigrated to the United States ten years ago.

He still respected the old ways, and even though he knew times were changing, he also knew the fundamental tenet of running any business was the same: to focus on supply and demand. Over the ten years he'd been in America, he had seen a change for the worse. So many guys desperate to get into the Bratva wanted it the easy way, and in their haste, would disrespect the chain of command. People like Yury. His family had moved to America the same time Misha had. But Yury had gone to school here, and to Misha's mind, he'd become more of a soft American than a hard Russian.

"They call me 'Russian Crusher' here in America. You Americans and nicknames."

"I'm not American! I'm Russian, like you."

"No! You not like me, Yury," Misha replied. "Crusher, I care not for name. Does this face look like one who care? No. Only good thing about these nicknames, Yury, is people talk. Always talking, talking... talking. You should have listened. You know why they call me the Russian Crusher?"

Misha lifted his large hand. "It very big, no? Once doctor told me when I was born, something wrong with me. Maybe I was a twin and eat him in womb. You see tendons in my hands are fatter than normal. Means I have grip like vise, like bulldog. Once I lock on, it can no be broken."

Misha grabbed Yury's right wrist. "Now this why people called me Crusher, Yury." He placed his other hand over Yury's right hand, cupping it. When he squeezed, Yury screamed in pain, thrashing in his chair. As Misha tightened his grip, everyone in the dark warehouse could hear the bones in Yury's hand snap. Blood streamed out between Misha's fingers, dripping onto the chipped concrete floor as Yury's eyes rolled back. He passed out from the excruciating pain.

Misha let go of the mangled hand and spoke to one of his soldiers. "When he wake, tell me. I not finished with him yet."

Misha opened a pack of Marlboro Reds, tapped out a cigarette, and placed it between his thick lips. Taking in a deep drag, he walked around the warehouse thinking. This had been a bad year for him. There was a traitor in his crew selling information to Homeland Security. The feds had busted eight of the last twelve drug shipments at the docks. That wasn't good. When there was nothing to sell, there was no money to collect.

He took another drag, holding the smoke deep within his lungs. He thought bitterly about the other gangs making moves in his territory. And now, to top it off, Yury had just fucked him.

Yury had tried to set up a side deal by dipping into the protection money he'd collected for Misha. The plan had been to buy meth off a Mexican gang, bring it into New York, and sell it to the West Spiders for a small profit, then return the original protection money. The West Spiders could smell the greenhorn stench of a chump out of his depth at the deal. They took the meth and kept their money.

Misha was furious when he found out. With other deals going bad, and so many of his imported drugs getting busted, Misha was falling behind in his payments to Russia. They were not known for being patient. The protection money would have bought him a few more weeks, but now that the protection money was gone, he had to find another way to replace it, along with everything else.

He inhaled the last of his Marlboro and flicked the remaining butt at the stained concrete wall. He needed one big score. Getting the cocaine was easy enough; he just needed money to get the ball rolling. And the cocaine had to be paid for upfront.

Misha heard a gargle coming from Yury as he regained consciousness. The next five minutes were going to be fun—for Misha, at least.

CHAPTER FIFTEEN

THE THICK METAL LADLE plunged into a simmering pot of gelatinous mushroom goo. Today's lunch at Bell was soup. Ross stood in line waiting for his turn. Like ants, prisoners marched together, moving as quickly as they could. One thing you didn't mess with in prison was feeding time. If you missed out, that was your problem. The staff went about their work—no conversation, no jokes, just serving and churning through the line.

As the soup went into Ross's bowl, he grabbed two bread rolls and a package of Lay's, keeping his head down and moving on like everyone else. The lunchroom could be a sanctuary from the normal violence of prison life, if you followed the basic rules of where to sit. The gangs had divided the room into camps, and each gang considered their corner prime real estate, one they were willing to control and defend with brutal violence. Trying to change corner ownership normally resulted in a full-blown riot.

Ross settled on the short bench in the middle of no-man's-land, his regular spot across from Father O'Grady. No other prisoners would join them; they hated Ross, but they were scared shitless of O'Grady. Ross had heard the stories about the young priest and the exorcism that had gone horribly wrong.

"Father." Ross nodded.

"Peace be with you, and good to see you again, Ross." O'Grady smiled.

That would be the full extent of their conversation. Ross grasped the spoon with his club-like fist; his hand was only good for punching now. Holding his spoon required more determination than anything else, but as long as he could make a fist and hit hard, his hands did their job. The soup tasted like dishwater, but it was warm, thick, and the bread did a good job of soaking it all up.

Ross looked around at the tide of colors flooding the lunchroom. There were three: orange, blue, and gray. New arrivals wore orange jumpsuits; the longer-term residents wore blue shirts and gray pants. Ross had just recently graduated out of his orange jumpsuit, which made him happy. He hated orange.

Every gang had their own style of wearing the assigned prison uniform. It was a subtle, yet effective, way of showing gang membership without the use of colors. Gang colors were banned in Bell.

West corner: The West Spiders

Prison uniform: Shirt unbuttoned, sleeves rolled halfway up. Pants rolled up to just below the knee. Socks pulled up.

Gang history: The West Spiders began in the 1960s. The first Spiders were swiftly established through a web of organized violence and strategic planning, which inspired chapters in other cities and several prisons. Their name was synonymous worldwide with American gangland culture, and they'd been the focus of many documentaries and feature articles.

When inducted into the Spiders, every member had a web tattooed onto a part of their body. The face was a privilege for only the most elite Spiders. Members had to earn that right, and if someone got a web tattoo on their face without earning it, the tattoo would be burned, then cut out of them.

Ross turned his head toward the gang of white supremacists, the White Fist. They saw anything in the South section as theirs by right and would go to war to defend every inch of it.

South corner: White Fist.

Prison uniform: Shirt buttoned up to the top, long sleeves buttoned down. Shirt tucked into gray pants.

Gang history: White Fist was a powerful force at Bell, as well as most other American prisons. A white-dominated gang, small in numbers but well-financed, and composed mostly of stone-cold killers. According to the FBI, White Fist gang members made up less than 1 percent of the prison population, but they accounted for 30 percent of all the murders within prison walls. One inflexible requirement to become a full-fledged member was to kill a black or Hispanic prisoner. Also, once a gang member was in, they could never leave. They spewed violence in the name of white purity and held a clenched fist in the air as a show of power.

Ross returned to his soup, dipped some bread in it, and took a bite. His eyes glanced east.

East corner: The Hispanic Czars.

Prison uniform: Shirts unbuttoned except for the top button, right sleeve on the right arm rolled halfway up. The left sleeve long and unbuttoned. Pants oversized and hung low.

Gang history: One of the oldest and largest South American street gangs in existence. A flood of Hispanic people in the 1940s didn't find America welcoming; instead, they often found themselves innocent victims of cruel violence by local bigots. The white police force turned a blind eye to the Hispanic calls for help. The Hispanic Czars formed to protect Hispanic people by any means available.

When becoming a member of the Hispanic Czars, inductees were ingrained with six important values: respect, honesty, unity, knowledge, power, and love. Each member was expected to abide by these values, though, from the outside it could seem rather hypocritical for a gang that murders and destroys families to uphold an ethically rigid value system.

They were known to play loud music and have parties—parties that could turn dark at any given moment if someone of high rank felt disrespected. Respect is everything, and they maintain a strong internal structure for obeying orders. To question orders means to disgrace those above you—those men who've fought and killed to earn their rank.

Ross returned to his lunch, neither happy nor sad that it was half finished. He picked up his packet of Lay's, crushed the chips inside the packet, dropped them into the soup, and mixed them in to thicken his meal.

As he took a spoonful of the new concoction, he avoided looking in the direction of the North corner. The gang that controlled it was the notorious M-16 and just about anything could set these guys off.

North corner: The M-16.

Prison uniform: Oversized gray shirts, buttons removed. Left untucked to hang over their pants.

Gang history: While new on the gangland map, they'd quickly become one of the most dangerous and violent gangs in operation, spreading to over forty cities across the United States. The M-16 was founded in the Salvadoran immigrant community of Los Angeles. Like their name depicts, early members solved problems with fully loaded M-16s. They spray painted the automatic weapon symbol every place they claimed as theirs.

Violence was their native tongue, and no one would receive a second chance or benefit of the doubt. If a member was going to fight, they fought to the death. Getting killed doing M-16 business would be seen as an honorable death.

They expanded quickly with no limits: drug trafficking, murder, extortion, racketeering, and even child prostitution. If they could make money off it, it was good business.

Scattered between the four main gangs were smaller groups and affiliates. In times of trouble gang leaders called upon them like soldiers, and once they chose a side, some serious shit had to go down in order to change allegiance.

Lastly, in the center of the room, were the tables designated for the unwanted scum—pedophiles, junkies, and assorted nobodies. No-man's-land.

Ross felt someone approach him from behind. He rotated the spoon in his hand, ready to use it as a weapon. Out of the corner of his eye he saw a lower member of the White Fist. The skinhead held a bread roll, which he placed next to Ross's bowl before backing away.

Ross knew what it meant. It was an offer to join the White Fist and be under their protection. If he ate the roll, it would show everyone that he accepted their invitation.

Ross wanted no part of any gang, let alone one with Marcus at the helm. He finished his lunch, got up, and glanced around the room. The other prisoners were waiting for his answer. He knew Marcus only wanted him as a pet, which would mean he'd spend the rest of his time being treated like a dog. Feeling all eyes on him, Ross ripped the roll in half and discarded it into the trash. Fuck those racist fucks.

CHAPTER SIXTEEN

IT WAS NOW OR NEVER, Steve told himself as he stuck Band-Aids over his forearms to hide his track marks. This morning he woke up in the bathroom with a needle in his arm and vomit down the side of his chin. He found the front door to his apartment wide open and whistling wind swirling two plastic bags in a lazy dance around the room.

Steve peered into the mirror and didn't recognize the stranger staring back. His face hadn't felt a razor in months, and washing his clothes now only involved a walk in the rain. He slammed his fists against the mirror, smashing it. Broken shards of glass tinkled into the sink. The sudden violence scared him. What was he doing? He had to change. Today was the day he was going to get clean, get his life back on track, and reclaim his family.

He had to go cold turkey, cut himself off from the outside world and sweat the drugs out of his system. He started to form a plan in his mind, and once Steve had a plan, he was good at following through.

In college, it was this drive and attitude that helped him get onto the football team, graduate with honors, and beat out hundreds of other applicants for a management role with Soda-Cola.

He thought about his football coach and the speeches he'd given back in the day. Steve closed his eyes and imagined Coach Helmsley standing in the room with him now. Coach Helmsley loved his coffee and donuts a bit too much, but he had a hell of a brain when it came to strategy and getting the best out of his players. His large face would go purple when yelling commands.

"Barker! What the hell do you call this place? It's a goddam trash bin. I wouldn't let my dogs sleep in here."

"Sorry, sir."

"Don't be sorry! Do something about it. When you take a shit, you either wipe your ass, or you smell of shit. Fundamentals, Barker. Do you want to smell of shit?"

"No, sir."

"What?"

"NO, SIR!"

"Good. Then time to clean that shit out. We need to do a whole lot of wiping to get you back where you need to be, son. You want that?"

"YES, SIR."

"Here's what you gonna do, son. You may want a pen to write it down, as I ain't gonna be repeating myself. First, we need a place where you're gonna sleep. That's all, just sleeping and sweating out that shit you put in your veins."

Steve went into the bedroom, dragged out the mattress, and pushed it into a corner of the lounge. Pillows and blankets soon followed

"Second, we need a visual reminder of why we are doing this."

Steve pulled out dozens of photos of himself with his kids and taped them to the walls around the mattress.

"Third, we need good food and lots of it so you don't have to go out. Water and soup, soup and water. Flush, flush, and flush out all that shit!"

Steve walked outside into the sun. For the first time in months, he felt alive. He sucked the fresh air into his lungs and took step after determined step down to the mini-mart to stock up.

He grabbed a dented shopping cart and dropped in two five-gallon water containers and twenty assorted cans of soup. The cart struggled under the weight and pulled to the right, nearly taking out a display of cornflakes. Steve carried on with his mission through the mini-mart, throwing in a few other must-haves like chocolates, cookies, and milk.

"That a boy, Steve," his imaginary coach hollered. "Once you get this lot home, you're in the game. And we're gonna win. What are we going to do?"

"We are going to win, sir!" Steve roared.

Passing the magazine stand, the latest issue of *New York Business Journal* caught Steve's eye. It featured a smiling photo of Justin Truth on the cover holding a bottle of Soda-Cola. GLOBAL MARKETER OF THE YEAR, the headline read.

Back home, the needle slid easily into Steve's forearm, and as the sickly substance swiftly entered his bloodstream, he felt sweet oblivion greet every cell of his aching body.

"Go fuck yourself, Helmsley..." Steve slurred as he drifted off into nowhere on his moldy old mattress.

CHAPTER SEVENTEEN

THE VISITORS ROOM AT BELL ISLAND hadn't changed much in the last thirty years. Foldout chairs sat in a long line in front of each visitor's booth, with one-inch-thick armored glass separating callers from the convicts. Visitors and prisoners conversed through archaic phone handsets. The booths were separated from one another with thick, wooden triangle dividers, and visitors had scribed jokes, pictures, and insults into the cheap wood over the years.

Justin sat on the hard chair and attempted to get comfortable. Today he wore Ksubi jeans, a white Henley T-shirt, and original Air Jordan V's with matching reflective tongue-and-rubber soles. He hated waiting, but in here he had to wait like everyone else. What he despised the most were the people he was forced to wait with. He couldn't stand the combined smells of stale body odor, fast food, and dirty clothing.

Justin came to Bell Island to visit Ross on the first Saturday of every month. He liked to tell him about events in his life that he couldn't share with anyone else. Killing his mother had left a hole, and Ross was the perfect replacement. It didn't matter what he told Ross because there was nothing he could do about it, and thanks to Amnesty International, no one could use electronic devices to record their conversations. Even so, Justin spoke in code words that he knew Ross would understand.

Finally, the doors opened on the other side of the glass and thirty inmates filed into the room and took their seats. Ross entered last.

"Hi, Ross," Justin spoke into his handset with an exaggerated smile.

Ross glared at Justin, his eyes burning holes into his skull. If it wasn't for the armored glass between them, Justin was sure Ross would try to kill him.

"Pick up," Justin demanded.

Ross didn't move.

"Pick up," he repeated.

Ross dropped his head back and stared at the ceiling. Justin's tap on the glass drew his attention back, and he held up a picture that always made Ross pick up. It was a photo of Justin with his arm around Ross's daughter. It had the desired effect.

"Good boy. So, how are you?"

Ross stared at him.

"I know, still in here, sucking cocks and benching the shit out of faggots as always. Check out your pecs! Didn't know you could get that much quality protein from prison cum. Look at you, Beast Man! Captain Roids!

"Anyway, enough about you. What a week I've had. My good friend Rip asked me to join his campaign to be the next governor of New York. That's pretty exciting. If he wins, I'll help him make decisions about how to best manipulate this entire state and country." Justin gestured for a guard to drop a copy of the *New York Business Journal* in front of Ross. "Ohhh. . . and would you look at that, you even get a mention, Ross."

As soon as Ross peered down at the magazine and saw Justin's grinning face, he tore it in half and tossed it behind him.

"You can keep it," Justin said. "I have a few more copies back at my place. I'm actually getting one framed for the office. Oh, and you should've seen what I did to this French girl last night. You ever play with asphyxiation? When you choke a bitch, nearly killing her, and then she cums super hard? It's a rush.

"By the way, a little birdy told me you've been in a spot of trouble," Justin continued. "It's so hard for a dirty cop like you to keep your nose clean, isn't it? You need to work on that or you'll never get parole. You have to show you're a reformed character, Ross. Getting into fistfights isn't going to help your case. I'm putting in a good word for you, though, you know. People like me don't have to change. There's something I want to tell you about. Just the other day I was walking the street with my green jacket on, you know the one. It feels so good to wear it, with all the memories and all. Anyhow, I was just walking, and this girl caught my eye. She must have been a teenager, tall, young, and sweetly dumb. What was that girl's name again? The one you were investigating?"

Ross's hands were shaking with restrained rage.

"She was just like her. Shit, I still can't remember her name. Not that it's really all that important, I guess. I followed her down the street for a while. She seemed interesting. I think I need to discover a bit more about her. I wonder if she can fly like what's-her-name did."

Ross suddenly lost control, picked up his chair, and smashed it against the heavy glass, sending bits of chair flying everywhere. He looked desperate for the glass to crack so he could get his hands on Justin. Ross didn't resist when three guards wrestled him to the floor, and when he looked up, Justin smiled broadly and blew him a kiss. "See you next month."

CHAPTER EIGHTEEN

BEFORE NICK OPENED HIS EYES, he knew the room would be spinning. All he could think about was water, any water. As he carefully opened his eyes, the motel ceiling emerged from darkness, and wind from an oscillating fan breathed down on him. He closed his eyes again and willed a glass of water to appear in his hand. It didn't. As he rolled off the bed, a sea of empty tequila and Corona bottles broke his fall.

Nick crawled into the bathroom, pushing bottles out of the way, and pulled himself up to the sink. He slurped water from the faucet in greedy gulps.

His thirst quenched, he splashed water on his face and adjusted his hair in the mirror. He noticed he was naked. He looked around the bathroom to see if anything jogged his memory… nothing did. He staggered back into the bedroom where a naked woman stirred under the bed covers before appearing to drift back into a heavy sleep.

The room was trashed. Nick's pants were slung over a lamp and his shirt crumpled under the bed, but his shoes and socks were neatly arranged by the front door, a curious habit he retained even during benders. He dressed in a hurry and searched his pockets for cash but found nothing. Peeling back the insole in his shoe proved to be successful. He found two folded-up twenties. He often hid money from his drunken self for these very occasions.

Nick went to wake his drinking partner, but then decided it would be better to let her sleep. He opened the motel door and stepped into the outside world.

The light was stark and bright; Nick felt like a vampire who should be sprinting for shade to stop himself from bursting into flames. He waited for his eyes to adjust, then stumbled from shady spot to shady spot until he finally reached the taxi line and slid into the backseat of a waiting cab.

"Where we heading, my brother?" the cab driver asked.

"Walmart," Nick mumbled.

"Sure you don't want me to take you home? You don't look like you should be shopping."

"It *is* home." Nick smiled to himself.

When the cab arrived in the Walmart parking lot, Nick dropped a twenty on the passenger seat and dragged himself out. He was home, as he called it. He didn't blame passersby for shooting him disparaging looks. After all, he did look like an extra from *The Walking Dead.*

Nick slipped through the front door and began his habitual purchases.

First stop: two coffees, triple black. He downed the first one fast and sipped slowly on the second.

Next stop: towel, body wash, deodorant stick, and razor … just what he needed to wash away the last three days.

Third stop: a charcoal suit, white shirts, tie, socks, and underwear. He didn't need to try them on.

Fourth stop: a generic cell phone to replace the one he'd lost; for all he knew it was still at the motel. He grabbed a black backpack, then headed to the checkout.

Nick pulled a collection of cards and random bits of paper out of his front pocket. One was a Walmart card loaded with his life savings, as that was the only way he wouldn't spend it all on alcohol during late night binges. If a bar accepted Walmart cards, he'd use it until it melted.

The cashier rang up the items and placed them into the black backpack. Nick polished off the last slug of bitter coffee and flicked the empty cup into a nearby trash bin. *Swoosh*—nothing but net. In celebration, he shot his arms up into the air and spun around on his heels.

Nick called Walmart home because he could do everything there that he'd do if he'd had a home. Every Walmart was a mini-village, complete with amenities for its many employees. Given its high employee turnover, Walmart's employees couldn't possibly know everyone who worked there.

Nick picked his moment and walked authoritatively toward a service door, catching it just before it locked. The back corridors were easy to navigate and signposts lined the way to the men's changing rooms.

He put down his bag, pulled out the phone from the box and inserted the SIM card, plugging it into the wall socket. A popular Katy Perry tune piped into the room through overhead speakers, and Nick moved to the beat while stripping off his clothes and dispatching them into the bin. He had a date with a shower, and the hot water didn't disappoint. He took his time slowly rotating under the steaming water.

Once freshly shaved and newly dressed, he checked his phone; it had finished backing up all his data from his private remote server. He sat on a bench and flicked through his emails looking for a new job. One opportunity in particular caught his attention: some children were hurt drinking a soda and the company wanted to find those responsible.

CHAPTER NINETEEN

JUSTIN LEFT ALEX in a deep sleep after a marathon of morning sex. She was alone in the king-sized bed while he sat in the kitchen sipping on a protein shake and surfing the web on his laptop. He had multiple screens open, scanning news feeds while also chatting to elicit friends on websites.

A notification slid in from the right side of the frame, an alerting him to an email from Gilbert Gruber. Justin closed all the windows and opened the email from the tall shadow.

"Baby! Where are you? I need you. . ." Alex called out, before he could read the email.

"I'll be there soon."

"Soon no good, need you now," she purred in her husky French accent.

"Wait a minute!"

"No, now, I need you."

Justin ignored her.

To: Justin.truth@thetruthfoundation.com
From: Gilbert.Gruber@gordonindustries.com
Subject: Trains.

Justin:

Peter told me he spoke to you at the Buffalo Club. It is great that you want to help us win the Iraq contract. You know how important the security of America is to Peter.

Sterling Incorporated and Phizz International have a tight working relationship. To win, we need to be tighter. What we need is for you to provide Soda-Cola at a competitive rate. I believe that if the price of a unit of Soda-Cola comes under a unit of Phizz, the contract will be ours. Work your magic.

And congratulations for the train invitation. There are many people that wanted that ticket. Each day, I am having to fend people off to get their hands on it. I hope that it will be you who will be joining us.

GG.

Justin read the email twice. Gilbert was straight to the point: if Justin didn't get this done—even if he came up with the ten million—he'd never get on that train.

Crash!

Something hit the bedroom wall. Justin could only guess what Alex had thrown.

Crash!

Another item hit the wall and broke.

Justin speed-dialed Montana and she answered on the fourth ring. He'd certainly trained her well.

"Sir," she answered.

"Montana, I need all the information about the partnership between Phizz and Sterling Incorporated," Justin barked down the line.

"What am I looking for?"

"Everything. I want everything that connects these two companies."

"Sure, I'll get onto it first thing tomorrow."

"Now," Justin growled. "This is your number one priority."

"I… I'll do it."

"Good girl, now tell me how much you love me."

"I… I love you…"

Justin ended the call and placed his phone on the kitchen table. Now he was now going to deal with Alex by bending her over his knee and painfully reminding her who was in charge.

OFFICER JARED HICKMAN APPEARED in Ross's cell and ordered him to follow. Hickman looked a bit green around the gills and Ross felt sorry for the guy, as he was one of the only guards who treated him with any humanity. Ross asked if he had done anything wrong, but just as Hickman began to answer, he vomited. The contents of his stomach carpeted the floor. Hickman weaved, and Ross grabbed him around the shoulder to steady him. As he wiped Hickman's mouth on the sleeve of his shirt, Hickman's eyes pleaded with him not to tell anyone. He knew the other guards and prisoners would use any weakness against him.

Once Hickman regained his composure, he asked Ross to follow him to E-block without asking any more questions.

The men walked in silence, navigating the halls, stairs, and security checkpoints to their destination. At E-block, they found Warden Parker pacing back and forth outside a cell, looking deep in thought with hands palm-to-palm as he tapped his fingers on the end of his nose. The warden wore an aged, medium-gray, three-piece suit, white shirt, and black tie.

"Warden Parker," Ross greeted him as they made eye contact.

"Smith," the warden replied, removing his frameless glasses. "Now I'm not asking you to do anything. If this ever got out, well… In all my years, I've never seen anything like it. I don't know who I'd get to look into this, whatever 'this' is. People don't care what happens inside these walls. You understand, Smith? But I care when no one else will. Bunch of animals. You understand, Smith?"

"I'm sorry… I don't understand?" Ross replied.

"You dealt with sick killers on the outside. That Beetle Butcher. He was one of yours, right? You got him when no one else could."

"I did help find him," Ross said.

"I want you to look at something in this cell and tell me what you see. What you think it could mean. Can you do that?"

"Sure," Ross said, his interest stirring. The warden waved Ross into the cell.

He entered cautiously, scrutinizing every detail with precision. There was nothing unusual about the two-man cell. It was cold and gray, with pictures of family, hot girls, and muscle cars on the wall.

What was unusual, though, was the sheer savagery of the murder. Blood dripped from a mattress into a congealing puddle of crimson mess beneath the bed. The man had lost all his blood through the gaping hole in his chest. Taking a step closer to the body, Ross could see the surgical brutality with which the killer had cut the hole. He wouldn't be surprised if the killer had used bolt cutters and a surgical saw for murder weapons. It appeared the killer had violently hacked and snapped his way through the rib cage to get to what he wanted: the heart.

The man's body was naked, the eyes taped shut, and eyeballs had been crudely drawn onto the eyelids. Ross could see no identifying struggle marks on the body. He leaned in to visually inspect the mouth, then sniffed it. The mouth area was slightly bruised and exuded a hint of chemicals. A rag soaked in a chloroform-like substance had been used to knock him out. Whoever did this had the time and experience to do a thorough job. The victim had known his killer, Ross thought.

Ross left the cell and approached the warden, who looked a little pale.

"What? Who did this?" the warden demanded.

"Whoever it was, he thoroughly enjoyed it." Ross fell instantly into his professional police voice. "This wasn't random. It was well-plotted, thought through, and then acted on. They knew what they were doing and why they were doing it."

"Some gang thing?" the warden asked.

"Not sure," Ross answered. "It feels too clinical to be a gang kill but if it is, we'll know soon enough. . ."

CHAPTER TWENTY-ONE

RIP'S HAND TWITCHED as he reached for the doorbell to announce his arrival. He didn't know what was behind the door, but he knew what to expect. This was going to be an evening of provocative adventure, fit for a member of the Knight's Round Table, the group they had invented for their alter ego adventures.

The small cocktail of pills he'd swallowed with a beer chaser on the cab ride over was kicking in. He could feel the collection of narcotics pumping through his body, making his cock harder than normal.

Rip didn't have a clue what the pills were. Justin had sent them to him two hours ago. There was a red, two blues, and a white hexagon one that left a bitter chalky taste down the back of his tongue. All he knew was he'd be as high as a motherfucker for hours, and his cock would be like a rock.

He trusted Justin like a brother, more than a brother if push came to shove. If it hadn't been for Justin at Harvard, Rip's life would have gone in a completely different direction, and not in a good way.

Rip glanced at his hand as it hovered in front on the button. He'd forgotten to remove his wedding ring. He didn't like to wear it when he was about to do what he was about to do. The ring was twisted free and dispatched to a dark corner inside his wallet.

The ring wasn't his only hang-up. Rip's father would never approve of any of this. It would be unseemly for a future president. Anything that didn't fit into Peter Gordon's methodically thought-out path to the Oval Office wasn't allowed. Yet here he was, about to go through with it once again.

Peter had gone to great lengths over the years to mold his entire family into presidential material, even selecting the perfect wife to be by Rip's side. She needed to be of the right status, from the right family, have the right temperament, and hold the right qualifications. Most importantly, she needed to have a face the American public would fall in love with.

Peter selected Barbara Benfell. Barbara was regal, blonde, and had an infectious smile. She was demure, yet walked with an air of confidence, and never seemed stressed or confused. She was educated and well-informed in the world of politics, spoke clearly, and answered questions competently. People loved her, and, to Peter, she was exactly what a First Lady should be: perfect in every way.

Barbara's family had earned a massive fortune from medical products; her great-grandfather had been prolific in his small lab. One invention led to another, and to another, and by the time her father took over the family business, it was a multinational company. Neither of Barbara's siblings, nor her cousins, needed to worry about earning a living, and so Barbara devoted her life to an assortment of charities.

Rip and Barbara met at a formal party arranged by Peter solely to introduce the two. Rip was immediately attracted to the tall blonde with the long, flowing hair, high cheekbones, and tall, slender frame. He imagined her as a Victoria Secret's model in another life. Both sets of parents agreed they'd make a great couple.

The two went on a date the following week and were a couple from then on. He thought he loved her—in the beginning—and was proud he never cheated on her. In fact, he never thought he would. But then one night, on a drunken rampage, a bartender caught his eye and he fucked her in a room in the back of a bar. Not because she was attractive, but because she had a great pair of tits and an interesting collection of finely inked tattoos. The way she'd sucked his cock had been intense, and the vigor with which her mouth had slid up and down his shaft had been mind-shattering. He missed the primal sex he used to have. Barbara tried, on the odd occasion, to perform oral sex on him, but it always felt more mechanical than passionate.

Rip felt guilty as soon as he shot all over the bartender's angel-winged tattooed tits, but he redeemed himself by proposing to Barbara the very next day. She was going to be the best thing that had ever happened to him, he'd told himself.

Barbara said yes and over the next six months planned the wedding of the century. Her mother, wedding planner, and best friend worked full-time to create an event that would raise the bar for weddings.

The wedding had been spectacular. Five hundred of their closest friends and relatives celebrated the unification of two powerful families to become the nation's most powerful family.

Rip felt he did well keeping it in his pants, though it didn't last long. The day after their third wedding anniversary, he felt a hole growing. A hole that he thought meaningless sex would fill. Barbara had started to annoy him with her politically correct answers and her cold exterior behind closed doors. Day by day he became more detached, yearning for another woman to talk into spreading her legs for him.

Then, during one drunken night out, while Rip was bitching about his lovely wife, Justin came up with an idea. He would pull together a night of excitement where Rip could do whatever he wanted. He called it the Knights Round Table. They would bring in some high-class hookers, pay them for their discretion, and fuck the living shit out of them. Make it an event for Lord Justice and Rip Rippington.

The following week they had their first Knights Round Table. It was such a success that they decided to make it a monthly occasion. Justin would theme it and organize everything—normally on a Sunday, as it seemed like a less obvious night for Rip to be out on a bender. They would drink, do drugs, and then spill into different rooms to fuck some girls. Often their sex feasts would involve masks, role-play, or porn, depending on the event's theme.

On Rip's birthday the year before, Justin arranged for five strippers to give Rip the night of his life. The theme was James Bond, and they had to fuck the information out of him.

Rip heard the doorbell inform those inside that he was at the door. In keeping with tonight's theme—horror movies—Rip put on his tight-fitting hockey mask just in time for the door to open and reveal four curvy women dressed as slutty high school students. He was in heaven.

CHAPTER TWENTY-TWO

MONTANA STOOD IN THE MIDDLE of the elevator, one arm wrapped tightly around her body as she watched the LED screen. She could feel the floors flying past as the elevator thundered upward, uninterrupted. Her stomach rolled as the elevator eased to a stop. The doors parted and a robotic voice announced her floor, welcoming Montana to exit. Montana stepped out, hoping that was the last voice she would hear tonight. She used her ears to scan for any signs of life, but all she could hear was the eerie hum of technology and its constant presence of white noise.

To make sure she was alone, Montana walked a lap around the floor, yelling out friendly greetings. When she was sure the space was as empty as it sounded, she tried the door to Kenny's office. It was locked. If anyone had the information Justin wanted her to find, it would be Kenny. The lock to Kenny's door was pretty simple; she'd broken into trickier ones before.

Using a nail file and two strong paper clips, Montana pushed the tumblers into place and twisted the lock. It turned on the first click and the door swung open.

Kenny had a corner office three times bigger than her own, and it featured enormous tinted windows. On one wall was a framed Stratocaster, signed by Eric Clapton, and the other walls were littered with framed retro band posters. In one corner was a high, round table with matching stools; there was also a foosball table and a fully stocked Phizz retail fridge. A four-seater black leather couch had a place of pride in front of the windows. Montana sighed with relief when she saw Kenny's laptop sitting in plain view on his desk.

Montana turned on the computer and, as she suspected, it promptly asked for his password. She had no idea what that was, but knew another way in. She pulled a flash drive from her pocket and plugged it into a USB port. This was no ordinary flash drive, but one Martin Goodby had given her when she was trying to get dirt on Justin. Martin was a genius hacker and knew everything about computers, password protection, and backdoors.

Martin's instructions were simple. She could hear his voice as if he were sitting next to her in his HAN SHOT FIRST T-shirt: "Plug it in to the computer you want to… peek into. The light will flash red, meaning it's cracking the password. This can take anywhere from thirty seconds to ten minutes. When it goes green, you'll have access to the desktop. Now, my young Jedi, don't use the search bars or anything on the desktop. This can be tracked and will be marked with timestamps. And you don't want no Boba Fett-looking dude hunting you down for the bounty on your head. Instead, you will see Darth Vader on the desktop; use the force and double click on it to open the flash drive.

"Inside the drive is my own custom-built search engine bar. It can do the Kessel Run in less than twelve parsecs, yup, that fast. Type in the key words of what you're looking for, and it'll search every file the computer has access to—servers, home computers, emails, Death Star. Anything this computer has ever touched will be revealed. Then just drag and drop the files you need into the Catcher Mitt icon and they will be copied over to the flash drive, leaving no trace or indication that anyone has ever seen the files. The light will flash red again and once it's green, it's all done. Remove the drive and the computer will shut down. Like Alderaan, it will be like you never were there."

Montana felt a hole in her stomach thinking of her friend. Justin had found out Martin was helping her and ruined his life by framing him for downloading child pornography. He was still fighting in court to prove his innocence.

The flash drive did its job, and she typed in the keyword—Sterling— which instantly revealed a list of folders. She highlighted them all and copied the folders over to the flash drive. A small timeline icon popped up counting down the percentage of data left to transfer.

Montana allowed herself to relax, watching the pulsing red light on the flash drive. She suddenly went rigid as she heard the ding of the elevator door as it opened. She stared at the flash drive, willing it to turn green. She inhaled deeply, telling herself to calm down, and that it would just be a cleaner at this time of night. Her mouth went dry as the steps stopped outside Kenny's door, followed by the unmistakable sound of keys jingling. Whoever was outside had keys to this room. There was no way Montana could explain why she was in Kenny's office, let alone snooping around his laptop. She glared at the flashing light: still red. If she pulled out the flash drive now, she'd lose everything. She needed more time; she needed a diversion.

Montana unhooked her bra, slipped it out of her white silk shirt, then hitched up her red skirt to make it even shorter and highlight her legs. The door opened and Kenny ambled in. He froze when he saw her, cross-legged on his desk, provocatively holding her white lacy bra.

"Montana?" Kenny managed to mutter.

She seductively ran a hand up her leg, over her breasts, along her cleavage and to her mouth, biting her finger. She slid off the desk and slipped her bra around the back of his neck, pulling him toward her.

"I wanted to leave... a little something... from me," she said in a husky tone. "I know you think a lot about what's under my shirt, right?"

"Montana, I..." was all Kenny could muster as Montana pulled his head toward her cleavage. Kenny could feel her nipples through her silk shirt. She looked over her shoulder and saw the light change from red to green.

"You like me, Kenny?" she moaned, pushing him back onto his desk and sending files flying.

"You're... incredible," Kenny huffed, wanting to touch her more. Montana took her bra and wrapped it around his head like a blindfold; then quickly retrieved the flash drive, which automatically shut down the computer.

"I want you to think about me, Kenny," Montana whispered. "I was going to leave my bra for you to find, then my panties, and who knows what else. Now I have to think of another surprise." She licked his ear and pulled away from him. She turned to show off her hourglass figure in more detail.

"I'll keep thinking, tiger," she purred, before strutting out of the room, closing the door behind her, and swiftly disappearing into the elevator as he called after her. She got what she was after. What she needed now was to get very, very drunk.

CHAPTER TWENTY-THREE

THE LOCK TO THE HEAVY cell door clicked. Ross's eyes sprung open, and he swiveled his head toward the door while wrapping a T-shirt around his fist in case of trouble. His cell door was never disarmed at this time of night. The only reason would be if Marcus was making a move in retaliation for Ross's lunchroom defiance. Marcus had a number of guards on his payroll and could easily arrange a visit this time of night.

Two guards entered his cell, patting their nightsticks playfully and with a hint of malice.

"Up!" Officer Ben Hoff hollered.

The twenty-year veteran guard was tall and barrel-like, with a large, round head and pig-like features. His cheeks were red, a web of broken blood vessels and patches of stubble he'd missed after a lazy shave. A black mole on one cheek, the size of a penny, stood out. It often bled because he constantly picked at it.

Officer Hickman hovered just behind Hoff, his eyes fixated on the spot where he had vomited earlier in the day; he was still a little pale. Ross had learned that Hickman had been the one to discover the butchered body. No wonder he lost his lunch.

"Now, bitch!" Hoff yelled. "Smells like puke in here! What you been doing?"

Ross unwrapped his fist and got off his bed. He surrendered his back to the guards by placing his hands flat against the wall. "Lunch didn't agree with me."

Hoff signaled Hickman to leave and gave the cell a search, roughly flicking items over with his nightstick while continuing to complain about the smell.

Hickman returned with a skinny white man. The new prisoner had black oily hair and a face covered in acne scars from his youth. His nose was far too big for his face and crooked from being broken too many times. The way his head moved in fast twitches resembled a rat smelling for cheese. His prison jumpsuit was oversized, and he looked like he was swimming in orange.

"Ross, meet you new boyfriend," Officer Hoff grinned.

"Friend?" Ross inquired. As a former cop, he'd always had a cell to himself, both for his safety and that of his cellmate.

"Too many fuckers committing too many crimes," Officer Hoff grimaced. "We're full, so he's in here with you. You can be butt-fuck buddies. He looks easy to break in."

"Hey, how you doin'?" the rat-like prisoner said. "I don't wants no trouble, man. Don't care what you done, okay. I just doing what I'm told like."

"Enjoy, old man," Hickman said, seeking approval from Hoff. Both guards retreated from the cell and signaled for the door to be locked again.

Ross stared at his new cellmate and cracked his neck.

"What's your name?" he growled.

"Jimmy Tootsie. People call me Toots."

"Jimmy, take off all your clothes."

"What? Shit. I ain't into that, grandpa."

Ross grabbed Jimmy by the throat, forcing him hard against the bars. "I don't want to fuck you, Jimmy. I'm making sure you don't belong to anyone."

"Wha… wha… what?"

"Strip now!" Ross growled.

Jimmy surrendered and Ross relaxed his grip, taking a step back. Jimmy slowly removed his clothes, stealing frequent glances at Ross.

"Turn around!" Ross yelled. "Where's your ink?" he asked, lifting Jimmy's arms. If this guy was a gangbanger or wanting to be one, he'd be marked.

"You're clean. Put your shit back on," Ross ordered. "As soon as you're dressed, we're going to play a game. I ask you ten questions and you give me ten answers. If I don't like what I hear, you won't like what

I'm gonna do to you."

"Sure, whatever. Fuck, man. You be crazy fucking intense for an old man." Jimmy muttered as he got dressed.

"Get down on your knees." Jimmy followed the order without question. Ross joined him. The cold concrete floor greeted his clicking knees with pain. He looked Jimmy straight in the eyes, with only inches separating them.

"This is how it works. I ask you a question and you answer it. Do not look away. You look me straight in the eyes. Your eyes go elsewhere, and I'll slap you. And I'll keep slapping you until you get it."

"Sure," Jimmy said. Ross slapped the side of his head so hard his hand tingled.

"Fuck!" Jimmy held his hand to his cheek. The skin was already changing color.

"You glanced at the floor!"

"Fuck, OK, OK, man. Shit, I didn't mean to. I ain't never had to look at anyone in the eyes before. You sure you ain't gonna kiss me?" Ross slapped him again.

"No more talking. Only answer my questions."

Ross needed to know if Jimmy was a mole placed by one of the gangs. By holding his stare, he could drill Jimmy for information and determine if it was true. Most people weren't great at lying; their eyes always gave it away. Facial movements told a lot, too.

"Question one. Is your name Jimmy?"

"Yes."

"Are you Superman?"

"What?"

Ross slapped him even harder. "Just answer the fucking question. Are you really Superman?"

"No, no, man, I'm not."

Ross continued his questions, reading Jimmy's face movements for any hint of a lie, confusion, or truth.

"Do I scare you?"

"I ain't scared of shit."

Ross noted the twitches and rapid eye movement. A lie.

"Did you kill my wife?"

"No, man, I don't know who she is?"

Jimmy's left eye focused, and there was no lip movement or curl. A truthful answer. It had to be; Ross had never been married.

"What's your star sign?"

"What's the bull? Taurus?"

"Are you sure it's not Cancer?"

"Yeah, I'm the bull and the Cancer thing is a crab."

Ross noticed the small twitches that indicated this was also the truth.

"Who put you here?" Ross fired his next question.

"Like who sentenced me, or those guards?"

"Who put you in my cell?"

"I just got here and they chucked me in here with a crazy old bastard," Jimmy said. "I don't know you, man."

"Who do you work for?"

"No one. I ain't worked in years."

"What gang owns you?" Ross scrutinized Jimmy's every move.

"I don't belong to a gang. I just got no money and these guys in suits had money so I thought 'Why not take their money, they wouldn't know.' But they did—a camera caught me in the act."

"Are you here to kill me?"

"I don't know you. But I kinda want to now!"

Ross stared at Jimmy in silence, watching him breathe. It was a stare-off, and when Jimmy dropped his eyes, Ross gave him another hard slap. Jimmy had passed the first test, but Ross would watch him like a hawk.

"You do anything I don't like and I'll kill you," Ross hissed, and returned to his bed.

CHAPTER TWENTY-FOUR

JUSTIN WAS THE FIRST to arrive. He wanted to make sure his friendly face was one of the first the other St. Mary's board members would see. Their meetings were more social than business. Each board member was highly influential, be it through family lineage, business connection, or political clout.

Tonight was a special. The board was officially granting him approval to build a memorial brick wall in the hospital's garden for his recently departed mother, The Sarah Truth Wall of Strength. Justin had commissioned one of the top designers in New York to create a stunning symbol of peace and love. The mosaic wall of crystallized quartzite stone would be an elegant, curved design; it would offer shelter from northerly winds, and the arched structure would create a cone of silence in its center. It would serve as a place for residents to bask in the afternoon sun. He would have loved to have a wing named after her—or rather, after himself—but the wall would do.

He scanned the room, assessing whether any particular patron could front him the "train money," and what story he could concoct in order to acquire it. Asking for business favors was easily slipped into conversation; they were business people, after all. But asking for actual money changed the relationship. The interaction would have to be handled delicately. One could never ask them for it directly; one would have to make them think it was their idea to offer.

After talking to a few esteemed members, Justin sensed the timing was off for making a sales pitch. Instead, he basked in their compliments on the wonderful design he'd proposed, as well as their condolences on his mother's tragic death.

Then Justin spotted Rodger Wellsworth, who had been with the board for fifteen years as a director in the property department in the state office. Rodger had been instrumental in helping Justin navigate the reams of bureaucracy red tape to get building permits for his construction site in record time.

"Rodger," Justin said, offering his hand. Rodger shook it and smiled as Justin proceeded to corner him.

"Justin… good to see you. Big night. I'm so happy we're having the wall built for your dear mother."

"Thank you, Rodger. She was everything to me. She is with God now, so I know she is happy in the light of our Lord."

Rodger was a staunch Christian, so Justin played to his religious fortitude. "I'm just glad that God gifted me the extra time she was in here. And through this, I met a fellow warrior of the Lord in you, my friend."

"Bless you too, Justin."

"Once again, thank you for your help with my construction paperwork," Justin continued. "That building was such a danger to the community."

"You're welcome. When you told me about how that unfortunate runner died on its front door steps, I had to do something." Rodger nodded with empathy.

"Yes, if more loose rocks had fallen, more people could have been hurt. I've ripped it down and we're in the stages of getting something beautiful built in its place."

"And it's great that you're going to use it for the kids."

Justin held back a grin. He'd told Rodger he was going to restore the building and open a Christian book center on the bottom level. It would be something his mother would have been proud of—a sanctuary for troubled children, a place where they could read the Bible and learn about the love of God. This was all a myth. Once it was built, Justin was going to sell it for a massive profit. The new owners could do whatever they liked.

"I'm working with a local priest to meet with the community to hear what they need," Justin said. "He'll be my eyes and ears on the project."

Rodger beamed. "We need more people like you in the world, Justin."

"I'm just doing the Lord's work, my good friend. And you have helped me more than I could ever repay you. What's more, you've shown the same kindness to my friends."

"As the good book says, 'Do not withhold good from those to whom it is due, when it is in your power to act.' All I've done is the same you'd do for anyone else in this room," Rodger said warmly.

Justin inwardly smirked. He would have killed his mother sooner if he had known that her death would have opened these doors this quickly.

CHAPTER TWENTY-FIVE

BEFORE JUSTIN STARTED at Soda-Cola, Montana could count on one hand all the men she had slept with, and she took pride in that fact. She didn't consider herself a prude, but if she was going to give her body to someone, they had to deserve it.

Now, she couldn't even remember how many men she'd slept with over the last few months. They'd morphed into one long, maleficent line of meaningless drunken sex.

A high-pitched whistling sound woke Montana. She opened her eyes and moved her head ever so slightly in the direction of the sound. She didn't recognize where she was. She brushed her matted hair away from her eyes as a naked woman breezed into the room. The woman was tall, with small, pear-shaped breasts, and long brown hair tied up in a bun. Her round, freckled face looked friendly.

"Morning, sweetheart," the woman said, revealing a sizable gap between her two front teeth. She joined Montana on the bed. "You sleep OK, sweetie?" She stroked Montana's hair and kissed her on the forehead. "You want coffee? Randy won't get out of bed until I bring him one."

Montana now realized that she wasn't alone in bed, and flashes of the previous night's misadventure hit her. A bar, drinks, more drinks. Talking, dancing, kissing, even more drinks. The cowboy couple, drugs, taxi, Randy fucking her while Dora cheered her man on, slapping his ass and joining in.

Friendly or not, Montana wanted out of there. She gathered her belongings, and without so much an excuse, stumbled out the front door and hurried up the street. She knew she looked exactly as she felt, a total mess.

She waved down a cab. Back at her own place, Montana hit the shower and drenched herself with scalding hot water. She knew she was spiraling out of control. The more she unraveled, the deeper she delved, and the darker she went.

She knew she needed help. She needed to see the only person who would understand. She needed to see Steve. He would know what to do, he'd save her from this spiral. She had wanted to contact him countless times, but Justin's threats always prevented her. Steve had also tried to get in touch with her, but to protect her family, and Steve, she'd ignored his attempts.

The hot water seemed to loosen up her mind. Suddenly she felt herself waking up. She felt the power of the hot water building up her resolve. Justin thought he had broken her—but he hadn't. She still had fight in her. Justin had no idea how strong she really was.

"Fuck Justin, and fuck his rules," she shouted at the shower head.

Out of the shower, Montana slipped into some comfortable clothes, her skin raw and tingling under the fabric. She popped open her bottle of Zoloft and Percodan and took two of each with a gulp of bottled water.

Twenty minutes later, Montana stood outside the door to Steve's apartment. The meds had kicked in, and she felt calmer. She closed her eyes and centered herself, then gently knocked on the door. Nothing. She glanced around then knocked a little harder. She heard movement, then the door creaked open.

"Steve?" She barely recognized him.

"Montana?" Steve, wearing only his dirty boxers, rubbed his blood-shot eyes.

"Can we talk? Want to get a coffee and a brioche?"

Steve silently dismissed her and disappeared back into his dusky apartment. Montana hesitated a few seconds, then followed him. The curtains were drawn closed, and a musky smell hung in the air. Stepping carefully over junk food containers and empty bottles, she made her way through the room.

Montana watched Steve collapse onto the couch with a beer in hand. He drained half the bottle in one swig. His beard collected the froth and he lazily wiped it away with the back of his hand.

"What would you like to talk about?" Steve asked.

"I just wanted to see if you're OK," Montana murmured.

"If I was OK? Sure. I'm OK. I'm better than OK. Thanks for asking. Next time you want to know if I'm OK, bring some beers."

"I'm sorry. Um, I'll go then." Montana placed her hand on the doorknob.

"I loved you, you know," Steve blurted out. Montana shot Steve a sympathetic gaze.

"I think you loved me a certain way."

"Fuck off with your emotional mumbo jumbo. I fuckin' loved you. I left my wife for you. I went after Justin for you. Everything I did, I did it for you. And what did you do for me? Nothing. Did you love me back? Not once have I seen you since I got released."

"Steve?"

"No! Fuck you. Go back to whatever cock you were riding before you came over here. I heard how much of a whore you've become, and I'm still not good enough for you!"

"This isn't you talking. The Steve I know wouldn't say these things."

"The Steve you know is dead. Long live the new Steve. King Steve!" He raised his bottle proposing a toast to himself and took another mouthful of beer.

Montana felt tears roll down her cheeks. There'd be no talking to Steve in this state. She opened the door, pausing.

"You're wrong, I did love you, Steve. But if you think love is all about fucking, you're as bad as Justin."

Montana walked out, leaving the door open behind her.

CHAPTER TWENTY-SIX

"THANKS FOR COMING, Mr. Harvey," Brendon Gibson said politely. "Would you like coffee?"

"Yes, three sugars, black, and lots and lots of coffee." Nick waltzed around the tightly packed office, picking up merchandise, inspecting it, then placing it down—somewhere else. Brendon watched him with interest while repeating the coffee order back to his assistant.

"You come highly recommended," Brendon said.

"Thanks." Nick picked up a SummerCrush cap from a cardboard box full of them. "Can I have this?"

"Sure." Brendon was in his fifties and a few pounds overweight from stress eating. His gray, thinning hair was parted to one side. His shirt was unbuttoned, due to the girth of his neck, and his maroon tie held it temporarily closed.

"So, Mr. Gibson." Nick flicked through assorted papers and reports on a low coffee table. "Just because I'm here, doesn't mean I'm going to help you. I'm not cheap, and only work cases I want to work." Nick folded a packing invoice into a plane and threw it into the air. It glided gently around the room. "I do things my way, and you don't have any say in that."

"So I'm told," Brendon said reassuringly. "I'm also told you get results."

Over the past year, Brendon had hired three investigators, and they'd all turned up nothing. Then an old friend mentioned Nick Harvey. The Ghost Hunter, he'd called him. Said he was hard to get, a little bit odd, but always solved the case.

Nick picked up an orange dimpled pen. "Can I have this?"

"Sure. I'm guessing you know about the SummerCrush tragedy."

"I do indeed, you big, bad corporation you. Hurting the youth of today with your tainted products."

"Someone did this to us. Someone tampered with and distributed those bottles of SummerCrush strategically around the country, with the deliberate intent to hurt us."

"And who would do that?" Nick asked, placing the pen inside his jacket pocket.

"That's what we need you to find out," Brendon replied. "Some sick people used the lives of innocent children to hurt us—and they succeeded. We are dying. Stores won't stock our products any longer, and consumers won't buy them. We only just break even now by exporting to the South Pacific islands."

"Why do you think someone did this to you?" Nick leapt onto the spare chair and it twirled around like an amusement park ride.

"We've gone over every inch of our factory and examined every contaminated bottle we could get our hands on. Someone went to a lot of effort to make us look responsible."

"Why?" Nick repeated.

"We don't know." Brendon shook his head, making his double chin wobble. "No one came forward to take credit. Once the newspapers stopped talking, there was nothing."

"I'm intrigued." Nick leaned forward.

"So, you'll help?"

"I think I might. I have a soft spot for children. And the people responsible for this should pay for what they did."

Nick got up, placed his hands on his hips, and walked toward the window, the warm sun spilling over him. He spun back to Brendon, lifted his hand, and spread his fingers. "There are five things I'll need before I decide whether or not I'll work with you."

"Sure, what are they?"

"Number one, money. You know from my email what I charge?"

"Yes, it's all signed off, and ready to go. Just so I get this right, your fee will be placed into your Walmart shopper account, and a weekly amount for incidentals into a cash account?"

"Bingo," Nick said. "Secondly, I don't work for you. I kind of have a problem with authority figures. So, you can ask me questions, just never tell me what to do, or how to do it. You do, and I walk."

Brendon nodded. He would agree to anything to find out what had happened.

"Thirdly, I need you to give me everything you already have from the people you've hired previously, and I'll decide what's important. Deal?"

"It's all yours," Brendon said without hesitation.

Nick smiled, turned, and headed toward the door.

"Wait!" Brendon called out. "What about four and five?"

"Once I figure those out, I'll let you know," Nick said with a twinkle in his eyes.

CHAPTER TWENTY-SEVEN

NO MATTER HOW HE moved the numbers around, Justin couldn't scrape together the ten million. He had sunk so much capital into his building project that there was no way that to retrieve it at this stage. It would take months to broker a deal. He had weeks.

On his laptop were an array of Soda-Cola accounts. He knew he could move money from each into an independent account, then borrow back those amounts through a ghost transaction, but the risk of being discovered was high. Yet, Justin's options were shrinking.

He ran through the numbers again. If he got it right, it would give him four million. If he added in his personal cash reserves, he would still be three million short. He rubbed his scar too hard. It started to bleed. He felt pins and needles run up the back of his neck.

Hey, buddy, why so blue? a familiar malicious voice whispered. *I know what would cheer you up. Why not go and strangle some streetwalker. Cave her skull in with a brick. You like that, buddy? It'll help, it always does.*

"I need to keep working on the numbers," Justin said. "I have to find a solution."

Work on the numbers while you work on New York's homeless epidemic. Drown some homeless prick in a barrel of water. Kick the teeth in of some raggedy disabled vet. Rip the jaw off some meth-head slut. You'd be doing them a favor. You'd be doing America a favor.

"Dirty scum, littering the city with their presence," Justin sneered.

They don't deserve to live in the same city as you, the voice encouraged.

"My city. My country. America needs me to sort out these social draining problems. If I don't, who will? They'll keep multiplying until we're worse off than a third world country in the Middle East."

America needs Justin Truth! Here's an idea! Ohhhh, this is a good one. You should invite that Jennifer bitch over. She was a tight piece of ass. No one will ever make her feel as good as you did. I bet she misses you like crazy.

"You're right, I made her cum harder than she had ever in her life."

Get her over and see where it goes. You could always show her fifty shades of black and blue.

"That sounds like fun. A red room drenched in her blood."

Yeah, buddy. You could keep her for a while first. Play with her, fuck her, make her your princess. Then decide how to end her worthless life once and for all.

Justin grinned from ear to ear as he scrolled through his contacts on his iPhone until he found Jennifer. He methodically typed each letter, imagining what he would do to her.

```
Hi, please read this. I miss you
so much. I'm lost without your guidance.
You were
```

A notification popped up, interrupting his text. It was an email from Black Wolf. Justin quickly deleted the text and opened the email.

```
To: Justin.truth@thetruthfoundation.com
From: Thebw316@gmail.com
Subject: Good times to come.
```

Justin, my good friend.

I'm going to be in New York. We should catch up and paint the town red.
It could solve all your problems.

BW

The pins and needles up the back of his head faded. He was back in the game. Jennifer could wait.

CHAPTER TWENTY-EIGHT

ONLY A FEW AREAS of the prison weren't controlled by a gang. The kitchen was one—food was too important to be disrupted in a turf war, so each gang had equal numbers working the kitchen to keep the peace.

The library was another. That was a blend of illiteracy, bravado, and having Father O'Grady as the librarian.

The workout yard was the most significant shared territory. Over the years, many different gangs had tried to take ownership. It never lasted long, as everyone wanted to work out. Strength was its own currency in Bell, and people would fight to the death to make sure they could get in their reps. One brutal gang war over the weights lasted five weeks until the warden removed the equipment and everyone lost out. They made a truce, and over the following months, the warden drip-fed the equipment back. The gangs had honored the truce ever since, and any person breaking it would have all the gangs on them.

Ross cracked open a can of Soda-Cola and poured it into a plastic container filled with instant coffee. He mixed it and watched it turn into a thick sludge. They called it Hypermud. It was a prison preworkout drink. He burped. It wasn't the best tasting concoction, but it did the job.

He surveyed the equipment. It was basic. The weights were heavy, rusty, and simple. The benches were always in high demand. In Bell, it was chest day, every day. Legs, not so much. Ross grabbed a power rack and stretched. Every work out, he worked his legs, believing that the key to all strength was in your base.

The Hypermud started to kick in. Ross felt a head rush from the caffeine spike. Stacking two plates on either side of the bar, he smoothly busted out ten Olympic squats.

"Ass to the grass," he said out loud to himself, adding "low as you can go" on the way down before thrusting to a standing position. Ross added two more plates, and unracked the bar, balancing it on his well-developed traps. He felt Jimmy before he saw him.

"I'm working out. Fuck off," Ross barked.

"Big boss man," Jimmy replied. "Thought you would be here. Hearing some fucked-up shit, man. Some Spiders don't like what you did to their boy."

"I don't care what they like," Ross grunted between squats. "They don't like it, they can step up and get knocked the fuck down."

"You need someone to watch your back." Jimmy swung his right hand as if it were a gun, flicking it randomly in all directions. "A friend to have lunch with who isn't a creepy Catholic child-killer. You heard what he done?" Jimmy crossed his heart and looked to the heavens.

"I don't need anything from you."

"Come on, man, you know you needs this. I'm offering to help. We's stuck with one another."

"You want to help, wait for the bench press over there. I'll need it soon. There's a system, but if you let someone push in, that's your fault. Hold your ground for me."

"You want me to wait in a line for you?"

"Do that or fuck off. Your choice."

Jimmy slinked off and grinned at the guys waiting to do a chest workout, but they ignored him. He looked like a toothpick in a forest of redwoods.

Ross stacked another couple of plates on the bar and vigorously continued squatting. By now his thighs were screaming at him, just the way he liked it. The harder it would be to walk tomorrow, the better. He looked over at Jimmy guarding his spot, not letting the muscle guys push him around. Inch by inch he got closer to the bench press. Ross kept on squatting.

Jimmy finally took control of the bench, sitting on it so no one else could take it. Ross meandered over to him, his legs in spasms from his last heavy set of squats.

"First, show me what you got, kid," Ross grunted.

"You want me to bench?" Jimmy asked.

"I may need a spot later, and you said you wanted to help, right? I want to see what you can handle."

Jimmy lay down as Ross mounted some plates onto the rusted bar, knowing they were going to be way too heavy. He moved to the head of the bench and looked down at Jimmy, who breathed in and out deeply, psyching himself up.

"You ready?" Ross asked.

"I got this," Jimmy said with gritted teeth as he placed his hands wide on the bar.

"Lightweight," Ross encouraged.

Ross helped Jimmy rack the bar, taking most of the weight, and guided it gently down toward the younger man's chest.

"And… up!" Ross shouted.

Jimmy tried to push the bar back up, but it didn't budge. He didn't have the strength to move it an inch. His arms started to wobble. The bar lowered even further. Dropping onto his chest. That's when he panicked.

"Fuck! Help, bro, fuck. Fuck! Fuck…!"

"You want me to help you? I thought you wanted to help me? I'm confused, Jimmy. I'll think about it and get back to you."

Ross strolled off, leaving Jimmy trapped under the bar, screaming all types of hell.

CHAPTER TWENTY-NINE

BLACK WOLF HAD PICKED the meeting place, a dark seedy bar off Baxter Street in the middle of Chinatown. It had once operated as a popular opium den in the late '60s. The walls were dark red with gold etched trimmings. Its wooden floors were blacked and scuffed from years of toil, and the lack of any ventilation trapped the smell of cigarettes, hash, and Asian spices.

The bar was empty apart from Misha, who was already halfway through a bottle of vodka. He heard footsteps approaching, as expected, and on time.

"Sit. You must have drink with me," the foreboding Russian insisted. Justin balanced himself on the three-legged stool next to Misha, not sure whether it was the floor or the stool that was on a slant. He placed an elbow on the cracked marble bar to steady himself. In front of the Russian were two narrow glasses and a bell-shaped bottle of vodka.

"Black Wolf told me—"

"Yes, Mr. Justin, I know. Man such as yourself not here to pick up wontons. Especially man in such dashing suit."

"I'm here to do business," Justin said dismissively.

"I here to do business also." Misha nodded. "I brought own vodka." He picked up the vodka bottle. "This bar only has shitty vodka water. Is for children, not men. Men drink real vodka, Russian vodka." He filled the two glasses to the top and knocked one back. His eyes forced Justin to pick up the other glass. Justin succumbed, drank it in one hit, and slammed the empty glass back on the bar. Misha refilled both their glasses.

"Our mutual friend said—" Justin started, but Misha raised his hand and cut him off.

"We talk business soon. No rush, Mr. Business. You have heard of saying, 'blind drunk'?" Misha stopped to knock back another vodka.

"This is true thing. When I was boy back in Russia, my father he work in factory. He was strong man. He work hard. Operate large machines. All day they go, loud and cranking, hard work for hard men. These machines grind all day, get very dirty. Not filthy dirt from ground, but metal dirt, sticky, very hard to clean, real black shit. Machines not like this dirt, if not cleaned, they break. Cost owner money. You cannot use water and soap. Best thing is hundred-proof alcohol. The boss, he buy big barrels of it for men to clean machines, stop them breaking down. Is good, but this hundred percent was also good for drink.

"My father, his comrades, they wait for the cleaning barrels to get dropped off. Crack it open, fill bucket each and take home. They replace what they took with water, as to trick boss, thinking they is clever. But boss, he find out. The machines, they not get clean and break down as the water mix was not good. He knows workers were drinking it and not using it. He get very mad about this. So, to stop them drinking it, the boss he put a poison in the barrels—taste very bad. This was also expensive ingredient, so boss only put it in some barrels, you know.

"The men, they discover trick boss had done, and decide one man his job would be to taste barrel. If it had poison, in a minute he be sick on ground, real violent. But when man not sick, they would break out buckets.

"On the nights my father come home with sloshing bucket, he sit in chair, listen to music. Pour himself drink after drink until bucket is empty. Soon he just be staring off into distance. I would go up, wave hand in front of his face, he no react as drink make him blind. In morning, he would get up and go to work, his eyes they slowly come back to normal.

"I had secret taste once. I remember how it burned my mouth. My head it started to spin and I threw it all up. My father he laughed—he know what I did. I never tried drink from his bucket again. When I grow older I would try vodka and, compared to that, it was like water. I loved my father. He was good man."

Misha continued reminiscing. "Many years later, I grow big and strong like him. I not want to work in factory like him. I want life with Bratva. Is better for me. So I must prove I was in Bratva for life. Prove everything before wasn't part of me now. I visit father with bottle of a hundred percent alcohol, like his buckets. We sit. We talk. We drink. He was so happy. I was so happy. Soon bottle was empty. I then lift my hand and put it around this throat. I squeezed. I crushed his throat. I kill him.

"I loved him more than anything. Just remember that. If I would do that with my bare hands to one I love, what would I do to one who I not love, and they crossed me." Misha paused, downed his vodka, and topped off the glass again. "You are businessman. I too, am businessman. Are you able to handle type of business I do, Mr. Justin? It is a long way from your business. . ."

"As long as I get my money back with the agreed interest, on the agreed date, I don't care how you do it." Justin polished off his glass like it was water, with no change of facial expression, even though his throat felt as if it had burnt to a crisp.

"Then we do business." Misha treated himself to another mouthful of vodka.

Justin got off the rickety stool, smoothed out his suit, and eyed the Russian. "You killed your father," he said. "I guess we have something else in common."

CHAPTER THIRTY

"ONCE YOU'RE WET, more rain isn't going to make you any wetter," Steve mumbled to himself as he continued to walk. The drugs were wearing off, it was dark, and he didn't know where he was. His arm itched from where he last shot up. He craved more.

The rain felt cleansing on his face. He opened his mouth wide, and his cracked lips stung as he tasted the raindrops. He raised his arms to the sky and spun round and round until he lost his balance and fell backward into a muddy puddle. Steve chortled as he waved his arms and legs as if making a dirty snow angel.

Over the splashing of water, he heard music; at first, he thought it was just his imagination. It was nothing like he'd ever heard before. There was an acoustic guitar, maybe a harp, and he wasn't sure what the other instruments were. A man was singing, his voice rich with emotion, dancing effortlessly over the notes.

Steve heaved himself out of the puddle and shuffled toward the music. It came from the basement of a run-down building covered in gang graffiti. Most of the windows had been smashed and were half-covered with cheap wooden boards. The stucco concrete walls were stained with black dirt and green mold from years of neglect.

He tried to look through a low window, but could only make out vague shapes moving through the marbled glass. He put his back against the wall and lowered himself down into a sitting position. This raspy voice had him mesmerized.

A hand appeared in front of Steve's face.

"My brother," a soothing voice said. "It sounds so much better downstairs."

Steve thought of every excuse under the sun why he shouldn't, but instead, he took the outstretched hand, and got to his feet.

"The name is Bearclaw," the man said, without an ounce of humor. He wore a plastic bag over his clothes as a makeshift jacket. His face showed signs of a hard life, and his long black hair lay flat against his head from the rain.

"I'm Steve."

"Hi, Steve. They have soup, too. I like soup, how about you?" His black eyes were kind, and his smile welcoming.

"Yeah, soup is good."

He followed Bearclaw into the building through a door that was barely hanging onto the frame, then down a dark flight of stairs. The only working bulb flickered as they passed through two double doors into a brightly colored room, a vast contrast to the darkly lit stairwell.

At first glance, Steve estimated there were fifty people in the room, all dressed in an eclectic assortment of secondhand clothing. The room was about the size of a basketball court, with multicolored fabrics hanging from stained walls.

At the front of the room was a band of sorts—a young man on guitar, an older woman playing a harp, another guy on bongos, and one more on an instrument Steve had never seen before. It was bright red and yellow and resembled a large bow with a wooden cup at the base. The man ran another bow across the string, creating high-pitched notes.

Fronting the band was the singer, a Native American dressed in black pants and jacket, a bright yellow shirt, and no shoes. Around his head was a matching yellow headband that kept his long black and gray hair out of his soulful, dark eyes. When he moved, Steve noticed that the singer only had one arm.

A plump, middle-aged woman with frizzy hair took Steve by the hand and led him to a table. Sitting on a burner was a pot of bubbling orange soup; next to it were a few bags of bread and assorted cups. She wrapped a heavy blanket around Steve's shoulders and served him some soup in a Styrofoam cup. It wasn't fancy, but it was the best tasting soup Steve had eaten in a very long time. Greedily, he grabbed a piece of bread, dipped it into the soup, and devoured it. He hadn't realized just how hungry he was.

Steve slunk to the back of the room, leisurely sipping more soup, watching the charismatic singer. Even though he had no microphone, his voice filled the room.

When the song ended, people applauded.

"Why, thank you, I didn't notice you all sitting there," the singer joked in his rich, velvety voice. The group reacted to his remark with scattered laughter.

"Before I start tonight," he continued, "I'd like to invite a new friend to our church. Her name is Penelope." He extended his hand to a young woman in the crowd. Her cheeks were sunken, and her body frail and weak. From what Steve could gather, she must have been on meth for a good year. The singer held her hand and turned her to face the group.

"Now Penny here—can I call you Penny?" he asked her. She nodded shyly. "Penny isn't from New York. She wasn't born here, raised here, or schooled here. Her family is back in Missouri. She came here with a man who treated her badly. They did some drinking. How we love to drink!" He smiled and opened his eyes wider as everyone erupted in laughter again.

"But the drinks soon turned to the drugs, and the drugs turned to more drugs, and we do things to get the drugs—things we don't like to admit to."

Steve rolled his eyes at what was about to come. He wasn't in the mood for a born-again lecture on the evils of drugs. He'd finish his soup and make a hasty exit.

"Let's not blame the drugs," the singer carried on. "Drugs are good. Drugs are our friend. They don't judge us, they make us feel amazing. It's the people who judge. We just need to be friends with the drugs and treat them with the respect we want for ourselves. The Soda-Cola we drink kills more people than any drug. You all know my fave, and no one has died from smoking it. It's God's gift to us, and what do we do? We ban it and make people take manufactured pills that hurt us even more instead of using what nature provides."

Steve found himself confused; this wasn't how these talks normally went, he was curious to hear more—and fill his cup with more of the intoxicating soup.

"Man, I loved drugs," the singer preached. "They helped me get through the day. Without drugs, I'd be dead by now. As most of you know, I lost my arm to them. But was it the drugs that did it? No, it was me. I did it to myself, and I have to stand up and take that on the chin. I no longer take the injection of pleasure, and that too is my choice, just as much as it was to put it in my arm.

"Penny, it's not the drugs that make us do bad things, it's the world around us. The world's most perfect plant is hemp, a gift from Mother Nature. Illegal. What? How can this be, when man-made drugs like cigarettes that kill millions of people are legal? Yet grass, which has killed no one, is illegal. Cotton manufacturers are killing our land. Again, it's legal. Hemp rebuilds our land and gives oxygen back, yet it's banned.

"That is why, Penny, you feel bad. It's the world around you that's telling you that you are wrong, when they are the ones in the wrong. If you want to do drugs, do them. If you want to get clean, get clean. We will not judge you. We will help you. Together we are stronger."

Steve wasn't quite sure what to make of it all, but he wanted to learn more. Finally, someone was making sense.

CHAPTER THIRTY-ONE

SOMETHING BAD WAS going to happen.

The thick air was the biggest giveaway. Some inmates appeared anxious and exuded a nervous energy. Their bodies were hotter, and they breathed quicker than normal. The oxygen in Ross's part of the prison was being used up faster, which made the air feel dense.

Ross crept his way down the stairs, away from his cell. The landing that separated the two floors of cells was busier than normal. From day one in Bell, Ross had been making a mental map of his surroundings and the people he saw. He memorized the times and occasions when certain faces would pop up. People are creatures of habit. But today, things were different. Faces he didn't normally see where popping up and hanging around, not moving in any direction.

Ross backed up to one of the concrete walls. If anyone came for him, he'd be able to take them head on. His eyes moved from person to person, looking for someone to glance his way for the wrong reason. Their eyes would tell him everything he needed to know.

Then it happened. Three members of the White Fist were on a gangbanger from the West Spiders. The guy didn't stand a chance. The three skinheads smashed him to the ground. They threw punches and kicks from all angles.

Four other West Spiders rushed over to help their fallen member and exchanged strikes with the three skinheads. The noise drew other prisoners to watch. From nowhere, a pack of White Fists swarmed the West Spiders and a brawl broke out.

It was now a case of throw down or run. Anyone who came close was a target. Inmates swung and kicked at anyone who moved. A siren wailed through the speakers. The guards were slow to react. They liked to watch the gangbangers beat the living shit out of each other.

In the chaos, a shiv was passed from one set of hands to another. The shiv was a toothbrush with a sharpened end, jagged enough to puncture flesh and rip into muscle.

The guards finally intervened. Their batons cracked skulls as they entered the fracas. Prisoners scattered in all directions, and Ross found himself caught in a sea of them escaping the scene. They twisted and turned him as he tried to watch all the angles for any sign of an attacker. He felt exposed.

Someone passed the shiv to the last pair of hands it was destined for—a low-ranking member of the White Fist with a freshly shaved head. He zigzagged his way through the tide of human bodies and made a beeline straight for Ross, his hand gripped tightly around the shiv.

Ross's senses screamed at him to find safety. He battled the crowd's hysteria, trying to make his way to a wall, only to be pulled in the opposite direction. More baton-swinging guards entered from another hallway, sending inmates doubling back on themselves. Ross was smashed in the back and fell down to the ground hard. He tried to cover himself from trampling feet. He had to get up. He fought his way back to his feet and pushed toward a wall.

He felt a hand on his shoulder and spun to defend himself. His eyes found those of the skinhead with an arm already in full swing, the shiv coming towards him. Ross tensed for the sharp impact. It didn't come. Jimmy slipped in between the two men with his back to Ross. The skinhead took a step back, dropped the shiv, and melted into the chaos.

Jimmy turned to Ross, holding his stomach, blood leaking out between his fingers. He fell against Ross while his eyes rolled back in his head.

CHAPTER THIRTY-TWO

WHEN NICK WORKED, he always booked two motel rooms—one for working, the other for sleeping and the odd one-night stand. The women he brought home didn't need to see what he was working on.

In the far corner he had stacked five office boxes on top of each other. They were filled with useless notes from the previous Summer-Crush investigators. He'd already gone through all the boxes, one piece of paper at a time, pinning only the useful ones to the Wall of Mystery.

Sitting on the motel floor cross-legged, he scrutinized his Wall. He'd created a collage of every photo and note about SummerCrush he'd found interesting. His eyes danced over all the information and followed the strings he used to link them all together. He saw someone do the "string thing" in a film once. He tried it, and it worked.

The securely fastened TV on the wall was alive with music and moving images. Nick channel surfed a lot, looking for anything of interest, then usually returned to a music channel. He liked to listen to music while he worked; it helped let his mind wander, gave it free reign without any time pressure. He worked with his own type of fuzzy logic, and his strong intuition would often see connections that other people missed.

A Justin Timberlake song came on. Nick felt the need to dance. He moved his feet to the music, and the room became his dance floor. He moved smoothly and hit the beat with grace and flair.

After the song ended, Nick strolled along the wall, his eyes darting around the notes and photos. The thing he hated the most about this case was the damage inflicted on the children. Most would be scarred for life. Why didn't anyone take credit for it? He found that bizarre. He couldn't believe someone would go to all this trouble and not to want the world to know they did it. Even terrorists want their five minutes of fame. The fact that no one had claimed responsibility made it odd and suggested the manufacturer must be at fault. After talking to Brendon Gibson, Nick was sure it wasn't a manufacturing malfunction.

Nick left his room on the third floor. It was time for a break and a snack. There was a collection of vending machines on the ground floor, so he headed down.

While sorting out money from the scraps of paper in his front pocket, Nick noticed that of all the soda brands on offer, not one was SummerCrush. He picked a Red Bull, and while waiting for the mechanical arm to deliver his beverage, he grabbed a Hershey's bar from the neighboring machine.

On his way back to his room, Nick passed a little girl with thick, curly blonde hair playing with a half-dressed Barbie. She looked up and smiled, revealing some missing baby teeth. Nick offered her a piece of his chocolate. She took it with a cheeky grin.

"Hi, sweetie," Nick said, dropping to his knees. "Where are your parents?"

A door to one of the rooms opened, and a man in a dirty white tank top and jeans emerged. He was in his late thirties, and judging by his unshaved face and disheveled appearance, he was going through a hard patch.

"Mandy!" he called. His daughter beamed at him and waved. "Honey, I've told you, don't leave the room without telling us." He looked at Nick, sticking out his jaw and narrowing his eyelids, which made him seem more menacing, the way a protective father looks when he sees a stranger talking to his daughter.

Nick smiled at him. "She's all good, sir."

"Thanks," the father said, bending down to pick her up. "I'll take care of her now."

As the pair headed back to their room, Mandy hesitated and waved. Nick sensed that she wasn't happy to leave. Something didn't feel right, and he made a note to himself to keep an eye out.

Back in his room, he put the last piece of chocolate in his mouth and drained half the can of Red Bull. He returned his attention to the Wall.

"Who would benefit from this? No one!" he bellowed out loud, and sat down in the middle of the room, sipping his drink. He watched the end of a music video featuring a young woman in cutoffs and a pink bra who bounced around a lot. The song sounded just like the previous tune, also performed by a hot young woman who bounced around a lot in her bra.

An insurance ad interrupted the bouncing. Nick groaned. He detested all forms of advertising. Especially blatantly condescending ones, like this one. It popped up every ad break, or so it felt. It was a collection of people—bad actors—telling him, "If you're like me, you should have the same insurance I do." He couldn't believe people bought this crap.

Another ad came on featuring a mother informing viewers how wonderful oranges were, and how oranges with bubbles were so much fun. OrangeFizz—the family fun favorite.

"Really? I bet it has no oranges in it." Nick laughed. He thought about it for a second. OrangeFizz would have benefitted from the accidents, but no one would take that sort of risk just to sell a few more bottles of carbonated orange. Or would they?

CHAPTER THIRTY-THREE

THE TWO BLACK DUFFEL BAGS felt heavy on Justin's shoulders as he marched through Central Park. He wore an Abercrombie & Fitch sport top and pants to match his mint condition, '80's maroon Converse High Top shoes.

He'd divided the money—all 3.1 million he'd borrowed from Soda-Cola—between the two bags. It was what Misha required to secure a sizable shipment of uncut cocaine. This was Justin's only option to earn the ten million in Peter's tight time frame.

Misha had agreed to do the money drop in Central Park. "People don't get shot in Central Park," he'd told Justin, who wasn't sure if this was a joke or a fact. Justin spotted Misha in the distance, sitting on a park bench feeding the pigeons. He wore black from head to toe, a half-eaten pastrami sandwich balanced on his knee.

The duffel bags made a deep thud as Justin dropped them on the ground next to Misha.

"Hello, Mr. Justin," Misha said, letting the Russian vowels roll off his tongue.

"It's all there," Justin said curtly.

"Good to know. I knew man like you would come through."

"You had doubt? I told you I meant business."

"Yes, Mr. Justin. You are a man who like money, and when you want it, you have to get it, no? I also like money. But much different reason, maybe, from you. I take it to make sure others do not. I make sure people not take food from mouth, and watch me starve." Misha threw more crumbs to the birds.

"This is what we agreed," Justin said, bringing the topic of conversation back to their deal. "And I get my cut first when it's pushed to your people. I have tight deadlines."

"Yes, you will. Once drugs in New York, very easy to sell. People have money and want now. Is good time to be selling; demand high, supply all-time low. Lots of coke not make it in."

"Yours will get in, right?"

Misha squinted at Justin. "You not trust me?" as he put his hand on his chest and smiled. "That is OK, a man cannot trust anyone, even himself. You sit. Listen.

"When I first come to America, it was like nothing I ever seen before. I was strong, for me to beat a man to death, is easy. Power wins a fight. But I see that most of men who had power were not strongest in the muscles. There was man who was second-in-charge. I would think I could just grab him. Crush his head. Take his money for me. Of course, I not do it. I not know why he had all this power. The more I watch, the more I saw he was strong up here in the brain." Misha leaned toward Justin and tapped him on the forehead. "He was always thinking, thinking. He would know what people would do before they do it.

"I got close to him, and he would share what he knew with me. He like to talk as I like to listen. He tell me that guy over there is going to lose money on that deal, meaning he will need to find more. He will skim some here and there. Do a deal with that guy. He will be found out, and he will have to pay a price. Maybe death. And he would be right. He knew them better than they knew themselves. He would have plans in place for when it happened, so he would come out on top. This was power. He beat people without his fists. He liked being number two. It gave him freedom, and not much stress, little stress but not as much as the boss.

"One day, he was drinking with woman, who all over him like cheap, dirty suit. He was married but that not stop him. To him, pussy was something you took when it was there. He fuck her. Mean nothing to him. He not think about her again until her boyfriend shot him in face. She was crazy bitch and her boyfriend even more crazy. They not know who him was, just some guy who not able to keep it in his pants. No gang thing, just a jealous man. He lost his power. Why? Because he trust himself. He should have made same plans for him, as he did for those around him. If he not trust himself, maybe he would not have fucked crazy bitch."

Misha stood and picked up the bags as if they were weightless.

"Do you trust yourself, Mr. Justin?" Misha stared off into the distance. "I don't. I not trust you and I not trust me. And that will be another thing we have in common, like dead fathers. As long as we not trust ourselves, not get greedy, we can live with each other. Have nice day, Mr. Justin. I be in touch." Misha strolled toward the bridge.

Justin remained on the bench, reflecting on what Misha had said. Justin trusted no one, but he did trust himself. Misha would find that out soon enough.

CHAPTER THIRTY-FOUR

MONTANA SPENT MORE and more time in her shower, sitting and feeling the hot water run all over her. No matter how hot the water was, she never felt clean. Nothing could wash away the emotional dirt. Her world had spun out of control. Nothing made sense any more.

Montana reluctantly left the foggy warmth of the shower, opened the medicine cabinet, and took out a small plastic bottle of high-strength sleeping pills. She twisted off the cap and tipped three pills into her hand. They looked so small and innocent. She slipped them back into the bottle and screwed the top back on.

She opened her walk-in closet, contemplating her collection of expensive dresses and shoes. Precious fashion items that she'd taken pride in buying and wearing.

Her eyes caressed the luxurious fabrics. She chose a red, strapless silk dress that she'd bought on a holiday in Paris. She'd seen it in a small store window and fell in love with it. The old woman had fussed over her as she'd tried it on. It fit her curves perfectly, and the long slit down the side flashed her toned legs seductively as she'd walked around the store. The dress held up her breasts perfectly and made them appear voluptuous. She'd felt like a movie star. The dress cost more than her flight to France but it was well worth it—or so she thought at the time. Since buying it, she'd worn it only twice.

She laid the dress out on the bed and carefully slipped on a black G-string in front of her full-length mirror, followed by matching stockings and a garter belt. She liked how they accentuated her body.

Montana sat at her makeup table and styled her hair in the light-bulb-framed mirror. She had a painstaking twelve-step ritual that she performed when applying her makeup. She took great care in making sure it was just right. She picked up the dress, slipped it on, and stepped into a pair of black Louis Vuitton high heels.

In the kitchen, she examined a smoky bottle of red wine she'd been given on her twenty-fifth birthday by her then-boyfriend. He was a merchant banker, and when presenting her with the bottle, went to great lengths to explain its rich history, suggesting it should be passed down from generation to generation. She removed the cork, filled her glass, and took in a mouthful. It was bitter and a little disappointing.

Montana swayed back and forth to the music as she walked back into her bedroom, her sound system playing Maroon 5. She reopened the bottle of sleeping pills and tipped it over until its entire contents were sitting in her cupped hand. She took a sip of wine, stuffed the pills into her mouth, and downed the entire glass. Her face screwed up from the taste.

She put the glass beside her bed and lay down. Her nightmare would be over now. She closed her eyes and listened to Maroon 5 lull her into an endless sleep.

FILE TWO:
CUT THROAT MERGER

THE CHUGGING FERRY PLOWED its way through pounding waves, spraying seawater onto Jill's face. She ran her tongue over her bright pink lips, tasting the salt. A beauty mark penciled above her lip was a new fashion addition. The ferry bounced again, causing her extra-large, black-and-white polka dot skirt to puff out.

She stood at the front of the ferry for the entire ride, wind rippling through her sixties-styled hair. Freshly dyed platinum blonde this morning, she wore a large pink bow to hold it in place. Eagerly, she watched the Iron Lady get closer and closer. She'd seen her many times in movies, books, and on TV shows, but to see her in real life was glorious. She polished off her ice cream as the ferry docked.

Like-minded visitors jostled one another to be the first to step foot on the iconic island. A hunched man pushed past Jill and for a second she thought it was Jeff. The guy shot a glance over his shoulder at her, rolling his eyes at her hefty frame. She was wrong; he was just another prick from the giant prick store.

She thought about Jeff a lot, not that she wanted to. She was glad to have him out of her life. How different it all would have been if two years ago she hadn't made a last-minute decision to pop into her cousin's party. Jeff was in the center of the room, beer in each hand, swaying slightly to the music. She remembered his gray Dallas Cowboys hoodie, stained with BBQ rib sauce, and how he constantly pulled up his loose-fitting jeans as he flirted with her.

She took him home that night, and things progressed quickly. Within the month, he moved in and a few weeks later convinced her to open a joint account for their expenses. The relationship ticked along nicely, so long as they didn't talk about money. Jeff found it hard to find steady work, but didn't let that stop him from doing what he wanted to do and paying for everything out of their joint account. If Jill asked him about his spending, he'd become defensive and abusive, so she found ignoring it worked best.

Jill stopped at the base of the statue and squinted up at the Iron Lady. She was elegant, bold, and strong. Everything Jill wanted to be. She bought a pretzel and Diet Soda-Cola from a cart vendor, sat on a park bench, and gazed out to sea, picking off crusts of salted dough. Once finished, she reapplied lipstick, made her way into the building, grabbed her ticket, and joined the back of the line. Climbing the stairs consisted of taking one step, then waiting five minutes for people to move before taking another. It was a slow and painful process.

Jill touched the side of her face. A layer of makeup hid the bruise well. Her hand trembled with the memory of her last argument with Jeff. She'd been at the grocery store. Jeff hadn't worked for a few months, and she wanted to make him a nice meal to cheer him up. Once the cashier rang everything up, they swiped her credit card, and it was declined. The cashier tried it a few more times, and every result was the same. Jill apologized profusely out of embarrassment to those around her and, once in her car, called the bank to sort it out. They informed her that her card was indeed maxed out due to a purchase that morning.

"I needed it!" Jeff had yelled as she'd asked him why he had bought a fifty-inch, flat-screen and a PS4. "It's on credit, I'll pay it back when I get a new job. Fucking boring being stuck here all day."

"I had just paid off the credit card. You should have asked."

"Like you ask if you should stuff your face with donuts. Want to bitch about something, bitch about how you can't lose weight."

"You know I have a slow metabolism!" Jill had screamed.

"Fuck off, you have sugar running through your veins, not blood. You're fat 'cause you eat shit. Don't tell me what I can and can't spend my money on."

"It's my money! You don't earn any. Who pays the rent, internet, groceries, and power? Me! What do you pay for? Nothing!"

"I should get paid for fucking you! Who else is going to do that? Disgusting pig," he sneered.

That was it, a crescendo to years of built-up abuse caused her to see red. She grabbed the closest thing in reach, an empty bourbon bottle, and flung it at Jeff. She'd never been good at sports, yet this time her aim was spot-on. Like a fastball, the bottle hit the side of his head, knocking him out of his chair. She didn't move; neither did he. The room was eerie-silent. She thought she killed him. Then he groaned and staggered to his feet, blood pouring out of the fresh wound, his eyes wild.

"Game on, bitch!" He removed his belt and whipped her, strike after strike after strike he beat her into submission. By the time the police arrived, Jeff was slouching on the couch, out of breath, nursing his bleeding head. Jill was huddled in a corner, traumatized. The welts over her body would sting for days. As the cops took him away, he pleaded self-defense from a crazy bitch. The neighbors who'd called watched from their porch.

The next morning, Jill emptied her secret bank account, one her momma had talked her into opening, and boarded a bus bound for New York. She needed to get away, and New York was a place she'd always dreamed about visiting.

Finally, Jill reached the top of the stairs and shuffled up to a small window looking out over the sea and to the hazy horizon. Her sore feet didn't think the view was worth it. She pulled out her travel notebook and crossed out STATUE OF LIBERTY. Next on her to-visit list was the 9/11 memorial, followed by the Empire State Building. She did another lap of the enclosed space, searching for anything worth a second look. There was nothing. The only shining light now was that the walk back downstairs had no line. A man in a dark suit pushed past her to get to the stairwell first.

"Sure, why not," she said. "You're way more important than me. Go save the world, jerk."

The man paused, then carried on through the exit door. Jill followed, muttering to herself about useless men. Halfway down the first flight of stairs, a voice stopped her.

"Hey, you," the dark-suited man yelled. He stood on the next landing looking up at her. He wore a grin that was more devil than man. He winked, then jogged down the rest of the stairs, three at a time.

Jill waited for him to go out of sight. As she moved forward, her foot remained stuck to the step. She tried to lean back to regain her balance, but gravity had other ideas, pulling her portly frame even further forward, ripping the thin buckle off the stuck Mary Jane shoe. Screaming, she tumbled downward, twisting and turning, snapping and cracking, until she came to a grinding halt. Her neck was broken, her eyes stared blankly at nothing, and her patent leather shoe was still stuck to the step.

The sticky glue residue that the dark-suited man had left on the step worked better than he'd hoped.

CHAPTER THIRTY-SIX

"JUSTIN, THERE HAVE BEEN SOME COMPLAINTS," Edward Chandler said as he sipped his Scotch on the rocks. He took his time, feeling the amber liquid warm his tongue before swallowing it. Such exquisite spirits empowered Edward with the courage to push his own agenda with Justin.

Edward was the chief financial controller of Soda-Cola, and the elected chairman of the Soda-Cola board. He saw things in black and white, no gray. He avoided meaningless emotional conflict wherever possible and let the numbers do the talking. He had asked Justin to come and visit him weeks ago, but Justin had only just now shown up.

Edward had a squished face with thick, round glasses and narrow shoulders. Justin stood a good head taller than Edward and often used his height to intimidate him.

"Some?" Justin leaned back in his chair. "If I didn't have 'some' complaints, I don't think I'd be doing my job, do you?"

"It's the type of complaints employees are making," Edward replied, taking another sip. "People are talking about this aggressive atmosphere you're creating. They're scared of losing their jobs over the smallest of reasons."

"I understand," Justin nodded. "You see, Carlton was sickly before I took over. He let a lot of shit slide and left me acres of dead wood to thin out. I have a vision for Soda-Cola, Edward, and you have seen the benefits of it. Did you enjoy the bonus the entire board received last quarter?"

"I did, indeed. Thank you."

"And I heard you used it to make a deposit on a rather nice beach-front property."

"Yes… a place I've had my eye on for a while."

"Carlton told me there was a bit of red tape, and some locals were making it difficult to build, so difficult that you nearly had to pull out and you would have lost everything." Justin leaned forward.

"Not really," Edward said. "Some paperwork got lost along the way; it was found, signed, and we didn't lose too much time. I just had to follow up on everything, double-check, and then triple-check."

"You knew what you wanted and went for it. A bit like what I'm doing. I have made changes here at Soda-Cola—big changes. Edward, let's be honest. You don't live in the real world and haven't for a long time. It's tough out there. The world is changing by the minute. Hundred-year-old businesses are going bankrupt overnight. The changes I'm making will make sure that beach house of yours will be paid off in no time."

Edward took another sip. What Justin was saying was true. Yet he still felt uncomfortable with the way Justin was going about things. He swirled his Scotch and took a larger mouthful this time.

"What can you tell me about the Young Lions?" Edward asked.

"Because of them, you had the deposit, and the funds to renovate your beach house," Justin continued. "They are young and hungry and motivated."

"Why give them a name?"

"They deserve it. They're the best, and it makes them feel proud and determined. Money is a great motivator. But when you're a part of a vision, that becomes more important than money. They want to be Young Lions. Other people want to be Young Lions. The name tells people that they're the future and that they're powerful and special. People on the outside will complain. And that's why we are having this chat."

"Their arrogance creates a hostile work environment, Justin."

"It creates competition. The strongest rise to the top, while the weak sit on the sidelines and bitch and moan. Of course they hate the Young Lions. These pussy-whipped weaklings can fuck right off and do better elsewhere." Justin stood, towering over Edward. "Why do Islamic terrorists hate Americans? Because we stand for peace and love, something they have no idea about. Should we care about what they think? Edward, should we care what these ragheads say about Americans?"

"No, but…"

"Damn right. We protect what's ours and will bomb the shit out of anyone who tries to take it away. We are a proud American company, Edward. You have been here for thirty years, and in that time have you let terrorists dictate what you can do with your freedom? Hell, no."

"Progress comes at a price," Edward said abruptly. "All I ask is for you to be more mindful of other employees and their feelings. We are a family company, and while profits are good, people are also important."

Justin grinned, stepping around the desk so there would be no barrier between them.

"I'm glad we've had this talk, Edward. I will take what you've said under advisement. We are on the same team, a team that is going to be extremely wealthy."

Justin extended his hand, palm up. Edward took it, wearily. Justin snatched it like a bear trap and held Edward's hand firmly.

"Stand with me and be rich, stand against me and fall," Justin said, holding Edward's gaze.

CHAPTER THIRTY-SEVEN

BLEEEEP... BLEEP...

I don't want to get up. The other girls make fun of my clothes. Momma. They say I smell. I don't smell. Why do they say that, why do they say I eat dirt for breakfast?

Bleeeep... bleep...

Do I have to wear this dress? It's not even new? People will know it's secondhand!

Bleeeep... bleep...

He really likes me, he asked me to prom. Should I go? He's kinda cute...

Bleeeep... bleep...

What? This is what he did, you should really promote me over Chad...

Bleeeep... bleep...

Take the offer on the table. If you don't, I will give it to someone else. There's the door. Stay or go. I won't stop you. Just know this is the best offer you'll get.

Bleeeep... bleep...

Hate him... Fuck him... Leave me alone. I can't do this anymore. I give up.

Bleeeep... bleep...

It's cold... What is this? Where am I? Please God, no.

Montana slowly opened her eyes and was hit with a bright white light. For a second she thought she'd made it to heaven. Then she recognized that smell; the chemical smell of a hospital.

Her vision slowly adjusted, and soon the hospital room came into focus, as did the concerned face looking down at her.

"Hey, girl," Steve said in a low, loving tone.

Montana tried to reply but her mouth was too dry, and her throat too sore.

"They had to pump your stomach. Try some of this." He lowered a plastic cup to her lips. She drank a small amount. It hurt, but helped a little.

"Wha… what happ-en-ed?" Montana asked in a mouse-like tone.

"I felt bad about how we last spoke. I wasn't in the best headspace, you know… I just had to apologize. I've being thinking a lot lately. I was walking the streets, thinking and walking, and before I knew it, I was near your building. I saw that the lights were on. It was a sign that I had to ask your forgiveness.

"I could hear music and found your front door unlocked. I called your name several times… it actually took me a good five minutes to step inside. And then I found you, saw the empty pill bottle on the floor, and freaked out. I called 911 and shook you until your eyes opened and did everything I could to keep you conscious. The paramedics arrived and it was touch and go for a moment, but they were able to pump out most of the pills."

Montana put her hand on Steve's. "Thank you," she whispered.

"We're going to have to talk about this, but not right now. Let's just be thankful you're alive."

"Jussstin," Montana said, squinting her eyes.

"Yes, we'll do something about him too, I promise you that."

CHAPTER THIRTY-EIGHT

STEVE LEFT THE HOSPITAL to let Montana get some sleep. Of all the people he knew, he never saw her as suicidal. He raised his arm to signal a cab and just as one pulled over he realized he didn't have any money on him. He waved it on and headed to the subway. At this time of morning it was easy to jump the gate among paying passengers.

The subway was a whole new discovery to him; for the past fifteen years he'd driven or caught corporate cabs. The train was packed shoulder to shoulder with people going important places for important reasons, like Steve once did. He smiled at a guy in a suit who he recognized as an intern at Soda-Cola. The intern looked through Steve as if he were invisible, whereas once he'd have spent hours sucking up to him.

Steve ran his hand through his bushy beard. He didn't look like the man who used to run a multinational company anymore. He had noticed beards were quite fashionable at the moment, but maybe ones that were better styled than his. His stop was fast approaching. He weaved through a throng of people until he was next to his former intern.

"Kid," Steve said. "Get out while you can."

Trekking up the long flight of subway stairs required a breather halfway. The lack of food and overuse of drugs had taken its toll on Steve's physical health. He had to stop the drugs today. How could he help Montana if he couldn't help himself?

He ambled back to his apartment. The door was open. This was not unusual, as he often left it unlocked so he didn't have to worry about losing his key.

"Steve?" a voice called out. A voice that used to sound so sweet, now sounded like venom covered in ice.

"Trisha, what are you doing here?" Steve asked his once-loving wife who was standing in the middle of the lounge. Her brown hair was longer than last time they'd talked, slightly parted to one side, and in a ponytail. Her slight frame was thinner than normal, and her T-shirt looked baggy. Her pencil-thin lips were tight with no sign of emotion, and her eyes just as cold.

"The kids were asking about you," she said. "They haven't heard from you in a while, and still like to think they have a father."

"Shit, I tried to call them yesterday."

"But you were fucking busy, right!" she snapped.

Steve was shocked, as his wife very really swore. She lifted her hand, and he saw what she was holding—a used syringe.

"You're not only a rapist, but a drug addict as well. Who are you? I gave you nothing but love and support, and this is who you really are? A fucking drug addict?"

"Listen…"

"No, you listen—stay away from me, and stay away from the kids. You so much as come near us and I'll have you arrested." She struggled for words. She wanted to sound tough. She opened her wallet and yanked out some money and hurled it at Steve.

"Go get yourself some more drugs, Steve," she said sarcastically, throwing the rest of her money at him until coins were all she had left. These too bounced off his head. She tried to storm past him, but he grabbed her wrist.

"Honey—"

"Don't you 'honey' me," she snapped, and gave his face a hard slap, catching his ear and sending him off balance. He dropped to one knee as the room started spinning.

"You make me sick," she cried. "I would tell you to get help, but what I really want to tell you is to go to hell." She slammed the door behind her. Steve got to his feet to chase her, but then dropped to his knees again, his head still spinning and his pride hurt.

"Fuck you!" he yelled, knowing she wouldn't be able to hear him. He looked at the money on the floor. "I don't need you or your fucking money."

He removed a shoe and sent it flying toward the door. Then he grabbed some of the bills and threw them too in a pathetic attempt to vent his anger, but they just fluttered helplessly in the air. Steve sat panting on the floor, watching the money land, note by note. Then a smile crossed his face and he began gathering them all up.

"All hail King Steve," he said. He was back in business.

CHAPTER THIRTY-NINE

THE ASSORTED CARDS, bills, and bits of papers sat on the bedside table as per usual. Nick scooped them up and stuffed them in his front pocket—that's where they lived. He glanced around his motel room, a final check for anything he might need. Nothing jumped out, so he exited and took the twenty steps into the room next door, his office.

Every wall of it was now covered in photos, scribbles and notes. Seventeen children had been scarred by SummerCrush; their faces reminded Nick of his own childhood: a sheltered upbringing in a small community of small-minded people who walked in small circles. He clenched his fists as he thought about his staunch, religious father, with his mean, vengeful streak.

Nick got the music channel blaring, then vigorously paced the room, letting his fingers move from one picture to another. He stopped at a picture of a six-year-old boy, Ethan, and his family. Ethan had been the first to drink a contaminated SummerCrush. This photo was taken three months before the accident and showed him with his mom, dad, and baby brother. The family had posed for the picture on an old tree stump in a neighborhood park. The proud father with Ethan on his lap was in his early thirties, still sporting boyish good looks. The mother, holding the baby on her knee, rested her head lovingly on her husband's wide shoulders.

Just from the picture, Nick could tell a lot about this family, but it was time to know more. He closed his eyes, letting the image wash over him, transporting himself into the scene. He was now in the park on the day of the photo as the mother directed the family into position. They were happy to see Nick, welcoming, wanted to share their dark secrets with him.

First to speak was the father.

I'm having an affair. God, it feels good to say it out loud. And she's not that hot, she's a six out of ten, but she has nice tits. My wife's a nine and so much hotter. I just like the fact I'm getting away with it—my wife and my whore. Living the American dream.

Oh, baby, the mother said. *I know, and I know who she is. I went to school with her. She was a slut then, and she is a slut now. You aren't special, baby, she'll open her legs to anyone who smiles at her. I'm choosing to ignore your little indiscretions in the hope you'll get over it. I don't want to be a single mother of two.*

Well, the father added. *I once got drunk with some guys from school while on a football trip, and we raped a girl.*

I can't stand my mother-in-law, the mother retorted. *I once spat in her tea while making it.*

Nick closed his eyes and opened them again. He stood in front of the wall staring at the picture. He ran his hand through his hair and messed it up, then shook his body to get the family out of his head. Their problems were their problems and he couldn't take them on. He cranked up the music and started to dance. This was the best way for him to clear his mind.

High on Nick's priority list was to check out the place where Ethan had brought his SummerCrush. The cops had already searched the shop, but they didn't have Nick's eyes or intuition. He booked a flight, grabbed his black backpack, and headed out of the room.

Mandy sat on the steps, holding the old Barbie doll. She smiled up at Nick. It was infectious and he smiled back, pulling a funny face and spinning around on his heels for her. She giggled and widened her smile.

"Mandy, honey," a voice called out.

"Yes, Daddy?" the little girl answered.

"Can you come in now, your mother wants to get ready."

"Yes, Daddy." She waved at Nick and waddled away. He noticed that she limped slightly, and anger boiled up inside him. Her father patted her on the head as she shuffled past him.

"Sir," Nick called out. "You have an amazing daughter, such a beautiful smile."

"Thank you, she gets it from her mother," the father replied proudly.

"Does she have an older brother?" Nick asked.

"Yeah, Taylor," he replied, slightly confused.

"Angry teenager?" Nick prodded.

"What teenager isn't angry?" The father laughed.

"True." Nick laughed back. "You have a good day."

The father nodded and closed the door. Nick saw a teenage boy stomping up the stairs toward him. His hair was similar to Mandy's, and their noses were identical.

"Taylor?" Nick asked, extending his hand.

"Yeah," Taylor replied, baffled that this stranger knew his name. Nick grabbed Taylor's hand, pulled him close and spun him into a rear chokehold.

"We're going for a walk," Nick growled, pulling the teenager back down the stairs.

Once they reached the ground floor, Nick released his grip and punched the teen in the kidneys. As Taylor crumpled, Nick grabbed him by the hair and wrenched him back up.

"I know what you've been doing to your little sister, fuckhead."

"She's a fucking liar!" Taylor screamed.

Nick followed up with another kidney punch that made Taylor double over onto the ground, tears welling up in his eyes.

"She didn't tell me, Taylor. She didn't need to." Nick dragged him back up and grabbed a nerve point under his jaw to make sure pain flared through Taylor's body. "This is your first and last warning. This is nothing compared to what I'll do to you if you ever lay a finger on her again. And I will know, Taylor. I will make you suffer like no one has ever suffered before. You will be begging me to kill you. And when I decide to end your worthless life, I will make sure you disappear and are never, ever found. This is your only warning!"

Taylor cried like a spoiled toddler, snot running out of his nose.

"What warning is this, Taylor?"

"My… my only… warning," he managed to stutter between sobs.

"And stop listening to that shit music. You are not black and not a gangsta. Delete all that shit. Only listen to music made in the seventies, right! Zeppelin and Dylan are now your bread and butter."

Nick released him, sending him crawling back up the stairs. Hopefully he'd never have to talk to Taylor again.

CHAPTER FORTY

IF IT WASN'T FOR JIMMY, Ross would have been the one bleeding out on the bleak prison floor. Ross had been able to halt the blood loss and keep Jimmy alive until help came. It was touch and go for the small man, but he pulled through and was recuperating in the prison infirmary.

Ross now had business with the White Fist. Marcus Wilson was their leader, and with seven consecutive life sentences to his name, he wasn't going anywhere soon. He was a megalomaniac who used swift acts of violence to keep people in line. Break one of his rules, and he broke you. No one sneezed within the ranks of the White Fist without his command. Marcus would have ordered the hit on Ross because of his public bread roll refusal.

The fledgling skinhead who'd failed to stab Ross was found later in the bathroom, beaten and covered in fresh shit. A message to the other members: what to expect when you failed Marcus. If Ross couldn't find a way to convince Marcus to have a change of heart, the attempts on his life would keep coming. He wouldn't be safe anywhere.

At lunch today, Ross kept his bread roll. On his way out, he slipped past a lower-ranked member of White Fist and, with a shiv of his own, stabbed the bread roll into the skinhead's shoulder. It was an invitation for Marcus to have a sit-down conversation with him. Now Ross sat patiently in his cell, waiting for the answer.

Prison-issued shoes sounded different on the concrete floor than those of the guards. On the floor next to Ross's bed was an old milk container that he used as a water bottle while working out. He pushed it over, letting the water gurgle from the bottle all over the floor. Ross focused his hearing and counted five pairs of shoes heading his way, four belonging to inmates and one to a guard.

Three burly, heavily tattooed skinheads stormed into Ross's cell. He raised his hands and placed them on his head to show that he just want-ed to talk. The men roughly searched his body to make sure he had no concealed weapons before Marcus appeared in the doorway. One of the skinheads threw a solid right cross. It struck Ross square on the jaw, sending him flying hard against the cell wall. Ross took the hit and didn't retaliate. His attention was on palming a small cable into his hand with-out being seen by his intruders. He got to his knees, placed his hands behind his head, and hid the wire from sight, trailing it down his back.

"Hello, Ross," Marcus said with dark amusement. He was in his late forties, just under six feet tall, and weighed a solid 180 pounds. Marcus had a gaunt face, with cold blue eyes that made people feel like he was ripping their soul out through their eyeballs. Ross felt the temperature in the room drop a degree. "You wanted to have a chat? I'm guessing that's what your little message was about, right?"

"One of your followers tried to kill me. I would like it to stop," Ross said promptly.

"Really? That sounds like you're asking me a favor? And I don't be-lieve we have any goodwill between us to warrant that."

"I have no beef with you." Ross kept his hands behind his head. Mar-cus stalked closer and stopped half an inch from Ross's face.

"You think you're too good for us? A dirty cop looking down his nose at his Aryan brothers? You want to be with the mud niggers, Ross?"

"I'm dirty. I don't need my dirt to spread. I know I'm never going to live long enough to ever get out of here. I need to know if this is the start of a war between us, and one I will no doubt lose?"

"You're a smart one. Yes, you will lose."

"For me it's not about winning, it's about creating change. If more come for me, I'll kill them, I'm a trained killer, Marcus, not some rape-bait punk. But it's not me you have to worry about. When the other gangs see what I'm doing, I'm sure they'll join in."

"You think they will help you? That's a joke," Marcus smirked.

"They won't help me," Ross replied. "But if there is blood in the wa-ter, they may just want a taste of it for themselves. You would then have a war on all fronts. I'll be dead. I don't care who dies after that."

"I could end this right here." Marcus shot his head forward so their noses were touching.

"You could try," Ross prodded. "Just think about it. You're in my house. Would I not have planned for this visit?"

Marcus flicked his eyes around the cell. For a brief moment Ross saw his cold exterior crack, but it returned just as fast.

"A dirty cop with a dirty mouth spurting lies and deception," Marcus spat. "Words are all you have. I am an eater of worlds, a destroyer of souls. You think you could do anything to hurt me? Many have tried and failed. I could cut you open right here, feed on your heart, and nothing would happen to me. No one would shed a tear. I fear no man, and a man like you should be praying to me as if I were God."

"You know what I did to Ezekiel," Ross reminded him. "Notice the water you're standing in?" Ross unclenched his fist, revealing two ends of electrical wires. Marcus's eyes followed one end of the wire to the water they were both standing in, the other trailing behind Ross.

"If I make these two wires touch," Ross said calmly, "I'll become a human fuse causing thousands of volts to pass through us, and we will both die. I'm guessing our hearts will explode in our chests, and our bodies will burn from the inside out, turning us black. You will die a nigger, Marcus; a black-as-coal nigger."

"You're bluffing, Ross," Marcus said, eyes glaring. "We both know that. You dare treat a god with such lies! You don't have any friends in here. I offered my hand and you slapped it away. If you do that again, I will call your bluff, and you will die. I will choose when and how. Right now, I choose to let you live for a bit longer. I give you the air you breathe, and I can take it away."

"And I thank you for it," Ross said.

"This is a reprieve—a man like you may not have many days ahead of him. Just be aware of that. You are one of us, Ross. The sooner you come to terms with it, the sooner you can rest in peace."

"Why would you want a dirty cop?" Ross asked, throwing the wires behind him. He had made his point. "As a pet to play with? Am I worth anything in here?"

"You have no worth. I do what I want—just know that. And there's a price for this reprieve." Marcus threw a jab, hitting Ross in the face, followed by a flurry of powerful punches that split open his lip and cracked a rib. Ross took each punch without fighting back.

Marcus left with his brothers in tow, leaving only Officer Hoff outside the cell. His face was white and covered in sweat.

"You have balls," Hoff said as he slid the door closed. "How much longer you'll have them is anyone's guess."

Ross collapsed on his bed. His body began to shake. He had been bluffing—the wires hadn't been connected to anything. If they'd decided to kill him, he would have been dead meat.

THE SMALL POUCH OF WHITE powder was securely tucked inside Steve's pocket. He tapped it every few steps to make sure it was still there. In his other pocket he had placed a tarnished silver spoon covered with burn marks and a syringe, all ready to go. His dealer had been happy to see him, telling him that they needed to hang out more often. Drug dealers love it when you have money.

Steve couldn't decide where he wanted to get high. He could take it home and enjoy it there in peace. Or he could head downtown and find an ill-reputed lover to join him. Getting high and fucking was awesome. You couldn't guarantee they were going to be hot, have all their own teeth, or not have a few random STDs, but once high, none of that mattered.

He was glad he and Montana were talking again. He still wanted her more than any other woman he'd ever met. But friendship would do, as it was better to have her as a friend than not having her in his life at all.

Steve wandered around for over an hour until he found himself outside Silver's church. The door was open, still hanging on for dear life. Steve had visited a few times since he'd first stumbled in on that rainy night. He liked to come and listen to Silver, and there was always tasty soup. The building had two levels, as well as a few rooms in the basement. The ground level was so run down that it was unusable, with exposed rotten wood, broken glass, and holes in most of the surfaces.

As he ambled down the abandoned stairs, Steve still couldn't decide what he was going to do with his drugs. He entered into the main room where Silver held his masses and saw him sitting in the middle, wearing a faded University of Maine T-shirt, in what looked like a meditation pose. He was crossed-legged with his only hand resting on his knee.

"Hello, brother Steve," Silver said without opening his eyes.

"Hello," Steve replied. "I just… was passing."

"Come sit with me. I was hoping to see you today."

Steve flopped onto the floor. "I can't stay long."

"You stay as long as you stay, and no longer." Silver smiled. "I am glad that you're passing by at this moment. Steve, this makes me happy. You've arrived just in time. Say, did you want to get high?"

"Umm…" Steve didn't know how to respond.

"You have drugs, yes? It's OK, there are clean places here to get as high as you want. It's safe."

"Thanks." Steve still couldn't get used to how open Silver was when it came to drugs.

"You know, your drugs won't be going anywhere. Today I was hoping you would stop by and help me. Would you like to help me first, and then get high?"

"OK," Steve said, rubbing his forearm.

"When you came down the stairs, did you see the walls? All the paint is cracking and peeling. I was thinking today would be a good day to fix up that wall with you, Steve. We can sand it back, then fill the cracks and paint it to look nice. Would you like to help me do that, Steve?"

"Sure. I don't know if I'd be any good at it, though."

Silver opened his soulful eyes and stood. "You are good already, so you can only be good. Come, let's paint."

For the next eight hours, Steve helped Silver without once thinking about shooting up.

CHAPTER FORTY-TWO

IT WAS A "NICE" NEIGHBORHOOD. The sun was shining, the trees were swaying in the light breeze, and the air was alive with the sound of chirping birds. The people who lived here smiled and waved at their neighbors. They had BBQs together and talked about the state of the country and football. They paid a premium to enjoy their American slumber.

After five minutes in this environment, Nick wanted to blow his brains out. It was all too fake for him. The grass was too well-manicured, the houses too tidy, and the streets too clean to be streets.

This is where Ethan had purchased his bad bottle of SummerCrush. Nick loitered outside the corner store, surveilling the area, searching for security cameras, nosy neighbors, or foot traffic, but found nothing. This store was a black spot, perfect for the crime that had occurred.

Nick strolled across the road, made himself comfortable on a park bench, and waited. He was in no hurry; whatever he'd find here would be found when needed. He closed his eyes and images of the store's customers invaded his mind, each person stopping and telling him one of their dark secrets. After two hours of confessions, it was time for him to check out the store with his own eyes.

An electronic *bing-bong* sounded as he entered the store. The fridges at the back were his first stop. Unsurprisingly, there were no bottles of SummerCrush to be seen; bottles of OrangeFizz were in their place. Nick grabbed a can of Red Bull and a bag of peanut M&Ms.

A middle-aged Chinese man with tortoise shell-rimmed bifocals stood behind the counter.

"Hi," Nick said and waved.

"Hello," the man replied curtly, but politely, wiping his hands on his green apron before scanning the can of Red Bull.

"How's your day going?" Nick asked.

"Day good. You want anything else? We have some good specials. Very good."

"Don't suppose you have any SummerCrush?"

"No, no more. That bad drink!" the man said in a nasal voice. He counted up Nick's items. "That be four dollar and fifty cents, please." The question had raised a sore point with the store owner, which was understandable. But Nick wanted more information.

"What specials do you have today?" he asked.

"Peanut Butter Cup." The storeowner pointed to the sale items. "What you really want? You reporter? I not bad guy."

"No. Investigator," Nick said, changing his voice to sound more sympathetic. "Tell you what—you talk to me about the day the bad drink was sold, and I'll buy the whole box of Peanut Butter Cups."

"I told police everything. No more. Bad for business. Who pay for the people who no buy things now?"

"I'm not police, just someone who wants to catch the guy who did it. That would be good for you, right?"

"Terrorist! That's what news say."

"What can you tell me?"

"I tell you, like I told everyone. Nothing strange. All same. Then boy get hurt. Not my fault."

Nick wasn't getting anywhere, and the store owner was just getting more and more worked up. The door bing-bonged again as two teenage boys jostled in, one in a cap, the other shaking his thick blond hair, both in loose-fitting jeans and skate-brand T-shirts.

"I have good store," the owner continued. "This bad for me. What I do? I work hard and now people stop coming."

"We still here, bro," one of the teenagers chipped in.

"Do you come here often?" Nick asked, intrigued.

"Most days when we need supplies." They looked at each other and cracked up. Their eyes were still red from the weed they had smoked an hour ago.

"Yes, bro, awesome choice." The cap-wearing teenager pointed at Nick's drink. "Red Bull is the bomb, bro."

Nick felt a tingle up the back of his neck. He was onto something here.

"I like it, I can't get enough," he said. "I'm Nick," he continued, holding out his fist for a fist bump. As the capped teen hit it, he made an exploding sound as he flicked his fingers.

"I'm Stan and this is Mason, bro." Mason stepped in and also fist-bumped Nick.

"Did you guys happen to visit the day the SummerCrush was sold?" Nick cracked open the Red Bull and took a sip.

"Yeah, bro, I think we even got on the news. We were in the background."

"I was doing the robot," Mason said, and demonstrated his moves.

"Yes! Awesome," Stan said, encouraging his friend.

"Anyone ask you about what you saw?" Nick asked.

"Nah, bro. No one talked to us."

"Did you happen to see anything?" Nick continued. "Even something tiny that seemed odd at the time."

"Nothing, bro," Stan replied. "Nothing at all. We only came in to get some Red Bull and Doritos in the morning. We had a late one playing GTA all night. I can play that shit for days, bro."

"We did try and get this old dude to buy a Red Bull," Mason added.

"Yeah, that dude. He was going to buy a soda, and we thought he needed a Red Bull. We're always trying to get everyone to buy it, especially oldies. It'll blow their mind."

"What was he going to buy?" Nick leaned in. That time of the morning, soda wouldn't be a huge drink of choice.

"Umm, took him ages but I think he got one of those ones that the kid got. The kid that was on the news."

"SummerCrush?" Nick allowed the universe to help him put the pieces together.

"Yeah, he didn't end up on the news, so he must have got a good one."

"Can you describe this guy?"

"Um, old. He even had one of those old-men hats. Golf ones you see in old films. Marko Brothers or something."

Nick turned to the shop owner. "Do you remember this guy?"

"No, I not think so. Lots of customer. I not remember everyone."

Nick was intrigued. "Thanks for everything." He dropped a few hundred dollars on the counter and handed the teenagers the box of Peanut Butter Cups.

"Yes. . . score!" one of them said.

"Grab some Red Bulls too, as much as you can carry. Go nuts until the money is gone. But you have to spend it in here."

"Double score!" Stan grinned.

Nick smiled at the storeowner and went to leave.

"Oh, there's one thing," Mason yelled at Nick as he reached the door. "He caught a taxi from here. Not sure if that's helpful or not."

CHAPTER FORTY-THREE

THE CONSTRUCTION SITE was silent. The tall, looming cranes were void of any movement. Ripped plastic sheeting flapped and snapped in the crosswinds. Exposed metal beams, cut and half-welded, collected rust. Piles of gravel had been dumped and abandoned. Trucks, pickups, and diggers were parked at odd angles like toys in a sandpit.

Justin stormed toward the foreman's shed. He glared at workers drinking coffee, smoking, laughing, and playing cards—doing anything but construction. Each one of them seemed to be joyous they were getting paid whether they worked or sat, and most preferred to sit.

He kicked open the door to the wooden prefab. The room was the size of a single garage, cluttered with desks, filing cabinets, a small couch, and assorted chairs. The walls were littered with building charts, calendars, and posters of FHM models.

"Hello, Mr. Truth, glad you could pop down." David smiled with large, veneer teeth that were too white for a man of his age. He was a solid man who wore double denim and a military-style buzz cut. His stubby fingers closed a magazine and dropped it on his desk.

"What is the meaning of all this, David?" Justin yelled as he advanced, only slowing when he noticed the presence of two gorilla-like men in the far corner, drinking coffee. Their faces were concrete slabs, void of any expression. Justin leaned menacingly on David's desk and eyeballed him.

"It's the union, Mr. Truth," David explained. "If it was up to me, I'd be kicking ass and making the guys pick up tools. Unfortunately, it ain't up to me. There are rules, and no matter who you are, you have to follow them." David leaned back in his chair. "You should take a seat, Mr. Truth."

Justin put his game face on. He knew the two heavies in the corner were visual aids to let him know this was more than just about unions.

"I know you're from the corporate world, Mr. Truth. The stuff you guys do goes over my head. I'm just a simple builder who does what he's told. The union guys came down, and there were a few things they didn't like. Until they're fixed, nothing can happen. I'm working on it and should get things cleared up in a week or two. A month, tops."

"A month?" Justin exclaimed.

"I know, it's a pain in the ass, and an expensive one. I have to pay all the workers out there until it's sorted. Which means you have to pay them. I wouldn't worry about it though. Once it's sorted out, I'm sure there'll be no further delays. That is, if the unions stay happy. You wouldn't believe what can happen once they get a bee in their bonnet. I remember this job on the Lower East Side, man, it ran two years over. I think the guy who started it went belly-up, poor guy." David leaned forward tapping the desk with his index finger. "That isn't going to happen here, I can tell you that."

"That's good to know." Justin eyed David. He could smell the bullshit coming out of his mouth.

"I know a man like you needs things done," David carried on. "And a man like you knows that sometimes you need to order in some extra, let's say 'grease,' to make the wheels move faster."

"What are you getting at?" Justin asked, knowing full well this was a shakedown.

"You're a businessman, Mr. Truth. It's time to do business."

"And what if I don't think it's good business?"

The two enforcers crept closer and looked like a wall of muscle.

"Like all business decisions, there are ups and downs," David explained. "You're a smart man, you know the right thing to do. These guys will walk you to your car—talk to them about what you think is good and bad business. Either way, I can't see work starting again for another eight weeks."

"Two months?" Justin shouted.

"Give or take a week. As I said, it's out of my hands."

Justin fumed. He breathed deeply and relaxed his muscles. "And to put it in your hands?" he asked.

David's sausage fingers fished out a crumbled-up piece of paper from his top pocket and handed it to Justin. "I think if you dropped off what's on that paper to these guys here every Monday, I'll be able to order in that grease, and things would be back to normal in no time."

Justin studied the handwritten numerals. Too many zeros attached. With what he had given Misha, he couldn't spare a dime let alone what David was demanding.

"Leave it with me," he grinned. "I shall take care of it."

Justin exited the prefab and dialed Misha. Having a Russian gangster to call upon could very well have its benefits.

CHAPTER FORTY-FOUR

NICK WAS IN A CAB on the way to his next destination. It had taken a while to flag one down because not many drove around these types of suburban streets looking for fares. This suggested to Nick that the old man must have been organized and prebooked a ride. The boys had never seen him before, so given how often they went to the store, and the type of community they lived in, the old man must be an outsider.

Nick decided that this old man was guilty. The man must have placed the contaminated bottle in the fridge and bought another one to cover it. A clever man wouldn't shit in his own house, he would've traveled from out of state. Meaning there was only one place he would have caught his cab to after leaving the store—the airport.

As the cab drove Nick over the I-90, he thought about what he could call the old man.

"Hello, old chap, hurrah and what-what, tally ho," Nick said to himself. "I'm an old man who likes to buy me orange soda in the morning while wearing me trusty flat cap, a cabbie cap, a Gatsby cap, a scally cap, a duckbill paddy cap and, by George, what they call it in New Zealand: a cheese-cutter. I'm an old gentleman, but not very gentlemanly. Gatsby Cutter is me name, dastardly tricks is me game."

Nick got out at the airport; it was twenty-three minutes from the store. It was possible for Gatsby to have dropped off the bottle and return to the airport within an hour. It was a snug little window, especially if he'd also been responsible for some of the other bottles. He just needed to find out if Gatsby had come from the airport.

Nick ambled around the terminal. There was no shortage of cameras. Unfortunately, airport security wasn't going to welcome him with open arms and let him loose on their backed-up footage. He needed an in; he needed to do security a friendly favor first.

Within ten minutes of searching, a hoodie-wearing teen caught his attention. The teen was far more interested in travelers than the departure/arrival screens.

Nick watched the teen slip in between two businessmen and slip out with one of their laptops tucked under his hoodie. Then he tracked him as he *zigzagged* through the airport to a narrow corridor and passed through a janitor's door. He waited. A few minutes later, another young guy in a green hoodie ducked into the same room with something tucked under his sweatshirt. A team of thieves were operating in the airport. He just needed to find the right security guard whose back he could scratch.

Circling the airport a few times, Nick finally spotted her. She was a voluptuous, African American woman with a badge. She had kind eyes, but her pouted lips told you she was not one to be messed with. She smiled at people walking past her. He was sure she'd be the type to repay a favor.

"Hi!" Nick approached her with a smile.

"Morning, sir," she replied matter-of-factly, sipping her Starbucks coffee.

"Look, Rhonda," he said, after reading her badge. "Can I call you Rhonda?"

"How can I help you, sir?"

"Would you believe I want to help you?"

"Look, sir, we're very busy. I ain't got time for games. Move along and have a nice day, sir."

"Not a game at all. I'm a PI working a case." Nick paused as Rhonda pursed her lips and placed a hand on her hip. "One that has nothing to do with the airport. I'm just in transit, and while I was sitting over there I saw something."

"What did you see, sir?" Rhonda retained her formal tone.

"Have you guys had a problem with bags, laptops, and small, expensive items going missing? Poof into thin air?"

"You wouldn't believe it," her voice softened. "Smooth operators they are, like ghosts."

Nick smiled. "I think I may be able to help you find these ghosts. It's kind of my specialty."

Twenty minutes later, Rhonda led a bust on the gang in the janitor's room, and forty minutes later Nick sat next to Rhonda's good friend, Paul, who operated the state-of-the-art security system.

"Is everything from the cameras backed up and saved?" Nick looked at the screens.

"Yeah, onto hard drives as well as the server." Paul nodded.

"Can I look at the cameras on this day and time?" Nick handed Paul a creased piece of paper with the date of the SummerCrush incident and the time frame the boys had seen Mr. Gatsby Cutter. "Love to be able to see footage of about an hour either side, if that's OK?"

"Sure, it'll take me a few minutes to bring it up," Paul said.

"Thanks for this, Paul, you're a lifesaver."

"Rhonda said you were cool, so you're cool with me." Paul smiled. "Just keep it on the down-low, you dig?"

"Oh, I dig." Nick knew this was a massive favor. "Is there a camera that watches all arrivals and departures?"

"Yeah, camera twenty-five," Paul said. "It's on arrivals and might be a good place to start; everyone has to walk by it to get out. It's a wide shot, so you'll need good eyes."

"I'm told my eyes are my best quality," Nick joked, and Paul laughed in return.

Not long into the footage, Nick spun his chair in circles and jumped to his feet, arms raised in victory. He'd seen what he'd hoped for: a guy in his seventies, distant from those around him, traveling by himself, and not looking for anyone to greet him. He was exactly as the boys had described him, down to the flat cap.

"Is there a camera that can get closer to that man right there?"

"Let's have a look." Paul brought up some other angles that were of better quality.

"Paul, my friend, you're a legend. Is there also a camera that captures people checking in?"

"Numbers twelve to seventeen would do that."

"Can we have a look at footage one hour after this point? To see if this man checked back in?"

"Sure." Paul was now excited as well, picking up on Nick's natural enthusiasm. He scrolled through the camera footage with intense focus.

Nick slapped Paul on the shoulder excitedly. There he was, the same old man heading toward another flight. He'd had just enough time to complete the round trip while putting a dirty bottle in place.

"One last question—can I get a list of all the incoming and outgoing flights around these times?" Nick now sported a massive smile.

CHAPTER FORTY-FIVE

THE SMELL INSIDE THE PRISON hospital had a toxic iron tang to it. No amount of bleach would wash it away. Too many liters of blood had been spilled, sprayed, and squirted onto its surfaces over the decades.

Once a week, Ross visited the prison doctor for his anabolic steroids fix, to maintain his muscles and prevent his body from shutting down. It was a dangerous cocktail, but something he was willing to do to stay alive in this lethal environment.

The man in charge was Dr. Theodore Long. He was a tall man with a thin, wiry frame that could easily be mistaken for a runner's build. Except he wasn't a runner; he just didn't eat much. The meds he "prescribed" to himself killed his appetite.

He was overqualified for the role; his own addiction to painkillers was the only reason he took the job. If he had turned it down, he would have lost his license, his income, and his home. He wore a uniform made up of a blue shirt, black pants, and a light green medical coat. The prison supplied it, and he liked that. It was one less thing for him to worry about. He ran as tight a ship as he could, given all the internal politics involved. So many hands washed so many other hands that you were forced to go with the flow.

Dr. Long injected the last shot into Ross's backside and deposited the empty syringe into the "recycling bin," reserved to be sold later to some desperate prison druggie. Dr. Long had developed a friendship with Ross. The men were about the same age, and they bonded as two old men stuck in prison.

"Same time next week." Dr. Long smiled through his snow-white beard.

"Thanks, Doc." Ross smiled and pulled up his pants.

"How's the investigating going? Or whatever the warden calls it?"

"Not easy, is what I would call it."

"I've seen some messed up stuff during my time here. What that guy did. . . That's two destroyed bodies now that I've had to write a report for."

"I know, the young Mexican kid this morning was—"

"Let's not talk about it. Even staff are freaking out."

"I told the warden it would happen again." Ross sighed. "He didn't listen then, he won't listen now. A third body will happen."

"He's an idiot," Dr. Long said, shaking his head. "You've got to make him listen."

"Sure, walk on water at the same time?" Ross joked. Dr. Long laughed.

"He's an idiot," Dr. Long repeated. "You should know, Ezekiel will be allowed back into the general population in a day or two. You did a pretty good job on him. They managed to reattach his eyeball. He'll have sight, but probably only eighty percent of it."

"I didn't do anything," Ross replied.

"No, of course you didn't. How's the hand?"

Ross lifted his hand and Dr. Long inspected it.

"Did you get any more movement back since the last time?"

"No more."

"Without breaking it and setting it in a cast for months, there's not much I can do," Dr. Long sighed.

"How's Jimmy doing?" Ross changed the subject. "Is he up for a visit?"

"He was very lucky. If you hadn't been there to stop the bleeding, he would have died."

Ross dropped his head. If Jimmy hadn't stepped in when he did, it would've been himself with a gaping hole in his stomach, his blood coating the floor.

"Come, he would like a visit, I bet."

Dr. Long used his key card to open the doors to the infirmary, and Ross followed. Every bed was occupied; prison life often led to time between hospital sheets.

"Ross!" Jimmy yelled out.

"Quiet!" Dr. Long shot back.

"Sorry, Doc, just got a bit excited to see my roomie."

Ross extended his hand for a bro shake, his arm slightly bent. Jimmy smiled as he grabbed it, then winced in pain.

"Just keep it down," Dr. Long said. "On second thought, I don't really care, I'm going for a smoke. Just don't steal anything. I'll know if you do and you'll be on my shit list, then who's going to stitch you up? Not me."

The doctor left the two cellmates to catch up.

"Why did you do it?" Ross asked sincerely.

"Do what?"

"Take that shiv that was meant for me?"

"Shit, I don't knows. Somebody gots to have your back, man. I was gonna get stuck anyway just for being in your cell." Jimmy laughed and once again winced in pain.

"We're cool, Jimmy," Ross said. "Thank you."

CHAPTER FORTY-SIX

MAKING PEOPLE SCARED of him was a part of the job that Misha liked. The more people feared him, the easier it was to get them to do what he needed. Justin had phoned him about a construction site problem. The local mob was strong-arming him. Misha normally would have told Justin to sort out his own problems, but he was interested in becoming closer to Justin. He found him intriguing. He also knew a lot about the protection racket.

Nothing built in New York is ever completed on time, or within budget. Often, many wheels have to be greased just to switch the power on, and they keep clipping the ticket along the way.

Misha did his research and found that the foreman was connected to a Lower East Side Italian crew, the Rossi family. Misha always did his research, as capping the wrong person was never good for business. Many a turf war could be avoided if people did their homework properly. The Rossi family were small-time, well-respected, and had connections to a few of the bigger Italian gangs.

A few calls later, Misha knew what the Rossi family required to get the construction site up and running with no further interruptions. The actual protection money the mob required was a lot less than what the foreman had demanded from Justin. The foreman had been greedy with Justin, and Misha just needed to put him in his place.

Misha got out of his car and cracked his knuckles. He told Sergio and Demetri to wait for him with the package.

"Can I help you?" a burly man with a monobrow asked him as he strolled into the yard.

"Yes, you can," Misha replied with his Russian drawl. "I would very much like to talk to Mr. David. He is boss, no?"

"You got an appointment?"

"No. But he would very much like to talk to me. Now. If I come back, that is not good idea. You will not be a happy man. Maybe broken, bloody man. We have understanding?"

"You stay here, I'll get him," the man said, sounding tough.

"Here is good. You be fast. I only stay here for few minutes."

While Mr. Monobrow went for his boss, Misha inspected an abandoned digger. He had used one similar once to make a problem disappear.

"What do you want?" a gravelly voice boomed at Misha. It was David, charging at him like a rhinoceros on heat. Misha sized up the solid man in his double denim.

"Hello. Come have chat with me," Misha said.

"I don't have time for this shit. Whoever sent you here has no idea what they're dealing with. This interruption is going to cost another week, and I'm thinking the union will be holding a few meetings, too, which again means more expenses."

"No. I think you is wrong," Misha corrected him.

"Fuck off, you Russian fuck! One call and it will cost your boss hundreds of thousands of American dollars. Greenbacks, pinko, not Russian rubles or bags of potatoes."

"Mr. David. All I want is us to have talk. You can huff. You can puff, but before you go, I want to tell you about my neighbor from home country." Misha waved him to follow. "Come, us walk and talk. Bring your friends, too. I not mind about company. As you see it is just me and four of you.

"When I was boy, neighbor of mine had bird. And bird it sing—and how it sing. People they come from all over village to listen. The notes sound like beautiful masterpiece. I remember, I sit in my little room and hear bird. It make me forget how starving I was. How cold I was.

"People want to buy bird. They offer lots of money. More money than as boy I knew could be. My neighbor, he not want their money. He want his bird. No amount of money could get another like it. One man, who was businessman like you, he want bird for daughter. He offered to buy it. 'No,' he was told. He threatened the man with violence. He was told no again. Now this man, did not like being told no. It sent message to everyone that you could say no to him. He decided he would take bird. From my room, I watch as he enter house, men argue. I made way to window like little cat with big eyes, I watch.

"The businessman he pull a knife, he stab my neighbor in stomach. Blood start to pour out, it was blood everywhere. Neighbor, he knew he was going to die. He whistle for bird, and it flew to him as he trained it to. He hold bird, the thing he love most in world, and bite its head off. Then he die with his dead bird. Now the businessman had no bird. All he had was dead man at feet. Bigger problem than no bird."

"I have no idea what this has to do with me?" David was confused. Misha whistled and Demetri walked onto the building site, holding hands with David's youngest daughter. David's eyes went wild. Misha grabbed David and clamped one of his arms behind him.

"Daughter is like bird. You have decision."

"Don't you…"

"Mr. David, you have job here, you make building happen smooth. I will give you money you need to pay the Rossis. Just them. None for you. You can tell them all about me. They know who I am. We have talked. As long as they get their money, you are just little fish to them. They not care what I do to you. We have understanding? Or shall I cut out little girl's eye for you? A reminder, every time you look at her, that you not listen to me, and was silly man."

"Don't hurt my girl." David sobbed in Misha's arms.

"Good. We have understanding. I is happy."

CHAPTER FORTY-SEVEN

ONE OF PETER'S PERSONAL assistants phoned Justin, informing him that Peter was expecting him for dinner at 7:30 p.m. and to arrive on time. She didn't ask if Justin was already busy—the world revolved around Peter Gordon, after all. As soon as she hung up, Justin told Debbie to postpone his scheduled meetings for the rest of the day.

Peter had never invited him to a personal dinner before. This was a big step forward in their relationship. He wanted to wear something extra special tonight to mark the moment. He was having a waistcoat and pants tailored to go with the new dinner jacket he'd won at a charity auction—the original jacket Brad Pitt had worn in *Ocean's Eleven*. He'd had it expanded to fit his stockier frame and felt great joy from knowing that he was more muscular than Brad Pitt.

At the tailor's, Justin looked at himself in the mirror and felt impressed. The tailor was worth every dollar he charged. He had an exclusive list of clients, and Justin made sure he stayed on it. The tailor needed to make some slight adjustments and told him the suit would be ready within two hours.

Next, Justin stopped at a trendy barbershop on Fifth Avenue to indulge in a facial and trim, while two pairs of Korean women treated him to a manicure and pedicure. Then he ventured up the back stairs for a deep-tissue Thai massage to loosen his tight muscles.

Two hours later, all dressed up and ready to go, Justin checked his watch. There was time for a drink before dinner.

The Blue Aqua Room was the perfect place: a popular hangout for talent agents, with plenty of young models desperate to be discovered. Justin strutted in, cased the joint, and took a seat in a booth by the panoramic windows overlooking the city. A cast of regulars soon joined him. Justin ordered three bottles of Cristal. His entourage filled their glasses while making sure the conversation revolved around how rich and powerful Justin was.

When it was time, Justin's personal driver, Dan the former Cab-Man, drove him to the Buffalo Room, showering him with compliments all the way. They pulled up to the entrance and Justin made a grand entrance through the double doors right on time.

"Justin," a voice called out.

Justin turned his head to its owner, Gilbert. The man was seated in an armchair and stood. He held up an envelope. "For you," he said.

Justin took the envelope and opened it. Inside was an embossed card.

JUSTIN, SOMETHING POPPED UP. I TRUST EVERYTHING
IS GOING TO PLAN. TALK SOON.
PETER

Justin slipped the note back into the envelope and slotted it inside his jacket pocket. He gave the Gilbert a charming smile. Inside he was a raging volcano; he loathed being stood up. He started feeling familiar pins and needles running up the back of his head. He rubbed the scar near his temple.

Back in the Audi, he told Dan to do a loop of the city. Dan knew where he needed to go—a rough part of town where groups of destitute individuals converged. The overpass created a natural barrier from security cameras and good Samaritans. A few hobos knew to hide when this particular car slowly rolled by.

Justin returned to the Blue Aqua Room forty-five minutes later. His fists were sore from repeatedly striking a vagabond in the face, treating his emaciated body like a personal punching bag. He ordered more Cristal as he surveyed the room for a titillating female to take out the rest of his aggression on.

CHAPTER FORTY-EIGHT

MONTANA SAT IN HER CAR. For the past hour, she'd been in the Phizz parking building, the car turned off, no radio, just sitting. She couldn't stop her mind from replaying what she'd done in her apartment. She hated that she'd put herself through that. If Steve hadn't found her and helped cover up her suicide attempt, everyone would know. Why did she do it? No. She didn't do it, Justin did it.

"Fuck you!" She yelled.

She couldn't see a way to get away from him.

"I'll cut your fucking cock off!"

There was a way.

"I'll fucking kill you!" She slammed her fists down on the steering wheel. Fucking kill him. Was that the only way out? Killing Justin would solve everything. A dead Justin would be a good Justin.

Montana pushed Justin out of her mind and got out of her car. It was time to face work. She felt nauseous entering through the front doors of Phizz International. She had been so caught up with Justin, she'd forgotten all about Kenny, creepy Kenny. Her eyes darted about searching for any signs of him. After her provocative interlude inside his office on that late Sunday night, he had become like a dog in heat, eye-humping her every time he spotted her. It was increasingly difficult to fend him off, yet she had to keep him close. A lovesick puppy was less likely to smell the dirt Justin told her to spread.

Montana made it into her office without being accosted, locked it, and breathed a sigh of relief. She removed the flash drive from her bag, placed in on her desk, and stared at it. All the information she had on the working relationship between Phizz International and Sterling In-corporated was right there. Justin had told her to follow up on a few leads, which she had done. From what she could gather, nothing they were doing was illegal. It wasn't a very profitable arrangement for the company, but it was worth it when it came to distribution and goodwill.

Her phone buzzed. The caller ID showed Kenny. Her hand nervously hovered above the handset. Finally, she forced herself to take the call.

"Hi, Kenny," Montana chirped.

"Montana, always a pleasure to hear your voice. Can you join me in my office?"

"Later this afternoon?"

"Umm, now would be good. I have Terrence Barclay here and he would like to meet you."

"Sure, I'll be right there." Montana hung up the phone. Her mind raced. Why would Terrence want to see her? She'd met him once during her interview process. Had she left anything behind when she'd copied the folders? Had they traced it back to her? Well, if they had, he wouldn't be talking to her—security would be escorting her from the building. Whatever they wanted to see her about, she'd have to think on her feet.

At the restroom on the way, Montana checked her makeup and practiced her game-face ritual. "I can do this and I will do it well," she repeated, facing the mirror. She'd learned this method in a self-help book a few years ago. She held her own gaze in the mirror and repeated the statement to herself until she believed it.

She knocked on Kenny's door and entered the office. Kenny was sitting on his couch. Terrance had perched himself on a single chair by the city-facing windows. Terrance had a '50s quiff of gray hair and an olive complexion. When he saw Montana, he got to his feet and flashed his pearly whites.

"Montana, great to meet you again." Terrence motioned for her to take a seat on the couch next to Kenny. "Kenny was just filling me in on some of the changes you've made, and it sounds like all of them are doing great."

"Thank you," Montana replied, sitting on the couch with her hands folded on her knees, making sure to keep a comfortable distance between herself and Kenny.

"I would just like to remind you how great it is to have you here," Terrance said. He cut to the chase. "You worked at Soda-Cola for a while and I was hoping to pick your brain."

"Sure, I can tell you what I know."

"I'm hoping what we talk about will stay in this room?"

"Absolutely." Montana nodded.

Terrence smiled again. "We have a good relationship with a company that services the military canteens stationed overseas. They serve food and quality Phizz products to the hardworking men and women of our armed forces. When you're in a hostile environment like that, a cool can of Phizz works wonders for your morale. It's not a huge moneymaker, but it's not about the money; it's about us helping those who are defending our freedom.

"Now, here's where you come in," Terrance continued. "The contract is coming up soon, and we've heard through the grapevine that Soda-Cola is working with another company to secure the contract. Normally we wouldn't be worried, as it's such a small part of our business. But profit is profit, and it's a component of our business that we'd very much like to keep. Is there anything you can tell us about Justin Truth? From what we hear, he sounds like a real little bastard."

Montana giggled. "I'm sorry, I think you'd find that he's a rather large bastard." All three of them laughed.

"What can you tell us?" Kenny chimed in.

"Justin makes lots of noise," Montana said. "Knowing him, this will just be one of a thousand things he'll have on the table. You guys have nothing to worry about. He talks a big game. He's consumed with competition. He probably just has one of his interns working on this. As you can see from my portfolio here at Phizz and the success I've had with my campaigns, I can beat him. If you'd like me to help, I'm more than happy to on my own time."

"No, that's all good, Montana," Terrance replied. "We just wanted to see what we might be up against."

"He's an ego-driven idiot," Montana continued. "That's what you're up against. He's smart, but his unrestrained sense of self-worth will be his downfall. He thinks everyone else is stupid. Work smart and you'll beat him."

"I told you she was a clever lady," Kenny said, placing his hand on top of Montana's. Her skin crawled. She quickly got up.

"Thank you, gentlemen. If you have any further questions, I'll be just down the hall." Montana exited the room, feeling their eyes on her body. Her fingers trembled, and she ached to go back in and bash their chauvinistic skulls in.

CHAPTER FORTY-NINE

NICK TOSSED A CAN of OrangeFizz between his hands, flipped it into the air, and caught it with the back of one hand, then spun it and snatched it behind his back with the other. A drink he'd never thought about; now it seemed to be everywhere. Its producers were the only ones to benefit from this whole SummerCrush mess, and not only did they benefit, they came out stronger. Nick tossed the can over his shoulder, kicked it with the heel of his shoe, and sent it flying onto the motel bed with a collection of OrangeFizz merchandise.

A new addition to his Wall of Mystery was an A1-sized map of the United States. A pin indicated where every contaminated bottle of SummerCrush had been reported. With the help of Rhonda, Nick had discovered that Gatsby's next destination was another pin on the map—Atlanta. Not only that, but he started his tour of terror from New York.

He traced his finger along the string on the map. Using New York as a starting point, he could plot a loop all the way back to New York. It was definitely possible for one person to hit all the places within a twenty-hour window.

His next question: Who was this person and why had they targeted SummerCrush? Surely it couldn't have been just to sell more orange drinks? People could have died from this… No, there had to be something more to it. The inner voice Nick had learned to trust told him that everything was connected, and all signs pointed to OrangeFizz. He had to go to New York and try to pick up Gatsby's trail there.

Nick's cell phone rang. It confused him at first, as he didn't give his number out very often. When it rang, it was important.

"Hello?" he answered.

"Is this Nick I'm speaking to?" a voice asked with careful diction.

"Yes, it is."

"It's Dr. Adrian here. I'm afraid I have bad news. Your father won't be with us much longer. If you wanted to say your goodbyes, you need to do so as soon as possible."

Three hours later, Nick was sitting on a plane heading toward the place he said he'd never visit again, to see a man he'd promised he'd never forgive.

CHAPTER FIFTY

MISHA DROPPED HIS CELL PHONE on the marbled kitchen bench. His life was hanging in the balance. It wasn't the first time he'd been in danger. It was part of the life he chose to live. He wasn't one to show fear or stress to outsiders; rather, fear was a dark beast he held inside himself that he battled alone.

Stark naked, Misha pulled out a bottle of vodka from the freezer and poured himself a tall glass, straight. Sometimes he yearned for the days when he was just muscle, breaking bones, crushing limbs, and busting faces. All he had to do in those days was think with his fists.

He knew he was too smart to use only his muscles, though. And besides, he liked to make his own decisions. After three years in America, the opportunity had presented itself for him to run the Bratva arm in New York. He'd grabbed it with both hands. He was going to grow his area and make a name for himself. Life had been good when he started, and success followed on top of success.

When the global financial crisis hit, it affected everyone, gangs included. Everyone fought harder to earn an extra dollar. Gangs splintered and invaded territories they normally wouldn't. Misha spent more time and money defending what he had instead of expanding it. As soon as he'd stop one gang, another smaller crew would knock on his door.

The vodka slid smoothly down Misha's throat, and he refilled the glass. He calmly paced the kitchen, feeling cool tiles beneath his feet. At a flick of a switch he could heat the tiles, but he never did. He liked the cold under his feet.

Over the past year, Drug Enforcement Administration Agent Rudy Jenson had taken a vested interest in Misha. He regularly dropped by Misha's import business to talk and poke him like a bear for his reaction. Rudy knew he was untouchable. If Misha touched a DEA agent, the entire department would be down on him like a ton of bricks.

Misha found it harder to trust anyone around him. There was a rat in his ranks, tipping Rudy off. Misha's shipments were busted way too frequently. What's more, Sultan, one of Misha's best earners, had gone freelance and set up his own crew. Misha considered this disrespectful and was now at war with Sultan over it. Many men had already died on both sides without any resolution in sight.

The longer Sultan remained alive, the more Misha lost face. He was sure this was why Yury had tried to pull his stunt with the meth.

Misha had just received a phone call from his superior in Russia asking why he wasn't providing as much money as he should be. Was he strong enough to run New York? Did they need to come over and check it out? New York was a strategic strong point, and if he couldn't do the job, there were others eager to take his place.

Misha sensed blood in the water, and the sharks were circling. Once the new massive shipment of drugs arrived and he was able to unload them, he'd have money to get Russia off his back, and more than enough to sort out his situation with Sultan.

"Baby!" a sweet South Carolina accent called out. "I need that big Russian cock of yours to play with." Misha chugged the last of his vodka and returned to his bedroom to pleasure his ex-*Playboy*-Playmate girlfriend.

CHAPTER FIFTY-ONE

STEVE OPENED HIS front door and once again she took his breath away. She only wore a tracksuit and a loose bun, without an ounce of makeup. It didn't matter what she wore; she always looked perfect to him.

"Come in," Steve welcomed her. Montana hid a few stray hairs behind one of her ears and entered. A few steps in, she threw her arms around him and squeezed him tight.

"I missed you so much," she sighed.

"And I missed you, too."

Montana let go and glanced around his lounge. "You cleaned up," she said. "For me?"

"For me, I think," Steve replied wryly. "I let my life fall apart for way too long, it's time to rebuild it now. Silver is helping me find what I need to find and lose what I need to lose."

"Silver?" Montana raised her eyebrow.

"He's this amazing man I've met. He runs a small church of sorts downtown. It's hard to describe. They show people ways to connect with their inner self instead of living how society tells them to. They help you grow into the 'real you' by encouraging you to let go of misconceptions."

"A cult?"

"No." Steve laughed. "It's a collection of ideals from different religions. Silver blends them and extracts only the good ideals, none of the bad ones. He encourages people to be the way they were born to be, without any judgment."

Montana smiled. "You look better, so it's obviously working for you. Just make sure you keep your eyes open. Places like that take advantage of people when they're—"

"When they're down and out, and drug addicts or losers?" Steve finished her sentence.

"That's not what I…"

"Montana, relax." Steve smiled and opened his arms to her. "Do I look like someone who would follow a Manson wannabe?"

"No… Sorry." Montana seemed to have something difficult to talk about.

"Coffee?" Steve offered.

"Yes, that would be lovely."

"I got these coffee bags," Steve said as he walked into the kitchen. "They're like tea bags but with coffee."

"Sounds good."

"So, we're going to kill Justin," Steve said offhandedly. Montana had hoped to hear those words, but when Steve said them out loud, she felt shivers run down her spine.

"I want to. No, I have to." Her voice was fraught with desperation. "It feels like the only thing we can do."

Steve searched the fridge for milk, opened a bottle and gave it a sniff. "How?" he asked.

"I think we should hire someone."

"Like, google 'Killer for Hire'?"

Montana smiled. Steve's humor was returning and he could tell she was glad. "I think I know someone I can ask," Montana said, tapping the bench in time to a popular Bruno Mars song.

"Milk and one sugar?" Steve asked.

"Just black for me, I like it strong."

"OK, I'll have your sugar," Steve said with a hint of a smile. "So you know someone?"

For the next two hours, Steve and Montana chatted about different ways to kill Justin. It felt good, really good.

ROSS FELT EYES TRACKING his every movement. Ezekiel would be released back into the general population today. Word had it he'd be out for revenge, and no doubt it would be bloody and brutal.

The West Spiders hadn't exacted retribution on Ross after the showdown in the shower. There was a rumor that the head of the West Spiders, Bizzy, was happy Ezekiel had lost so shamefully. In fact, all of Ezekiel's supporters turned their back on him the minute they saw him dragged out of the shower, unconscious.

The murmurs were that Ezekiel still wanted to be top Spider, but to do that, he would have to win back those lost supporters. Ross reasoned that the most effective way to win them back would be to do what he failed to do the first time—kill the dirty cop.

Ross didn't see Bizzy as a man who'd let someone take power from him. Bizzy would need the inmates to see him tame Ezekiel and put him back in the pecking order. He could strip Ezekiel of his membership and cast him out to fend for himself. Without the West Spiders, all the other gangs would want to make the great Ezekiel their bitch.

The way Ross saw it, Ezekiel had two options: fall back in line or fight for leadership. Ezekiel wouldn't be the go-quietly type.

Wars are often won before a single shot is fired. Great generals know where and when to fight, when to take the high ground, when to flank, and when to make a stand. The last time Ross and Ezekiel fought, Ross had predicted the shower as the place where Ezekiel would attack him, the watery battlefield. It had worked then, but it wouldn't work again. No doubt Ezekiel would have learned from that.

Thanks to the heads-up from Dr. Long about Ezekiel's imminent release, Ross visualized all the potential places he could get jumped: his cell, the library, the lunch room, and the yard. Ross had a defense strategy for each location and knew which weapons were available to use. In his experienced hands, everything could be a weapon.

Ross made his way to the yard on full alert for signs of Ezekiel. Inside the workout area, he hid weights where they might come in handy. He put a dumbbell against the mesh fence; in case Ezekiel dropped him with a hard body shot, he could come up swinging with it as a knuckle-duster. He made sure to balance a heavy plate on a rusty bench with one edge peeking over the side to flip upward and send hurtling at an attacker, if need be. He filled his pocket with crushed-up chalk to throw in Ezekiel's eyes at close range.

Finally, as Ross anticipated, Ezekiel made his move. While Ross racked a couple of plates onto his bar, Ezekiel charged toward him, heaving like a Brahma bull and sending dirt flying into the air with each stomp. Men tumbled out of his way, and spectators swept along behind him. Ross kicked off his shoe to access the shiv hidden in its sole. He picked up a hand weight, gripping it tight. His knuckles grew white.

Ezekiel slowed his pace and flexed his muscles, his chest rising and falling with every deep breath. Neither man took their eyes off the other. The gathering crowd remained silent as Ezekiel gradually closed the distance between them. Ross stood tall, holding his ground.

Ezekiel made the first move, extending his hand.

"I have no heat with you, pig," Ezekiel grunted. This was a public display of an apology. Ross cautiously raised his hand and grabbed Ezekiel's. The handshake was solid. Neither of them asserted dominance. It was merely a sign of respect—and an acknowledgement that there wouldn't be any violence today. They dropped their hands and smiled.

"By the looks of you, you need a workout partner," Ezekiel said, pumping his pecs.

"You know someone who can keep up?" Ross asked.

"No, I know someone who will kick your ass until you're in shape like this." Ezekiel raised his arm to flaunt his massive bicep.

Again, both men smiled, and for now, they weren't going to kill each other.

CHAPTER FIFTY-THREE

MONEY IN, MONEY OUT. Red and black.

Edward Chandler was an accountant by nature; everything needed to balance. He controlled the finances at Soda-Cola and, under his watch, the company stayed in the black.

He didn't work in the present, as he believed it was too late. Instead, he planned a year ahead, watching and setting market trends, and making plans for potential situations. This meant that when the global financial crisis hit, he was ready, as he had Soda-Cola streamlined for the dip in the economy.

In Edward's mind, people in a company were just like numbers to be moved around. Lose some here, cut a bonus there, and bring in younger, hungrier individuals to remove older, more expensive workers. Even so, Edward cared about people. He had to make tough decisions to ensure the survival of the company. But if the company was in good shape, so were the employees.

Eight years ago, Edward was voted head of the board, a job he took very seriously. And like everyone else on the board, he'd voted for Justin to replace Carlton. He'd weighed up the pros and cons. On paper, it was the best choice, and he was happy with the decision.

However, since Justin had taken over, cracks had started to appear and whispers about Justin's unorthodox leadership style began making the rounds. For one, he'd replaced the entire management team with the Young Lions, whose testosterone-driven meetings were pushing the boundaries of good business etiquette.

Edward wasn't impressed when Justin dismissed his concerns and instead went on a tangent about record profits and negotiating with ter- rorists. From what Edward had heard, Justin still hadn't addressed the situation with the Young Lions, and they were still running roughshod over everyone. The Young Lions were well on their way to becoming an elitist boys' club, and that wasn't something Edward had signed up for.

Jade, Edward's daughter, had started with Soda-Cola after graduating from college four years ago. She wasn't one to gossip, but she would tell her father about whatever she saw or heard about Justin or the Young Lions. Like her father, Jade saw things in black and white, good and bad, right and wrong.

Edward recalled one incident involving the Young Lions that had nearly made her quit. She'd walked in on a pair of seminaked strippers making out on an office desk for the enjoyment of the men in the room. She made an official complaint through the proper channels. To her disgust, HR did nothing about the incident. Edward believed his daughter and was disappointed with himself for originally backing Justin and offering him the CEO position.

Edward knew it wouldn't be wise to bring up his concerns about Justin at a board meeting. Justin was a master at manipulating people and telling them what they wanted to hear. His fellow board members would be more forgiving of Justin than he was. They loved the increased bonuses.

Edward opened a spreadsheet he'd been working on for the past few months. The thing about numbers was they never lied; they always added up. But to Edward, Justin didn't add up, and for the first time in his years with Soda-Cola, neither did the numbers.

CHAPTER FIFTY-FOUR

THE FRONT DOOR SQUEAKED open exactly the same way it had since Nick's childhood, grinding on its rusty hinges.

The living room smelled of spoiled food. Crap lay around everywhere. The aged couch had just enough room left for one person; laundry, magazines, and dirty plates covered the rest.

As Nick pulled open the heavy, cream-colored curtains to let the sun in, particles of dust spun in the light.

Nick's father was staunchly religious, and like most religious people Nick knew, he only believed in the principles he wanted to believe in. For a start, it was fairly obvious that he didn't equate cleanliness to godliness. From where he stood, Nick could see the kitchen through a serving window, and the movement of flies indicated that the stench in there was far worse than in the living room. He felt great satisfaction knowing how much filth his father spent his miserable days in.

Nick had very few happy memories of growing up in this simple, two-bedroom house. He delicately touched the hole in the wall next to the front door, a constant reminder of his mother. One day when Nick was five, his father rushed home and caught his wife in bed with her younger lover. He beat them both mercilessly and threw them out onto the front lawn, yelling that the devil had taken over her body, and that he'd kill her if she ever showed her face again. She never did.

Afterward, his father slammed the door, punched the hole in the wall, and warned Nick that if he ever disgraced the house like his "she-devil" mother had, he would suffer an even worse fate.

Nick wished his mother had taken him with her. She'd gotten her freedom, while he had to live with the consequences of her mistakes. Anytime Nick spoke out of turn, or did anything his father considered blasphemous, his father beat him and told him that it was for his own good. He blamed his wife, for it was her who'd made Nick dirty in the eyes of God.

Footsteps approaching from the bedroom startled Nick, and he yanked his hand away from the hole. The intruder's stomach preceded him, followed by the rest of his body. The portly priest opened his arms wide and closed in on Nick.

"I'm so glad you could make it," Father Wayne said, squeezing Nick tight.

Nick detested many things about Father Wayne, and one of them was his inability to keep his personal distance. Nick pushed away and meandered around the room, a safe distance from the man's foul breath.

"I thought my father had a cleaner once a week," Nick inquired.

"Oh, he did, a member of the congregation was doing a spectacular job for him. She dropped in twice a day, made him the most marvelous meals too. But you know what your father can be like. He took a dislike to her. Expressed in certain words that he wanted to do everything himself and told her to not return. I tried convincing him to see the errors of his way, and to welcome her back. He declined, and was very determined about his decision."

"So, you could talk him into donating this house to the church when he dies, but not into someone stopping it from turning into a pigsty?" Nick shook his head in disbelief.

"It was your father who approached me about donating the house," Father Wayne explained. "Your father is a truly godly man and wants to bequeath what he can to the church so that others will benefit from his generosity. We all have free will. He can change his mind, Nick. If you want the house, you can converse with him about it, if it's not too late."

"I don't want this house, and I don't want anything to do with this town," Nick said dismissively. "Now if you'll excuse me, I want to go and see him."

"May God be with you, my son," Father Wayne said solemnly as he removed a handkerchief from his pocket and wiped his brow.

Nick pushed open the door to his father's room where the smell of dying flesh hung in the air like a foul fog. His father's body was riddled with cancer, and a machine next to his bed had a plastic lung that pushed air into his body to help him breathe. The device was loud and consistent, like an industrial printing press.

"I'm here," Nick said, hoping his father could hear him. "To make things clear. I didn't come to see you. I came to watch you die."

CHAPTER FIFTY-FIVE

IT FELT GREAT TO WAKE UP and have purpose. Steve opened his eyes and smiled as the sun peered in through his window. He'd left the curtains open so the sun could act as his natural alarm clock.

His bed now had fresh sheets; his room was vacuumed, dusted, and spotlessly cleaned. Books were on the bookshelf, clothes in the drawers, and shoes in the closet. He swung his feet onto the floor without fear of standing on a needle or a piece of trash.

Walking into the living room, the air didn't greet him with the smell of stale body odor. He didn't have to worry that he'd left the front door wide open or that he'd find some random junkie asleep in a corner. His couch was no longer hidden under a blanket of fast-food wrappers.

Steve jumped in the shower and lathered his body with scented soap, then massaged both shampoo and conditioner into his scalp. He had forgotten how good it felt to be clean. He was back to having two showers a day.

Wiping the steam carefully off the broken mirror, Steve looked at himself in the remaining shards, seeing himself clearly for the first time. He did like the beard, and he liked the new him. It could do with a trim though, to make it more presentable.

Small clumps of hair landed in the sink, whisked away by running water. Steve smiled at himself in the mirror. He enjoyed the face that smiled back. He'd come a long way during the last few weeks, and today would mark the next step. He removed the top of the toilet tank and pulled out the little plastic bag of heroin, spoon, and syringe he'd stashed there—just in case.

His fingers trembled anxiously as he opened the bag. The temptation to use the last of the heroin was enticing. Thousands of tiny voices inside his head yelled at him, pleaded with him, told him that one last hit would be fine. One more wouldn't make a difference. It would be a waste not to use it.

He flushed it and waved as it circled the bowl. No, he wouldn't need that shit anymore, and that was his choice.

Steve opened the closet; the smell of new clothes greeted him. He'd gone shopping with Montana the day before. He slipped on a pair of blue jeans, a crisp white T-shirt, and casual Converse sneakers. He felt better than he had in months.

He headed into the kitchen and opened the fridge to a selection of healthy foods and juices. He made himself a salmon bagel with cream cheese. Then he ate it, cleaned up, and left the kitchen gleaming.

He locked his front door and set off to the church. He had some ideas he wanted to run past Silver. Steve knew the church had a lot of potential, someone just needed to make it happen—someone like him, who wasn't a drug addict.

CHAPTER FIFTY-SIX

RUDY JENSON LOVED what he did, but some would say he had a death wish. He liked to put himself in the thick of the action. If there was going to be a fight with a drug dealer, he'd try to be there, and most of the time he even provoked the confrontation. Rudy detested drugs and anyone who had anything to do with them, whether it was the manufacturer, the seller, the pusher, or the user. Anyone who was part of the drug problem was his problem.

When he was in college, Rudy's youngest sister attended a party where she was pressured into taking some pills. "Harmless pills," they'd told her. She reacted badly to the chemicals. Her body overheated, and her heart abruptly stopped. She died before paramedics could help her. Another statistic in the war on drugs.

This was the key driver for Rudy to turn his back on football fame and do everything he could to become one of the guys who'd never let this happen to anyone else's family. His friends tried to talk him out of it. He'd just been selected all-American, and pro scouts were interested in recruiting him. But football didn't matter to him anymore.

With this newly found drive, Rudy's C grades shot up to straight A's. He joined campus security and volunteered at any opportunity to gain law enforcement experience. Once a star on the field busting tackles, now he busted former teammates for drug infractions.

From college he was accepted into Basic Agent Training at the DEA and graduated in the top 3 percent with honors. His request for more military training positioned him in the Cardamom Mountains in Cambodia to hunt down MDMA manufacturers. After three years in the trenches, his life took a turn when a bullet exploded his calf muscle. After a year of painful rehabilitation, he could still walk, but with a nasty limp.

Rudy transferred to the New York office. He wanted to remain in the thick of the action, and New York was the place to make his mark. And so he did. In his first year, he'd made more busts than any other agent before him.

Gangs regularly threatened his life, but they wouldn't follow through out of fear from reprisal. DEA agents were a tight-knit unit—touch one and the rest would go to war. A small number of agents had membership with an unsanctioned team called the Black Eagles. If any agent was shot or killed, they'd swoop into action, hitting the guilty without mercy, and leaving a trail of bodies as a warning to everyone else. The government denied that the group existed, but Rudy knew the squad well. He'd been a founding member.

Rudy was excited as he exited his car outside the fish depot. He was going to drop in and see how Misha Ivanov was doing. Rudy was in the mood to dance, and Misha was one of his preferred partners. He didn't hide behind his badge when he was dealing with scum like Misha. He did it face to face with the intention of taking away any power these types thought they had.

Rudy slowly meandered through the warehouse, loving the dirty looks the workers shot him.

"Misha… Misha… Misha," Rudy called out, pushing through the plastic flaps into the service hangar. "Can you hook me up with some drugs, please? Whatever you have in stock would be great."

"We only have fish," Misha replied, shooing away the men he'd been standing with. "You know that is all I do."

"Fish, drugs, drugs, fish. I can see how you get confused." Rudy kicked over a bucket of ice and fish, sending the contents skidding along the chilled concrete floor.

"I am honest businessman. No donuts here, officer."

"Shame, I could go for a nice cocaine-glazed one about now. Anyway, I was hoping to talk to a friend of yours. Is Yury around?"

"I have not seen him for few weeks."

"No one has. Maybe he's on vacation."

"Maybe," Misha said.

"He wouldn't be sleeping with the fishes now, would he?" Rudy kicked a fish, sending the scaly sucker sliding along the floor.

"He like to fuck ugly, maybe he like to have sex with fish."

"You crazy Russian," Rudy grinned as he lifted his knee and slapped his thigh. "And people say you don't have a sense of humor. Misha, you are wasted here. You should be up on the stage."

"You are welcome."

"Well, if you happen to see Yury, can you tell him I wanted to say 'Hi.' And some guys he knows also want to say hi. Some black street punks dealing meth. No idea why they would know Yury, if he is just a fisherman like you."

"Maybe they like fish, everyone like fish. Even pig like fish, I'm sure."

"I'll keep looking," Rudy replied. "I'm sure he'll float to the surface any day now."

CHAPTER FIFTY-SEVEN

MONTANA WAS ALL TOO familiar with the steps leading down to Mazed. She knew to avoid the third-to-last step if she didn't want to slip. But today she was only coming back to explore the prospect of having Justin killed. She pushed open the door and braced herself for the flood of bad memories. The heavy base of a '70s disco song greeted her like an old friend—an unwanted one at that. Montana steadied herself in the doorway.

Another unwanted memory grabbed her by the wrist. "Where you been, baby?" the bouncer asked with a lisp, the large gap between his missing front teeth expelling extra air.

"Under a few rocks," she replied.

"I have a hot rock cock all ready when you are, baby."

"I better get drunk as quickly as I can then," she replied matter-of-factly.

He laughed. She laughed back. Then she slipped into the bar area. Her eyes bounced around the place searching for Maggot. He'd bragged about "taking out" people a few times. He was a regular at Mazed, so he shouldn't be too hard to find.

Her eyes adjusted to the light, and once again she was shocked to see so many of the patrons she knew. Their faces and stories flashed through her mind, causing bile to rise into her throat. The more she started to feel like her old self again, the more her recent actions sickened her.

The unwanted friend she was looking for slid up behind her. "Moaning Montana, what brings you and me together?" Maggot asked, his hands pulling her hips back toward him. She pushed herself off him and walked to one of the leather booths in a corner. Maggot followed and dropped himself next to her.

"I have a problem that I think you can help me with," she said.

"Been dreaming of my cock, have you?" Maggot replied as he grabbed her hand and forced it to feel his junk.

"Baby, your cock is the best I've ever had between my legs, but now I need your other talents… I want a man dead!"

"You want me to beat up an old boyfriend?"

"No, I want a fucker killed. You said you were a killer."

"Now this isn't asking to borrow a cup of sugar." Maggot sat up straight.

"That's good, because I got as much sugar as I need."

"This ain't for you, girly, now why don't you get us a few drinks, and I'll pretend you never asked."

"Fuck off," Montana said coolly, glaring at him without blinking.

"What? You think you all that, bitch?"

"You heard me. Are you the man you boasted to be, or are you all talk like the rest of the sick fucks in this place? You don't have the balls for shit, do you?"

Maggot grabbed her by the throat. "Now you listen fucking closely, girly," he growled. "Do not fuck with me. I'm not one of your suit-wearing panty-sniffers. You play with fire and I'll burn your face off!"

"I want a killer. I have money," Montana hissed, not backing down or showing any pain. Maggot released his grip. Montana gasped for air.

He rubbed his chin, staring at her. "Stay. Don't move," he ordered, sliding out of the booth like a serpent chasing its dinner.

Montana ordered a white Russian, hoping the milk would help soothe her throat. Three drinks later, the sore throat was gone—either that or the vodka had kicked in. She wondered, if Maggot didn't return, whether searching Google would actually offer up a hit man. She'd heard about the Dark Web, the murky underground of the internet. That was an option.

Maggot did return and hunkered down across from her. He held a torn-off piece of paper between his thumb and forefinger.

"Text 'New York Dreaming' to this number, and in the next forty-eight hours they'll message you back. Do what they say, go where they say."

"Thanks," Montana said, snatching the paper.

"Don't thank me. You have no idea what you're getting yourself into."

"Oh I do, and I can't wait," she shot back in such a cold voice she was sure Maggot believed her.

THE PRISON LIBRARY WAS L-shaped, with a single keylock door granting access. Shelves of books ran along each wall, while reading desks and freestanding shelves filled the rest of the space. Two smaller rooms were attached in the center—one for the librarian, the other acting as a storage closet where decades of broken books, shelves, and Bell Island memories had been dumped. The warden had given Ross permission to use the cramped storage room for his growing investigation. O'Grady had helped him move boxes around so Ross could fit in a single desk.

Books, books, and more books surrounded Ross. He ordered in some specialty editions that could only be accessed through the Behavioral Analysis Unit and the National Center for the Analysis of Violent Crimes. It felt good to get back into police work. It gave him purpose. The irony didn't escape him that, as a prisoner himself, he was investigating the death of other prisoners. He could understand the logic, from Warden Parker's point of view. Murders like this had a habit of sticking to those around them like a bad smell. A series of grizzly, unsolved murders would affect the warden's reputation, and his ego wouldn't stand for it.

There was a polite knock on the door. It was Father O'Grady; he was twenty-eight and had been an actual priest on the outside. "I've never seen so many new books in all my time here," O'Grady said.

"Thanks, Father," Ross replied, taking the book, checking out the cover, and assigning it to a pile. O'Grady placed his hands on his hips and inspected the case notes on the walls. He had taken an interest in the case, and in Ross too.

"You think you'll find this guy, the Heart Collector?" O'Grady asked.

Ross glanced up and nodded. Ross had heard controversial stories about O'Grady from other prisoners. He wasn't sure what to believe, but he knew that O'Grady wasn't trying to kill him, and at least he spoke like a normal person.

"Who do you think did it? Any suspects?" O'Grady continued.

"I guess in here, everyone's a suspect."

"Everyone, you say." O'Grady pointed his finger in the air. "But we can rule you out, right?" He pointed at Ross. "Or is that the twist? Should I be worried?" O'Grady scrunched up his face in mock horror. He deepened his voice. "The only person no one suspected of being the killer was the detective in jail convicted of murder who was tracking down the murderer, and who was, in fact, the murderer himself. Coming to a cinema near you this fall."

"What?" Ross shook his head, laughing.

"Sounds like a good movie to me," O'Grady smiled. "Need any help?"

"You are helping. How long have you been running the library, Father?"

"About five years now. When I got sent to the big house, the warden gave me the opportunity to rebuild the library," O'Grady explained. "Before my arrival, a good proportion of books had been burned and destroyed in a 2012 'shotgun' riot. You may have read about it—it lasted five days before order was restored. There's no budget, but I do what I can."

"You're doing good, Father." Ross returned his attention to his anatomy book.

"May God be with you, Ross," O'Grady said as he let himself out.

"Thanks, Father. Has anyone told you that you look like James Franco? And not in a good way." Ross winked.

"Maybe once or twice." O'Grady laughed as he left the room.

CHAPTER FIFTY-NINE

NICK STOOD MOTIONLESS outside his old school. He'd hated every tormented minute here. It wasn't just the other students. The small-minded teachers had been just as hard on him too.

He remembered his first day of school. Mr. Reece asked the class if they had any questions. No one did. He encouraged his students, so Nick had shot his hand into the air. He wanted to know why Mr. Reece didn't hold hands with his boyfriend and kiss him in public. "That would make your boyfriend happy," he told him. The class laughed, and Mr. Reece flew into a rage. He caned Nick in front of everyone to teach him to respect his elders and not to make up vicious lies. Homosexuality wasn't spoken of in their small town. Many years later, Nick saw Mr. Reece on a gay pride float in New Orleans and guessed that he hadn't been ready to be pulled out of the closet by a five-year-old that day.

Looking back, all the things his younger self used to say now made him laugh. Words and images would just pop into his head, and seconds later he'd say or describe them. He couldn't keep anyone's secrets, and most of the time this caused problems. Secrets are secrets for a reason.

Nick struggled with schoolwork as a child. If only his gift for reading people transferred to reading books. He often found himself too distracted by the mental static those around him gave off to fully take in academics. Sometimes he thought classmates were talking to him, but when he replied, they'd tell him they hadn't said anything. His low marks prompted his father to get out his belt and beat the devil out of him even more. "The devil is stupid," he'd say, which was why Nick was stupid too, and why he'd say stupid things.

His teenage years were the worst. A hulking classmate, Buddy Baldwin, took it upon himself to torture Nick every waking moment. When a redneck bully with a low IQ torments someone, you can rest assured it's not done with skill. Buddy would push him over, hit books out of his hand, call him a fag in class, and laugh at his own jokes. More than once, Nick considered ending his own life. He didn't think anyone would miss him. His father actually may have been thankful that Nick took care of his own "devil-ridden soul." But if he were to kill himself, he would hurt the one person he cared about. The one person he would miss. The one person who made all the shitty things in his life bearable—Kirsty Hawkins. When she was around, life was just better. She'd talk to him, ask him to go exploring, and share her feelings about life.

Kirsty was a tomboy, the only girl among four older brothers. She had big brown eyes, long flowing auburn hair, and pixie-like features. Her big heart matched her outer beauty. Her family moved to the small town when Nick was twelve. He'd felt a connection with her the day they met after Buddy had chased Nick up a tree. She climbed the tree to sit with him. Once Buddy got bored and left, she walked home with Nick. From that moment, they walked to school together every day. His years of getting harassed prevented him from thinking their friendship could ever go anywhere special.

Buddy also liked Kirsty. Nick's mind flashed back to the last day he walked into this building. Buddy destroyed everything that day.

Nick could feel the anger build up inside him. He needed a drink now, and then twenty more.

CHAPTER SIXTY

JUSTIN ENTERED THE extravagant ballroom, taking it all in as if it were arranged just for him. The room was an ocean of wealth, with men in tuxedos and women in flowing ball gowns.

Tonight, Rip was formally announcing his political campaign. The event had to be grandiose. It had to visually convey that he'd already won. Rip and Barbara sat regally at the head of the room, easily accessible for guests to wish him well and compliment her beauty.

Alex dazzled on Justin's arm, her sensual black hair pinned up into an elaborately braided bun. A long, seductive split up the side of her tight black dress flaunted her body. This dress had to be worn with confidence, and Alex did it to perfection. She was an accessory Justin used flawlessly.

"I need a drink!" Alex ordered in her French accent.

"Soon. First we need to make the rounds." Justin smiled.

"You walk, I will drink." Alex departed Justin's side and strutted toward the bar, turning heads of both men and women alike. Justin resisted grabbing her by the hair and dragging her back. With her stunning looks also came the attitude of doing whatever she wanted.

Justin let her go as he spotted Peter in a corner, deep in conversation with an assembly of distinguished men. They were nodding and grinning as Peter told a story. These men would be the controlling forces behind many a corporate merger, and the decisions they made would affect thousands of people. They had the sort of power Justin knew he would have one day.

The group of men laughed, and Peter gave one of them a jovial slap on the back. The joke had gone down well, and they were all in great spirits. Peter glanced Justin's way, motioned for Justin to join him, and excused himself from his present company.

"Glad you could make it, Justin," Peter said.

"I wouldn't have missed this for anything. Rip is going to make us all very proud."

"Yes. Yes, he will," Peter confirmed. "And will you make me proud?"

"I will," Justin reassured him.

"Are you sure? I see you haven't deposited the pledge yet."

"That's all taken care of. I'll earn a little bit more interest on it before it's all yours." Justin explained smoothly.

"I can always offer it to someone else." Peter gazed around the room.

"I've got this."

"As long as you understand." Peter changed the subject. "And how is the other issue I asked you to look into?"

"They won't know what's hit them. I've already secured some intel from a person on the inside."

"You trust this person?"

"No, I don't. What I trust is that the person won't do anything to make me angry with them."

"Fear is a strong tool. It makes people do stuff they never thought they would." Peter looked Justin straight in the eyes. "What are you afraid of, Justin?"

"Nothing."

"Are you sure?" Peter prodded.

"I fear nothing, as I know I can achieve everything," he maintained stubbornly.

A smile crept across Peter's face. "A man who is not afraid, has a lot to fear. Remember that."

CHAPTER SIXTY-ONE

MONTANA NEVER LOOKED at her phone as often as she had in the last thirty hours. She'd been checking constantly to make sure she didn't miss any incoming messages. She normally only checked her phone a few times a day.

It buzzed in her hand, and her eyes shot to the notification. She let out a deflated breath. A text from her mother. Since she'd left the hospital, Montana's mother had been messaging her more frequently than ever. She told Montana she was concerned and felt that her personality had abruptly changed. She knew something wasn't right with her.

Montana's phone buzzed again. A message from a colleague inviting her to drinks on Friday night. She ignored it. Having a few drinks with people from Phizz was the last thing she could face. Kenny would no doubt hunt her down to paw her.

Her phone buzzed. Her mother again, asking if she had got her previous message. She quickly replied that she was doing well, then she carried her phone to the kitchen and held it while she foraged in the fridge. She wasn't hungry. She closed the door and nervously paced between the lounge and the kitchen.

She started to doubt if the number Maggot had given her was even a real number. Should she call it? No. Did she really need a hit man? She was smart. She could find another way to kill Justin. She could make it look like self-defense.

Her phone buzzed. It would be her mother again. She could wait… Montana snatched up her phone. She froze. It was the message she'd been waiting thirty hours for.

```
Corner of West 112th Street and Broadway.
One hour.
```

THE CAB STOPPED outside the diner. Montana was thirty minutes early. Her heart thumped in her chest like it wanted to escape. This was the place. This was it. She was going to do this. She made the impatient driver wait a minute before paying him while she controlled her breathing.

Stepping out of the cab, her head spun. She felt too much on edge to walk directly into the building. She took a deep breath and wandered along the road, looking at stores without seeing them. An older lady walking a schnauzer bumped into her. The dog barked. Montana waved her on. A couple sitting at the restaurant next-door looked up, concerned. The dog barked again.

She leaned against the wall for support. She'd run meetings where millions of dollars traded hands, commanded interviews on *Good Morning America*, and delivered detailed presentations in front of thousands of people. She could do this. "I can do this, and I will do it well, I can do this, and I will do it well," she repeated out loud.

She returned to the diner and saw a free booth near the back and made a beeline for it. Within seconds, a waitress appeared to take her order—in between chewing gum and tapping her pad with a pencil. She spoke with a thick accent that Montana didn't recognize.

Montana said the first thing that popped into her mind. "Coffee."

"No food? You know you can get coffee anywhere," the waitress replied.

"What's good?" Montana replied politely.

"Nothing," the waitress said with a hint of a smile, and it made Montana laugh. "Look, lady, I'll get you the grilled cheese. It's as close to good as you gonna get. You will like, but if you no like, it's OK too."

"That sounds great," Montana said. "Her coffee arrived. She sipped it. It was a weak, brown liquid that only loosely resembled coffee. She picked up the menu. Put it down. Picked it up again and placed it down on a different part of the table. She moved the condiments around, placing them at right angles to each other, then turned the menu over. She opened a sugar packet and added it to her coffee. Stirred it. Rotated the coffee cup in circles. Stirred it once more. She wanted to look at her phone to see if they'd messaged her again. Her phone remained untouched.

Montana's grilled cheese arrived, but as soon as she saw it, she knew she wouldn't eat it. There was no way her stomach could handle that right now.

"A grilled cheese for me? You shouldn't have," a man's voice said.

Montana looked up at a guy in sweat pants and an I LOVE NY T-shirt sitting across from her. He picked up the sandwich and took a large bite.

"I'm sorry, I'm expecting someone," she said.

"Yeah, you are," the stranger managed between chews. "Me, Miss Montana."

"Are you…?" Montana's eyes went wide, and her body turned rigid, as if she were about to go into rigor mortis.

"I'm the man of your dreams, sweetheart." He winked mischievously and took another bite.

"I wasn't expecting…"

"You thought I was going to be wearing black, with sunglasses and a pencil-line beard? Look, babes. I dress like this because no one's going to remember me. Just another stupid tourist. Good work on the grilled cheese, by the way." He shoveled a handful of fries into his mouth.

Montana swallowed hard. "You will do what I asked for?"

"Not me, sweetheart. I'm a middleman. I'm here to decide if this job will go any further. You know what a tire-kicker is? Let's say it happens a lot. My friends don't like to have their time wasted. My time is fine to waste. Lady, are we going for a drive together?"

"I don't have a car."

"That was a metaphor to go with the tire-kicking. I've done better. Are you one hundred percent sure you want to go for a drive with me and my friends?"

"Yes!"

The man scarfed the last piece of sandwich, then stood. "I'll tell you what. I'll talk to Bob. Then if it's good with him, it's good with me. Then I'll get in touch with you about money, meeting Bob, and yada yada." He snapped his fingers and pointed at her. "Who's the lucky Joe?"

"Justin Truth, works for Soda-Cola. I want him to suffer. Make him beg for his life, and then hurt him some more. Hot pokers, sharp knives, break his bones, poke out his eye, castrate the bastard! Whatever you think will make him scream. Then kill him."

"Calm down, if you have the money, honey-cake, we can do anything you want."

"One more thing," Montana took in a deep breath. "I want to be there."

"You pay me enough, foxy, you can pull the trigger yourself."

CHAPTER SIXTY-THREE

THE OLD BASTARD WAS hanging in there, and Nick was sure it was only to piss him off. Each day, Nick went to his father's house and listened to the machine puff and wheeze air into his father's lungs. Each day Nick told him to hurry up and die. The smell never got any better, nor did his anger ever recede.

Often, Nick would slam the door, walk to the edge of town, and hit up Lass-Whoo's, a simple cowboy-themed bar that was as tacky as the name suggested. As he basically started living in the joint, he became friendly with the bar staff, especially Michele, their assistant manager. She came back to his hotel room most nights.

"Must be that time of the day!" Michele greeted Nick as he pushed his way through the swinging doors.

"When you dress like that? How can I stay away?" he smiled. Michele's denim shirt was cut low, showing off her cleavage, and her Daisy Dukes were tight and short. She lined up five shot glasses for him as he took a seat at the bar.

"What time did you leave this morning?" Nick asked.

"Honey, I left last night. You kinda passed out on me, so I drove home." Michele was ten years older than Nick, knew what she liked, and was very vocal about it.

"Sorry about that."

"You got nothing to be sorry about. I shouldn't have poured you so many double shots last night."

Nick smiled and greedily hit the first shot back.

"How's the old man doing?"

"Hanging in there. I bet God and Satan haven't decided who is going to have him yet. One thing I'm sure of, neither of them will want him."

"And once he's gone, you'll be gone, too?"

"Yup, you knew I wasn't staying."

"Baby, I knew you were leaving the minute you arrived. Just got to get as much fun out of you as possible before then." She leaned over the bar and planted a kiss on his forehead. She smelled of strawberries and it turned him on like hell.

"What time you finishing?" he asked, knocking back the second shot.

"Same time as always, as soon as the last drink has been bought." She smiled and placed clean wine glasses on the shelves behind her.

"The boys are back!" a gruff voice bellowed.

Nick froze. His blood began to boil. Since he'd been back, he hadn't gone out of his way to find trouble, yet trouble had just walked in the swinging doors with three friends in tow.

"Beer now!" Buddy yelled as they settled down at a table. Nick slowly turned to sneak a peek at his teenage tormentor. It was Buddy all right. Judging by their worn and dirty clothes, Nick assumed Buddy and his friends worked as a road gang.

One of the waitresses pulled four beers and delivered the foaming glasses over to the men. They greeted her with derogatory remarks.

"Are you as wet as this beer?" one of the men sneered.

"She's pretty, but my cock in her mouth would make her beautiful," boasted another.

"Can we order you as takeout?" a third chimed in.

Nick didn't recognize Buddy's foul-mouthed friends. The muscles in his jaw tightened, his teeth ground together, and his hands formed into fists.

"It's OK, sugar." Michele gently rested her hand on his shoulder. "They come in once a month. They make a bit of noise and that's about it."

Nick turned back toward the men. Buddy had put on a lot of weight since school. His face was pudgy, and the broken blood vessels were a dead giveaway that too much booze was the reason. His arms were big and solid, presumably from manual work. The group downed the beers quickly and yelled for more.

Nick got up, stretched his back, and rotated his head a few times to iron out kinks in his neck. The waitress placed the last beer on her tray, and before she could protest, Nick lifted the tray. "I'll take them over for you," he said, setting off toward the rowdy men. "An order for four baboons who think treating women like shit makes them more manly." Nick dropped the tray on the table, causing the beers to slosh over the sides of the glasses. The men shot back in their chairs to avoid the spillage.

"Who the fuck are you?" one guy asked.

"Fuck off, midget," another yelled.

"Why don't you climb back up the hole you came out of, so you'll wake up tomorrow with your own teeth." That was Buddy talking.

"I'm sorry," Nick said. "How about I pay for the drinks, and you lot can fuck off. You're stinking the place up. You sweaty, slimy, disease-ridden, septic, gelatinous, hold-my-nose-because-I'm-going-to-throw-up pig fuckers." He had their full attention now. One of the guys began to stand up, but Buddy motioned for him to stay put.

"I know this prick," he growled sarcastically. "I went to school with him."

"Wow, and here I was thinking you were dumb as dog shit. Well done." Nick clapped.

"Watch your mouth, cunt. I have no problem slapping the taste from it."

"Tell you what," Nick gestured. "Why don't you come outside with me, and we can talk about the old times."

Buddy's memory seemed to kick in about the things he had done to Nick in the past. He smiled, revealing a set of yellow-stained teeth. He stood up, towering over Nick.

"Let's do this," Buddy smirked. He picked up a beer, downed it, and let out an exaggerated burp.

Nick took a few steps back and led the way, and Buddy and his friends followed on his heels—as did half the bar.

The fenced-off parking lot behind Lass-Whoo's mainly consisted of burnout marks, litter, and a scattering of small rocks from the broken asphalt. Only a third of the parking spaces had vehicles in them, giving the men loads of room.

Buddy instantly played up to the bar crowd that gathered around them. "You'd have thought I'd have beaten this out of you during our school days, boy." Buddy puffed out his chest.

"We are very different people now," Nick replied. "Well, I am anyway. You're just as fat and stupid as you've always been—maybe even fatter."

Buddy threw the first punch. Nick easily weaved under it. He struck back with a hard kidney punch. It surprised the big guy, and he winced. Buddy threw a few more wild haymakers. Nick ducked, then surgically hit the same kidney with three more punches.

"Is that all you got, fag?" Buddy roared, to hide the pain he was feeling.

"I haven't even started," Nick snarled. "This isn't just for me, it's for Kirsty too."

Buddy launched at Nick's waist and tried to use his size advantage to wrestle Nick to the ground. Nick timed his knee perfectly. *Crack!* He connected it with Buddy's chin. Buddy hit the ground hard. Dazed.

Out of the corner of his eye, Nick saw one of Buddy's friends try to ambush him from behind. Nick dropped to one knee, thrust out his elbow, and hit the guy square in the balls. He followed with a knee lift to the bridge of the coward's nose. The man tumbled backward and slammed onto his back. Blood poured out of his broken nose.

Another of Buddy's cohorts half-heartedly rushed in with apparently no idea what to do. Nick easily deflected a feeble punch with his raised forearm. His left jab hit the guy's temple. A spinning back elbow knocked his attacker out cold, leaving one last Buddy supporter standing. Glancing at his beaten friends on the ground, it seemed to dawn on him that he was out of his league. He held up his hands as a sign of surrender and retreated.

Nick could hear Buddy wheezing, trying to sneak up behind him. He twisted and hip-tossed Buddy to the ground. The big man groaned. Nick went into full mount, his knees trapping the fat man's arms against his body. He took full advantage. Elbow after elbow rained down. Blood gushed. Cartilage snapped. Buddy's face became a bloody pulp.

Michele's screaming pulled Nick out of his blind rage. He staggered to his feet, blood dripping from his arms, and stared down at the mess below him.

"I liked her, you fat piece of shit." Nick couldn't stop his body from shaking. "She didn't deserve what you did. And I sure as hell didn't either!"

CHAPTER SIXTY-FOUR

"I DID SOME RESEARCH into this place, your church," Steve said to start the conversation.

"You did?" Silver dipped his brush into the white paint. They were standing in the warm sun, covering up some fresh graffiti on one of the church walls.

"I did," Steve continued. "And did you know that 'we'—and when I say 'we,' I mean 'you'—can get a massive grant from the government?"

"I received some money when I started here, Steve."

"You did, but that wasn't meant to be a one-off fee. It was meant to be a monthly payment."

"I'm not sure about that. Just getting anything has been a great help. This is just a place to help people who have nothing." Silver slopped more paint in circles.

"I called a few people, and it seems all we need to do is some paperwork," Steve encouraged.

Silver stopped. "Paperwork is the devil's work in my mind."

"It's just paper and ink," Steve paused. "We can use your history to our advantage too."

"I don't understand? I have no history." Silver put his brush down and gave Steve his full attention.

"Silver, I hate to point out the obvious, but you're American Indian, or do you prefer 'Native American'?"

"Which will get me some money, so I do not need to paint?"

"Both."

"I've always picked you as one of the smart ones." Silver laughed, and Steve joined in.

"My people screwed your people pretty bad, and now the white man is trying to make up for it. As a Native American, you and your people have an official religion, and there are teams of people who have to make sure that this religion isn't lost. There's a huge pool of money just sitting there waiting to be doled out."

"I don't know any of the spiritual ways, Steve. I just want to help people. Not sure I know what to do?"

"You don't need to know. Let me help you by doing the paperwork. The money you'll get can be used to buy this place. It's for sale, and I'm not sure too many people are lining up to buy it. There is even a government department that will match what you pay and provide an interest-free loan for the rest."

"What can I say?"

"Nothing. I want to do it and it's what I'm good at—getting ideas together and making them happen."

"It's time for a break," Silver interrupted. "Come, let's get a drink and celebrate. We'll thank whichever God you like for bringing you here, Steve."

"No, I have to thank you. If I can help you and help others the same way coming here has helped me, then that is all the thanks I need. Also, we've only just started. We can't have a break just yet, can we?"

"Steve, the journey can't be judged by how much rest we take along the way."

Both men laughed. The truth was, Silver just hated painting.

CHAPTER SIXTY-FIVE

JUSTIN ENTERED MONTANA'S apartment without knocking and planted himself on the couch. He dropped his feet onto the coffee table with a loud bang. She'd only just returned home from the gym and was surprised to see him.

"Bring me a drink," he ordered. He'd bought Montana a $10,000 bottle of 650-year-old Dalmore whiskey and insisted it be on permanent display to remind her she belonged to him.

She retrieved the bottle, scooped a few ice cubes into a thick tumbler, poured the whiskey, and served it on a coaster in front of him.

He lifted the glass, inhaled its fine scent, and took a sip.

"Now that's what I call quality." He placed it back down on the table—next to the coaster. "What do you think of my tie? It's pure Italian silk, handmade. It's the quality things in life that make all the difference."

Montana's fingers trembled. She leaned down and traced her finger along the tie.

"It's so soft," she whispered. She playfully wrapped it around her hand, pulling Justin closer. His eyes went wide with excitement. The pounding tribal beat of her heart consumed her. She yanked him up. Choking him. From behind her back, she whipped out her serrated kitchen knife. She thrust it up into his exposed neck, ripping an artery and staring him in the eyes as the color drained from his face.

"I'm told Ryan Gosling gets his ties made by the same tailor." Justin brushed an invisible piece of lint off his tie.

Montana steadied herself and retreated back to the kitchen, the tribal drum beat fading.

"Ryan… Gosling." Justin repeated.

"Good to know," Montana said vaguely, as she stared at her hand, minus the knife. Still imagining Justin's blood on it.

"What's new with Sterling and Phizz?" he inquired.

She composed herself and rejoined him with a bottle of water. "They know you're putting a deal together with a competitive pitch. They must be a bit nervous because they called me in and asked a few questions about you, and what you're up to."

"And what did you tell them?"

"I played it down." Montana sat on the armchair across from Justin. "I told them you had your fingers in many pies, and that this would be just another one of them."

"For them to ask means they feel threatened."

"I told them I'd work with them on whatever they were doing and give them as much info about Soda-Cola as I could."

"Good girl." Justin reached over and ran his hand up her thigh. "I went through all the files you sent me. Nothing was overly helpful. At least you tried."

"Really?" Montana asked, annoyed.

"You get that," Justin said dismissively.

Montana stood to get out of Justin's reach.

"Lucky for you I have an idea." Justin said. "I'm thinking we could use you against them. I'll have a fake contract drawn up showing what our pitch will be. You can pretend that you got it through a friend. I'll fire someone to make it more legit. One of your close friends who still works at Soda-Cola should do the trick."

Montana glared at Justin. He continued, unfazed. "If they think we're going in high they may just undercut us enough to keep it close. And in reality, we'll be going in at a fraction of where they are now."

"That could work. Not sure you need to fire anyone, though. I can make it look like I pulled in some big favors."

"It makes the information more valuable if someone got burned for it." Justin took another sip and dropped the glass back down. "Did you just finish a workout?"

"I did. Getting back into the gym."

"I like that you're taking care of yourself. You really should take a shower."

"Good idea. I'll have one as soon as you leave."

"Why wait? You should do it now—and leave the shower door open. I want to make sure you clean every part of that body."

Montana hovered in the doorway, looking at her block of knives on the kitchen bench.

"Now is good," Justin insisted.

She closed her eyes, removed her sweatshirt for him, and sulked toward the bathroom. The sooner he was dead, the better.

CHAPTER SIXTY-SIX

SWEAT BEADED ON Jimmy's forehead. The walk back to his cell felt like a marathon; each step replayed the pain of getting stabbed. No one was kept in a prison hospital bed longer than absolutely necessary, and there was no wheelchair to escort you out on your exit.

He'd been punched and kicked a few times, but getting stabbed was a whole new experience, and like no pain he'd ever felt before. The initial stab wasn't so bad, not that he remembered much. It was the healing pain that really hurt. Even now, he was in constant agony. The painkillers weren't doing shit for him. A part of him wondered if the doctor was just giving him Tic Tacs and keeping the real meds for himself.

For the next four weeks, three times a day, he would have to make the trek back to the nurses' station for antibiotics. While it felt good to be out of the hospital bed, it wasn't so great to be back in general population.

Jimmy was scared. Prison wasn't the place for him. He wasn't a bad person. Sure, he had stolen things, told lies, and pulled a few cons to get money. He wasn't a killer, a thug, or a bully, though. He'd been stupid, and that is how he ended up here—by chasing the easy money.

With each step that Jimmy took, he felt as if his wound was ripping open again. He stopped a few times to check that blood wasn't seeping through the dressing. It wasn't.

He found the door to his cell open and walked in on Ross and Father O'Grady talking.

"...too random not to be, unless they wanted it to look like that," O'Grady was saying. "Would the Heart Collector be thinking that? Sending you a message? Changing the third victim slightly so you'd notice. He's playing with you. He has to know you're looking for him, surely."

"Look at you, all acting like a criminal investigator," Ross quipped back.

"I've seen a few cop shows," O'Grady retorted.

"Same," Ross smiled. "The new victim is the same, it's just the eyes—"

Finally Jimmy cleared his throat, interrupting the conversation.

"Jimmy!" Ross roared, giving the slight Italian a careful bear hug. Jimmy winced, but enjoyed the affection.

"All good, boss?" Jimmy asked, looking at Father O'Grady.

"Jimmy, have you met Father O'Grady?"

O'Grady extended his hand, but Jimmy ignored the offer.

"You're the one who killed the boy, yeah?" Jimmy asked with a stone-cold stare.

"I didn't, it was the demon inside him that did that," O'Grady corrected him.

"Your hands, Father."

Ross interrupted the heated exchange. "Come, sit down, Jimmy. I bet the doctor told you that you still needed bed rest? I found you a few more blankets."

Jimmy stooped his head and hobbled toward his bed. "Thanks, boss. Yeah, I think I may needs some sleep. Just try nots to kill me in my sleep, Father, you know, mistaking my snoring for the devil."

Ross looked at Father O'Grady apologetically. O'Grady waved him off and they left Jimmy to rest, continuing their conversation down the hallway. Jimmy closed his eyes, even though sleep wasn't going to come anytime soon.

CHAPTER SIXTY-SEVEN

STEVE GRABBED A BASKET as he entered the small convenience store. Where once he saw this store as dark, smelly and crammed, now he thought it was bright, exciting, and humming with activity. As he moved through the store, he chatted to an old Hispanic man about his favorite piece in chess, the rook. Then he had a lively discussion with a young mother on the food her toddler would eat, and listened to a young man explain why Steve should support the New York Mets.

Silver encouraged his congregation to talk to everyone they came across in their daily lives. "No matter who they are," he'd say, "give them five minutes of your time, and you will both be rewarded." It was difficult at first for Steve to approach strangers, but after a while it became like second nature. Talking to a stranger made every journey more enjoyable, and that was the point.

"We are in such a rush to get to our graves," Silver would say. 'Let's arrive in our own time."

Steve felt his love for Silver grow immensely with each passing day. He didn't know much about Silver's past, as Silver had a way of turning the conversation back onto you and before you knew it, you'd shared secrets you'd never told anyone before. He would listen patiently and always give simple yet effective advice that made everything right.

Silver founded the church three years ago, not long after he'd lost his arm. Based on no particular religion, he brought together ideas and symbolisms from a plethora of different sources. Silver's own take on Native American philosophy formed the foundation of his life philosophy and church ethos. Most of his philosophies were common sense, conveyed in easy terms that people understood.

Tonight, Steve was leading a group for teenage runaways. Silver had given him a list of food to buy so he could make dinner for them all. He had most items already; he just needed dry pasta and a large container of butter. Everything Silver prepared used copious amounts of butter.

"Get the fuck down!" a voice yelled. "I'll fucking kill you!"

Everyone in the store hit the floor. A young man wielded a handgun at Dong Kim, the store owner. The gunman's arm jittered. Steve recognized those shakes. The young man was coming down from drugs, and it obviously wasn't a good trip.

"Give me the money, man!" He continued his tirade. "Hurry the fuck up!"

Dong Kim handed over money from his register. The thief looked at it in disgust.

"Where's the rest of it?" he demanded. "You think I'm stupid?"

"That is all we have," Dong Kim whimpered, bowing his head submissively.

"Don't fuck with me, man. I will fucking put a bullet between your fucking eyes."

"That is everything! Please, I beg you…" Dong Kim pleaded, holding his hands up in the air.

"You're a fucking liar!" The young man pulled the hammer back on the gun.

"My friend, stop. I have what you need," Steve said calmly. The man spun around and pointed his gun directly at Steve.

"You wanna die, hero?"

"We're all going to die at some point." Steve put his hands in the air. "It's one thing we can't control." Steve felt Silver's words rolling off his tongue.

"What?" The gunman tilted his head like a dog.

"Death. It comes to all of us. It might be my time today. And if you're the one who's responsible for that, then so be it."

"What? What the fuck are you talking about?" the gunman stammered and looked around, wild-eyed.

"I wonder if today is my day? Maybe I have lived this long to die and save my friend Dong Kim. He is a good man. He has a family, wife, and four kids. He enjoys building Lego sets, watching *The Chase*, wants to stop biting his nails. I've wasted my life, so it's a good trade." Steve pulled up his sleeves to show his half-healed track marks. "I've been where you are, you know.

"I tell you what, I'll do you a deal," Steve continued. "If you want to kill someone, kill me." He gently stepped toward the young man. "If you kill me, you take the money and you run. You run fast, and you hide. But you will be caught, my friend, we both know that will happen. Or you put the gun away and take a walk with me. I have a friend who can help. If you don't like what we talk about, or where we go, you kill me and whatever happens, happens."

Steve slowly placed his hand on the gun, lifting it so the barrel rested against his forehead. "It's an easy shot," he told the gunman. "You do what you need to do."

Stillness hung in the air as everyone held their breath. The young man lowered the piece and allowed Steve to take the money from his clenched fist and hand it back to Dong Kim. Steve placed his basket in the man's hand in its place.

"I just need to get some more things," Steve said. "Hold that and I'll be right back. And if you want something, feel free to put it in the basket. Get up, everyone," Steve said to the people on the ground. "You can finish your shopping. Sorry for any inconvenience."

When he returned, the young man had put a Mars bar in the basket.

"On my account, Dong Kim." Dong placed the groceries in a plastic bag without taking his eyes off the young man. Steve pulled out the Mars bar and gave it to the young man.

"Do you like soup?" Steve asked.

CHAPTER SIXTY-EIGHT

A MEETING WAS SET, and all Montana could think about was what to wear. She told herself she was being silly, yet how do you dress when talking to a hit man? In the movies they always dressed in black. She had a lot of black clothing. Maybe her trench coat?

The real reason she thought about clothes was to take her mind off the dirty deed ahead. A battle raged in her mind. Once Justin was dead, would she really be free? Could she return to her normal life, the one she had before Justin had fucked it all up? What if she was caught? Could she handle prison? Could she live with blood on her hands?

She poured herself a fourth glass of wine, took a sip, but couldn't taste anything.

Montana decided on simple black pants and a black turtleneck top. This guy wouldn't care what she was wearing. It wasn't a job interview. Her phone beeped—time to leave. She drained the rest of her wine and headed downstairs to an awaiting taxi.

The ride went by in a blur. The buildings morphed into one. She felt less afraid than she did on the ride to the diner a few days earlier. Maybe she was coming to terms with being a murderer. The taxi arrived at the Empire State Building, and the place was alive with tourists pushing and lining up everywhere, talking and yelling in all manners of accents.

She waited to get her ticket. She waited to get into the elevator. She waited in the elevator. She waited to get out of the elevator and waited to walk toward the open air.

As the doors opened, Montana felt the cool breeze on her face. She hadn't been up the Empire State Building in years and had forgotten how breathtaking the view was. She spotted the Phizz International Building and sneered at it.

She did a loop of the floor until she found the designated meeting spot for her contact. As she waited, she listened to a conversation between a young couple next to her.

"If I threw this quarter over the side," the young man said, "it could kill someone."

"No!" his girlfriend exclaimed in a dramatic tone.

"It's totally true. The speed at which the coin would fall would build up such momentum that it would become like a bullet. It would pass right through a person's head. People have been killed like this before."

"People?" the girl asked sadly.

"Yeah, that's why there are signs. Don't feed the birds and don't throw coins," the boyfriend said convincingly.

A third voice only Montana could hear joined the conversation.

"Do you think a coin could kill a man?" the voice asked Montana.

"It's just a myth, isn't it?" she said, and turned to the voice. It belonged to a man in his fifties wearing a security guard uniform. His face had deep lines that didn't move as he talked. His small, peg-like teeth looked like they were stained from coffee and cigarettes, and she could smell the mixture on his heavy breath.

"It's a myth that still exists," he said. "And yet hundreds of people throw coins from this very place every single day knowing it probably won't kill anyone, but they get a thrill from it all the same." The guard peered at Montana with heavyset, emotionless eyes. "I'm Bob. Are you looking for a thrill, or are you looking for a kill, Miss Montana?"

"A kill!" Montana replied without a second thought.

The guard stood in silence, gazing out over the city. Montana could feel drops of sweat running down the side of her face. Finally, Bob spoke again in his monotone, husky voice.

"I'll take the job, Montana. This man Justin Truth will be eradicated, and his blood will be on your hands."

"I have no problem with that," Montana replied. "Did they tell you I want to be there when it happens?"

"Yeah, but it will not be a fast job. My team has many preparations to make. No ties, no leads. He will be missed. It has to be a smooth act. Once we have him, you'll be messaged the location. Go there immediately. We will then execute him in front of you."

"Can I do it?" Montana couldn't believe the words coming out of her mouth. "Can I kill him? Can I be the one to kill that son of a bitch?"

"You really want to go down that road?" the guard asked.

"I do."

"That will cost you twice as much."

"I can live with that."

The guard placed a coin into Montana's hand along with a surgical blade.

"Bloody the coin and throw it as far as you can. This will be our contract. Once I see the coin fly, I will start the process and it won't end until Justin is dead." And with that, the guard evaporated into the crowd.

Montana looked at the shiny coin, then cut her thumb and squeezed droplets of blood onto it. She sucked her bleeding thumb as the coin flew into the New York skyline. It had started.

CHAPTER SIXTY-NINE

THE BARBELL HIT the ground, making a loud clank. Sweat poured off Justin as he took a gulp of electrolytes. Angus, his personal trainer, had pushed him hard today. His muscles were going to feel it tomorrow. Angus gave Justin some final feedback on his form and congratulated him for surviving the workout.

Justin showered, then dressed in front of the full-length mirror so he could admire his chiseled body. Angus knew what he was doing, and Justin's ripped physique was the result.

As he ran a hand through his damp hair, the familiar itch in the back of Justin's brain flared up, and the sickly-sweet whisper made itself heard.

Good work, buddy, it said. *Getting strong, looking good. I know you've got more gas in the tank.*

"What can I say? I'm a machine."

What do you think about getting in another workout? Someone who needs to be taught a lesson.

"I know just the person." Justin grinned.

He emerged from the gym wearing his gray sweatpants and hoodie. Dan was waiting; he hadn't moved from where he'd dropped him off.

"Number one boss man," Dan greeted him. "Where would you like to go? Some pussy?"

"I feel like going for a drive out to Jennifer's place," Justin replied.

"Very good. Yes, she still want Justin cock! You the man, sir."

It had been fourteen months since Justin had talked to Jennifer, but he'd been keeping tabs on her and tracking her actions and whereabouts all along. He'd hired a private investigator to tap her phones and installed pinhead cameras in her bedroom. Justin hadn't just broken her heart, he'd ripped it out and stomped on it in front of her. Still, he didn't want her to be with anyone else.

The Audi parked across the road from Jennifer's city apartment.

"Let's just wait here for a bit," Justin said, eyeing up the building.

Dan obliged and turned the engine off. Justin hid in the shadows of the backseat and watched the building. He was in full predator mode, waiting for his prey to arrive.

Without a word, Justin pulled up his hood and slipped out the door. Jogged across the road and dropped his shoulder to bump into a guy carrying a bouquet of flowers.

The guy spun around. "Excuse me," he said sarcastically. Justin stopped. Keeping his face hidden inside the hood.

"I'm sorry, I didn't see you there," Justin snarled. "If I had, I would have done this." Justin shot out a jab, flattening the guy's nose. Blindsided, the man dropped the flowers. Justin threw two heavy body blows to the guy's floating ribs. Mr. Flower Guy collapsed to the cold ground, groaning. Justin dragged him up by his shirt and slammed him against a brick wall. In a Muay Thai clinch, he cracked him as hard as he could in the balls with a knee lift. Mr. Flower Guy hit the ground, vomiting.

"Never fucking come near here again," Justin hissed. "She's all mine, do you hear me? I see you again, you're dead."

CHAPTER SEVENTY

THE BEDROOM WAS QUIETER, devoid of the verbose breathing machine. Nick's father now had to breathe unassisted. He struggled for air. His body shook as he gargled down a small pocket of air into his lungs. Failing to expand them, the air slipped back out his mouth. He lay still before jerking and gulping for more air.

Three men stood watching: Father Wayne, Doctor Austin, and Nick.

There were tears in Nick's eyes, not from watching his father take his last gasps of air, but from the memories and scars the old man had inflicted on him.

Seeing Buddy at the bar had opened the dam of emotions he'd felt for Kirsty. He hadn't thought about her for years, on purpose. All the drunken nights had helped drown out the memories of her. Now they escaped and flooded out of him, reminding him in great detail why he'd run away from his hometown all those years ago.

Kirsty was Nick's best friend, and the only person he'd ever felt truly connected to. They hung out after class and talked about everything—their hopes and dreams.

He remembered admiring Kirsty's body as it bloomed. Her curves caught the attention of all the boys, including a couple of the male teachers. She could have chosen to be with anyone, yet she chose to hang out with Nick.

Nick often shared with her what he emotionally "picked up" from people, the things he "knew" about them—their secrets, and that he didn't know why he knew these things just by looking at people. Kirsty marveled at his hidden talent and the connections he made purely through his intuition. She encouraged him to trust in himself more. Believe in himself.

Their favorite place to talk was in the grandstand overlooking the football field. A gentle breeze would waft in the alluring aroma of jasmine across from a neighboring field. It was perfect, until one evening when Buddy crashed in on them. He stumbled up the stairs, drunk.

"Kirsty," Buddy yelled. "I thought you were going to come to the movies with me."

Irritated, Kirsty rolled her eyes. "I never said I'd go."

"I told you I would take you," Buddy replied. "Why are you with this fag?"

"Leave us alone," Nick piped up.

"Fuck off!" Buddy retorted.

To get away from Buddy's abuse, Nick took Kirsty's hand and led her down the stairs.

"Come back here!" Buddy bellowed. "I didn't say you could leave." He bounded down the stairs after them and shoved Nick in the back. Nick tumbled uncontrollably and landed face-first into the dry dirt below.

"Time to go." Buddy grabbed Kirsty's arm. She squealed as his tight grip hurt her wrist.

Nick had never fought back before, but hearing Kirsty in pain filled him with righteous rage. Without fear, Nick jumped to his feet and punched Buddy as hard as he could. Buddy didn't flinch. He released his grip on Kirsty and shook his head with eyes open wide and lips stretched across his teeth in a lunatic smile.

Buddy threw a looping right hand. *Crack!* Nick rocked back and dropped to the ground. Everything went dark; all he could hear was mumbled static. A cloud came into view, as if he were looking at it through a pinhole. The black hole slowly widened, neighboring trees and a building came into focus. Nick couldn't remember where he was. Sound slowly crept back. A scream. His head rolled in its direction. He made out a moving shape under the bleachers. He closed his eyes, stared again. Buddy was on top of Kirsty. Holding her down. Thrusting into her. She was pleading for him to stop. He was laughing.

Nick staggered to his feet. Screamed as he ran at Buddy. Hit him with everything he had. They tumbled to the ground. Free of Buddy's weight, Kirsty curled up in a ball and sobbed uncontrollably. Buddy rolled to his feet, pants flapping around his ankles, his erection exposed.

"What the fuck do you think you're doing, fag?" he roared. He lunged at Nick, hitting him in the stomach and wrestling him to the ground, then flipped him over so he got a mouthful of dirt.

"Fuck you!" Buddy yelled in his ear. "You ain't nothing but a bitch."

Buddy pulled down Nick's pants, exposing his backside, and pushed his cock hard against his ass crack. Guiding it with force.

"No! Please!" Nick cried in desperation, but Buddy ignored him and plunged his cock deep inside Nick's anus. The pain shot through his body like a hot knife, and he felt his rectum rip. Blood seeped down between his butt cheeks as Buddy thrust into him, calling him "a dirty fag" with each push.

After Buddy came inside Nick, he stood and hissed at him with menace. "Fucking fag! Who's the fucking man now."

Buddy wrenched Kirsty up by the hair. "This is your fault, bitch! Say anything and I'll kill you both. You fucking know I will." He then dumped her back on the ground and stomped off, pulling up his pants and tightening his belt.

Nick had told his father in this very room what happened earlier that day. Instead of showing compassion, his father blamed him, accused him of asking for it and of bringing shame onto him and their family again. Unable to take any more, Nick ran from the house and the town, and never looked back.

A hand rested on Nick's shoulder.

"He's gone now," the doctor said softly. Nick wiped his eyes, nodded, and stood over his father's lifeless body. He cleared his throat and spat on his father's face.

"Burn in hell, you bastard!"

CHAPTER SEVENTY-ONE

THE VISITOR'S ROOM at Bell Island wasn't a place Ross spent much time in, and he was pleasantly surprised not to see Justin sitting on the other side of the safety glass. Instead, this time his visitor was a slender man in an ill-fitting black suit. The man's arms were wrapped around a worn, tan briefcase that sat on his lap. His head bobbled on a slight angle, and he watched Ross through thick, black-rimmed glasses.

"Hello, Mr. Ross Smith," the bespectacled man said into his phone handset. "My name is Walter Smith. We're not related," he chuckled, revealing slightly uneven teeth. "I work for the FBI. Oh, I love saying that... F. B. I. I'm actually not a field agent yet. I'm working on that, though, and hope to get my badge sometime this year."

"And I should care?" Ross fired back.

"I was hoping to talk to you about two things, Mr. Smith. I've approved many books from our depository to be sent here to you. I must say, I normally wouldn't send these books to a prison, as they're extremely valuable and rare. Usually only the FBI can access them." Walter leaned his head back, looking down his nose at Ross. "I didn't have to approve them."

"Yay, good for you," Ross sarcastically replied.

"When I heard that you'd requested them personally, I decided to cut through some of the red tape and make sure you got what you asked for. That wasn't easy, I can tell you."

"Thanks, I didn't know."

"That's all good, Mr. Smith. You're a bit of a special case."

"I am?" Ross asked, leaning back in his chair to relax his back muscles.

"I'm a student of the game. I live, breathe, and eat my job, Mr. Smith. So many cases come across my desk that I have to file. I know where everything is, and where to find it. It's a specialist job."

"Like a librarian?"

"No," Walter shot back as if insulted. "I do deal with books and files, and I do spend a large amount of my time in the record room. But I'm a research analyst and a recorder of information."

"So, a librarian."

"Can you please not say that? I have come here to help you, not to be insulted."

"I'm sorry. I'm not sure what you want?"

"As I was saying, I have approved a fair number of books for your perusal, and most of them revolve around profiling serial killers. I'm surprised you would need them."

"Why is that?"

"You cracked the Beetle Butcher, a case that looked uncrackable with the info that was available. I've read all the research, interviews, and files. The speed with which you solved that case was pure genius. I'm impressed." Walter removed his glasses, drawing attention to his left eye, which was slightly lazy and made him appear cross-eyed. He cleaned them with a handkerchief and slipped them back onto his nose. "That brings us to my first question. I would like to know how you did it. I've dealt with hundreds of these types of cases, and I need to understand how you did it."

Ross had been asked the same question more times than he could care to remember, and he was going to give this guy the same answer. "Just plain good old detective work, my friend. I got lucky."

"And what else?"

"That's it."

"It can't be." The man sounded aggravated. "You couldn't have just randomly found him without any clues or leads."

"There were clues, and I found them," Ross said. "That's how I did it. Plain and simple."

Walter let out a deep sigh. "Maybe we can talk more about it later. The other question I have is, why do you need these books?"

"There's a murderer in here—a sick person killing prisoners." Ross was happy to talk about the case at hand. "I don't think it's just about killing, there's something more to it. More people will die."

"Guilty men will die?" The young FBI man's eyes widened.

"Guilty or not, they deserve justice just like everyone else."

"Why do you care? You will die in here too."

"It's the right thing to do," Ross snapped. "I may be in here, but that doesn't mean I have to leave my humanity on the outside."

"I can help you, Mr. Smith." The visitor clearly appeared happy with himself. "Excuse my questioning. I just wanted to know that I'd be helping you for the right reasons, and that you wouldn't waste my time. I've heard about what's been happening in here, this Heart Collector. If I hadn't, I wouldn't have allowed any of my precious books to be sent here.

"You interest me, Mr. Smith. You're a killer who wants to catch killers himself and save the innocent, while it makes no difference to your own personal well-being. I find that intriguing. I thought you might like to read this." Walter removed a manila folder from his briefcase. "Here are some cases you may find interesting, and I have even created a profile of your killer." Walter signaled Officer Hickman at the end of the visitor's aisle to approach and handed him the folder. He then returned his attention to Ross.

"Once you've read this, we can maybe talk about the Beetle Butcher some more?"

"Help me catch the Heart Collector before he kills again," Ross said, "and I'll think about it."

CHAPTER SEVENTY-TWO

STEVE FOUND THE brown-bonded leather chair he favored and waited for his latté. He hadn't been in the Book Café for a while, but it still gave him the warm fuzzies to be there, surrounded by written scriptures alive with stories. He noticed a collection of books on the Elizabethan-style dark oak coffee table. He picked up a random book: *Harry Potter and the Goblet of Fire*. He'd read the entire series to his youngest child. To find the time to read aloud for half an hour each night before she went to bed had been tricky, as work often required him to work late. But he was glad he'd stuck with it. It was a memory he held onto with great fondness. He missed his kids more than anything. Once he got really clean, he would find a way to become part of their lives again.

His latte arrived, and so did Montana. She sat opposite him, her face beaming. Steve glanced at the barista and signaled him to start making Montana's coffee.

"I think I have someone," she announced, rubbing her hands together.

"You have someone?" Steve wasn't sure what she meant.

"To take care of our 'rat' problem."

"Ahhh, that Soda-ratola." Steve took a sip of his latte, while moving his eyebrows up and down to emphasize his play on words.

"He wasn't what I expected," Montana said. "But then I didn't know what to expect in the first place. He's going to get back to me with a price."

"How much are you willing to pay?" Steve crossed his legs, resting his hands on his knee.

"I don't know but it'll be worth it."

"You know I can't help with the money side of things right now,"

Steve said.

"Oh, Steve, I'll take care of everything. I just need you to support me through this." Montana reached over and placed her hand on his.

Steve nodded, picked up his latte, and gazed at a London planetree through the café window. A squirrel wound its way round the trunk to an overhanging branch. It balanced itself on the swaying branch before jumping to a neighboring tree.

"You're looking good, Steve," Montana said. "You know, the beard suits you. You should have grown one years ago."

"I should've done a few things years ago," Steve laughed, then looked deep into Montana's eyes. "You don't have to do this, you know. What you don't do is equally as important as what you do. You should come and see Silver. He'd be able to help you more than I can."

"That's OK." Montana looked at Steve lovingly. "Killing the rat will do that."

"Killing the rat or is the rat killing you? When it dies, would you die as well?"

"Is this you talking or is it Silver?"

"It's me."

"Are you sure? Since you've joined this group, you don't talk like you anymore." Montana sat back.

"I talk the same, it's just that I now have new words to use."

"I'm happy that Silver is helping you, Steve, but you need to watch that you don't become one of his brainless followers."

Steve leaned forward. "Montana, have you thought about leaving this all behind and moving to Australia? Starting all over again?"

"No, I want my old life back. I'm not sure what you're getting at?"

"I've been talking to Silver about this. . ." Steve admitted.

"You told him?" Montana shot back.

"Not in so many words, but in a roundabout way. He's so wise, Montana. We should stop while we have the opportunity."

"No, we agreed. This is what we're doing!" Montana shifted around in her chair, visibly agitated.

"I've thought about it long and hard, but I'm sorry—I can't help you with this rat anymore. I was weak when I said I would. Weak people do weak things. To be strong, we need to make strong decisions. Let's be strong together, Montana."

"What?" Montana looked incredulous.

"I don't care about Justin," Steve explained. "If he hadn't done what he did, I wouldn't be where I am right now, and where I am now is where I'm meant to be."

"Is this some kind of a sick joke?"

Steve stood and kissed Montana on the top of her head. "It's no joke. It's time to move on. I can't be an enabler for you anymore. I love you in the way you want me to love you. Like a friend, and as a friend I ask you to stop this. Come with me to see Silver—tonight."

Montana didn't look at him. Steve nodded to himself, wanting her to stand.

"My door is open to you, like my heart is open to you," he sighed, and left, alone.

CHAPTER SEVENTY-THREE

RAIN THUNDERED DOWN, hitting the parked four-wheel drive with such force that the windshield wipers were useless. Frustrated, Misha tried his binoculars again; the Port of Bayovar was one mile away. In this weather, it felt more like ten. He sat in the passenger seat with his local contact in Peru. The drugs were late, which Misha didn't like, and his companion picked up on this.

"It's this weather, you know," Ricardo said, rolling a matchstick from side to side between his lips. "People can't drive when it rains. Their brains don't work so good." Ricardo had a round head and large, protruding ears, and a full face of dark stubble.

"They is coming?" Misha asked, trying his damnedest to see what was going on through the sheets of water. It looked like the last load was being placed in the hull, and the workers were getting the ship ready to depart.

"Yes, of course, they will be here. Look, I call them again."

Just as Ricardo was about to pick up his cell phone, he received a text and smiled.

"They had a flat tire. Only in weather like this do you get a flat tire, no? Anyway, it's fixed and they will be here quick smart. Don't worry, the captain will not leave without the cocaine, my friend. His life isn't worth it."

Misha caught sight of four black Hummers with tinted windows speeding toward the ship, crashing through puddles. This could only mean one thing: a raid. The Hummers skidded to a halt on the wet concrete. The doors flung open. Armored men jumped out with automatic weapons at the ready. The ship was locked down. Nothing would get on or off.

"Fuck, fuck, fuck." Misha's companion repeated.

"Call your men," Misha sneered. "Stop them. Tell them go to safe house. Not here."

"Yes, fuck!" In his native tongue, Ricardo contacted his men and told them to avoid the port and to go to the backup location.

Misha saw one of the guys in uniform limping in the rain. Rudy. The DEA agent had waited until the very last minute to make the bust. If not for the flat tire, the drugs would have been in the process of being hidden in one of the containers.

This convinced Misha that he definitely had a traitor in his crew. It also meant he'd have a huge problem getting the uncut cocaine into New York in time. He'd let Justin believe that Justin was the only one with a deadline. If Misha wasn't able to settle his payments to Russia, he'd be as good as dead himself.

Misha's companion slammed the vehicle in reverse. The back wheels spun in the mud as he sped away from the port. He crosscut his way through back roads to make sure they weren't followed. Misha was quiet on the ride; he was thinking. He needed to find another way to get his drugs into New York. He cracked open a can of Soda-Cola and took a huge gulp. Then it hit him.

FILE THREE:
SODA-COCAINE

IT WAS THE FIRST FRIDAY NIGHT of Spring Break, and the Wilson Brothers' traveling fair was packed with a mixture of excited adults, yelling teenagers, and shrieking kids. The combined sounds of voices morphed into the music and blared from all corners of the field.

The sun inched below the horizon, and electricity buzzed through multicolored lights, hiding how old and rickety the rides actually were. Balloons ducked and weaved around the park as people moved from ride to ride, sideshow to sideshow.

Laura McCoy screamed excitedly as the last member of the Fabulous Seven arrived. She and her friends had been planning this night for months, what they were going to wear, rides they would dare to go on, and what boys would fall over themselves to talk to them.

It didn't happen often that all seven friends were allowed to go out together without a parent tagging along. The girls huddled and compared their accessories, spending money, and the drama their parents gave them on the drive out. They took selfies to capture the moment, each girl posing perfectly.

Laura's long blonde hair set her apart from her friends. She'd been growing it since the age of five. It was lustrous, straight, and went all the way to the hem of her miniskirt. She washed it often and brushed it 120 times every night. She'd never been tempted to cut it, only trimmed it now and then to keep it healthy. Her hair defined her uniqueness in the world.

When the animated movie *Tangled* was released, Laura became obsessed with it. She would dress as Rapunzel for any fancy-dress occasion, even birthday parties. Her mother was her biggest fan and helped create elaborate Rapunzel costumes. Young girls meeting Laura in the street of her small town would call her "Rapunzel" and want a photo with her.

She loved the attention, and every Saturday she'd dress up just to have her photo taken with her groupies at the mall.

The next step had naturally been to open an Instagram account. At first she simply posted pictures of herself dressed as Rapunzel, then she started adding photos of herself with her fans. Her account popped up on some cosplay websites, and her following skyrocketed. She knew exactly how many fans she was gaining each day and losing even one follower made her terribly depressed.

As she grew into a teenager, Laura's body blossomed and she started getting cheeky with her hair and curves. Fewer of her pictures now showed her dressed as Rapunzel, and as getting "likes" became her obsession, she began to show more skin, realizing that the more playfully sexual she appeared, the more likes she'd receive. Before long, Laura was mostly posting pictures of herself in revealing clothing with her hair suggestively draped around her body. If a particular photo didn't get enough likes, she'd delete it immediately.

One of the Fabulous Seven spotted a group of cute guys in line for the Ghost Train, and Laura squealed with excitement. Giggling and egging each other on, the girls quickly lined up behind them and tried to get the guys' attention by totally ignoring them and talking as loud as they could about how awesome they were.

When their turn came, the girls crammed into the ghost carts. During the ride, they overreacted to every spider, ghost, or vampire that popped out of nowhere. Wherever the guys went, the girls followed, or tried to get there before them. Before long, a game developed between the two groups, merging them into one. They laughed and flirted up a storm.

The giant Ferris wheel called to them; from the top of the ride they'd be able to see the entire town. It was also a good way to pair off into smaller groups. Laura had her eye on Benjamin; he played football and was also the captain of the basketball team. She made sure she'd be able to softly flick her hair into in his face throughout the ride.

They joined the long line, and snacked on cotton candy while complaining about having to wait. Fredrick sat in the tiny booth to the right of the wheel. As the operator, his job consisted of pushing the yellow button to load, and the green button to set the wheel in motion. Tonight he wasn't thinking about the job though, instead all he was thinking about was the half-bottle of vodka in his trailer that he would polish off that night and whether Sarah from the hoop-toss sideshow would let him fuck her again. He'd been working for the traveling fair for three years. It was an easy job, and it allowed him to indulge his drinking habit.

Roddy's task was to load people on and off the wheel. He was twenty-two and focused on making his job more interesting by seeing how many points he could score in a night in a game he called "Touchdown."

He tried to get in triple figures most days. Touching a girl on the hip scored three points, on the butt five points, and a boob hit seven points, with three bonus points if the boob touch became a three-second hold.

With the last carriage loaded, Fredrick hit the green button and zoned out. The wheel would automatically stop after ten rotations. He ran his hand through his greasy hair and put his red cap back on to cover his eyes.

Roddy saw some young MILFs at the end of the line, so he wandered down with a measuring stick to check their kids' heights and grab some easy points on the mothers. As he passed Laura and her friends, he ran his hand along the girls closest to him. Three hips, two butts—that came to a total of sixteen points.

Laura felt the hand on her bottom but couldn't see whose it was so she turned back to the conversation she'd been having. They were working out who would be the breakout star of a current boy band rumored to be breaking up.

At first she didn't feel her hair being touched, as it happened so often. She also didn't notice the guy in the dark gorilla suit sneaking in behind them with his squeaking banana. Nor did she notice as he lifted up her hair and wrapped it around one of the slow-moving carriages.

Suddenly, Laura's head jolted back. She tried to pull it forward, but the grip was strong and pulled her back even farther. She tried to see which of her friends were playing this trick on her—if it was Benjamin, he wasn't going to get even a kiss now!

She shrieked when she realized what was really happening. She grabbed her hair and jerked it in an attempt to free it from the carriage. Her hair was stuck. The Ferris wheel began dragging her over the cheap chain that acted as a barrier between the line and the ride. She screamed louder as she was lifted off the ground. Her friends screamed too. Soon the entire crowd screamed and pointed at Laura as she rose up into the air.

Roddy turned to see what the commotion was about. He dropped the measuring stick, ran toward Laura, but missed her as she was pulled up and out of his reach. He yelled at Fredrick to stop the ride. When Fredrick saw what was happening, he slammed his hand down on the red emergency stop button, and the wheel came to a screeching halt. This caused the carriages to swing dangerously backward and forward, ripping the hair from Laura's skull. Tumbling downward, she landed hard and was impaled on a rusty pole railing.

At the back of the crowd, the gorilla jumped and clicked his heels together in victory, then skipped off to his hired car.

CHAPTER SEVENTY-FIVE

THE MERE THOUGHT of having a twenty-dollar phone in his pocket—one that you could pick up from any old electronics store—made Justin feel uncomfortable. It wasn't because it was a burner phone that Misha had given him. He just didn't like cheap things. What if someone saw it and thought it was his actual phone?

There was only one number saved on the phone, and only one person knew that number. When it vibrated, he knew to answer immediately. He kicked everyone out of his office, then fiddled with the buttons trying to remember how to operate a low-tech device.

"Misha!" Justin barked abruptly.

"Mr. Justin, we have slight problem," the Russian voice crackled.

"A problem?"

"Yes. Not as big problem as it could have been. Police raided boat."

"You are fucking joking!" Justin shouted down the line.

"This is no joke. Is no laughing matter. Our stuff is OK. It did not make it onto boat. So that is good. Police find nothing."

"What?" Justin asked, not sure what exactly was happening.

"Police they raided boat. Stuff was not on boat. They did not find stuff. Stuff is safe."

"That's good." Justin breathed a sigh of relief.

"What is not good. We still have to get stuff to New York."

"Find another boat," Justin urged.

"Yes, but not so easy. Now many eyes are looking. But I have plan. Plan that is good and will work."

"What is this plan?" Justin sounded skeptical.

"Your fizzy bubbles, it is sold in lots of places. It not be hard for you to see if boat you use is close. Can pick up."

"You want me to use a Soda-Cola vessel to pick up the stuff?"

"Yes. We have understanding. I have man who say lots of sugar is picked up in area. Soda-Cola sugar boat is good."

"No, we don't have an understanding," Justin shot back. "It's not going to happen." His mind raced. It was bad enough that he'd borrowed money from Soda-Cola to do the deal. There was no way could he use the company's delivery ship to bring the drugs in.

"You will make it happen, Mr. Justin. You have deadline. You will find boat. Call me when you know boat going to be here." And with that, Misha hung up.

Justin stared at the phone in his hand. "Fuck!" he yelled, as if it were the phone's fault.

He got onto his computer and fired off a couple of emails. He sent the first one to Guy Chambers, the head of IT. Guy had shown himself to be handy in certain situations and he'd easily be able to find out which boats were in Misha's area and carrying Soda-Cola products. The second email went to Black Wolf. If there were a way to have the drugs picked up and sent to America, he'd know it.

CHAPTER SEVENTY-SIX

GUY CHAMBERS LIKED COMPUTERS. He understood them better than he understood people, and a keyboard under his fingers felt as natural to him as taking a breath. On his desk were three screens, and each screen had multiple windows open, and each window had scrolling code. He absorbed it all while continuously searching. He was on a mission.

Over the last year, Guy had transformed himself. He'd dropped forty pounds. Gone was the long, oily hair he'd had since his teenage years, as well as the goatee, oversized T-shirts, and sweatpants. He cleared up his acne-prone skin and visited a dentist who removed years of grime and installed invisible braces to fix his crooked bottom teeth.

He went to the gym five days a week now, toning his muscles with the help of a personal trainer. He no longer survived on pizza and an endless supply of Soda-Cola, but instead had healthy meals delivered to work and sipped filtered water.

Now that his energy levels had increased and his mood improved, he looked forward to seizing each day. He also dressed better, as clothes now flattered his slender new shape. It was all thanks to Justin Truth.

After their first meeting, Guy wanted to kill the son of a bitch. No one had ever spoken to him like that at Soda-Cola. He'd returned to his office, shaking and feeling like a scared ten-year-old kid that had just been beaten up because he was fat. But even though Justin threatened him, he'd also given him a completely different view on life; a view that only money and power could provide.

Guy took his wife to the restaurant Justin had made arrangements for and the staff treated them like celebrities. They enjoyed Michelin-star quality food and wine, and on the taxi ride home, they'd laughed and kissed like teenagers on their first date.

The next day, Guy looked at himself in his bedroom mirror and was disgusted by what he saw. Someone like Justin would never look like this, he'd thought. If he wanted to enjoy nights like that again, he would have to change, so he decided to do whatever Justin asked of him.

He even started to model himself on Justin, from the way he dressed, to the way he walked and talked. Nothing Justin asked for was too much. Guy ran his team tighter than before and made sure he was at Justin's call 24-7.

Guy's full attention was now on Justin's latest email. He'd fired Guy a random question about Soda-Cola boats in the region of Colombia that were headed for New York in the coming weeks. Nothing was ever random when it came to Justin, though, so Guy's priority was to provide him with a quick answer. He wanted Justin to be proud of him.

CHAPTER SEVENTY-SEVEN

THE NEWS WASN'T GOOD. Black Wolf wasn't able to help him. For the risk, Black Wolf needed a huge cash payment upfront and time to pull together a plan to get the coke safely into New York. Justin couldn't give him either. Justin could see his train ticket inching out of his grasp. His phone buzzed. It was Guy.

"Mr. Truth. I have run a diagnostic report of all the boats that Soda-Cola owns or hires."

"And?"

"There are three shipments due in New York over the next two weeks."

"Do any of them pass by the coordinates I sent you? And can they be here two days before the requested date?"

"There is one. But..."

"But what?"

"It's not going to be easy. I don't want to overstep the mark, but I'm guessing that you wouldn't want this to show up on the boat's log? The boat stopping..."

"What do you mean?" Justin asked, knowing full well what Guy meant.

"Sir, I'm... I'll help no matter what. You tell me what to do, and you can consider it done. I want to be your guy, Mr. Truth. You can trust me with anything."

The line went quiet as Justin rested the phone against his forehead and rubbed his scar. There had to be another way, yet he couldn't think of one.

"Yes, Guy," Justin finally said. "It has to be untraceable."

"The way around this would be for someone who knows the computer system inside and out to mess with the ship's guidance computer.

If the captain were to play along, the boat could manually sail to where you need and be back on track by the time the guidance system was up and running again. In other words, you'd be creating a black spot. As long as it's done within the tight timeline, it will appear not to have moved."

"So it's possible? Not to be tracked?"

"It is, but the system would have to be hacked on the ship. This means someone like myself would have to be on a plane in two hours to meet the ship at its next port and be there ready to do whatever needs doing."

"I guess you'll be flying out in two hours then." Justin sounded determined.

"That's what I expected you might decide, Mr. Truth. I've already booked a flight and will be leaving for it any minute now."

"Good work, Guy."

"Thank you, sir."

"And Guy, you will be rewarded for this. Do we have an understanding?"

"Yes, sir."

"Guy, do we have an understanding?"

"I understand. This never happened, or any trace of this."

Justin ended the call. As soon as the drugs were cleared, he'd have to take care of Guy—he knew way too much.

CHAPTER SEVENTY-EIGHT

THE COUNTRY-CLUB HOUSE was the unofficial boardroom for some of the biggest deals that went down in America. Membership was limited, and you had to pay a premium for it. Carlton had been a member for over thirty years, with Soda-Cola picking up the tab.

His health was improving, and he felt like a new man. Some of his gray hair was growing back thick and strong, his head was clear, and his sense of humor had returned sharper than ever. Whenever he thought about taking a more active role in Soda-Cola, he went for a round of golf, and by the eleventh tee he talked himself out of it.

Something inside the Soda-Cola building made him sick, and he convinced himself that it was stress. Now he just attended board meetings, played golf, and lunched with other heads of corporations that had retired or were close to it.

Edward Chandler couldn't play a good game of golf, even if his life depended on it. No number of lessons could cure his uncoordinated limbs. At the club, he was notorious for how badly he played and the length of time it took him to complete the course. On too many occasions, other members had been stuck behind him, waiting for him to finish a hole in thirty strokes. And these weren't the type of men who waited. Carlton had to persuade the club chairmen to allow Edward to keep his membership, provided he stuck to the driving range.

One ball sailed high in the air and hit the 200-yard mark easily, while the other ball crawled along the ground, barely making it twenty yards.

"Are you still seeing Woody to work on your drive?" Carlton asked as he pushed the button to automatically drop a ball onto his tee. Woody was the golf club pro and worked wonders on most people's game.

"Once a week. Can't you tell?" Edward smiled slyly.

Both men chuckled.

"I bet Woody can't balance the books of a multinational company, though," Carlton quipped.

"I'll take that bet," Edward said, as he hooked a ball, sending it flying hard right. Edward pushed a button for a new ball and decided now was a good time to talk serious business.

"I want to ask you a few things about Justin," he began.

"Ask away," Carlton replied.

"Do you trust him?"

"I'm loving the dividend checks I've been getting since he took over, that's for sure." Carlton laughed.

"I'm hearing rumors about the way he's running the day-to-day operations," Edward swung his club short. It thumped the ground, knocking his ball off the tee. "There are a lot of unhappy people."

"It's a tough job." Carlton sent a ball skyward, exceeding 250 yards.

"You did it well." Edward repositioned his feet and measured the distance from the ball with his club. He visualized his swing and pictured the ball soaring into the sky.

"I had thirty years on my side," Carlton replied as he cracked another lofty ball. "When I started, lots of people didn't like what I was doing. I retrenched a quarter of the staff in my first twelve months. Today's market is even tougher. You've seen the forecast. It's not good."

"I don't trust him," Edward said bluntly, slicing another ball. "My daughter told me a few things…" Edward paused. "I'm just giving you the heads-up, but I'm sure Justin has embezzled company money; in fact, over a million dollars."

Carlton stopped midswing and lifted his head.

"That's a serious accusation."

"What he has done is craft a beautiful financial web of deceit. The only reason I picked it up was because I was searching using a new forensic algorithm. Something wasn't right about the numbers; I knew he was up to something."

"And what do you want to do about it?" Carlton asked, putting away his golf club. He was no longer in a mood to hit a few friendly golf balls.

"It should be handled internally. Once I have all the information, I'll call an emergency board meeting, present the damning evidence, as well as a swift exit program for Justin. Minimize the damage."

"Agreed. We've only just recovered from last year's scandals. Once you have it all locked down, I'll personally invite Justin to face his crimes."

CHAPTER SEVENTY-NINE

MONTANA'S HEAD FELT HOT as she entered Kenny's office and closed the door behind her. He stared at her with puppy-dog eyes, and she could feel him undressing her in his mind.

"I have something for you," she said. "But I'm not sure I should be giving it to you." She held up a file.

"Sounds intriguing," Kenny smiled, circumnavigating his desk toward her.

"This doesn't exist. Once you see it, you can't unsee it."

"A bit like you." Kenny's eyes widened.

"Kenny. A good friend of mine got fired over this. She works… worked at Soda-Cola. She said Justin brought her in to work on their military pitch against us. She worked eighteen hours a day on it for weeks. She's good—amazing, even. Yesterday, he pulled her into his office and told her to use our friendship to get Phizz information. Something to help them win. When she said she wouldn't, he fired her and had her instantly escorted out of the building. They didn't think of searching her, as it happened so quickly. If they did, they may have noticed a flash drive on her keyring. She gave the flash drive to me this morning over breakfast with the words FUCK JUSTIN. This is the printout."

Kenny moved in closer and placed his hands on Montana's hips.

"What do you want me to do?" he asked. Montana picked up on the double entendre. She lifted up the file again and tapped it against his chest.

"What I'm giving you is highly illegal," she said, trying to distract him. "If any of this gets back to Justin, he'll have a whole horde of lawyers coming after us."

"I'll take care of it," Kenny replied, taking the file with a naughty schoolboy grin. Montana hated that Justin had been right about one thing: that someone lost their job because of what was in that file did make it more exciting to read. Kenny drifted back to his desk, opening the file.

"This is their entire pitch," he murmured after a while.

"Correct."

"Not just that of Soda-Cola, but also of Peter Gordon's company and what they're offering."

"Indeed," Montana nodded.

"We can undercut them with this. At the end of the day it's about numbers, and all we have to do is be zero-point-one cent cheaper to retain the contract. Going by this, we could actually ask for more and still win. They've really overshot the mark—they've obviously been greedy and hoped that some backroom handshakes would swing the deal."

Kenny lifted his head, clapped his hands, and shimmied his shoulders.

"This is dynamite, Montana. Fucking dynamite."

CHAPTER EIGHTY

The motel room was just as Nick had left it. He hovered outside the door, wishing he had thrown out the half-eaten pizza and chicken wings before flying home to watch his father bite the dust. He forced his body to ignore his nose, ran in, gathered up the rancid leftovers, chucked them in the trash, and dropped the trash can outside. He took a breath, leaving the front door open to bring in fresh air.

While the air cleared, Nick sat on the stairs and checked his cell phone for emails. He deleted some he would never read and deleted more he should've read, then sent a brief email to Brendon Gibson letting him know the investigation was going well and that he was making progress.

His thoughts drifted back to Kirsty. He wondered where she was now and what she was up to. Once he solved this case, he thought he might track her down and see if she wanted to meet him for coffee. He suddenly laughed out loud. It was quite a strange thought that after all this time, he'd ask her out for coffee.

On the flight back here, he'd decided it was time to visit New York. Gatsby Cutter had started and ended his journey there, he was certain. He checked his room; the air was less pungent. Holding his breath, he hit the room like a human tornado, pulling down the Wall of Mystery and cramming it into his backpack. He'd rebuild his investigation on a new wall in New York. Solutions sometimes came from two random clues finding each other in the bottom of his bag. The truth wanted to be found, and it usually found ways to be heard.

As he left his room, Nick saw little Mandy and she was giggling. He could tell by the spontaneous way she moved that the threat to her big brother—that he'd kill him if he ever touched her again—had worked.

Mandy ran up to Nick and hugged his leg, as if she knew he'd made her brother stop. Her father appeared and he too seemed in better spirits than before.

"Good to see you again." He smiled. "My little girl has taken a real shine to you, mister. She wouldn't stop asking where you were after the last time we bumped into you."

"I had some family commitments to take care of," Nick said, stroking her curly hair.

"Nothing bad, I hope." The father looked concerned.

"All for the best, to be honest." Nick shifted his attention to the little girl and went down on one knee to be at her level. "And it's good to see you, gorgeous girl. I know you're being a good girl for your dad." She smiled and nodded.

From the corner of his eye, Nick clocked her brother about to exit their motel room. He was dressed differently, less angry and black, and had a new haircut. Gone were the long fringe and bad attitude. When the boy saw Nick, he dropped his head and went back into the room.

"Well, little one, I have to say goodbye."

"But you just got back?" she pouted.

"I know, it's my job."

"Where you going?" she asked.

"New York," Nick said. "There's a ghost there that needs to be caught."

"I don't like ghosts," Mandy said, giving him a warm hug.

"Neither do I, sweetie, neither do I."

CHAPTER EIGHTY-ONE

THE PHOTOS IN THE report were graphic. For a second, Ross forgot that he was looking at real people whose lives had been cut short by some sadistic murderer.

He glanced from picture to picture. The victims in the photos were all women, aged in their early twenties. All of them had green eyes, short brown hair, long legs, and small breasts. In fact, they looked so similar, they could've easily been related. Each victim had been abducted and repeatedly raped over three days before being killed. They'd had their eyes removed and their hearts clumsily hacked out. Over three years, five bodies had been discovered in shallow graves before their killer was caught.

A forensic profiler had studied each of the gruesome crimes and then issued a potential profile of the killer.

The perpetrator is most likely a white male, as all the victims have been white, and sexual criminals often gravitate toward people of their own skin color.

Removing their hearts points toward heartbreak. Someone has broken his heart in the past and he does the same to them as an act of revenge.

Removing the eyes stops them from looking at him. This could be because he is ashamed with what he's doing. Another reason could be that he doesn't like his victims looking at him as if he is an anomaly, potentially due to an unusual facial or body feature or something else that makes him less attractive.

The perpetrator held his captives for three days. This could mean that he only had three days before anyone would miss him, for example, his wife or family members.

He is likely intelligent and might often be seen as moody and unap-

proachable. He thinks of himself as smarter than others and is frustrated that they don't recognize his perceived intelligence. He is a loner and would have used his own vehicle to dump the bodies, as he would've felt uncomfortable using a rental car.

He wants to be involved in the investigation, and there's a good chance that he has visited the crime scenes, called helplines, or volunteered to help. Doing so will stroke his ego and let him know what the police have found out.

Based on this information, the investigators had used traffic cameras to create quadrats around the dumpsites. A license plate that appeared in three of the quadrats led them to the killer, James Russell.

The profile had been close to spot-on. Ross skimmed over the arresting officer's notes.

James Russell was a twenty-nine-year-old white male. His front teeth were abnormal and protruded out at right angles. In interviews he'd revealed that while growing up, an older sister constantly abused him, making him perform sexual acts on himself in front of her. She called him her "dirty little monkey that no one would love." She wore heavy amounts of eye shadow and laughed at his performances so hard she would tell him her heart might explode. He became introverted. Not knowing what it was to be loved, he eventually married a woman twice his age who was controlling and aggressive, like his sister. The only time he had to himself was when his wife visited her family up north for a long weekend every second month. He wasn't allowed to go. He had to stay home and look after her collection of cats. He used this time to plan his crimes. The victims resembled his sister, and he took his hatred of her out on them.

Ross returned the case and pulled out the second one Walter had given him. This involved a killer who'd painted eyeballs onto his victims' eyelids. When caught, the killer talked about the "hate" he saw in their eyes when he attacked them. By painting new, "friendlier" eyeballs onto their eyelids, he hated them less.

Ross went over the files a few times and scrutinized every single detail about why and how the men had committed the murders. There were certainly many similarities between these cases and his current one. The way the killers treated the eyes revealed a lot about their mental state; none of them liked how they thought their victims perceived them.

At the back of the folder was an envelope with Walter's profile. It was clear, focused, and detailed. Ross nodded to all the conclusions. As he read it for the umpteenth time, one line stood out: *The killer wears a uniform, to work and to the world.* No one sees him for what he is. Remove the uniform and discover the monster.

CHAPTER EIGHTY-TWO

STEVE'S WATCH TOLD HIM that he'd been sitting in the plastic seat at City Hall for four hours and seventeen minutes. He knew he would be in for the long haul and had brought along a Jim Thompson novel and some snacks. He was determined to get the allocated money owed to Silver's church from the government department.

He tried not to think about how disappointed Montana was with him. She didn't seem to understand how much he had changed. For once in his life, he was happy, truly happy. It was time to leave the past behind and live in this moment.

Steve dressed up today to show he meant business; a suit and tie spoke volumes. The last time he'd worn a suit was in court. His beard felt itchy against the collar of his crisp, white shirt. Sitting by his right foot was an aged leather briefcase—a gift he'd received on his thirtieth birthday. Everything he needed for today was filed within it.

There were no empty chairs in the waiting room; they were filled with a collection of people from different cultures, religions, and walks of life. Each person had been issued a number on their arrival. An overhead LED screen showed which number could now proceed to a room or cubicle. Very rarely did Steve see someone leave a cubicle smiling.

Silver had told Steve that he'd be wasting his time. A few years earlier, he'd gone down there to look into some church funding. He'd gotten lost in the paperwork and been bounced around from department to department. But if Steve had learned anything from the corporate world, it was how to cross the t's and dot the i's. He looked forward to the challenge.

"Ticket number H2545, please proceed to room seven. Ticket Number H2545, please proceed to room seven," a robotic voice announced over the PA system. Steve put his book away and calmly made his way toward room seven.

"Good morning," Steve warmly addressed the lady behind a desk stacked with forms and files. She wore her dark hair in a bun and used a generous amount of blusher. The two empty, large Starbucks coffee cups in the bin were apparently her way of enduring the morning.

"Good morning, sir, and how may I help you today?" she said curtly.

"My name is Steve, and yours?"

The lady smiled, and with her eyes partially hidden behind large fake eyelashes, pointed down at the embossed name plaque next to her PC.

"Patricia Mills," Steve smiled. "May I call you Patricia? I'm looking into some funding for a church I'm supporting."

"That's great. To apply for funding, you need to go online and print out a RD47 form. Fill it out and bring it back—then I'd be more than happy to help."

Steve nodded. He knew paperwork was the backbone of any government department, and fortunately he'd done his research. He gently placed his briefcase on the table, popped the locks, and pulled out the RD47 form he'd already completed.

"Here you go, I thought you might need this," Steve chirped.

"Well, aren't ya a helpful little bee." She started to read the form while twiddling a pen around in her right hand, stopping occasionally to tap it against her teeth. Steve watched her eyes as she scrutinized the form, wondering if she'd be trawling for the tiniest of reasons to point out that he was required to submit more paperwork. Her eyes found something, and the corners of her mouth curled upward in victory.

"I'm sorry, sir, you've missed a signature from the founding member on page four. Until you can provide this, I cannot enter the information into our system."

Steve smiled. He'd been prepared for this, too, and handed over another form.

"Well spotted," he said kindly. "I was going to get Silver to sign it, but if he had, it would have created another problem. You would have found that he also needed to sign a DF56A, and having him sign the original RD47 would mean he would have to come down here in person to have you witness it. Signing the DF56A, and having a Justice of the Peace witness it, saves him the hassle of coming in and being told that after he signed it, he'd need the aforementioned Justice of the Peace signature as well before you could process his request.

"As soon as we would have organized all that, you would have entered it into the system. Enter problem number three: you would have found that the RD47 was outdated and so would have to be replaced by the DW47, as it was specific to Native American religions. I have also printed this out, and filled it in with the correct signatures." Steve placed the appropriate forms on her desk.

He continued: "About this time you would have told me that I'm in the wrong place and had to go to the Federal Building to fill out a blue AIN07 form. Doing this, and then completing the yellow AIN05 form, I would be sent back here, as it falls under American religion and not American Indian religion. I've also prepared these forms." Steve handed those over.

"And here's the kicker. Even after all this, I'd still have to wait twenty-one days for the request to be processed, only to receive a letter to say that this file was already open, that all the extra formalities I'd provided weren't needed, and all I needed to do was have his tribe elder sign off on form Ind2020 that Silver is a member of his tribe. And so here they are."

Steve placed the final form on top of the others. "Once you've entered all this, you will see that the church has been in arrears of payments for two-and-a-half years. You will then issue a check to the church and set up a monthly payment to go into this bank account." Steve presented a deposit slip and placed it on top of the forms and pulled out his book.

"Don't mind me, I'll just do some reading while you get on with it. I'm thinking there's a lot of processing to do. People to call, and protocols to set in motion. At least two hours, if you don't dawdle. I'm here to help if anyone gives you the runaround."

Patricia stared at Steve, unsure of what to do, so she did something she hadn't done for a long time: her actual job.

CHAPTER EIGHTY-THREE

NICK LIKED LAGUARDIA airport. It was a hive of activity; a truly international destination. Like a ninja, he cut and weaved his way through the maze of people until he found the gate that Gatsby had used to fly to Chicago. It was a busy spot—the turnover would be higher than college students at a strip bar.

Nick pulled the wad out of his front pocket. Rhonda from Chicago O'Hare Airport security had given him a contact at JFK. The help he'd given her in busting the thieves helped her get a long overdue promotion and move up a few pay grades.

After a quick stop at Krispy Kreme, Nick navigated his way to the security room's side door. He texted the number Rhonda had given him and waited. Two minutes later a hefty man with a cheerful face and thick ginger Afro opened the door. His shirt was half-tucked into his pants, which were still hanging loose; his snakeskin belt wasn't doing its job.

"You Nick?" he asked.

"I am, you must be Ging?" Nick was thrown a little by the name.

"I am Ging. Only a man with hair as beautiful as this could have that name," he smiled.

"Rhonda suggested I buy you some of these to share with the other security guys." Nick held up his large box of donuts.

"She said that?"

Nick tried his best to sound like Rhonda. "She said, 'If you don't buy Ging a big-ass box of donuts, he ain't going to be helping nobody. And he ain't gonna share no donuts with no one. And he should get a goddamn haircut already.' I think those were her words."

Ging cracked up. "Damn, that girl knows me well. I can't let you in, but tell me what you need and I'll see what I can do. Might take a bit, have to sneak it in around real work."

Nick pulled out a folded piece of paper from his back pocket. "Any help will do," he said. "All you have to do is check the footage and see if you can spot this guy at gate forty-eight." Nick unfolded the paper to show Ging a security camera photo of Gatsby Cutter. "I've written down the date and rough times he was here."

"That should be fine." Ging took the paper. "What exactly are you looking for?"

"How he arrived at the airport, anyone he may have spoken to, and whether he made any calls. I just want to find out who he is and where he's from."

"I'll flick you a text when I have anything. This is all private info, bro, and there's no way you can tell anyone you got it from me."

"You have my word, and another box of donuts."

"Make them all double chocolate with custard." Ging smiled.

CHAPTER EIGHTY-FOUR

EVEN THE SCARIEST INMATES at Bell Island were afraid of one man like no other: Father O'Grady.

No gang messed with him. Hard men would move over to let him pass, and no one pushed in front of him or took anything that was his. Even the warden treated him with kid gloves and had given him the library to run and do with as he pleased. He was the only prisoner who could move about the prison without fear.

Why? Because he'd seen the face of Satan—and killed him.

A five-part Netflix documentary delved deep into the case, using actual court footage. A movie was in the pipeline by the same studio that produced *The Conjuring* series. Pictures of the bloody, mutilated body of the young boy he performed the exorcism on still popped up as dark memes. Father O'Grady was famous for all the wrong reasons.

O'Grady placed the last box in the corner, pulled the desk away from the wall, and rolled in a second chair. He'd spent the morning creating more working space in the storage room. It was looking more like an office. Ross joined him, sat at the desk, and made fun of him for cleaning. O'Grady retorted with his own joke before placing a pile of newly delivered books in front of Ross.

"These arrived for you this morning, from Walter," O'Grady said.

"Thanks, Father." Ross skimmed the cover of the books. *Hearts, Eyes, and Why* was another murder profile book that dealt with body parts, while the one underneath it was titled *Satan Lives and Religion Dies*.

O'Grady sat down across from Ross and picked up *Satan Lives and Religion Dies*.

"I'm in this one," he said.

"Really? I didn't ask Walter Smith for it," Ross apologized.

"I know," O'Grady smiled. "We've chatted about most things, but you've never asked about this. The large Satanic elephant is in the room wherever I go."

"It's not really my business…" Ross wasn't sure how to respond.

"It's OK. Just look at how I'm treated here. I don't fit in. People don't know what to do around me. You're different. In your company, I feel normal." Both men looked up and smiled. "Well, as normal as a priest in jail convicted for killing a possessed boy can be," O'Grady added.

He passed the book to Ross, who checked out the cover and flipped through some pages. O'Grady had started this line of conversation, so he decided to go along with it.

"Why did you do it?" Ross asked.

"It was the right thing to do. God delivered this boy to me in order to help him. You don't know that you've met someone who is possessed by the Devil until it actually physically happens. God put me to the test and asked me to step up."

"I'm not a religious man, Father. Could it have been brought on by, say, a brain tumor? Or a psychotic episode triggered by a mental disorder, like schizophrenia?"

"I've read all the reports. When you're in the presence of pure evil, you feel it. I didn't go out looking for a possessed person to perform an exorcism on. It is the last thing any member of the cloth ever wants to face. When God wants you to do something, you do it. Working for the Lord isn't a choice."

O'Grady took a deep breath. "I haven't spoken to anyone about what happened in that room. The holy war I battled. The book you're holding is what the documentary series is based on—no, I haven't watched it. The book discusses the medical reports, contains interviews from people who'd been close to the boy—his parents, brothers, friends, and other members of the church and school. The writer pushed me to tell my side of the story. But my side is God's side. I didn't feel I needed people to get behind me."

"Sounds like you want to get something off your chest now, Father?"

"Maybe I do, Ross. Reading all these books you've been sent makes me think that maybe people should know my side. There's human evil, but the biggest evil is still Satan and how he has used science to hide what he does."

"You want to tell me about it?"

"Maybe. Maybe one day I'll tell you what it's like to be in a room with Satan, so if you're ever in that same position, you'll know what to do."

Officer Hickman appeared in the doorway and stared at the two men. "Sorry to interrupt, Father, but the warden wants to see Ross. Now!"

CHAPTER EIGHTY-FIVE

THE TRAIN CAR WOBBLED from side to side as it thundered down the tracks, deep beneath the streets of New York. Nick sat, his body swaying to the rocking beat. Ging had worked some magic for Nick and found footage of how the old man got to the airport: the subway. Nick was one step closer, now he needed to find out where the old man had boarded the train. He'd sent Rhonda a text, thanking her for her help. She'd replied instantly, calling him Sugar Lips.

He rode the train's loop to and from the airport. Over and over. Each journey, he'd sit in a different compartment to see what else he could feel. Nick continuously asked himself why the old man had caught the subway to the airport. He found that when he asked the universe the same question repeatedly, he naturally opened himself up to receiving the answers. Even if he just picked up on the smallest clue, it usually led to another, more significant lead.

Reading people was one thing, and reading places was another. Like people, places were packed with detailed information that they wanted to share with the right person asking the right question. Nick believed that everything left an imprint, and that every event or action was re-membered. This train wanted to share what it knew; Nick just had to sit in the right place at the right time and be open to receiving the answer.

Riding the same train back and forth as if it was Groundhog Day meant some of the train's security guards became suspicious of Nick and started asking him questions—what he was doing, whether he had a ticket. The words *potential terrorist* still hung in the air over New York from the Twin Towers. When faced with these questions, he showed the guards his unlimited-ride MetroCard, told them about Gatsby Cuter, and asked them whether they recognized him in the photo. Each time, they'd shake their heads; of the thousands of people they saw each day, this guy didn't pop out.

So, Nick continued to smile and sit and wait patiently, enjoying the company of New York's finest crazies. He started to give the regulars nicknames and memorized when they got on, how long they stayed, where they sat, and when they got off.

First on his list of "usual suspects" was Plastic Bag Sally, a lady in her late fifties with wild gray hair. She lugged around at least ten packed plastic bags full of more plastic bags. Next was Butterbean, a giant of a man who moved about as if he were a mouse. He always wore head-phones stooped over his head and mouthed the words of whatever he was listening to. Billy Goat, a tall skinny guy with a few teeth missing and a long pointy beard amused Nick as he was always laughing and slapping his leg at jokes no one else could hear.

Another regular of note was Mumbler, a stocky Hispanic man in a black hoodie who oscillated between mumbling to himself, getting angry, yelling at no one in particular, getting scared, and going back to mumbling.

Most of these people sat in the same spot at the same time. Then, as if a silent warning went off, they'd move, apparently aware that security would be in any minute to kick them off.

Nick found that approaching the crazies got him nowhere. Instead he sat quietly and let them strike up a conversation with him. On their terms, they were happy to share bizarre stories of things they'd seen, places they'd been to, and how they'd ended up in New York.

Snowball was a regular who typically kept to himself, rubbing dandruff off his head onto the floor while singing Christmas songs. Today he seemed to be in a good mood and chuckled away, smiling over at Nick. Nick reached into his pocket, pulled out a Hershey's Milk Chocolate bar, and tossed it over to him. Snowball looked down at the chocolate in his lap and laughed some more.

"Damn, my good sir, what for you don't want this?" Snowball eagerly picked up the bar.

"I just thought you might want it," Nick said, pulling out another bar. "I was going to eat this one instead."

"I think I will join you in participating in the eating of such dining experience. The label may say Hershey's, but it's not caramel."

Both men unwrapped their bars and Nick broke off a bite-size piece while Snowball devoured almost half of his in one bite.

"Who you be, and what for you be riding the train?" Snowball asked. "I sees you a lot these last days."

"I'm just looking for someone, and they sometimes take this train," Nick answered.

"They do not have a telecommunications device on their persons that you could converse with them on?"

"I don't have their number."

"That is a problem that one is not wanting to have, not in a day and place like this."

"I do have a picture of them," Nick said hopefully, and reached into his back pocket.

"Ah, photographic information. Could you not scan it into machine of quantum processing, and have their location reported back to you?"

"If only I had such a machine," Nick said.

Snowball laughed and ate some more chocolate, in little bites this time, while talking. "I bet you do. You should get one. I actually invented such a machine once. Got stolen by the CIA. Crack goes the chocolate in my mouth. Munch, munch. It's good just like the way the good things in life are manipulated into little bites of information, shared above us in waves of energy and spikes. I see it all."

"Can you have a look, and maybe tell me if you've seen him?" Nick asked.

"I see everything, man. Not just through my eyes but through the pores in my skin, and my brain processes it all. I see sounds in waves of color a lot, and I see smells in glows."

Nick pulled out his folded piece of paper. "Here's what he looks like."

Snowball snatched the paper and ran his eyes over it as if it were a contract. He started laughing. "This one tough old man."

"Yeah… why do you say that?"

"I saw this old man give a street urchin the beating of his life."

"This guy?" Nick sat forward.

"He was wearing the same clothes as this photographic evidence shows me. I told you my brain process all. I was sitting just yonder there, under the heating vent, and it happen right there." Snowball pointed at the ground between them. "And once he finished inflicting the beating, he dispatched him from the train. It was rather grandiose."

CHAPTER EIGHTY-SIX

ALL THE TEXT said was:

    The Queen is away. Let's get fucked up

Rip was supposed to slow down his extracurricular activities, but instead he pushed for more, upping the excitement levels. Any time Rip wanted something, Justin had to pull it together. It was the nature of their friendship and it had worked for Justin so far, but he was getting sick of it. He had outgrown babysitting Rip.

He had more important plans on his mind than getting Rip wasted and laid tonight. Guy was now on the container ship and checking in every thirty minutes about hacking the locator and making sure the cargo would be picked up. Guy needed more money to buy silence. Justin gave him $25,000 for this purpose.

Justin felt like he was losing control; too many people were involved now for his liking. He just had to kill someone; that would calm him down for sure. He opened the link to the cameras he had in Jennifer's bedroom. She was alone, watching a movie on her laptop. He called her cell phone from his burner phone. He watched as she looked at her phone, not recognizing the number. She answered it.

"Hello?" she said.

Justin remained quiet, staring at her.

"Hello? Who is this? Is this you, Brad? What happened?"

"Bitch!" Justin growled in a deep voice.

Jennifer ended the call, dropped her phone on the bed, and pulled her knees to her chest. Justin watched her for a few more minutes, then an idea came to him. He was Justin Truth, and Justin Truth didn't sit around waiting for things to happen, he made them happen.

He fired Rip a quick text.

```
The royal court is waiting.
Many a pig will be put on the spit.
Dan will be over shortly.
```

He eagerly made some calls to get things rolling. Tonight was going to be an extra-special evening. He was going to need some high-class hookers, a large bag of coke, copious amounts of Dom Pérignon, and a few extras. . .

CHAPTER EIGHTY-SEVEN

SITTING OUTSIDE THE Warden's office always made Ross feel like a naughty schoolboy waiting for the principal. No matter what time the appointment had been set for, the warden would keep Ross waiting. Classic little power games.

After an hour, the warden's secretary opened the door and invited him in. Ross thanked her and took the visitor's seat. The warden was behind his mahogany pedestal desk. With his head rested on his entwined fingers, his elbows on the desk, and eyes closed, the warden basked in the afternoon sunlight that streamed in through the thirteenth-century-inspired stained glass windows.

"Warden," Ross said.

The warden remained quiet.

The warden's office was referred to as "the Bell Room" because the warden had, on display, an assortment of antique church bells he'd collected from all over the world. Each bell had a plaque with a blurb about it that Ross couldn't read them from his seat—not that he would. Behind the warden was the largest bell, the original bell the island was named after. To the left of the bell was a fire exit door. He wondered if the warden rang the bells in the event of a fire to warn everyone. The idea made him smirk.

Finally, the warden spoke. "Myself and the Lord hope that our trust in you hasn't been misplaced. Are we close to solving this problem?" he said, as if a dead person was just as much of an inconvenience as a lightbulb that needed replacing.

"We are. It's one of your guards," Ross said.

"What?"

"Going by the profile, it has to be," Ross said matter-of-factly.

"This place is full of killers and you come back telling me it's one of my guards? This is not the time for you to be grinding axes," the warden thundered.

"I'm not judging people as one or the other. You asked me to look into it, and that's what I'm doing."

"Are you? Or is this a way to get back at the system? Are you trying to put an even bigger wedge between people in authority positions and those who need to be told what to do? They can't operate under normal rules. This is just what they want to hear, and next thing you know, the whole place will be going up in a riot like animals!"

"I haven't told anyone about this," Ross said, trying to calm the warden.

"Don't you dare raise your voice at me! You're still just scum here, Smith. Another number, another prisoner. Do not take my charity for weakness."

Ross sighed. The warden was right. He was still seen as a dirty cop, as bad as the other inmates. Ross wished he had some jellybeans to offer him.

"I'm sorry." Ross sank back in his chair. "It's this killer, he's got me wound up. I'm grateful for your generosity. How about I leave this for you to read over. It's a profile of the killer. He's—"

"I'll read it when I have time." The warden cut him off. "And if I decide to push it further, I'll share it with my senior staff and see if any of the prisoners fit the bill."

"Just the prisoners?" Ross asked gently so as not to set the warden off again.

"For now!" The warden's eyes moved to the door.

Ross meandered to the door. He stopped and decided to try a different tack.

"Sir, I want to thank you for asking me to help you with this matter. It shows great compassion, and true leadership. Everyone talks about how gifted you are at running a place like this. This is not an easy job, not with all the scum, murderers, and rapists in here. You're so gifted one could be forgiven for thinking that God looked upon you as a son."

The warden leaned back, basking in the glory of Ross's words. Ross continued. "You have great staff here, too. Even before I arrived, people in the force waxed lyrical about them, and the qualities you brought out in them. I don't want to show you disrespect by indicating that one of them is, you know, a bad apple. Sir, these serial killers are master manipulators. The only reason I'm this close to finding the perpetrator is because of the help you've provided. Allowing Walter Smith from the FBI to visit and share his wealth of information has been a godsend."

"Walter who?"

"Walter Smith, he's been helping me by sending out books and case files. He was in here last week. I thought you'd arranged it?"

"If someone from the FBI visited my prison, I would be the first to know about it. Who is this Walter Smith?"

Ross sat back down, confused. He asked himself the same question: *Who the fuck is Walter Smith?*

CHAPTER EIGHTY-EIGHT

DAN, THE FORMER CAB-MAN had stepped up in the world. He wore an Armani suit, Mermin black leather shoes, and a gold Tag Heuer wrapped around his wrist. The smell of his Ralph Lauren aftershave still crisp, he beamed at Justin in the rearview mirror, a new tooth completing his smile.

Two weeks earlier, Justin had given Dan a preloaded credit card to make himself more presentable. If he was going to be Justin's full-time driver, he had to look the part; glamorous and complex. Justin gave him the day off to get what he needed. Paying for all of it with Justin's credit card made Dan feel wealthy for the first time in his life.

Back in India, growing up with six brothers and sisters, his family struggled to put food on the table. Each family member had to work to scrape together what they needed to survive each day. In the Indian caste system, Dan would never be allowed to make it out of the slum. He was taught from a very early age that people with money are far superior to everyone else.

From his first ride in his cab, Dan knew that Justin was special: he was Kshatriyas, a ruler and warrior. To be in the presence of such a great man filled Dan with pride. He liked to watch Justin get women, he liked to watch Justin outthink his competition, and he liked to watch Justin enforce his dominance over lesser men.

The road outside Rip's bachelor apartment was bumper to bumper. There was no place to pull over or park. Outside the entrance to Rip's building, Dan arrogantly stopped the Audi in the middle of the road and turned on his hazard lights. Traffic behind him ground to a halt. Cars now trapped honked furiously, and divers angrily waved at him to move. As Rip approached, Dan jumped out of the driver's seat and proudly held open the passenger's door for him. Once Rip was seated, he closed the door and drove them on their way.

Dan adjusted the rearview mirror so he could sneak glances at the two men. He listened to everything and mimicked what he heard to improve his English.

"Lord Justin Justice, which dragons will we slay tonight?" Rip excitedly rubbed his hands together.

"A species we have yet to encounter, Sir Rippington," Justin said with a knowing pout.

"I'm intrigued. What are these creatures?"

"You'll have to wait and see. Good things come to those with power." Justin smiled, offering Rip a large line of coke.

Dan mouthed the words *good things come to those with power* to himself.

A few lines of coke later, they arrived at their destination. Dan leaned out his window and swiped a security card to gain access to a gated parking lot. Rip recognized the location. Once Dan parked the car, Rip leapt out of the vehicle and embraced the fresh sea air.

Moored at the pier—lights shining, music pumping—was Peter Gordon's luxury yacht. Dan opened the car door for Justin, fetched two suitcases from the trunk, then followed the two men onto the yacht. Dan greedily stared at the five gorgeous models lounging around the top deck, all dressed like slutty mermaids. He placed the suitcases in Justin's cabin and got another view of the goddesses before returning to the pier. He waved enthusiastically as the yacht cruised out of the harbor.

"Good things come to those with power," he said.

SNOWBALL CUT HIS STEAK lengthwise, then across each strip to make cubes of meat. He stabbed one cube with his fork and nibbled at it like a rabbit. He'd ordered a two-pound steak. Just the steak.

"Did any of your friends see Gatsby?" Nick asked.

"Nicolas, I am afraid that the answer you are seeking is not one that I can provide. There are numerous of my fellow traveling companions that have many such skills. There is one young lady who is able to talk without moving her mouth; her voice is one that only your soul can hear. This other gentleman of impeccable distinguished behavior can converse with any animal that pitter-patters on four feet." Snowball stabbed more meat cubes and swallowed them, one after the other, without chewing. "Yet for all their talents, none were able to confirm that they knew of the movements of the man you seek."

"It was worth asking, thanks for trying," Nick said.

"The question is still out there. Just because I have not communicated the answer to you does not mean that I have not told you in another time portion. At any point the line of time could bend, bringing us all together. I have seen my past self on a collection of occasions. My future self is a pompous jerk. Steak is good. Chewy. Salty. Must have a nourishing morsel more." Snowball nibbled on another piece.

Nick took a sip of his coffee, tapping the cup with his index finger. His eyes shifted around the diner. What could he do next? It seemed as if Gatsby had disappeared like a snowman in July. A waitress appeared at their table, balancing a tray of beverages. She placed a drink down.

"One soda," she smiled, moving onto the next table.

"That is most wonderful of you, miss," Snowball waved.

"I didn't know you ordered a soda?" Nick inquired.

"Just because I have no memory of placing an order, does not mean it is not my order. Maybe it was that righteous future me. He often will do unquestionable deeds for which I do not know, until I become him, then it will all be revealed." Snowball sucked up a mouthful of soda. "I did prefer when orange was orange, and not colored bubbles of fancy."

Nick wondered if that was the answer. Had the old man delivered him to where he was meant to be? He'd become so focused on finding him, instead of finding out why. Everything Nick had discovered along the way pointed him to OrangeFizz. If someone connected to OrangeFizz was the instigator, New York would be the best place to start searching for them. It was the home of OrangeFizz after all. Nick pulled out his phone. A Google search of OrangeFizz businesses would give him names of suspects he could visit. People near the train line would be an ideal place to start. He grabbed some napkins to note down his findings.

"Good work," Snowball said. "I too shall take one of these flimsy pieces of paper and work out the directions one must move in, to arrive at the place one must be in, to see who of us, in what time, ordered the soda."

CHAPTER NINETY

STEVE HAD DELIVERED THOUSANDS of presentations over his career. But standing in front of this gathering of twenty-seven new church attendees made him more nervous than he'd ever felt before. This was to be his first speech inside the church walls, and the first time he'd talk to a group to share the church's values.

While preparing for this talk, Silver encouraged Steve to bare his soul to the group. To do so would enable his soul to grow. It would help him to reach those he wanted to help in a way they would be open to and understand. To use not just words, but words that mattered. Silver was here tonight, at the back of the room serving up soup to their guests. He'd set the bar high, and Steve wanted to make his mentor proud.

Steve was barefoot, wearing a simple blue T-shirt and shorts. "It's not what you wear, it's where your heart is," Silver told him. The group of newcomers he was about to address had given up on life. Most were drug addicts, alcoholics, abusers, or victims of abuse. They were people who slept in doorways, who scavenged for food in restaurant dumpsters, and survived off money Good Samaritans dropped their way.

Steve cheerfully gazed around the room. Like him, the room had had a makeover. The backdated money he'd secured from the government had been put to good use. The holes in the walls had been fixed and painted, the once water-stained ceiling was back to its majestic self, the brand new ducted central heating was on, and the newly laid carpet still smelled fresh. He scrunched his toes in the fibers.

"I'm a fuckup," Steve began. "Every morning I woke up, and I was reminded what a fuckup I was. I'd lost my wife, my kids, my job, my friends and my self-respect. And since I was a fuckup, I didn't have to try. My new way of looking at life was, 'how could I fuck up more than the day before?' If you're going to be a fuckup, why not be the biggest fuckup you can be? I challenged myself daily on the fucked-up scale. Pretty soon no fuckup felt fucked up enough." He removed some items from a pocket: a metal spoon, a syringe, a piece of cotton, and a lighter.

"I was offered heroin and I fucking took it, and took it, and took it, and. . . you know. I fucking loved it."

Steve used the syringe to suck up some water and squirted it into the spoon. He dropped in a Tic Tac-sized bit of black tar heroin. He used the lighter to heat up the bottom of the spoon, causing the heroin to dissolve into the water. He then took the piece of cotton, rolled it up in a ball, and placed it in the spoon, where it instantly expanded like a sponge.

He inserted the syringe into the cotton, pulled on the plunger, and slowly sucked up the heroin, using the cotton as a filter. Steve held up the loaded syringe for the group to see. He then took a bit of elastic and wound it around his bicep to make a tourniquet, pumping his fist to make his veins swell up.

"I'm not a fuckup because I used this." He tapped his vein of choice, then inserted the needle into his arm. His body screamed for him to push the plunger, to send a warm wave of divine pleasure through his veins. "I'm a fuckup because I used this to forget the person who I was. Everyone's a fuckup. You just have to love the fuckup you are."

Steve pulled the needle out of his arm. Some junkies in the audience drew in a loud breath—they couldn't believe he'd pulled a loaded syringe out. Steve held the syringe up. "And I've found out, I like the fuckup I am, when I don't fuck it up with this." Steve squirted the heroin into the air. "Each of you will be different. We're not saying 'no' to drugs. We are asking that if you want to get loaded, do it for the right reason. Everyone is a fuckup. Let's just be the best fuckups we can be."

Steve walked into the middle of the group. "This is not about me standing here and just talking to you, it's about us talking to each other. Learning from each other.

"Now let's do a little exercise," he continued. "Pick a person you don't know and tell them about yourself and vice versa. Choose one thing you're sad about and one thing that makes you happy and share it."

The group started to talk among themselves. Steve looked over to

Silver, who gave him an approving nod.

A newcomer approached Steve. "Can I talk to you, please?" he asked, while wiping his runny nose on the sleeve of an old Dodgers sweatshirt.

"Of course you can, we're all equals here," Steve assured him gently.

"You made some sense, man," he nodded. "But, did you, you know, have to squirt all that heroin onto the floor?"

Steve pulled out the rest of the stash and handed it to him. "You can have it if you like."

"Really?" The guy didn't need to be asked twice; he grabbed the black tar and stuffed it in his pocket. "I was going to have a smoke outside. Can I talk to you some more? I like the idea of being the best fuckup I can be."

Steve felt exhilarated. The rush he got from helping others far outweighed the rush from any drug he'd used.

CHAPTER NINETY-ONE

JUSTIN RESTED ON the top deck of the seventy-foot yacht as it docked, sipping coffee and picking from a platter of fresh fruit. The approaching Manhattan skyline reflected off his sunglasses, hiding his red eyes. He was immaculately dressed for the day ahead, having selected a purple tie with fine silver thread weaved through it. Only he and the crew were up; everyone else was still below. He'd left his two mermaids to sleep off their hangovers in his cabin, while Rip, still wearing his pirate eye patch, was passed out with the other three hookers.

The yacht's engine rumbled, slowing its drift. A crew member threw a rope to lasso a bronzed cleat and guided the vessel gently into position. The moment the yacht docked, Justin gave the captain directions, then departed while checking his phone for any new notifications. Every time he checked his phone there were more urgent problems he needed to address.

Dan was parked exactly where he had dropped them off. Justin slipped into the backseat of the car, replying excitedly to a text.

"Mister. . . sir," Dan beamed. "You party like motherfucking gangsta last night?" He tapped his hand on his forehead. "Up to here in pussy, no doubt."

"Whatever you think it was like," Justin boasted, "it was better."

Justin pulled out his burner phone and messaged Misha to make sure everything was on track at his end. Guy had worked his magic on the ship to create a black hole for a flawless pickup. The cocaine was scheduled to arrive this afternoon, at the latest. Justin reminded Misha he needed the bulk of his share of the sale by 5:00 p.m. Friday.

Justin wasn't usually one to feel stress. Bet for the first time in a long time, he was nervous. He went over the plan in his head, making sure all the angles were covered. He gave himself permission to smile. He was good. Better than good—he was fucking amazing.

Dan pulled into the underground parking garage at the Luxor Apartments, parked in Justin's premium spot, and opened the door for him.

Dan smiled. "Welcome home. I will wait and take you to work."

"Take the car to get detailed first," Justin said. "The salt air isn't good for it. On the way back I need you to pick up some things. I've messaged you a list. I've got a Skype call I have to make upstairs in five minutes. Be back here in two hours."

"I will make sure everything is done extra good, sir."

Justin watched the Audi disappear up the car ramp. He wasn't aware of the black panel van pulling up behind him, nor did he hear its side door slide open, and didn't notice as two men jumped out and homed in on him.

CHAPTER NINETY-TWO

THE SOUND OF AUTOMATIC WEAPONS getting locked and loaded gave Rudy goosebumps. He loved this part of the job. Balls to the wall, strike while it's hot, and bust them bitches!

The botched Peru raid had pissed him off. His contact told him they'd gone in too early, that the drugs had been delayed due to the storm. If they'd waited ten more minutes, they would have caught the smugglers loading it. There wasn't much he could do about it. Not all busts went down as planned. Today would be different.

On the oil-stained floor in front of him was a dismantled Barrett .50 Cal sniper rifle, a personal favorite of his. He picked up the bolt carrier and depressed the catch to pop out the bolt. It was spotless. He cleaned the bolt face anyway.

Twelve hours earlier, Rudy's inside man sent him a message that a commercial cargo ship was smuggling Misha's drugs. Rudy scrutinized the vessel on their database and asked the Coast Guard to double-check its positioning. The ship's log reported a problem on board, that their navigation had gone down for a few hours, and this had temporarily halted the ship's progress until it was rebooted. According to the records, the vessel never went near land during that time.

Rudy rotated the accelerator in his hands and popped it to release the ride. He cleaned the ride with a Teflon cloth, then slid it back into place.

The ship was due in New York this afternoon. It had been leased by Soda-Cola and wasn't the type of vessel one could just thumb down for a ride, especially a drug pickup. It would have required some powerful friends in high places in order to smuggle the drugs on board midroute. Rudy wasn't aware Misha had these lofty corporate connections. But his inside man was adamant that the drugs were on board, and that if this bust went down, Misha would be left ruined—and the results would ripple through the Russian underground.

Rudy picked up the upper receiver and slid the barrel into its firing position.

With all the information at hand, Rudy decided to make the call, and hit "go" on today's mission. A storage warehouse on the port was sequestered as their base of operations. He briefed the entire team an hour ago, assigning them to positions around the port. The ground crew were with him in the warehouse; each member running through their own preraid rituals. They would follow Rudy anywhere, out of respect. He never asked anyone to do anything he wouldn't do himself. He didn't hide behind a desk, paperwork, or corrupt systems. He was upfront and straight with everyone, no matter what their rank. Everyone knew where they stood with Rudy. Busting the bad guys was all he cared about.

He clicked the two receivers together at the front, pulled the bulk groove back about halfway, then snapped the receivers together.

There was internal pressure on Rudy to pull back on his aggressive actions of late. He had been warned that a few high-ranking DEA officials were concerned with his tendency to go off-script and break protocols. Rudy's reply was simple: fuck off. He did whatever was needed to get the job done. Rudy didn't trust the system that he himself was a part of. He wasn't deaf to the rumors concerning DEA agents who were more invested in running drugs than stopping them. If anyone tried to derail him so they could profit from the drug cartels, it was only going to end one way: Rudy putting them down.

Rudy locked in the pins, inserted a loaded mag, and sighted the rifle. No one was untouchable. If anyone was helping Misha, even tying his shoelaces, then they had just graduated to his shit list as well.

CHAPTER NINETY-THREE

HER PHONE BUZZED. It was a text from Bob:

1334 West Hampton. Cargo bay 45

This was it. It meant they'd already started to torture Justin. She had asked them to stretch it out, to break him down, to make him suffer. She wanted him broken, distraught, to beg her to kill him.

Montana hastily changed into sweats and running shoes, tied her hair back, and jumped in her car. Her destination was in upstate New York, an hour's drive away. As it was the middle of the day, she might get there sooner. She dropped her foot down, and the car roared into life. Once Justin was dead, she decided that she would resign from Phizz, sell her apartment, move to her hometown, and do the stereotypical American thing: get a regular nine-to-five job, meet a regular guy, fall in love, and start a family. Never think about Justin Truth ever again. Her hands tightened on the wheel.

She thought of Steve. She'd dreamt about him a few times over the last week. She'd been mad at him; more than mad, downright angry. As the days went by though, she started to understand his reasoning. He had just pulled himself out of a very destructive cycle. She was proud of him. Once this deadly task was done, she would visit his church and ask for his forgiveness, maybe even chat to Silver about finding herself again.

Montana was in such a daze that she nearly overshot her turnoff. It was easy to miss the forgotten road in between overgrown bushes. Her car fishtailed into the road, and she continued toward a condemned complex, the Summit Mall. It had been built big; its developers heralded it as a shoppers' destination. Unfortunately, shoppers never stopped there, and it went bankrupt five years ago.

A rusty wire perimeter gate had been roughly wrenched open, allowing her to enter the derelict area beyond. There were three main buildings, and each was three stories high with external walkways connecting them. No Trespassing and rusty Hazard signs dotted the abandoned structures. It was like a cemetery for bankrupt businesses. She tore across the expansive weed-ridden parking lot and toward the back of the buildings. She drove past rows of identical cargo bays with rusted roller doors. Stenciled numbers were the only visual difference separating them. The store names had been long since removed.

Number forty-five came into view, a large green circle freshly spray painted on the service door. This was the right place. She parked in the cargo bay. No matter what she did now, Justin was dead. This was her last chance to walk away, pretend she had never started it, and move on with a new life she'd create. They had her money. All she had to do was put the car into reverse, do a U-turn, and keep driving.

She turned her car off, removed her sunglasses and stepped out of the vehicle into the bright sunshine. With tentative steps, she climbed up the stairs, and nervously stood on the platform. She gave the door three quick knocks, followed by two slower ones, and again three quick ones. The door swung open. Silhouetted in black was a solid man that was built like a door himself. He was dressed in black army fatigues, gloves, turtleneck, and an ammunitions vest. His face was hidden behind a woolen balaclava and reflective orange Special Forces goggles. He didn't say anything. Montana brushed some stray hairs behind her ear. He grunted and took a step back, giving Montana enough room to enter the dark building. He handed her a phone, then pulled the door closed behind her. Small portable lights provided the only source of illumination. Montana spoke into the phone.

"Hello?"

"Hello, Ms. Cruz," Bob replied in his dry voice. "Justin is waiting for you as agreed. There are rules you must follow. My men are here to make sure everything goes to plan. Do not ask them any questions. Kill him, then leave. Tell me you understand."

"I understand," Montana replied, nodding at the orange-goggled enforcer.

"Good. Hold out your hand."

Montana lifted her hand, uncurling her fingers. The enforcer dropped a small round squishy glob onto her palm. She prodded the white sphere with her thumb, examining it. She shook her hand hurriedly, flicking it away. It was an eyeball.

"Mr. Truth had a bit of bravado at first," Bob said, "We cut out one of his eyes to show him who was boss. He changed his tune after that. It became all very real for him. We then gave him decisions on different body parts. They could be broken, burned, or cut from him. If he didn't choose an option, we would do all three.

"To simulate drowning, his head is currently shrink-wrapped, and he can only suck in small amounts of oxygen by means of a thin straw. Every breath he takes is a struggle and he feels as if his lungs might implode. It's like waterboarding, but the older, uglier, meaner brother.

"It is now up to you. Every ounce of pain we have inflicted on him has been because of you, Montana. You started it. You will finish it. We have injected him with an amphetamine. This means he'll be lucid for you. He will understand and feel everything you do to him. Shoot him. Stab him. Cut him. Slice him. Castrate him. Garrote him. Kill him, Ms. Cruz."

Bob ended the call. She returned the phone to the orange-goggled enforcer. He slipped it into one of his vest pockets, then grunted for her to follow him. He led her down a flight of stairs, along a dark, winding corridor. The air felt damp and smelled strongly pesticide. Another orange-goggled enforcer stood guard in front of a heavy iron door. He nodded as they approached, and lifted the locking arm, pulling it open with a deep screeching of metal grinding on metal.

The room was pitch black. The enforcer grunted. Montana cautiously took a step into the void. She stopped. Took another step. Stopped. She could hear something move in the middle of the room; a scraping on the floor. Four spotlights suddenly came on with a loud boom, as electricity surged into the powerful bulbs. She was momentarily blinded. Bright white spots pulsing, clouding her vision. She stumbled to regain her balance.

As the spots faded, she saw Justin. He was slumped in a wooden dining chair, his wrists and ankles tightly bound with black duct tape. His expensive three-piece suit was ripped, lacerated skin exposed, and dark patches of blood soaked the fabric.

The door slammed shut behind her. The steel locking arm clicked back into place. She kept her eyes on Justin. He reacted to the sound of her footsteps, lifting his head to meet her eyes. His bludgeoned face was squeezed tight by the shrink-wrap. His chest rose and fell with shallow breaths. He started yelling at her in a muffled, garbled mess.

Montana took her time circling him, taking it all in. The smell of his singed flesh was strong and intense. Dark globules of blood dripped from where his fingernails used to be. His right ankle was broken so badly that his foot pointed the wrong way, and his fractured shin bone ripped through jagged skin. A boastful Italian silk tie hung loosely around his neck. She wrenched it from him, wrapping it around her fist, the purple now flecked with crimson.

"Hey, baby boy, what's the matter, you got a boo-boo," Montana teased. "You want me to kiss it better, run you a bath, get you a glass of Dalmore to take the edge off your hard day? How about I break your fucking nose?" With the tie wrapped tightly around her fist, she punched Justin's face. His head rocked back. It hurt her hand. Yelling, she punched him three more times; on the last blow, she heard his nose crack.

She dropped the tie to the ground, rubbing her bruised knuckles.

"You like that?" Montana said in a hoarse voice. "How do you like your baby girl now? Is she a bit naughty? Do you want to punish me? Put me over your knee? … Fuck you… Fuck you, and what you did to me for your own fucking amusement. You fuck. You fucking fuck. You fucking piece of fucking shit! God, I have thought so much about what I would say to you at this very moment, some brilliant speech to make you understand why. The funny thing is, I know no matter what I say, you won't understand. It would only be a waste of energy and air. You have no heart; you're an emotionless desert, void of any human decency. An endless black hole of bullshit. You're an off-the-Richter narcissistic sociopath with no redeemable qualities. The greatest gift you can give humanity is to not exist anymore.

"I've killed you so many times in my head. Every time I saw you, I saw you die. I saw you die at my hands. I saw the world made into a better place."

Montana pulled out a leather-sheathed Bowie knife she had tucked inside her pants. Its wooden handle was been intricately carved with images of wolves and eagles. "This belonged to my grandfather, and his father before him. My father presented it to me when I turned twenty-one to remind me of where we came from. For years, it just sat in a drawer. I didn't have any idea what to do with it. Then it dawned on me last week—the reason he'd given it to me, why it had been handed down from generation to generation, was to end your life."

She slid the knife from the sheath, light reflecting off the cold, polished steel. She ran the ten-inch blade over her fingers, feeling its titillating sharpness. She waved the blade in front of Justin's face, taunting him. Reflecting light into his one remaining eye.

"I could do so much to you, babe."

She trailed the blade down the front of his shirt, cutting off the remaining buttons. Then ripped his shirt open, exposing his bruised and battered chest. She placed the tip of the knife between two of his ribs, and applied pressure until the knife penetrated the skin. Justin's body jerked from the pain; he sucked his stomach in to avoid the blade. He made a deep-throated groan as the knife punctured and collapsed his right lung. She pulled out the knife and slapped him across the face with the side of the blade, leaving a bloody imprint. Her hand trembling with anger, it was time to end it; she didn't want to play anymore. It was time to free herself and move on.

She moved behind him, grabbed his sweat-soaked hair and yanked his head back, presenting his neck. He thrashed to escape, but the binds were too tight, his body too weak.

"You did this to you, Justin, and you fucking deserve it!" Montana held the blade against his throat, just below his Adam's apple. She gripped the handle tighter, then sliced across the skin, splitting it open. Blood seeped out. Justin thrusted his body forward in the chair in one final attempt to escape. The chair moved an inch. Montana's eyes widened as adrenaline surged through her body. Every muscle in her body tightened. She returned the blade to his bloodied neck in a frenzy. Deeper and harder, she worked the knife. Back and forward. Cutting and hacking. A torrent of blood now streamed out of the new gaping wound. His body convulsed one last time, then went limp.

She dropped the knife onto the hard concrete floor, and the sound echoed inside the small room.

CHAPTER NINETY-FOUR

AFTER A FEW DEEP BREATHS, Montana's legs went weak. She dropped to her knees, praying she wouldn't pass out. Her body shook. Her heart raced. Her eyes wept. She stared at her hands; they were like crimson gloves, dripping with silky blood. She frantically tried to wipe them clean on her top.

Montana had been fantasizing about killing Justin ever since the Soda-Cola 110th birthday celebration. She imagined the power she would feel herself regain by taking his life away. But now that she was immersed in his blood, she felt neither happier, nor sadder. Instead, the void inside her suddenly seemed to start growing. Killing Justin hadn't filled it yet.

For now, she would tell herself that, over time, the sun would shine warmer and the birds would sing sweeter. That she would wake up tomorrow feeling lighter. She would have breakfast and it would taste beautiful. She would call her mother, tell her she loved her. She would walk through the park, smell the flowers. She would go and visit Steve. They would reconnect. He would embrace her, understanding why. Then she could start her life over.

One of the enforcers towered over her, giving her a fright. She didn't hear him come in. She could see her own reflection in his orange goggles; she was covered in Justin's blood.

"I didn't think you'd go through with it," he said.

Montana wiped the blood from her chin, but only added more in the process. The man inspected Justin's body. He poked the lifeless head. It flopped to one side and rolled back to its original position. More blood oozed out of large gash.

"I'm proud of you," he said. "Slicing someone's throat open isn't as easy as you see in the movies."

Montana went to swallow, but stopped. There was something about the man's voice, the way he stood, that felt familiar. She blinked; nothing changed. Why was he talking to her? The man returned his attention to Montana. She shook her head. He nodded. She dropped onto her backside. He removed his goggles. She pushed herself backward with her hands and feet. He pulled off the balaclava and gave her a wink.

Montana screamed.

"Red looks good on you." Justin grinned. "Where are you going, baby? I'm not mad, actually I'm a little turned on." Justin bent over and picked up the tip of the knife with his thumb and forefinger, dropping it in a sealable plastic bag.

"Who…wh…oo… who…?" Montana stuttered, staring at the body she'd just butchered. Justin ripped the plastic wrap from the corpse, discarding the dirty film to the floor.

"You know, I thought you and Steve were friends. I bet he didn't think you were going to cut his throat like some backstabbing bitch."

"Steve?" Without the wrap, she could make out some of Steve's features under the purple swelling. They'd shaved him and cut his hair similar to Justin's before the vicious beating. Tears streamed down Montana's cheeks, and her throat clammed up.

"I was highly surprised to learn that you were trying to put out a contract on my life. I have friends in very low and dark places, Montana. I let you run with it—I wanted to see how far you'd go. And you went all the way, baby. You tapped into your inner killer." Justin clapped his hands slowly. "Well, this 'narcissistic sociopath who has no redeemable qualities' has some important business to attend to. Hate to love you and leave you, but I think you may need some quiet time with Steve here. I know the grieving process is important. I'll be back in a day or two. See you soon, babe."

Justin left, closing the heavy iron door behind him, locking Montana in with Steve's body. The lights went dark. Montana could no longer see Steve; all she could hear was his blood dripping onto the floor.

CHAPTER NINETY-FIVE

JUSTIN INSTRUCTED THE mercenary outside the iron door to watch over Montana; she was to stay in the filth she'd created for herself until he decided what to do with her.

They'd grabbed Steve outside his church last night; another mercenary had easily lured him out alone. While torturing him, Justin cheerfully told Steve that Montana would kill him. And that if only she had listened to him, none of this would have happened.

Justin pushed open the service door into the warm sunshine, jumped from the platform, and continued past Montana's car to the awaiting black panel van. His burner phone rang. Hopefully Misha had good news this time.

"Misha," Justin answered, as he shut the van's passenger door behind him.

"Hello, Mr. Justin. How was meeting?"

"It went well. Actually better than I thought," Justin said, signaling to the driver to put his foot down.

"Is good. I have word from captain. Boat close. Is docking sooner than planned. We have to move fast. As people say. Time is money."

"I'll be there as soon as I can."

"You not need to come," Misha said brusquely. "My men, take care of it."

"It's best if I'm there," Justin insisted. "It's my ship, and my money. Now I shouldn't have to ask this. Are you a hundred percent sure that there was no leak?"

"Is hundred percent no leak on my side. To make sure, I told men that drugs be arrive tomorrow. As soon as boat is in dock, I will call them, men will action fast. No time for police to get involved. No need for Mr. Justin to get hand dirty with unloading."

"I want to be there. We can open the container together."

The phone went quiet for a moment before Misha responded. "OK. I wait. Be quick smart. Like rabbit."

Justin stuffed the burner phone in his pocket as the panel van thundered away from the Summit Mall. It was still a workday for him, so he used the hour drive to the docks to make some calls and answer urgent emails. He flicked Rip a text to see how he was doing, phoned Debbie to move his meetings around, and contemplated contacting Carlton, who still hadn't returned his call from two days ago. He was about to phone him again when he saw they were approaching their destination. Carlton could wait, Justin decided.

The panel van swung into the docks, turned down a side road, and hammered along a commercial, dusty back road to the meeting point: an isolated area where old shipping containers were stacked waiting to be turned into scrap metal. Justin pointed Misha out to the driver, and the van pulled up across from the large Russian. Justin and the driver got out.

"Mr. Justin, is new look?" Misha said, looking sideways at Justin in his black fatigues, his typically manicured hair messed up from wearing his balaclava. "I call men now. Or you like for us to unload by ourselves?"

"Get them down here." Justin smiled. "Today is my day."

CHAPTER NINETY-SIX

RUDY WAS PERCHED in an observation point overlooking the Soda-Cola ship, watching through binoculars as it went about its docking procedures. He'd stationed five snipers at strategic spots around the expansive port, and each kept him updated. As soon as Misha entered the port, Rudy would know.

The entire port ran along the Hudson River, encompassing an area of approximately twenty-five miles. Rudy had strategically broken it down into key areas, constructing a net around the Soda-Cola ship. Once Misha's crew were within Rudy's dragnet, he would seal the area, leaving them no way to escape. The harbor would be cordoned off, the roads out would be blocked. The port's own high-security steel fence completed the trap.

Below Rudy was a mini-city of stacked containers. A troupe of RTG cranes maneuvered through the container buildings, sorting, stacking, and rebuilding. Behind him was a collection of private units, warehouses, and dumping grounds for marina equipment. To his far right, seven miles away, was the container graveyard where Misha was.

"The Bear is on the move," Rudy heard through his earpiece.

"How is the Nest?" Rudy asked his team, wanting to know what was happening at Misha's import business, three miles away in a group of commercial fishing warehouses.

"Something is going down," Blake replied. "The whole place just emptied. I'm counting twenty men in assorted vehicles rapidly leaving the Nest."

Rudy was excited. For a moment, he'd suspected that he had been played again. Earlier in the day he'd received conflicting intel that the shipment was due in tomorrow and he should pull out. Now he was glad he stuck with his gut and the original information.

"How's the Bear?" Rudy asked.

"Heading toward the Woods."

"Stations everyone!" Rudy commanded his team. "The Woods are about to come alive. Wait for my order!" Rudy needed the convoy of incoming cars to be inside his cordon. Once they were in, no one would get out.

"The Bees have entered the Woods," a voice snapped in Rudy's ear. This was it; Rudy focused his binoculars on the line of cars tearing toward the pier. The lead car stopped near the ship, and men piled out.

"How's the Bear?" He asked.

"The Bear is in the Woods," a voice replied.

"The Woods is go!" Rudy ordered. "Close off the roads. No one gets in or out. We want Misha alive. I repeat: the Woods is go!"

The DEA sprang into action. From the far side of the dock, seven patrol boats with wailing sirens sped into position, creating a line that separated the ship and anyone trying to get out of the harbor.

On each of the port roads leading out, armored Hummers weaved together to create a wall of steel. Road spikes were slid across the road and armed men took up positions behind the Hummers.

Two helicopters with snipers mounted in position descended from above the horizon. One hovered above the ship, the other positioned itself over the main entrance. This was the widest road to protect; in the unlikely event that a car broke through the roadblock, the chopper was there to stop them.

Ten ground units hit the ship from different angles, firing random shots with their assault rifles to indicate they meant business. Three cars split from the convoy; the helicopter above the ship fed their position to the roadblocks.

Rudy's earpiece sent him constant updates. He hobbled up the ship's boarding ramp as fast as his crippled leg would allow. The ship's captain rushed to contain the situation, getting in Rudy's face.

"Show me your papers!" he insisted.

Rudy pulled them out from under his DEA-branded bulletproof vest and shoved them into the captain's chest, knocking him on his ass. "We have reason to believe you have a large shipment of narcotics on board,

Captain Crackhead."

"Impossible!" the captain replied, struggling back to his feet. "This is an American ship. We have our rights."

"When it comes to trafficking drugs, you have no rights. And if you get in my face again, being arrested for obstruction will be the least of your problems."

"The Tree has been located," a voice sputtered through Rudy's intercom device.

"Give me your location; I'll be there ASAP," he replied urgently.

Five minutes later, Rudy stood in front of the forty-foot container holding bolt cutters. "It feels like Christmas, boys," he joked as he cut the security bolt off with a dull clunk.

CHAPTER NINETY-SEVEN

MISHA'S PHONE LIT UP like a Christmas tree. It was a raid! The appearance of choppers in the sky and the cracking of distant gunfire confirmed it.

"Motherfucker," Misha growled.

"I think those are your DEA friends," Justin sneered. "You remember the ones you said didn't know about the shipment."

"No. Not possible." Misha replied. He knew of only one person who could be the traitor.

"They will know which container it's in," Justin continued. "It's only a matter of time before they open it. We have to move fast!"

"We cannot get to drugs now."

"I don't think you happened to notice, but we are not going to the ship. They've been watching you." Justin turned to the driver. "You know where to go."

"Understood." The driver focused on the road ahead, his eyes flicking to the wing mirrors to make sure no one was following them.

"Turn right here," Misha ordered as they reached a T-junction. The driver hit a hard left instead, sending smoke and rocks flying.

"Is dead end, idiot," Misha snarled. "Right road is road to city."

"You got us into this shit," Justin glared. "I'll get us out. If we go that way, we'll hit a roadblock. They control the only way in and out. They are corralling us toward them."

The van continued along the side road, going deeper into the port's dumping ground.

"Then we are rats in cage," Misha stated.

"We are far from rats!"

No one was following yet. No doubt the DEA was waiting for them to drive into one of their roadblocks. Instead, the van barreled toward a restricted section near the back of the port, hugging the buildings' shadows to hide their movements. At the end of a side road, they crashed through a mesh gate. The driver controlled the van with expert precision. He switched gears, increasing speed as the road delivered them to a dead end. They had reached the end of the port. It was a private dumping ground for old boats, repair equipment and rusty trailers enclosed by a staunch metal security fence constructed from half-inch bars with coils of barbed wire on top. The driver spun the wheel in his hands and aimed the van at a stack of large wooden shipping crates, five wide and three high.

Misha shook his head as the van increased its speed. He knew the van couldn't dent the solid bars, even at this speed. The van crashed into the middle shipping crate. Misha braced himself. More wood exploded. The van didn't stop. He saw daylight on the other side. The van wobbled, straightened, and shot up a side street toward the main traffic, leaving a trail of broken wood behind.

Misha peeked out the black-tinted window. Steel bars had been removed in a perfect escape hole for the van.

"You cut hole?" he asked surprised. "When?"

"I told you, I'm not a rat, and I'll never be caught in a cage," Justin replied coldly, his eyes firmly on the road.

The driver continued through a warren of twists and turns. Conversation halted. For now. A mile from the port, they entered a parking garage and headed down to the basement level. The rubber wheels squealed on the concrete as the van skidded to a halt. The driver jumped out first, then jumped into the front of a neighboring furniture-moving truck. Misha followed Justin.

"I have safe house we can go to," Misha said.

"We have somewhere to go to first... and how safe is your safe house?"

"Watch mouth, Mr. Justin," Misha threatened. "I have no problem in kill you here."

Justin composed himself. He knew the Russian would do it without blinking.

"We will work together," Justin assured him. "After you." Justin held open the passenger's door for his companion. Once all three men were in, Justin exchanged nods with the driver—they both knew where they were going. The truck eased out of the parking garage; no reason to draw any unwanted attention.

Misha didn't like sitting between the two men, and he didn't like what was going to happen once Russia discovered that he'd lost drugs to the DEA yet again. He would have maybe seven days before they'd send someone to replace him. Whoever they sent, Misha would ask him to shoot him in the forehead. Die like a man, on his feet.

The truck stopped in front of the entrance to a gated private marina. Justin handed the driver a swipe card to activate the security gate. It rolled open, allowing the truck to slip in. Misha looked around confused. "We is going back to ship?" he asked.

"No," Justin replied. "This is a pier. A friend of mine has a very lavish yacht here."

The truck parked in a reserved area near the spacious yacht. The men piled out. Misha stood next to Justin, admiring the vessel. "Yes, we escape by sea," he nodded.

The driver went to the back of the truck and pulled up the roller door. Three men emerged from the dark space.

"What?" Misha whipped out his gun, feeling a double cross coming on.

"Put that away," Justin yelled. "We need to move fast if you want your drugs."

"Police have drugs," Misha reminded him.

"Maybe," Justin grinned, ignoring the gun pointed at his head. He took a step back and glanced at the yacht. "After what happened in Peru, I didn't trust your people, Misha. If they gave you up once, it means they'd do it again. I couldn't risk losing this shipment, so I took matters into my own hands."

Justin headed toward the yacht, encouraging Misha to follow. Misha trailed, keeping his gun pointed at Justin.

"A yacht like this can come and go unnoticed," Justin continued. "Last night I had a special crew take me and some party friends out on this baby. My friends didn't last long, as some of the drugs they took, well, were fast-acting. I had my man on the cargo ship work with the captain; he was more than happy to get the narcotics off his ship."

Justin lifted a hatch at the bow, revealing tightly wrapped bricks of cocaine.

"You? Took drugs?" Misha lowered his gun.

"I did. Now let's unload it and get to your people," Justin encouraged Misha. "We're still on track."

CHAPTER NINETY-EIGHT

THE HEAVY CONTAINER door swung open and sunlight spilled in, revealing nothing. Rudy peered into each corner, but no matter how hard he looked, the container was empty.

"Is this the right number?" he asked.

His second-in-command confirmed that it was. "Double-check, rip this place apart, it must be here somewhere!" Rudy shouted. "And get me the captain—he's going to talk to me, even if I have to beat it out of him."

One of Rudy's officers came running toward him.

"Sir, the captain is in his cabin. He's on a Skype call with his lawyer. He's taken the fifth, and we can't talk to him again until his lawyer is present."

"Fuck! How the hell?" Rudy wasn't happy. "Where's Misha? Find him. It's on here somewhere…"

"We can't find Misha," a voice blurted through his earpiece. "The black panel van he was in has vanished. It never reached the ship or the roadblocks."

"What? Find it now! He has to be here somewhere. Start sweeping the areas. Get the choppers searching. Those roadblocks stay active. Nothing gets in or out."

Rudy hobbled into the center of the empty container. His temperature was rising. He knew he'd been played, and it hurt. Two massive operations had both come up empty-handed, which meant he had a lot of internal explaining to do for the cost and man hours. This was just the excuse some of his crooked superiors had been waiting for to kick him in the guts. They'd warned him to back off, yet he pushed ahead. He had definitely underestimated Misha. Or did Misha have help?

CHAPTER NINETY-NINE

WHO THE FUCK WAS WALTER SMITH? Ross couldn't get the question out of his mind. The warden was right—if an FBI operative had entered the prison, he would have been told. Ross sat on his bed, rubbing his hands over his face, his eyes closed. He would do this when he was thinking really deep, pushing away the outside world.

Walter had never shown Ross a badge; he only said he was with the FBI, and Ross went along with it. He'd given Ross special access to FBI files and info, so he'd seen no reason to suspect him of anything. The profile Walter showed him was too good and too detailed to be anything but professional. Why would Walter give him this if he wasn't FBI? How would he know all this case information?

The killer wears a uniform, to work and to the world, Walter had written.

From what Ross had seen in Bell Island, the only thing separating some of the guards from inmates was their uniform. To the world, guards are seen as protectors; to the prisoners, they're seen as predators. The uniform hides who they really are.

The way the Heart Collector had slipped in and out of the murder scenes? Only guards had that freedom. Yet, the warden wouldn't budge. He informed Ross that he'd gone over all the information and concluded his guards were innocent. His reasoning: the murders conflicted with rostered schedules. Of all the guards, not one name had been rostered on each and every time a murder happened. Meaning it wasn't possible.

Could the warden be right? Was it a prisoner? Only an inmate like Marcus could get close. When he threatened Ross's life, he did say he could "rip out his heart and no one would care." But Marcus would need guards to help cover his tracks, and they would talk. Whoever was doing it didn't leave any such trail.

Ross nodded to himself, rubbing his eyes with his palms. He kept coming back to Walter's profile; there were three guards who fit. He dismissed the warden's findings, as his roster system was unreliable at best. Father O'Grady had even acquired pictures of the three suspects for his investigation file in the library. O'Grady was handy in getting most things; he had a way with working the prison system.

Ross stood up, paced, sat down, and rubbed his face in his hands some more. What was he missing? It had to be a guard, unless… Ross shook his head as a new theory offered itself up. No, it couldn't be? *Unless it wasn't a guard?* Ross went cold, his face resting in his hands. *Unless it wasn't a guard?* How could he have been so blind. *Unless it wasn't a guard?* He had been under his nose the entire time. In fact, the killer had even inserted himself into the investigation.

He had never asked O'Grady to help. He was always "just there." He also called his time in Bell, "God's work." He was always smiling, welcoming, and able to move freely. Both guards and prisoners left him alone and ignored him. Was his religion his uniform?

Remove the uniform and discover the monster.

Ross suddenly felt compelled to head to the library in search of clues as to whether his suspicions could be true. Ross had taken O'Grady on good faith that he didn't murder the young boy, but what if he had killed him and was as crazy as Jimmy believed? Ross had completely overlooked O'Grady's fit with the profile. That he was the profile.

A few yards from the library, Ross stopped. The voice at the back of his head, one that only a veteran cop knows, told him something was wrong. He reached to pull his gun from his holster, then remembered that he didn't have one; it was just muscle memory kicking in. He dropped his arm to the side and put his back up against the wall. A nose can often tell a person things before their eyes do, and there are certain putrid smells a cop can never forget.

Ross gripped the library door handle. Gently turning, he inched it open to peek inside. There was movement out of his line of sight. He pushed the door enough to slip in as quietly as he could. His breathing controlled, he looked for any signs of danger. He didn't have to look hard. The horror scene unfolded right there in the center of the room. Father O'Grady lay on a reading table with his chest cut wide open and the last tendon of his heart severed.

"Freeze!" Ross yelled at Officer Hickman, his police muscle memory kicking in again. Hickman was naked, squatting on the table, hunched over his victim. He lifted his head and smiled as if he were in a '50s sitcom.

"Hi, Ross, I've been waiting for you." Hickman pulled out the heart and raised it to his lips. "Do you understand love, Ross?" He opened his mouth, and bit into the heart, as if it were an apple. Blood spilled down his chin and onto his bare chest.

"You're one sick bastard!" Ross blurted. He couldn't think of anything else to say.

"Sticks and stones," Hickman replied. "I'm talking about love. I never truly understood it until Caesar explained it to me. Take this man, this beautiful young man of God. We had a cosmic connection of love. I could see it in his eyes. He loved me, not you. I watched you two getting close—you thought you could steal him from me? From me!"

Hickman jumped to the floor, his body hunched, his torso heaving, his eyes wild, with O'Grady's heart still in his hand. In jerky movements, Hickman straightened out his spine, like he was growing, unfolding taller. He snatched a military knife off the table. Ross took a step back, keeping his eyes firmly focused on Hickman.

"Put the knife down," he said calmly. "I can get you help."

Hickman strolled toward Ross, his feet slapping the concrete, leaving bloody footprints behind him. He wielded the knife at Ross as if he didn't have a care in the world.

"I could just give you the knife. If you asked nicely?"

"Can I have the knife, please?" Ross asked in a friendly tone.

"Decisions, decisions. What to do?" Hickman put the knife to his lips and licked off some blood. "Should I give you the knife or stab you with it?"

Ross heard distant footsteps down the hallway heading their way.

"Sounds like we will have company soon," Ross said. "Give me the knife, and I'll let you put on some clothes before they get here." Ross reached out his hand, willing for Hickman to hand over the weapon.

"Ooopsie me, I'm all naked. Well, I suppose I could do that. Or not—I still have enough time to cut you up a little before they get here. I know these halls well. I'd say we have at least ninety seconds. How much could I do to you in ninety seconds, Ross?"

The footsteps got closer. Hickman moved his head around as if he were looking at a gallery of paintings. He hunched once again and swayed in looping steps about the library. His body language was so different to the Hickman that Ross knew—the Hickman who had vomited in his cell.

Hickman shuffled toward Ross, dropped the knife at his feet, and backed away again.

"Take it, it's yours." Hickman sighed. "I've had enough fun for one day."

Cautiously, Ross reached out, keeping direct eye contact with the killer. His fingers wrapped around the handle as he took control of the weapon.

"I guess I should put my hands on my head," Hickman offered. "Isn't that what cops say, even crooked ones?" Hickman placed his hands up behind his head.

"That's a good idea." Ross pointed the knife at Hickman. "And maybe put some pants on."

"I like the way I am. Do you have a problem with naked men, Ross? I don't want this to be uncomfortable for you. I have an idea." Hickman returned to his table of horror. He sorted through his macabre instruments. He discarded a pair of blood-stained bolt cutters, dropped a surgical saw to the floor, and threw a scalpel over his shoulder.

"Don't fucking move!" Ross yelled. Hickman spun to face Ross. In his hands were two connected zip ties—a basic form of handcuffs. He placed one over his wrist and tightened it for Ross to watch. He then put his hands behind his back, slipped the second one on, and tightened it.

The footsteps got even louder, and Ross estimated there were at least five people moving at pace.

"It will be pretty busy in here soon," Hickman said. "Now here's a question for you, Ross. Why are they coming? Did you tell them?" Hickman raised his shoulders, looking comically confused.

Ross suddenly felt eerily exposed and tensed his muscles, gripping the knife tighter.

"They're guards," Hickman announced. "I called them. Oh, and Caesar wanted to say 'Hi'."

"Caesar?" Ross asked, as Hickman thrust his head downward, straight onto the knife, the sharp blade effortlessly penetrating the skin under his jawbone. Out of instinct, Ross steadied Hickman's body to catch him. Hickman pushed himself harder onto the knife.

Two guards crashed into the library first, followed by the others. It then dawned on Ross what Hickman had set up and how the scene now looked: a crooked ex-cop, an unarmed guard's hands bound behind his back, kneeling, executed by a knife in the throat. Before Ross could say a word, a guard clocked his head with a baton. Ross stumbled; a second swinging baton put him down. As his body hit the ground, the name Caesar echoed in his brain.

AN IMPRESSIVE CHANDELIER dominated the center of the room with the sparkle of a million stars. The freshly polished marble floors gleamed with reflections as tail-coated waiters swanned around balancing trays of champagne, replacing drinks with a magical fluidity. A majestic fireplace stacked with wood crackled with luster. Ladies in their finest gowns converged together like a kaleidoscope of butterflies, and distinguished gentlemen huddled like of a rookery of penguins. It was a night to be seen; it was a night to be captured; it was a night to be spoken about.

Tonight at the prestigious Waldorf Hotel, Peter Gordon was hosting an exclusive cocktail party for the people connected to Rip's campaign. Peter had chosen the Waldorf because of its history—a history that was steeped in presidential candidates. Peter stood personally at the bottom of the sweeping stairs, warmly welcoming each and every guest.

"Good to see you, Justin," Peter said.

"Good to see you, and to be here," Justin replied.

"You earned your ticket." Peter acknowledged, looking around the room. "What do you see?"

"Money."

"Indeed. I was once told money is the god of our time, but I believe power is stronger than money. With the right power, you control the currency, you own the gold, meaning you govern the gods."

"God isn't power, power is God," Justin stated.

"Correct. Justin, what you are part of is power, pure power. Not everyone can have it. I see something in you. It's become very clear that you belong with us, with the Gordons."

Peter produced a small, dark green box and offered it to Justin. "This is for you, son." Justin felt hidden emotions welling up inside him—Peter had never called him that before. He opened the box; inside was a Rolex GMT Master, the white gold face glowing in the light. Both Peter and Rip had the exact same watch.

"I need men like you," Peter continued. "Men of fortitude, men of intelligence, men who know how to get things done. No doubt you have heard we were awarded the military contract this morning. Sterling is scrambling to pull it back. They won't. You played a key role in helping."

"It was my honor. I only did what you asked of me."

"You did it well."

"Anything you ever need, I'm happy to be of service."

The room's assembly erupted in a round of applause as Rip and Barbara emerged at the top of the stairs.

"It has taken two hundred years to get here," Peter said. "I generally feel this is one extraordinary moment in the history of the Gordon family. Our family name will be printed in bold in the history books of America, forever."

"I believe that," Justin said.

Peter put his hand on Justin's shoulder. "This is just the beginning. I will make you richer and more powerful than you've ever imagined."

Justin smiled. "Yes, this is just the beginning," he nodded. He had big plans, and even Peter would be surprised if he knew just how big those plans were.

WHEN SILVER FIRST OPENED his church, he'd given himself three months. At first, people came for respite from the cold or the rain, or until they drifted off to another place. But one or two souls returned, and within a few months he had a congregation of sorts. If people wanted to join in, they could; everyone was welcome. Some abused the openness, but most didn't, and everyone appreciated Silver's generosity and kindness.

Those three months had turned into six, and then into twelve, and now over three years had passed. He'd lost count of the number of times the power and water had been shut off. But he always found a way to get it back on, even for just a few more days. It was what it was, and regardless, Silver was happy.

Things had changed dramatically over the last few weeks, however. Steve had cracked the bureaucratic Da Vinci Code of City Hall. The backdated money owed to the church was paid in full, and the monthly payments increased the church's good fortune. Silver joked that the church bank account now had more zeros than he had fingers. The building was in a state of transformation. A full-service kitchen was being installed, book shelves had books, and central heating now kept every room comfortably warm.

Silver opened the front door and smiled as the door swung in silently on well-oiled hinges. It was nice to have a front door. He strolled down the hallway, his shoes squeaking on freshly polished wooden floorboards. He placed grocery bags on the communal kitchen bench, then removed all the items. He had choice cuts of meat, fresh vegetables, and assorted dairy products. They all easily fit into the commercial-sized fridge, with room for more, lots more.

He folded the paper bags, tucked them under his arm, and walked up the rebuilt stairs to the top level. In the three years he'd occupied the building, he'd never used this floor. The old rotten stairs had been too risky to climb. One of the newly accessible rooms had been turned into an activity room for kids. The paper bags were perfect for turning into masks, astronaut helmets, or a thousand other things young minds might imagine.

He dropped the bags on a rainbow-painted desk, then returned to the ground floor, stopping outside the double doors that led to the new service room. No longer were sermons confined to the bitter basement; two weeks ago they moved everything to the bigger, newer, friendlier room. Silver had gone out himself to buy colored fabrics to hang from the walls. Steve had told him he planned to install a projection screen to show movies and use for services. Silver was more excited about watching football on it, though.

He noticed the room's timetable had been ripped off the front of the door, leaving only corners of yellow paper taped behind. Silver pushed open the door and saw the discarded timetable on the floor. He picked it up and instantly forgot about it, his attention grabbed by the fabric ripped that had been ripped off one of the walls and dumped in the middle of the room, apparently to make room for graffiti: DON'T DEAL IN OUR AREA CHURCH CUNTS! This made no sense to Silver; no one in the church dealt in drugs. It was a safe area for everyone, even gang members. He couldn't understand what might motivate any of them to vandalize the church.

The timetable hit the ground again as Silver ran to the mound of fabric. Someone was cocooned within it. He dropped to his knees to tear away the fabric from the half-hidden body of a man wearing only a loose T-shirt and shorts. Though the man's face had been horrifically beaten, Silver recognized his friend. Steve didn't deal in drugs. He was getting clean and helping others to do the same. There was no reason for a gang to kill him. Tears welled up in Silver's eyes and he started to sing a song his grandfather had taught him. It was to help guide Steve's soul on its journey to the other side.

JUSTIN RECLINED IN THE BACK of the Audi, marveling at his new Rolex as if it had magic powers. His iPhone vibrated—a text from Alex:

```
Baby man. Fuck me tonight. I bring
friend you bring drink and drugs.
lots of coke and lots of fuck
```

Justin replied:

```
I'm in the mood to fuck hard.
Be ready.
```

Dan entered the Luxor's underground parking garage then stopped suddenly. He couldn't park in Justin's spot. A car was already there, a black Hennessey Venom GT.

"Some asshole be parked in your spot, sir," Dan said. "I get the motherfucker towed."

"No, you won't," Justin said.

"You must let me at least key that son of a bitch."

"I would prefer if you didn't," Justin smiled. "I just brought it, all one-point-two million of it."

"Jesus, motherfucking Christ, shit, cunt motherfucker what? Fuck."

Justin got out, quickly followed by Dan, to check out his new toy.

"Where should I park the Audi, mister sir?"

"At your place. It's yours."

"No, motherfucking way sir. Thank you, sir!"

"Keep doing what you do, and I will give you a life others can only dream of."

Justin took his time to inspect the Venom from every angle, running a hand down the side of it. This was a serious piece of machinery. He was going to have to christen it; bending Alex over its hood was called for.

While waiting for the elevator, he got a notification from his private email account. All it said was *Hi* and then it deleted itself the moment Justin opened it, leaving no trace it had ever been there. A subtle power show. He was impressed. Caesar had reached out to him, finally.

Justin opened the door to his apartment and smelled smoke. He flicked on the lights, revealing Misha reclining on one of his leather chairs. A cigar in one hand, a large glass of vodka in the other.

"What are you doing here?" Justin asked.

"I thought I would come say hello. Well, hello."

"How did you get in?" Justin inquired, as he checked his alarm panel on the wall.

"You not only person who can get things done, Mr. Justin."

Justin unbuttoned his jacket and flexed his posture. "We both have what we need. Our arrangement is over. We don't need to keep in touch. So, thanks for dropping by, and all the best for your future endeavors."

"I think we stay in touch. You very good at what you do. I was surprised. I knew you were prick, but prick with brain, is rare thing. Now you are on way in politics with friend Rip. I think we must continue work relationship."

"I don't think so."

"You no think?"

"We're done here," Justin persisted.

"No, we is done, when I say we is done. And I not think I say those words. We just start." Misha tapped his cigar on the side of his glass, the heavy ash falling into the vodka. He stood, eye to eye, with Justin. Neither man backed down. Misha dropped the glass onto the polished concrete. It shattered, sending the ashy liquid everywhere. Neither man's eyes shifted off each other.

"I happy to continue work with you, Mr. Justin," Misha said, giving Justin a few light slaps on his cheek. Justin wanted to explode and throw down with the Russian. He resisted his urge. Misha smiled and brushed past Justin, heading toward the front door. As Misha opened it, he casually added, "I have left present for you in bathroom."

Justin's iPhone rang.

"You are popular man. I will see you round, like donut," Misha smirked, leaving the door open behind him.

Justin stood motionless, his iPhone continued to ring.

Kill him the wicked whisper said. *Fuck that Russian cunt. He's not American. He's a tick feeding on the blood of real Americans.*

Justin nodded.

Kill him now, he won't be expecting it. Now is perfect. Sneak up behind him and cut his head from his body. Who will miss a Russian cock sucker? No one. Justin Truth, cleaning up American one disgusting immigrant at a time.

Justin took a step toward the door, but stopped. Now wasn't right. He didn't know enough about Misha and whether he had any connection back to himself. He answered his phone. It was Carlton. He'd finally found time to call Justin back.

"Hello," Justin said as he meandered toward the bathroom.

"Justin, we need you in the office. We're having an emergency board meeting." Carlton's voice sounded urgent.

"Can it wait?" Justin pushed open the bathroom door with his foot.

"No, sorry. We need your leadership with this problem."

"OK, I'll leave now. See you soon."

In his bath was a recently departed woman. Her throat was contused, completely crushed. Justin recognized Misha's wife from her spread in *Playboy*. She must have been the leak. Problem sorted.

NICK TOOK A BITE Of his third hot dog of the day; this one was dinner. He made himself comfortable on a park bench under a street light and unfolded his tourist map of New York. He'd circled all the stops on the airport line where Gatsby Cutter could have boarded the train. Added to Nick's custom map were little sketched stars that represented places of interest to him. Each star was the home and the office of different suspects on his OrangeFizz list. Gatsby may have had a meeting with the person or people who hired him before he'd set off on his poisonous mission. There was a chance that this type of meeting could have been at their home, office, or a place close by. In Nick's experience, people didn't travel too far from familiar surroundings.

Nick took the last mouthful of his hot dog and rubbed his hands of sticky sauce crumbs while looking across the road at the Luxor Apartments. He was interested in one of the people who lived there: Justin Truth. From the limited amount of research he'd done on the guy, he appeared to be a corporate superhero. There were streams of online marketing articles on him and his successful career.

Around the time of the SummerCrush tragedy, Justin had also suffered a personal tragedy. His mother was murdered by a bent cop who'd been trying to extort money from Justin. Nick had found pictures of the cop, Ross Smith. He compared the pictures to the one of Gatsby; they were two completely different people. No connection there.

While looking into Justin, another name had popped up: Steve Barker. He'd worked at Soda-Cola before he was arrested for rape. If he could step over that line, could stepping over the line to discredit his company's competition be just as easy? Steve's apartment was a forty-minute walk from the Luxor. Nick checked his map for a rough direction to set off in. His stomach gurgled. The hot dog wasn't digesting so well. He could wait on the bench a little longer for it to settle. If needed, he could sneak into the Luxor and use their bathrooms.

While thinking of ways to sneak in, Nick noticed a bear of a man exiting the Luxor. Judging by his stone-carved features and black attire, Nick picked him for Eastern European.

"I shall call you Ivan," Nick said aloud. "Ivan the Big and Strong. If you have problem. Ivan will fix problem, no problem. No problem too big. Break problem into no problem."

While doing this type of surveillance, Nick often gave people he watched nicknames and created potential stories about them. It was a great way to entertain himself and pass the time.

A minute later, Nick recognized Justin racing past him in a vehicle that was more spaceship than car.

"Justin Truth, a man on a mission," Nick said. "By day he sells So-da-Cola to the thirsty people of the world. By night, he dresses in purple Lycra, and with his effervescent 'bubbles of doom' cannon, he battles alien invaders as… Pop-Man!"

JUSTIN WAS THE LAST TO ARRIVE. The atmosphere was tense, and by the way people were whispering amongst each other, he could sense that no one knew why they were actually here. The usual smiles and handshakes were strangely absent.

Justin glanced at Edward, who smiled smugly back. Edward tapped his hand on the table to get everyone's attention.

"It is sad news that brings us all together here tonight," Edward began. "It has come to my attention that one of our own has been embezzling company funds."

The board members looked at each other in disbelief. Edward walked around the table and placed a black folder in front of each member.

"I have compiled the damming evidence, and you can see it for yourself, in black and white. The total sum in question is close to three million dollars and was not easy to trace. In fact, it was so well concealed that it took me weeks of digging to get to the bottom of it." Edward returned to his seat at the head of the table and stared at Justin, who still hadn't opened his folder.

"I'm utterly disappointed in Justin Truth," Edward stated.

Justin could feel all eyes on him; judging eyes. He coolly opened the folder and flicked through a few pages while rubbing the scar on the side of his head with his index finger.

Reveling in his financial forensics work, Edward continued. "Justin, this is a serious crime. You have destroyed any trust I have in you. This is how it will be handled. You will resign forthwith, and all links to the company will be severed. You will vacate your position on the board. You'll surrender your shares. You will not be paid out for them. The money you stole will be paid back to Soda-Cola in full."

Edward slid a gray folder with SILVERMAN, CLEAVE AND CAREY

embossed on it across the table to Justin. "You will sign these papers, and then be escorted off the premises. If you do not sign, criminal proceedings will be brought against you immediately with the full force of the entire company. Justin, your services are no longer required."

Justin closed his folder and spun it into the middle of the table as three security guards entered the room, along with two lawyers.

"You got me." Justin smiled. "That is, if any of this is true."

"You know it's true!" Edward fired back. "Read it, it's all in the folder."

"I don't need to read it, I know it's fabricated." Justin addressed the board. "Fellow board members, what you have in your hands is an orchestrated litany of lies. Edward is a desperate man, playing a very dangerous game. When a man is drowning in as much debt as Edward, even the most honest man can become disreputable. He is clearly setting me up, and it all makes sense now."

"What?" Edward said. "I'm not drowning in debt. You are the delusional one. You can't talk your way out of this. I have damming evidence."

"Do you? Or is it fabricated like this charade you organized tonight? How long have you been planning this little ambush? Whispering in dark places, behind our backs. Not long ago, I went to Edward with some anomalies I picked up in the Soda-Cola accounts. Edward dismissed my findings and got rather aggressive. He told me in uncertain terms that I was to slash staff, dismantle the Young Lions, and up the board's performance bonuses even higher. He made it very clear that if I didn't do what he said, he would turn you all against me and find someone for my position who would do as told. I was confused by why he would demand more money, since I have exceeded all profit forecasts. Then while talking to Rodger Wellsworth, a close friend of mine who is on the board of St. Mary's and works at the State Department, he let it slip that Edward had defaulted on multiple land tax payments. I assured Rodger that it must have been an accounting error."

"This is preposterous! I've always paid on time."

"I have paperwork that proves the opposite. It's in a folder on the server. After my chat with Rodger, I started digging myself. I'm not a financial wizard, such as Edward, so I asked Guy Chambers to help. He pulled the system apart, searching for what the anomalies I originally discovered could be. He started to untangle it all, tracing hidden payments that had been funneled into a shell company that Edward himself had created. What was it called—Beachside Dreams limited?"

"That's a legitimate company I have created for tax purposes," Edward said.

"You created it to hide the money you stole from Soda-Cola. I can only assume you were using it to offset debts and extend your credit, hoping no one would notice. The way you bounced around the numbers was incredible. At the start it was tiny, but over the last two months, you must have become greedy."

"Nice story, Justin. No one here believes a word of it."

Justin logged into the boardroom's computer, bringing it up on the big screen.

"Edward, one easy way to prove me wrong. Beachside Dreams must have online accounts. A man like you would be precise."

"Those are private, my own personal business," he stammered.

Edward could feel the room turning on him. There was nothing wrong with the Beachside Dreams accounts, apart from it was running at a loss. He was ashamed at how badly he had misjudged the housing market. He was in debt, not as bad as Justin was making out, but sharing would prove his innocence. Edward logged in.

"As you can see, it's not hugely profitable, yet. We are in the development stages; once the houses go up, the profit will be more than respectful. It's my retirement plan."

Justin approached the screen on the wall and tapped on an account that displayed no information. "What's this one?" he asked.

"That would be… I'm not sure," Edward replied, confused. He clicked on the link and brought up a list of transactions—starting with $3.6 million in credit.

"Now, Edward, how much did you say I embezzled?" Justin asked sternly. "There is way more here than you accused me of."

"I've never seen that account before in my life!"

Justin took control of the computer and scrolled down. "These transactions go on for over a year. It's worse than I thought." Justin addressed the room. "You bastard! How long have you been planning to set me up?"

Carlton got to his feet. "I'm not sure what is going on here, but we will get to the bottom of it."

Edward's face turned white. This was not how he'd envisioned this meeting would go.

"Edward, you have two choices," Justin said, taking control. "You can explain yourself to a judge, or sign those papers that you put on the table for me. You get the same deal you gave me, but since I'm not a bastard like you, I'll let you keep your shares. You have five minutes to decide."

Conversation erupted. The board members spoke over each other and tried to ask Edward questions. Justin leaned back in his chair, delighted in the chaos. As Edward glared at him, Justin lifted his Rolex and tapped it.

When Justin took over Carlton's position, he'd foreseen Edward as a future problem who would need to be removed. When Edward became vocal about his side business of beachfront homes, Justin seized the opportunity to disrupt the process, costing Edward money. He'd then convinced Guy to hack into Edward's accounts and create a hidden account within Beachside Dreams. Only Justin could see it when he logged on. He had actively used it to create a trail of payoffs. Justin had made sure the money he "borrowed" could be traced through Beachside Dreams' account, before giving it to Misha. He'd transferred the money back a few days ago. On the drive to the board meeting, he'd activated the account, making it visible on Edward's own login.

Time was up. Justin stood and offered Edward a pen. Edward was frazzled, searching for friends in the room, finding none. He snatched the pen, his hand trembling as he signed the forms.

"All the best for your future endeavors, Edward," Justin grinned. "Now don't let the door hit your ass on the way out."

For his own amusement, Justin told the security guards to escort Edward from the building. Damn, it felt good to be Justin fuckin' Truth!

CAESAR WAS IN HIS THINKING ROOM. It consisted of twelve mirrored walls that formed a perfect dodecagon. The floor and ceiling were made out of thick tempered glass. Lights backed the panels, illuminating them. In the center of the room stood a brown leather antique barber's chair, lovingly restored to mint condition.

Caesar sat, rubbing his thumbs back and forth along the tips of his fingers. The room was designed to feel like a clock, with the chair at the center. Time captivated Caesar; it was the one thing he couldn't control. People and events and jobs and actions and plans and life and death were all easy enough for him to manipulate, but time was the one thing that eluded him. No matter what he did, he couldn't make it go any slower or faster.

Caesar continued to rub his fingers and carry on the conversation in his head. Caesar wasn't his real name, the name he was given at birth. It was the name the collective within his head agreed on. At the age of five, he discovered that he had a second personality living inside his head. This personality talked to his prime personality, and they shared ideas—a bit like having a best friend always by your side. Even at his young age, Caesar knew he shouldn't share with anyone that he had an invisible friend, as he didn't consider anyone around him smart enough to understand. As a result, Personality Number Two remained hidden.

The two personalities gave each other secret names. His prime personality was called "Julius," the second one "Augustus," so together, naturally, they were "Caesar." And even though they were joined by one body, their minds worked independently. Julius could watch a film while Augustus read a book, for example, yet Caesar could commit facts from both activities to memory and easily recall them if needed. Caesar forgot nothing.

As he grew older, Caesar realized that he actually had two more personalities, Tiberius and Claudius. Each added their own unique view on situations, and like Augustus and Julius, they could operate simultaneously as well. The one thing all four of Caesar's personalities had in common was their fascination with murder. To them, holding the fate of someone's life in their hands—murder—was the epitome of control.

He practiced on local pets and wild animals he caught, burning the evidence of his experiments with death. Then eventually the four personalities decided they wanted to go all the way—a human life. They had all agreed they didn't want to be caught, so they needed to study how to get away with it.

By the time he was thirteen, Caesar had consumed every piece of information on the topic that he could order through his public library—any book that related to serial killers, profiling, and murder. He'd scrutinized how the killers were caught and which mistakes they made. He'd investigated some unsolved FBI cases and solved them for his own pleasure, keeping their identities to himself. He'd take road trips to visit the killers in their natural environment, watching them from afar. He'd keep tabs on them, record their movements, and be there when they were eventually caught. At one stage, he knew the identity and whereabouts of seven of the ten most wanted serial killers in the country.

Caesar left his chair and stood in front of the mirror at the three o'clock position. The face looking back at him wasn't his own; it was that of Walter Smith. He pushed against the mirror, and it opened up a door to a brightly lit room featuring a large collection of clothes, makeup, and props. It was the type of room you'd find in a West End theatre, and he'd used many of the items for different disguises over the years.

Once inside the room, Caesar removed the crooked-teeth plate off his own perfect ones, pulled off the oily hairpiece, and popped out the contact lens, which he'd used to make his eye appear lazy. Seconds later his ill-fitting shirt was off, and so too were the cheap pants that itched his legs. He stretched his weary limbs and yawned.

Caesar was now looking at Caesar.

He was the most prolific serial killer to walk the streets of America, and no one knew he existed. There were just rumors, no evidence.

Every move he made was set far ahead, and he never left a trail, unless he wanted to create one on purpose.

When Ross Smith stumbled upon one of his followers, the Beetle Butcher, he was intrigued, and Caesar was rarely intrigued these days. *How did Ross do it?* all his personalities had asked at once. *How did he solve it with the minimal clues he had?* When Ross was convicted of murder himself, Caesar wanted to play.

It had been a risk to go see Ross at Bell Island; having his follower, Hickman, on the inside made it easier. Caesar had wanted to look Ross in the eye and experience the man. He expected more though, as Ross had, unfortunately, given little away in their chat. Caesar knew Justin Truth was involved. Justin was a person Caesar had been keeping tabs on since his Harvard days with Rip.

One of his cell phones vibrated and he took the call, selecting the right voice.

"Hello. That is right… Good to know… Thank you. I thought so too. Bye."

There was a new addition to this little game. A Nick Harvey had just inserted himself into the mix. Caesar thought of all the possible games ahead. This was going to be fun.

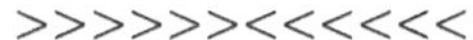

IF YOU ENJOYED CRIMINAL TRUTH, I need your help.

I write because I like creating stories, characters, and twisting plots that make my readers need to read just one…more…page…

If you crave more twisted tales from the world of Justin Truth, please consider leaving a review for Criminal Truth on my Amazon website. Your review, which need only take a few minutes, will help other readers discover the world of Justin Truth, which, in turn, will help me be able to create more twisted stories for your reading pleasure.

Help more readers discover the Truth, write a review today.

Thanks!

FRACTURED TRUTH

BY
KARL WILLIAM FLEET

NORRIS THATCHER WAS A HAPPY MAN, a simple man. A man that liked things, all kinds of things. He was constantly in a hurry. Where he was meant to be often seemed more important than where he was. To get there, he shuffled forward in little steps, scuffing the soles of his shoes. His face was always grinning a grin that showed all his teeth, as he believed "a happy face made a happy person."

"Hello, kitchen," Norris said as he entered the small room. "Hello to you too, table, chairs, and kitchen things. Going to be using some of you soon."

Norris always talked to himself. He need to verbalize everything he did as it gave his life a running commentary.

"Can't wait to listen to you," he said to the radio perched on the windowsill. His small brown eyes squinted behind thick glasses as he searched for the ON button. "Where are you, talk button? Always hiding." He finally found it. "Brilliant. It's good to know what's happening in the world. Important to know. Time for breakfast." Every morning he enjoyed the same breakfast: a cup of weak tea, a boiled egg, and three pieces of whole grain toast lightly smeared with his own honey.

For his entire life, Norris had lived in this house with his parents. Now he lived alone. He lost his father first; he'd suffered a heart attack while working on a Thursday. And not long after, his mother went to bed one night and never woke up. Norris missed them both terribly. He also missed their monthly family trips to visit trains, always on a Sunday. Norris loved trains, but he loved model trains the most. To him, they were the best type of trains. He spent all of his spare time building and adding new trains to his impressive collection.

Norris finished his breakfast. "That was rather good this morning," he said, getting up from the breakfast table. "Must remember to clean the plate and leave it to dry. A clean dish is a good dish."

At the sink, he turned on the tap and waited for his favorite part: adding the bubbles. "Not too much to waste, just enough to wash," he said, squirting in the dish soap.

Once he finished the handful of dishes, he pulled up the sink's plug. "Bye-bye, water," he waved. "Time to get to work. If we all work together, we can achieve great things."

Norris left his house and walked the twenty-one left steps *and* twenty-two right steps to his spacious double garage. He unlocked the door and turned on the lights.

"Hello, Norrisville," he said to everyone. Norrisville was home to his model trains and over ten thousand miniature people, each individually painted by Norris. The enormous display took up the entire garage.

"Hello, Bob Blueman," he said to a man painted in a blue suit. "Are you taking Bob Jr. out on the train? I think they are running on time." Norris flicked a switch to set his trains off on their circular journey. He could watch the model trains for hours as they ran through mountain ranges, deserts, and a New York-inspired metropolis.

Today was Saturday, the best kind of day for Norris. It would be a busy day for visitors to Norrisville.

"Who is coming today?" he asked, and he opened the logbook to find out. Sometimes Norrisville would attract people from distant lands; the most visitors he ever had in one day was forty-five. That was a splendid day. He counted the names on his fingers, "Fourteen people today," he said proudly. "That's nearly three hands."

He liked visitors, he liked to talk, he liked to listen. He liked people, he liked everything.

Norris was saving up for a big trip to England. They had some amazing train collections over there, and he was extra happy that they spoke English too.

Norris read all the names in his logbook again, smoothed out the day's page, and placed a pen in the book's gutters to keep it open. He could now go and check on Henry.

Bees were his latest hobby. He thought they were amazing. The world needed more bees. It made him happy that his bees were helping the world one flower at a time.

He called all his bees Henry.

A few weeks ago, a man stopped by and asked him about his bees. Norris enthusiastically told him all about them. That man worked for the local newspaper and wrote a story about Norris and his bees. Norris had carefully cut out the article and stuck it to his fridge. He was very proud of it.

Norris went back to his house to get into his homemade beekeeper's gear: white pants, white cotton top, and black rubber boots. Just like the pictures of beekeepers he'd seen in books. Last, he put on his hat. A football helmet he'd covered with netting he'd found on his mother's wedding dress.

Once dressed, he opened the back door and waddled to the far end of his property.

"Hello, Henry," he said. "It's a lovely day for flying around and visiting all the flowers. Hope you have worked hard and have some yummy honey for my toast." Norris noticed a number of dead bees on the grass. He dropped to his knees. "Ohh, Henry! Henry! What's the matter?"

They didn't answer, so Norris got back to his feet and rushed to his hive to see how his other little friends were doing. He didn't notice a small detonator attached to the hive's lid. As he pulled the lid off, the detonator went off with a loud bang.

Shooting out from the hive, bees angrily swarmed and attacked him.

"Henry! No! Henry!" he yelled at his buzzy little friends. They engulfed him. Panicked, he spun in circles to shoo them away. Blindly swinging, he stumbled, tripped, and toppled onto the hive. The fragile box shattered under him, sending the entire colony on the attack. His thin white pants and shirt weren't much protection from the bees' multiple stingers. As he twisted and turned from the painful jabs, he accidentally knocked off his netted helmet. The bees dived at his face, pumping their venom into Norris's soft, exposed flesh. Their poison caused his skin and throat to swell. He rolled ferociously on the ground to lose his attackers, using up all the air he had in his lungs. He flopped onto his back and his vision blurred as he reached his fingers out toward the sky.

His hand was heavy and covered in bees.

"Hen-ry…" he gargled, as determined bees crawled into his mouth and stung his swollen tongue. His arm collapsed to the ground, and he turned an asphyxiated shade of blue.

A dark figure recorded the entire dance of death that he'd, in fact, orchestrated. Caesar had set him five deadly tasks to complete in order to determine whether the man was worthy of Caesar's royal favor. Each task consisted of a simple phrase; it was then up to the man to impress Caesar with his brutal interpretation of it.

The first was: *Task I: To be, or not to be?*

One down.

Four to go.

THE SODA-COLA INTERNATIONAL BUILDING, one of the tallest structures in New York was built in 1995. It stands at an impressive 813 feet, with over 1.8 million square feet of floor area and is home to more than 7,000 Soda-Cola employees spread throughout its sixty floors. One of those employees sat outside the CEO's office.

Guy Chambers, was head of Soda-Cola's IT department, a position he used to instill fear into people within the company. "I control their computers, I control them," he'd boast to friends. The rule didn't apply to Justin Truth, however. In fact, no rules Guy could think of applied to Justin Truth.

Guy fidgeted in his seat and played games on his phone to distract himself. Justin wasn't expecting him, and that was part of his plan. Today was the day he was going to be a man, a man like Justin. He would do something bold and unexpected. For this special occasion, he wore his best charcoal suit, white shirt, and black tie. He noticed Justin had been moving from bright colors to blacks and grays lately. And like most of the ambitious men in the building, Guy took his fashion cues from Justin.

Perched behind her desk, Justin's personal assistant, Debbie, peered at Guy. He could feel her eyes on him and glanced up from his *Clash of Clans* game. They exchanged smiles; his nervous and wide, hers small and curious.

Guy's stomach rolled, making him wonder if he should take another trip to the restroom. He'd already been five times in the last two hours.

Debbie's phone beeped. "Mr. Truth will see you now."

"Thanks, Debbie."

Guy stood, straightened his shirt and tie, closed his eyes, and breathed in deeply. He knocked on Justin's office door, waited a few moments. then entered.

Justin didn't look up from his computer, continuing to work as if Guy were invisible. Guy knew the routine: he would have to stand and wait for Justin to acknowledge him before he could sit. You never interrupted Justin, and he had to initiate conversation.

As Guy stood quietly, he admired Justin's charcoal suit, no doubt worth thousands more than his own. Guy gazed at the faint scar on the right side of Justin's face. The mark ran from his temple to just above his cheekbone. He often wondered how Justin got it. Guy had contemplated giving himself the same scar. He rubbed his right temple where he wanted it. Once, while drying the dishes at home, he caught a glimpse of himself in a carving knife. As he admired his newly styled, Justin-inspired haircut, he told himself that he also needed a scar like Justin's. Impulsively, he placed the knife on the side of his head, where Justin had a scar, and sliced the skin. He instantly screamed and dropped the knife. His action drew drops of blood, but not hard enough to scar. His feeble attempt healed and disappeared within days.

Finally, Justin looked up from his computer and leaned back in his chair.

"Sit," Justin said.

Guy sat, resting his hands between his legs. "Um, sir. Look…" Guy paused. His palms were sweaty, his mouth dry. He knew this would be hard, but he could do it. Be like Justin. He summoned all his courage. "I would not like to die, disappear, take a dirt nap," he said.

Justin leaned in and squinted his eyes slightly. "What?"

"I'm scared," Guy said, looking at his shoes. "You know, about dying."

"Guy, we all die sooner or later."

"I know, it's… I just don't want to die because you have decided it's time for me to go."

"Guy? What are you talking about?"

"Sir, I know who you are and what you are capable of doing. I've helped you get to where you are now, and I know there is a much darker side to you." Guy lifted his head to look Justin in the eyes.

"Guy, you don't know anything. But right now, know that you are pissing me off."

"No, don't get me wrong." Guy raised his hands in a defensive pose, his voice rising an octave. "I'm not trying anything on. I'm here to let you know, I'm one hundred percent committed to you. I don't care about what you have done or the things I've helped you do. My life, the life you have given me, is a life I never dreamed of having. Without you, I'm a pathetic loser. I'll do anything to keep what you have given me. I will do anything to prove to you that I can be trusted and that you come first."

Justin held eye contact. "Guy, I have no idea what you are talking about."

"I'll do anything," Guy pleaded, physically shaking. "Anything you ask. Look at me? Do I look like that fat slob that walked into your office three years ago? No. That man is dead, and this is what has been reborn. This is all because of you. That's why I'm here."

"I'm glad my leadership has inspired you," Justin said. "I have things to do, but I'm glad you came to me. Let's talk again soon."

Guy stood, weakly. "I'm here for you, anything, anytime." He bowed, he had no idea why, then hurried to the office door. He needed air. He twisted the door handle to leave—but the door didn't open. He rattled the handle to escape; it remained locked.

His body shook uncontrollably as he turned back to Justin, who stared at him intently.

"Do you know anything about Genghis Khan?" Justin asked.

"A little," Guy said, wiping sweat from his brow. "He was a king, a brutal ruler."

"He was more than that. More like a god. He once said, 'The strength of walls depends on the courage of those who guard them.' What do you think he meant by that?"

"That… that a wall is just a wall, but who guards the wall makes it strong."

Justin nodded, then deliberately blinked, as to say "go."

Guy tried the handle again—it opened. He quickly left and closed the door behind him. He leaned back against it, his shirt soaked. Only time would tell if he had done the right thing.

JUSTIN CLOSED HIS LAPTOP, pushed his chair back from his desk, and stood. He slowly removed his jacket and placed it on the back of his chair. He needed a new shirt. During Guy's little discourse, Justin had tensed his bicep with such force that it had ripped his sleeve.

Guy was right to fear for his life. Justin had been thinking of ways to remove him—and everything Guy knew. He just hadn't worked out the best way to do it, in other words, a way that was worthy of his time. It was obvious Guy worshiped him and would crawl over broken glass to lick dogshit off his polished shoe. So why would Guy would bother broaching the subject? Either he was dumber than Justin originally thought, or he was growing balls.

Slice off his tiny balls and feed them to his wife, the wicked whisper said. It'd gotten more demanding of late.

"I don't want to touch them," Justin replied.

Make his whore of a wife do it.

"It has to be a clean accident," Justin stated. "He's too close. Can't have any TV-wannabe cops sniffing around. Besides, his digital talent is handy."

You don't need him. Justin Truth doesn't need any help. They are all bitches, and Justin fucks bitches. Don't be weak!

"I'm not!" Justin flexed his muscles, tearing his shirt even more. "I rival Genghis. Greater than Alexander and more ruthless than Ragnar. I'm building an empire of which they only dreamed!"

The whisper remained quiet.

Justin opened the door to his personally designed restroom, which he'd outfitted with a sauna, spa bath, wet room shower, exercise equipment, and free weights.

He stood in front of the mirror and checked out the damage to his shirt. It'd also split across the back. Not the first shirt he'd ripped lately. He removed it. Watching himself undress turned him on. He got hard.

Shirtless, he rested his palms on the marble sink top and leaned toward the mirror. His eyes were a little bloodshot. He was stretching himself, surviving on barely three hours sleep a night. He needed to take better care of himself.

You should take care of Montana, the whisper encouraged.

"I know where she is."

She hasn't messaged you back. That alone warrants carving the bitch up with her grandfather's knife.

"She loves me." Justin thumbed his chest.

She tried to kill you, the whisper taunted.

"That's how I know. Only love would push her to that extreme, push her to do something she never would have believed she could. I saw her eyes when she sliced open Steve's throat. She liked it. She understands. She'll be back in New York soon, begging me to fuck her."

Justin turned his back from the mirror. Next to him, a fully stocked closet of designer clothing ran along one wall. He pulled a crisp white shirt from the rack and slipped it on. He buttoned it up while walking back into his office.

Justin was back in the zone, going through all the latest forecasts for Soda-Cola, one reason for so many late nights recently. Soda-Cola's share price had dropped, and sales across the board were down. The worst dip in twenty years. He didn't understand why. With everything he had done, the company should be booming.

You know why this is. It's not you.

"That fucker Carlton. I bet he had help from Edward to hide how badly he had been running the company. Without me taking over when I did, Soda-Cola would be bankrupt."

Justin knew he would find a way to streamline the business even more. There was no way he'd let Soda-Cola go down under his leadership—that would be unacceptable. The entire company, every single person, would work harder or be replaced.

Justin rubbed his scar. "You know what?" Justin said.

I can only imagine, buddy, the whisper replied.

"I need a break. Let's see if we can cross off one of Caesar's tasks before I fire some deadwood from around here."

You are the man, Justin Truth. All day! Everyday!

NICK HARVEY WHISTLED WHILE HE WALKED along the cracked sidewalk, a brown paper bag full of treats cradled under his right arm. Not a vegetable in sight. The trick was to never eat healthy so your body never knew any different—that's what Nick told himself.

He was staying in a budget hotel on E 170th Street, near the border of the Bronx and Crotona Park; close enough to Manhattan to work the case, but far enough away from its vibe.

His problem with Manhattan was the people: angry people, angry loud people, angry loud annoying people. Just too many of them clashing with each other, and the static they emitted put him on edge. He thought of himself more as a California kid and felt that folks on the West Coast were just a little bit nicer. When he finished this case, he would hit up the West Coast for as long as his money lasted.

He felt closer to solving the case of who contaminated the bottles of SummerCrush, a popular soft drink that went nasty for a few children two years ago. In all, eighteen bottles containing tiny shards of glass had been drunk. The tragedy caused a media storm of negativity to rain down on the manufacturer. The manufacturer's top executive, Brendon Gibson, had hired Nick, the Ghost Hunter, to find who was responsible.

The afternoon sun stretched out his shadow. As usual, he looked like he stepped out of *Reservoir Dogs*, sporting a fitted black suit, white shirt, and today, a light blue tie.

Nick stopped. He took a few steps back and glanced down an alley. He'd spotted something in his peripheral vision that needed another look. Three teenagers dressed in red and black: WestSpider colors. They surrounded a small boy in baggy clothing. One teenager booted the boy hard in the chest; his body bounced as he hit the ground. Tears instantly welled behind the boy's glasses as he turtled up to protect himself. The leader snickered as he strutted around the boy, then gave him a heavy kick to the spine. The boy squealed in pain. He received another kick. He squealed even louder.

"Can I help you?" Nick yelled out.

"Fuck off, faggot," a lanky teen shouted back.

"Keep walking, cocksucker," another added.

"I wasn't asking you," Nick replied.

"This is Spider business," the leader said. "This little bitch gots to learn that these streets aren't free. He gots to pay, and since you've decided to get involved, you now need to pay the Spiders' tax too."

"Sure," Nick chirped. "How much? Want to make sure I pay enough."

"All you have, bitch!" the leader said, pulling out a knife. "That's every motherfucking dollar you have."

Nick placed his brown paper bag down and opened his wallet. "I have about four hundred. Is that enough?" He strolled directly toward the gang, pulling the money out from his wallet.

From the ground, the boy shook his head at Nick, warning him to run away while he could. Nick's smile widened, waving the notes in front of him like a fan. The shortest of the gang members stepped in to grab the money. Nick turned sharply, making his extended elbow connect with the guy's nose, breaking it.

"Fuck!" the teen yelled. His hands shot up to his face and he checked the painful damage.

"Who should I give it to?" Nick asked, turning in a circle. The lanky teen stepped in to grab the money. Nick pivoted. The teen tripped over Nick's foot and stumbled head first into his friend's groin. Both went down, one teen holding his nuts and nose; the other rubbing his head.

"Sorry," Nick said. He extended his hand as if to help the tall teen up. Instead, he cracked the youth in the side of his ear with his well-placed knee.

Acting confused, Nick turned to the leader. "They don't want my money? You have it." Nick shuffled toward the leader with his arm outstretched, waving the notes.

The leader thrust his knife at Nick, who easily sidestepped the blade, catching his would-be attacker's arm between his own body and bicep.

Nick slapped the money across the leader's face. "Take my damn money, what's wrong with you? Everyone has to pay tax."

The leader fumbled to pull his arm free. Nick spun him around and trapped the knife behind his attacker's back, then twisted the wrist to dislocate it, and disarmed him. With a boot to his ass, he sent the leader flying into his cohorts.

"How did I get this?" Nick asked, while he comically blinked at the knife in his hand. "This is yours. Want it back? Catch!" he said, drawing his arm back to throw the sharp blade. The teens scrambled to their feet, pushing past one another to get out of the alley as fast as they could.

"You're fucking crazy!" the small boy said while Nick helped him up.

"Yeah." Nick shrugged. "I get that a lot."

CHAPTER FIVE

LEFT ELBOW TO RIGHT KNEE, right elbow to left knee, down, pause, and repeat.

"…four-thirty-seven…." Ross grunted.

His abs were screaming at him to stop and he wasn't even halfway through his set. Being stuck in solitary was no excuse to miss a workout. Without weights, he just did high-volume sets instead.

At Bell Island, the inmates referred to solitary as "the Hell Hole" or "the Hell Island Hole," which summed it up well. It was a musty, windowless, concrete box, deep under the main prison. A fluorescent light in the ceiling intermittently crackled into life and buzzed and flickered in short bursts. Each room contained a single steel cot bolted to one wall. No pillow, no blanket. On the opposite wall was a stainless steel crapper, which was clogged the day Ross got hauled in and still was. Its stench made the air heavy and repugnant.

He was having trouble putting the pieces together. Why had Officer Hickman thrown himself onto Ross's knife to kill himself? Apparently the guard wanted to die at Ross's hands and wanted Ross to know that his death was a message from Caesar, a person Ross had never, ever heard of. Did the incident have anything to do with Walter Smith? Or was Justin Truth involved? This was the second time Ross had been set up for murder, and it pissed him off.

He channeled his anger into sit-ups, grunting as he quickened the pace.

Today, Ross would be released back into general population. He stopped mid-set when he heard the sound of his cell door unlock with a heavy *clunk*. Two guards entered with well-oiled AR-15 rifles pointed directly at Ross.

"Hands behind your back, now!" one guard ordered.

Ross rolled onto his front and rested his hands on his lower back. Cold steel greeted his wrists. The cuffs clamped tight, then a few more strained clicks made sure they were extra tight, pinching his skin.

"Stand up!" the other guard snorted.

Ross awkwardly fumbled around on the floor and used his forehead to help push himself up onto his knees. He moved slowly and carefully so as not to give either guard a reason to inflict painful discipline.

The warden stood behind the two guards, his head peering over their broad shoulders. Ross noticed he held a handkerchief over his nose and mouth, probably in an effort to filter out the odor inside the cell. He gagged a few times.

Ross finally made it to his feet, amused how green the warden looked.

"Sir," Ross said.

"Smith, I'm letting you back into general population today," the warden preached. "This is because I am a man of God and have mercy in my soul. I want you to know we will be watching you. Any sign you might harm another prisoner or one of my staff, and you'll be back in here faster than the wind can change."

"I didn't kill him. You know that," Ross said.

"Do not dare to contemplate what I know. You know nothing about what I know." The warden fired back. "You're a stone-cold killer who butchered a defenseless man. You are devil scum."

"No, I didn't," Ross growled through gritted teeth.

"Don't you dare raise your voice to me! You killed him and you killed all the others."

"That's not true! Hickman murdered those men!"

"He did not. You did. You killed him to cover up your murders."

"He was a psychopathic killer." Ross replied. "I didn't kill him. He set me up. Who is Walter Smith? Who was this 'Caesar' he was working with? You need to contact the FBI. Something isn't right."

"You are what isn't right. You're a cold blooded murderer. You are a disgrace to the law and everything I hold moral. I don't think you can change. You are truly evil." The warden removed his rimless glasses and cleaned the lenses with his handkerchief. "I haven't come here for a discussion. I came to let you know I've put forward a request to have your sentence changed from life to the death penalty. You shouldn't be allowed to live after what you've done."

"I didn't do it, you stupid fuck!" Ross said, exasperated.

A guard stepped in and thrust the butt of his rifle into Ross's forehead, splitting it open. His vision went blurry. He dropped to his knees. A wave of nausea swept over him and he threw up.

"You will be punished in the eyes of the law, and God can decide what to do with you next. No doubt, he will send you straight to hell."

JUST NEED ONE MORE HIT? A little more of the Truth sounding good about now? Don't worry, you're not alone. Go where others have discovered even more of the Truth: karlwilliamfleet.com.

Sign up to be a Truth Seeker today and receive ongoing bonus short stories, behind-the-scenes snippets, audiobook chapters (with author's commentary), plus loads more exciting stuff—all exclusive to Truth Seekers.

And, as a special collector's edition extra for Truth Seekers, I'll send you an exclusive Blood Red Hand Print Cover of 01: Corporate Truth eBook, signed by myself.

We do need your email address to send you all this awesome stuff. Don't worry, I guard email addresses from people like Justin—I'll never sell or give them away. And of course, you will have the option to unsubscribe whenever you wish.

And... you never know, one day you might find your own name within the pages of the Truth Files. Passionate Truth Seekers have been known to make appearances...

THIS BOOK WAS NEVER PLANNED.

When I first had the idea of writing about the exploits of Justin Truth, I thought there would be three books in the series. Their original titles were: Corporate Truth, American Truth, and Global Truth. Each book tackled a different era of Justin Truth's life, with a ten-year story span between each novel.

After I finished an early draft of Corporate Truth, I shared it with some family and friends to test the waters, see if the book made sense.

Of course, since they were family and friends, all their feedback was glowing. They all asked for the next book in the series, which at the time I hadn't written. But I did have my 30-year story arc idea.

I would explain this idea: "Book Two" I would say, "is set ten years after the events of Book One. It picks up when…" And I would smile at how clever my story was.

"But what happens next?" they would ask.

"So," I would start again. "it's ten years later…" And thus, I would explain the idea again.

"No," They would interrupt me. "What happens next? To Ross, Montana, Steve…"

"Umm, forget about them. It's ten years later and besides they aren't even in Book Two. A completely new cast of characters, Only Justin returns and—"

"What? But. No. What happens next?????"

After this exact conversation with many different people, I started to think "Yes. What does happen next?"

What you are holding in your hands is the answer to that question.

Without this question from family and friends, the entire series would have been completely different.

This is a big, heartfelt thanks to these special people for asking the perfect question at the perfect time.

I hope they are happy with my new answer.

KARL WILLIAM FLEET has been fascinated by story and the act of storytelling since childhood.

Born in NaeNae, Wellington, he moved to Auckland in his teenage years, where he later attended college and discovered advertising as a career option. Intrigued by the creative process, he completed a bachelor's degree in business marketing, with a major in advertising.

During his advertising career, Karl tapped into his love of storytelling and quickly discovered success. In his first year within the industry, Karl won an opportunity to represent New Zealand at Cannes in the Young Lion's competition. In his second year, he won a rare and highly coveted Gold Pencil award at the One Show. The publication, Campaign Brief, soon named Karl their "Number One Australasian Advertising Creative" for his accomplishment of winning the largest number of international advertising awards between the period of 2008-2009.

While writing ads, Karl also dabbled in writing scripts for short films. One of them, "Signs," found a special place in people's hearts and has been viewed over 10 million times on YouTube.

Karl's love for storytelling even led him down the most unlikely of paths: professional wrestling. As his alter ego, Curt Chaos, he defied the odds and became the New Zealand Heavyweight Champion. He held this prestigious belt for one year and thirteen days—the third longest title run in New Zealand's history.

Karl then had a crazy idea to write about an ultimate "negative protagonist,"

Justin Truth. As the negative protagonist genre is one of the hardest to write, Karl went back to university and earned a master's in creative writing to help build Justin Truth's world. Karl spent the next three years writing, crafting, and editing Corporate Truth, Criminal Truth, and Fractured Truth.

Everything Karl's learned from advertising, wrestling, and earning his master's degree comes together as a creative and unique form of written prose that he calls "binge reading."

He released the first three volumes of the Truth Files at once so readers can binge read to their heart's content.

He hopes you'll enjoy his stories as much as he enjoys creating them.

www.ingramcontent.com/pod-product-compliance
Lightning Source LLC
Chambersburg PA
CBHW021058110726
47900CB00007B/1925